MAIN

THE WINDY HILL

Recent Titles by Harriet Hudson from Severn House

CATCHING THE SUNLIGHT
QUINN
SONGS OF SPRING
TOMORROW'S GARDEN
TO MY OWN DESIRE
WINTER ROSES

THE WINDY HILL

Harriet Hudson

This first world edition published in Great Britain 2004 by
SEVERN HOUSE PUBLISHERS LTD of
9–15 High Street, Sutton, Surrey SM1 1DF.
This first world edition published in the USA 2004 by
SEVERN HOUSE PUBLISHERS INC of
595 Madison Avenue, New York, N.Y. 10022.

British Library Cataloguing in Publication Data

Hudson, Harriet, 1938-
    The windy hill
    1.   Women food writers - Fiction
    2.   Manuscripts - Fiction
    3.   Detective and mystery stories
    I.   Title
    823.9'14 [F]

    ISBN 0-7278-6028-3

Typeset by Palimpsest Book Production Ltd.,
Polmont, Stirlingshire, Scotland.
Printed and bound in Great Britain by
MPG Books Ltd., Bodmin, Cornwall.

One

W ho was it this time?

Rachel threw open the front door of the cottage. Clearing out a home, saying goodbye to her past, was not the best job in the world, and she wanted to finish it quickly. There were too many memories here of the last awful twelve months, and each interruption delayed the moment when she could say: Hey, it's over. I'm off to find a new life. New lives were usually easier to dream of than find, but the hunt would begin just as soon as she could make it.

'I've tracked you down at last.'

The man on the doorstep looked all prepared to step inside and make himself at home, but she was willing to swear that she'd never seen him in her life before. He was about her age, thirtyish, slightly taller than she was, perhaps five foot seven; he was thinnish, lean of face and bright of eye – but she didn't know him.

'Who?' she asked politely.

'Who am I, or who are you?'

'Who are you, please?' Rachel noticed the way his enquiring eyes seemed to be summing her up, and decided she disliked him.

'Adam Paynter. You came into our Never Alone shop.'

'Your what?' Then she remembered that she had dumped half a dozen black bags and a couple of suitcases full of her mother's possessions in the nearest charity shop in Canterbury last time she was there. Chilford itself was too small a village to have charity shops – or any kind of shops, save a general store.

'In Canterbury. Remember? You left something I thought you should think twice about.'

1

'I don't remember seeing you there. How did you get hold of me?' It was ridiculous to be so suspicious, and it wasn't like her. Another sign that she was due for a new life.

'I wasn't there,' he said patiently. 'That's why you didn't see me. I run the charity, and have a whip through everything as a matter of course. I had a hell of a job tracing you, but here I am, thanks to an old bill left as a bookmark with your name, Mrs Margaret Field. And here's the suitcase.'

'Oh no! Not that.' Her heart sank. Some old possessions refuse to give up and go away. This battered suitcase had accompanied her parents and herself on many a childhood holiday, and now here it was dumped back on her doorstep, laughing at her.

'I'm not Margaret Field. She died in February. I'm her daughter Rachel. Do come in.' She tried to make it sound hospitable but she was aware she'd failed miserably.

He seemed not to notice. 'Thanks.'

He filled the narrow hallway in the cottage with its low ceiling as he followed her into the living room. She looked round despairingly but was able to push enough rubbish off one chair for him to sit down. He didn't take advantage of it, however. Instead he squatted over the suitcase, throwing back the lid.

'*Voilà!*' he declared theatrically.

Rachel glanced into the suitcase. 'I don't see any rabbit jumping out,' she observed.

It was empty. Puzzling, but it brought an odd relief. When she had found it in the attic, it had been stuffed full of old photos and letters, most of which she had bundled up more tidily and put aside to check through on the proverbial 'rainy day', which so far had not come. She'd been tempted to throw the lot away, in the interests of seeking her new life, but decided she should check them first. Mum had been an only child, and, so far as Rachel knew, she would be the last of the Carter line – that had been Mum's maiden name. It was looking as though she would remain so too. The shock of François' duplicity had made her abandon rosy notions of happy-ever-after and two point something children.

2

'Sorry. Couldn't resist my Magic Circle trick,' Adam said. 'Look.'

She watched, as he undid a zip fastener running so flush with the inside of the suitcase that she hadn't noticed it. Now, of course, she remembered it well. It was the 'secret pocket.'

'What's in it then?' Rachel was annoyed at hearing the quiver in her voice. Perhaps Adam heard it too for he glanced at her sympathetically.

'Well, what is it?' she repeated as patiently as she could.

'You take it out.'

For a moment she hesitated, then decided to play his game. It might hasten his departure. She got on to her knees, reached into the pocket and took out a manuscript of some sort in a transparent plastic bag.

'Go on, take it out,' he said encouragingly, as she hesitated again. 'I did.'

Curiosity made her obey him. She found herself staring at a script on thick paper, loosely tied together through the punched holes with green ribbon. The top page was blank.

'Go on,' Adam urged again, 'or have you seen it before and decided you really don't want it?'

'No. I didn't know it was there.' But still she didn't open it. Why should I? she thought. This is mine. I can look at it when I like. Then she remembered that she'd given it away, and she acknowledged that this man had some rights in this too. So she turned over the top blank page and caught her breath at the sight of what lay before her.

'Yes,' he said, 'I thought you'd want it back.'

She didn't even react to the self-satisfaction in his voice. She was too spellbound by what she was looking at. It was a square of brilliant gouache, an original, delicately executed painting of a hillside, with blossom on a large apple tree; scattered by the breeze, some of the blossom lay on the green grass of spring, amongst a few bluebells. There was a sense that the breeze was still blowing those petals around, and had just paused for one second before the artist. It wasn't a peaceful scene, for there was a sense of urgent movement in it, filling Rachel with excitement and at the same time a weird desire to forget she'd ever seen it. Underneath was a copperplate handwritten inscription stating the obvious: The Windy Hill.

It was a picture that demanded something of the viewer, and she had no energy to give anything at present. This sweetness of life caught at her throat, as if challenging her to say: This is real. This could be yours. Conscious of Adam's eye on her, she forced herself to turn to the next page. This was a simple title page typed on an old manual typewriter, on paper now yellowing with age: Repasts of Delight. A Book of Crandene Recipes by Alice Carter.

Yesterday her path forward had seemed simple: she would put the house on the market as soon as probate came through, then move away, far away from Kent to begin her new life. She'd been looking forward to it. So how come she suddenly felt trapped, as though the tentacles of the past still had the power to affect her life? And they hadn't. It wasn't possible.

'Are you all right?' Adam was looking at her in concern.

She managed a faint smile. 'Yes, sorry. The effort of clearing out the house.'

'More than that I think.'

'A bit of a shock,' she conceded unwillingly. 'Alice Carter was one of my ancestors.'

'If you know of her, why is this a shock?'

'Did I say shock?' Rachel was puzzled. She'd said it instinctively, but had no idea why. 'I meant I've had an overdose of family history recently.'

'It's an interesting one if it produces this.' He spoke politely, as he nodded towards the script. *Too* politely.

'Yes, but it's *my* family history, Mr Paynter. I'm grateful to you, but I've a lot to do.' She was standing up, trembling. Was it with irritation, or just from an overwhelming wish to be alone? Whichever, it was irrational and she knew it.

Adam Paynter stood up too, but with no sense of having taken offence. 'I'll go. Don't worry, Miss Field. Bereavement takes people in funny ways. Testaments to the past – like this script – are a good way to force oneself to face it.'

'The past affects nothing,' she said, fiercely protective of that new life awaiting her somewhere out there.

'Wrong. Sometimes it's the way to the future.' He strolled to the front door and she watched him walk down the garden path to his shabby van, with Never Alone painted unprofessionally in blue on the side. What on earth did he mean by the past being a way to the future? Professional claptrap probably, which boiled down to nothing. Looking back was only a way to excuse oneself from the effort of marching forward in her view. And marching forward was the path she had always enjoyed taking.

She'd used to laugh with Mum about doors slamming in her face. Another one will open, Mum would say. Don't look back. Who wants to stare at a closed door? So Rachel hadn't. Not when Dad had walked out on them, not when Marjorie had married Kevin, which meant the end of their joint sandwich business, and not even when François had dumped her so unceremoniously in France.

'There'll be another *poisson* in the sea for me somewhere,' she'd joked with Mum, even though she wasn't too sure about it.

So where next this time? It was a puzzle, that was for sure. She'd had her fill of France and working in restaurants, but England didn't seem to offer much in the way of an open door either. Still, she'd had no reason to take out her frustration on a casual stranger who'd merely tried to help, and she was consumed with guilt at the way she'd treated him. She rushed down the path, looking for the van, and saw Adam just pulling out. She reached his window just in time.

'I'm sorry, Adam. I really am. I'm just a grouch at the moment.'

He pulled back in, switched off the engine, and considered this. 'Shall I come back in? I'd like to know more about that cookery book.' Then he glanced at her. 'I need not,' he pointed out. 'I can go right now. You're still forgiven.'

It would mean more talk about that script, Rachel realized, though she was unsure why this pile of paper presented a problem.

'Yes,' she said. 'Do come. You never know your luck. I might raise a cup of coffee.'

'Sure? It's your family after all.'

5

Rachel grinned at him. Perhaps he wasn't so bad. 'Alice Carter might be, but Crandene belongs to everyone.'

'Mighty grand words, ma'am. But you're right.' Adam was serious. 'I have to admit, that's what got me going when I first saw that typescript. The word Crandene.'

The name Crandene meant something to most people, but Rachel had always felt a very slight proprietary interest in it, ever since she'd learned as a child that her mother's aunt had been the second Lady Beavers, wife of the owner of Crandene. This had not meant much to her then, since she had no idea what Crandene or being a lady meant, save that it sounded grand and far from the Field lifestyle. What had struck her imagination was that this forebear had once been the cook at Crandene, and had landed up married to its owner. It planted the idea in her mind that one could change one's life; it was not one of steady progression from A to B. That there was always tomorrow had remained her hopeful attitude.

Crandene Place was on the western side of Kent, in the lush and green Weald, where the estate sat snugly in its nest of valleys and hills. It had once been a medieval castle, but the Civil War had put paid to that. What ruins remained had been incorporated into the rear walls of the late seventeenth-century mansion that took its place. This had had a chequered history until the Beavers family bought the estate and restored and added to the house in the second half of the nineteenth century; the new owner, Major General Gerald Beavers, VC, became the first Baron Beavers for his services both in the field and to the government. Since then the Beavers family had prospered, keeping both military and political connections intact. It became the tradition that the elder son should become a soldier and then take his seat in the Lords. The second son could follow the career he chose – provided it was the army or politics.

The heyday of Crandene, so far as the public image was concerned, however, was the 1930s, when it became a social weekend rendezvous for both military and political figures, with the occasional dash of the theatrical and artistic talents of London too – providing a service that neither Whitehall nor London's clubs could offer. This was partly because it became renowned for its cuisine. At a time when French food dominated the high ground, Crandene stood out for the excellence of its English cooking.

Rachel had heard little of it for years though. 'Who runs Crandene today?' she asked Adam. 'The National Trust?'

'No. A foundation. The house and grounds are open to the public but his lordship still lives in a wing or in a house on the estate, and runs the foundation with a board of trustees. I met one of their fundraisers at a seminar recently.'

To her surprise, Adam didn't seem to want to pore over the script. Instead, turning down the offer of coffee, he suggested they walk up the hillside to the rear of the cottage, a gentle slope of the North Downs. Only a field divided the cottage garden from the hillside, a field her mother had constantly feared might go for development, but which had so far escaped. Rachel was only too eager to agree to Adam's suggestion. Out in the open air she might feel better able to cope.

'You're never alone with a hill to look at. Is that it?' she managed to joke, as they walked through the garden. The daffodils were giving way to her mother's prized double tulips now, and seeing the sprouting rose bushes and honeysuckle she felt an unexpected qualm about leaving them. Wasn't it treasonable to leave her mother's beloved garden to a stranger? No, she told herself. No. But the honeysuckle swayed in the wind as if shaking its head at her perfidy.

You, Rachel, are definitely going bonkers, she told herself, now glad of Adam's presence ahead, in case she began to muse about delaying the sale of the cottage.

'I suppose,' she shouted to him as he negotiated the footpath between the growing crops, 'I might be related to his lordship by marriage somehow. Good old Alice managed to marry one of them at some point.'

'Perhaps that makes you a countess.'

She laughed. 'I don't wish. Alice was only my great-aunt, married to the third baron, and they didn't have children. She was his second wife.'

'So you do know something about her.'

'That's all I know. I told you, it's past.' Over, gone with the wind. Yesterday's stories fluttering into the eternal dustbin.

'We all leave talking till it's too late. It's inevitable.'

'Is it?' She was being fed the professional line and wondered if she minded. She was beginning to feel better for being with him so she let it go. 'You must be very good at your job,' she added, meaning it.

She caught Adam unawares for he turned round, looking startled, out of his role of official comforter.

'Perhaps. But it doesn't make what I say insincere.'

'Touché.' She grinned at him. 'Truce?'

'How about a ceasefire?'

'Do you get a lot of flak thrown at you in your job? Whatever it entails,' she added, realizing she was only guessing at what Never Alone did.

'Masses. That's why I wear bulletproof clothing.'

'Be careful you don't catch it on that barbed wire,' she called as he came perilously close as he swung his leg over the stile.

'I won't. Shall we sit and admire the view?'

She peeled off her anorak and flung it on the grass. 'Here, sit on this. I'd hate to see grass stains on those posh trousers.'

'That's rather patronizing of you.' Nevertheless he took advantage of her offer.

'Sniper fire, sorry.'

'Forgiven . . .' A pause, then he answered her query, 'Never Alone offers company to people angry at being old, angry at being singled out for severe, maybe terminal illness. Or angry at being childless, angry at being parents, angry at being bereaved, or even angry at being alive.'

'Is there a cure for anger?' She wondered if he thought *she* was angry. She wasn't sure if it was true. After all, she believed in going forward, not complaining over the cards dealt her.

'Sure, there's a cure, but it lies in the person, not in our charity. All we can do is alleviate the pain, not cure it.'

'How did you come to set it up?'

'I started it four years ago because there was a need,' he replied promptly.

'That's all?' she asked when he stopped.

'Yes. Anyway,' he continued briskly, 'that's work. I want

8

to hear more about Alice Carter. I'm sure you must know a little more than you're telling me.'

'I don't think I do.'

Below them she could see her cottage, and in between the trees the roofs of the rest of the village, looking far away from this lofty position. It occurred to her that for the first time she was thinking of it as *her* cottage, not Mum's.

'Then let's think about the manuscript,' Adam persevered. 'I would say those could be the recipes Alice Carter used at Crandene in its heyday in the 1930s.'

'Probably.' It was a reasonable conclusion on his part, and would force her into co-operation.

'If Alice was your mother's aunt, how old would that make her in the thirties? When were your grandparents born?'

'My mother was fifty-eight when she died.' With some surprise, Rachel realized she had spoken of it quite naturally. The usual pain hadn't come. It would undoubtedly return, but this afternoon there was a reprieve. 'And her father fought in the Second World War. He was Alice's brother.'

'So to be at Crandene in the 1930s Alice would probably have been an older sister.'

'I suppose so.'

'Think about it. Your grandfather could have been born during the First World War, or earlier. Let's say 1910. An elder sister could well have worked her way up to become chief cook and bottlewasher at Crandene in the 1930s.'

'But he wasn't born in 1910.'

'How do you know?'

'Pops is only in his late 80s now.'

'*Is?*'

'Yes. He's in a retirement home in France.' Pops had been too mentally and physically frail to come to the funeral, but he was alive, and she could see him any time she wanted to.

'Hey, Rachel. You've been holding out on me. You'll be telling me next Alice herself lives next door.'

'No, and so far as I know there are no other descendants. Anyway, why should I have told you about Pops?' she added indignantly.

'You could go and ask him all about his older sister.'

9

'Why?'

He sighed. 'You know you're interested in this script. Any dumb-bell would be.'

'Thanks.'

He laughed. 'Serves you right.' He turned towards her and settled down, propping himself up on one elbow. 'Anyway, Alice had probably forgotten about it and handed it with a lot of family junk to her brother, who gave it to your mother when he went into the home. There, how's that for sticking my nose in?'

'Possible,' Rachel conceded. This was all going too fast for her. 'But why are you so interested in this script? It's only recipes.' Recipes were the tools of her profession.

'Maybe. But it's for you to find out what's so special about it. If that lovely thing were mine, I'd want to know about it. It represents more than just recipes.'

'You're doing your professional act again,' Rachel warned him.

'No. In your place, I'd like to know a whole lot more about Alice Carter, that's all. Firstly, why begin a cookery book with a painting of a windy hill? You know what I think, Rachel? That it's there because love was in the air. But what's it doing in a cookery book?'

April 1912

Alice Carter walked along the gravel path up to the big house. Each crunch of her boots on the gravel made her more nervous. Each step took her further away from Mum and Dad and the kids in the small cottage in Cranbridge village where all eight of them lived crammed in together. 'The shoe', Mum cheerfully called it, and she was the 'old woman who didn't know what to do'. Alice supposed that Mum was old, at least thirty, maybe forty, but she was always singing and her face was lovely and soft, so she didn't look it. Dad worked for the estate as a carpenter, and so had Mum before she married Dad – only not as a carpenter of course; she was inside staff, like Alice was going to be now she was nearly fourteen.

She was lucky to get the job. Being a scullery maid at

Crandene Place wasn't like being one elsewhere. You had prospects. If you worked hard, you would become an under-kitchenmaid, then head kitchenmaid. Anyway, she had no choice. She had to leave home now. Emmy and Rosie weren't babies any more. The family needed the room, not to mention her wages. If you lived in the Big House you got board and food too, as well as the money. A whole £6 a year. She tried to convince herself that life was going to be wonderful, but failed. She felt forlorn, and kept her black bag close, for it reminded her of home. She was no stranger to Crandene, of course. She'd seen the house many times from the outside but now it was different. She was going inside to stay. She was to live here for ever. She shut her lips together very firmly to stop the tears coming.

She was nearly there now, and the way ahead was looking ever more daunting. This wasn't the drive the family used of course; this was the pathway to the back entrance of Crandene Place, but even the route the tradesmen took was imposing enough, past the greenhouses, then the vegetable gardens, the dovecote, the apple store, the coal house, the laundry, everything that made the big house tick over – like the innards of a clock, Dad said. Tick tock, tick tock and the family's life was organized. The hands were the family who showed Crandene's face to the world, but they couldn't do that without the innards working too. So, Dad said, they were all part of the same big clock at Crandene. And now she, Alice Carter, would be a tiny part of this ticking clock.

She had reached the door to the kitchens now, where the tradesmen called and which all the servants used. To her relief, no one in the grounds had taken any notice of her even though she was wearing her Sunday best hat, as Mum had insisted, and she had been glad of her anonymity.

'Go on, my love. It won't bite,' a passing groom said encouragingly.

The door very nearly did bite. It was opened by the tallest man she'd ever seen and involuntarily she curtsied. He was so smartly dressed in uniform she wondered if he might be his lordship, whom she'd heard had been a military gentleman. 'If you please, sir, I'm Carter.'

11

'Carter?'

'The new scullery maid.'

The face looked scornfully down at her. 'Follow me.' The back was turned and she followed this god along the passageway, aware of storerooms on either side, and one much larger room. At last the god knocked on a door.

'The girl is here,' he announced to its occupant, ushering Alice in, and leaving her in a large room, with a table and armchairs. An imposing woman clad in black stared at her in silence from behind a writing desk. Then slowly she rose to her feet, her bombazine gown rustling. Alice did not dare look her in the eye, so she gazed down at the chain round the lady's waist, with a bunch of enormous keys hanging from it. The lady came closer, inspecting her in silence.

'Leave your bag here,' she eventually commanded. 'John will take it up later. You'll be sharing with Lily.'

This meant nothing to Alice, save that her precious bag, her link with home, was being taken from her. 'Are you her ladyship, ma'am?' she asked timidly.

The forbidding face seemed to relax a little. 'I, Carter, am Mrs Cheney, housekeeper at Crandene. I trust we shall see little of each other, Carter. Do you know why that is?'

Alice shook her head, wondering if the lady had taken an objection to her face.

'If our paths should cross again, it means you have not proved satisfactory. Do you understand?'

'Yes, ma'am.'

'Yes, *Mrs Cheney*, if you please, Carter. Now, follow me.'

Another formidable back to follow. Cowed, Alice meekly obeyed, and was led into the main kitchen. No doubt about that. The heat of the ovens was stifling though welcome on this chilly spring day, and the smells coming from them were almost as good as from Mum's tiny oven back home. But there were copper pots and pans, people and noise everywhere, and everyone seemed to be shouting. One man – obviously the cook from his white cap and apron – was shouting much louder than everyone else.

'I work with imbeciles. *Mon Dieu*, it is insupportable.'

To Alice's horror a soup ladle was flung straight in the face of one of the girls – a kitchenmaid? – who burst into tears. Her tormentor seemed to regard this with great satisfaction, but it terrified Alice.

'The new scullery maid, Monsieur Trente. Carter is her name.'

The man stopped his tirade for a moment, suddenly deferential to the housekeeper, and Mrs Cheney left Alice with him. He had a belly on him, and a moustache; Alice didn't like the look of him – especially the two beady black eyes that fixed themselves on her.

'Carter,' he roared, 'for me you work hard. There is the scullery, Carter.' He pointed to an adjacent room. 'We shall see what you can do. The scullery is your home, but I am the king. I am king here of all the kitchens, and I reign over you all. I am *le roi*. Who am I, Carter?'

'His Majesty the King, sir,' Alice replied, bewildered.

'Very good. You are more intelligent than you look, new scullery maid. Now, go to the scullery and *scull*!' he roared. 'Do not waste more of my time.'

The scullery seemed a refuge after the kitchen, despite its bleak stone sinks and scrubbing boards. A skinny tired-looking girl, with a red nose and straggly hair, was working at one of the sinks. She looked up as Alice came timidly in.

'Not much, is it?' she said brightly. 'But it's home. All we've got. We've got a tap, which is more than some could say. My name's Lily to you, Spratt to them. Worked before, have you?'

Alice shook her head.

'Clean's the order of the day here, or it's the order of the boot. He's a devil, that 'un in the kitchen. Not a speck on his blessed pots and pans. Beastly black-lead the stoves, and scrub, scrub, scrub the floors and tables. I tell you, no cockroaches dare come in here. Anyway,' she sniggered, 'knowing him he'd cook it. Cook anything, these Frenchies will.'

The ordeal before her seemed worse than she'd dreamed of in her worst nightmares, so Alice clutched eagerly to the fact that Lily seemed friendly enough.

The rest of the day passed in a blur as Alice struggled to help Lily diminish the huge pile of pots and pans with a minimum of hot water – which she had to venture into the kitchen to collect in brass cans from where they were heating on the stove. Sometimes she was allowed one, sometimes she was shouted at to leave it alone. There seemed no rhyme or reason to it. As fast as one pile of pots was clean, the next arrived, with Lily continually expanding on how Monsieur Trente was a chef, not a cook. A cook would have been under Mrs Cheney's thumb, but as a French chef the position was more complicated and sparks would fly. 'Then he takes it out on us,' Lily added with relish.

By the time servants' supper was served, Alice was too tired to care if she ate or not. The larger room she had seen to one side in the corridor was the servants' hall where they ate their meals – the lower servants that is. The upper servants never joined them save at dinnertime when they came in in a procession just for two courses and then left again. It sounded very strange to Alice, and she found the lower servants formidable enough, let alone the high and mighty upper ten. The meal was held in silence, she couldn't even talk to Lily. Although Mum had explained what the household was like, she didn't think it would be as bad as this. It was like being sent outside for being naughty when she was young. So, she just ate her meal and then followed Lily back to the kitchens. Their dinner was at midday but the family had luncheon at midday and dinner in the evening, and what with all the plates of food, footmen rushing around, and noise and hubbub, the scullery was indeed a haven.

'We have to get all the washing up done before we go to bed, so it's no use you looking as if you could drop where you stand,' Lily informed her merrily, as yet another plate-bucket arrived full of dirty crockery. 'And we still have to clean the kitchens. Cheer up, it don't take as long as it sounds.'

But it did. Alice's last job was to take a pile of plates to the butler's pantry with careful instructions as to where that was. She found it all right, and was relieved that there was no sign of Mr Palmer the butler, a terrifying individual whom she had yet to meet, though she'd been told about this august person. In her tiredness, however, one of the willow pattern bowls slipped

14

from the pile, crashing on the dresser and smashing on to the floor in small pieces.

Appalled, she stared helplessly at the results of her crime.

'Crumbs,' said a voice behind her, 'you've started well.'

She spun round to see a lad grinning at her. 'Ain't seen you before. Who are you? No, don't tell me. You won't be here long enough for it to matter when old Palmer sees this.'

She burst into tears, seeing herself dismissed on the spot.

'Look,' he said with alarm, 'I was only joking.'

'No, they'll tell me to go,' she moaned. On her first day, this had to happen.

'No, they won't.' He came over to inspect the damage. 'Tell you what, let's give this lot a funeral, so they won't notice it's gone till it's too late to find out who did it.'

'A funeral?'

'I'll bury it, just you see.'

'Put it in the rubbish, you mean?'

'Not on your life. They'll see it there. You'll get us both the order of the sack then. Go on, just leave it to me. You get on and put the rest away.' He quickly shovelled up the bits into a paper bag and vanished. Alice carefully replaced the rest of the china, breathing a sigh of relief when the last was safely in place. She waited fearfully in the silence, scared that at any moment she'd be discovered. Just as she was thinking she'd have to rush back to the kitchen to help Lily, however, the lad was back.

'There, buried outside the veggie garden, and I said a prayer over it. You never know, it might grow two new plates.'

That brought a smile to her lips. 'Thank you,' she said.

'Think nothing of it. You just keep smiling, and life will look a lot grander in the morning. Just you wait.'

'Who are you please?' she asked timidly.

'Me? I'm the lamp boy, rising steward's footman when I'm sixteen next month. Very important job, lamps. Why, on my half day off the family all sit in darkness, 'cos no one else can clean and trim them but me. If I left Crandene, they'd have to get this newfangled electricity put in.'

Alice looked at him doubtfully, wondering if he were joking again.

'Don't worry,' he said encouragingly, 'you'll do. It's hard-going at first. I was only a bootboy when I came here. Twelve, I was. Now see where I am, Miss . . . er . . .'

'Carter. I'm Carter.' Or was she Alice? She couldn't think clearly for tiredness.

'Nah. That's not what the rector said when he chucked the water in your face.'

'Alice Carter.'

'That's better. And I'm Harry. Harry Rolfe.'

~

'You will try to find out more about it, won't you?' Adam asked as they tramped back to the cottage.

'I'll think about it,' Rachel teased him, shouting against the increasing wind.

'Cop out. At least *look* at Alice Carter's script.'

'When I have time.' She wasn't going to be badgered by anyone, not even Adam.

'Today.'

'Perhaps.'

'Sorry. I know it's tough to have to face the past, just when you're longing to get on with the future. Will you let me know what you decide to do about it? Even if you want to put it in a drawer for your grandchildren?'

'Yes, I will.' Why did he have to be so damned under-standing?

'We'll meet again, Rachel.' It was a plain statement. No question in his voice. Because of her, or because of this cookery book? She didn't know, and it didn't much matter. He wasn't her sort. She wasn't sure after François who was her sort, but it wasn't Adam.

She watched him drive off and went back into the silent cottage. She'd promised to let him know her decision, and that was fair. As she returned to the packing she'd been engaged in when he arrived, she still found herself thinking about him – especially as he seemed to assume they'd be meeting again. He was nice enough, she supposed, but then he had to be in his job. It must make him a kind of deus ex machina, who

16

descended from the heavens to sort out people's lives, and then disappeared again, satisfied with his work – or washing his hands of it. Maybe that was the role he thought he was playing with her. She hadn't been given a clue as to what made the real Adam tick, but did she want to know?

I admit, she told her reflection in the mirror, to a certain curiosity, even if he's not my sort. Her face stared back at her, framed in brown curly hair, and she wondered what he saw when he looked at her. She wasn't short, she wasn't tall, she wasn't wildly beautiful, but she wasn't, she supposed, unattractive. Certainly François had thought so. '*Mon coeur,*' he would whisper, cupping her face in his hands, 'the eyes that laugh, the eyes that love, the eyes that live . . .'

Yes, well, her eyes hadn't done too much of any of those things recently, and he'd been a snake anyway. She wondered how Adam had seen her. As an average woman, or as an obstinate customer for his charity? Did he even see her at all? Did she care? No. She had not been aware of any electric currents tingling between them, or of any physical sign that either of them existed for the other. There was nothing between them.

Except a cookery book.

Two

'Could I please speak to Adam Paynter?'
It had been nearly two weeks since she'd met him, and a lot had happened in the meantime. Or rather a lot had been decided. At last her new life had a signpost pointing towards it, and she was impatient, first to fulfil her promise, and secondly to get going.

His voice on the phone sounded pleased to hear from her, even if there had been an infinitesimal pause as though his brain were clicking into action over who she was.

'I keep my promises,' she laughed. 'Any chance of your coming over one day soon? Lunch might be on offer.'

'Every chance, I'd say. Tomorrow?'

'Done. Twelvish?'

On that first evening when she had her first real look at *Repasts of Delight*, she had placed it on the one decent-sized table in the cottage, which served for dining, working, coffee, tea and general dumping ground, after clearing it of everything else. There it had lain with its initial blank page staring up so innocently at her. She forced herself to turn over the mesmerizing picture of the apple tree, then over the title page to the dedication. She'd spent a moment or two on that. It was dedicated, *'To Sam, Remembering November 15th'*, and she made a mental note to ask Pops if he knew who Sam was – Lord Beavers, probably. Then came an introduction, followed by the typed recipes, each set out with its name, its list of ingredients followed by comments and cooking method. Nothing unusual in that, but there were plenty of things that were.

There were two main aspects that amazed her, and kept her glued to the task. The first was the sheer interest and range of the recipes. For a start they were firmly entrenched in an ancient English tradition of food, yet they were written down at a time when English cooking was generally considered the pits and merely the fare of the masses, stemming from a sub Mrs Beeton tradition, that had suffered from the deprivations of World War I. True, there had been the occasional voice crying in the wilderness – Dorothy Hartley's *Food in England*, Mrs Leyel's *The Gentle Art of Cookery*, Dorothy Allhusen's *Book of Scents and Dishes*, and Florence White's *Good Things in England* came to mind – but by and large French cuisine was the aspiration of society gourmets. She had known of course that Crandene was renowned for English not French cooking, but she hadn't expected anything like this.

Rachel had had an overdose of French cooking in the three years she had lived in France, and what she saw in this script began to reawaken all her former excitement for food. Alice Carter had clearly been doing her homework on the history of English cuisine. What leapt out of these pages was not the perfect shepherd's pie, or how to achieve the ideal cooked joint of roast beef, as she had stupidly assumed. Instead, greeting her were spices, herbs, fascinating conjunctions of sour and sweet from medieval days, syllabubs and tansies from Georgian, and comfits and 'banqueting stuffe' from Tudor palaces, all presented together in simple terms adapted for 1930s ingredients and methods. They were not King Henry VIII's or Richard II's recipes, but Alice's, built on the traditions of the past. Her eye slid over almond milk and rose-flavoured sauce for fish, shellfish salamagundi, ham with curd cheese and mint, baked onions with cinnamon. The recipes left Rachel gasping, and longing to try them out.

The last page in the script was a quotation from John Ruskin, beginning: 'Cookery means the knowledge of Medea and of Circe and of Helen and of the Queen of Sheba'. All these recipes bore testament to that. Queen of Sheba she was not, thought Rachel, amused at the thought of her making a triumphal entry to Handel's music bearing one of Alice Carter's dishes in her hands. Nevertheless she was giving a mental trumpet toot. The realm of cooking was awaiting her once again. Here was her crown handed to her on a plate. Or rather in a suitcase.

19

The second most striking aspect of the script was that the picture at the beginning wasn't the only one in the book. Each page, almost each recipe, was decorated with pen and ink drawings, each a minor masterpiece in itself, some with a caption in immaculate copperplate handwriting. Each section also had a number of watercolours like the one at the front of the script, only smaller. The combined effect was of a sense of life, of colour and drama as if Alice Carter were trying to speak to those who saw her script. If so, what was her message, Rachel wondered? The joyousness and abundance of this world, yes, but there was more than that, for the storms seemed to be represented as well.

It was hard to see the relevance of many of the illustrations. Some were landscapes, in sun and storms, some were humorous, such as the two figures wandering hand in hand at the seaside with pies as heads; in another, captioned Uriah's Humble Pie, one pie covered its face with thin pastry arms; in another two plates with smiling faces on them fondly regarded each other, while further down the page one plate with tears on its painted face regarded its smashed partner. Others were beautiful studies of garden or wild flowers.

It was an odd mixture and Rachel could see no connecting link or order. Perhaps there was little relevance to the text. They were just what they seemed: illustrations to make the book spectacular to look at as well as to cook from.

Rachel hadn't been able to concentrate on the cottage with Alice niggling at her mind, and instead she had dashed into Canterbury to visit the reference library to find out whether it had ever been published. When her excitement was sharpened even further, since Sam proved not to be Lord Beavers, who had been a Robert, she had decided it was time to call in Adam.

He arrived for lunch exactly on time.

'Come in.'

She had dressed up for the occasion, not exactly in full evening dress, but a skirt at least. After all, this lunch was for Alice – as well as for Adam. Alice, having lived through the twenties, would have approved of its short length and Adam seemed to have no objections either. She noticed his eyes flicking to her legs.

'I see we're both doing smart casual,' he observed. Clad in blazer and light trousers he too presented a different picture from the jeans and sweater of their last meeting. In fact, he looked rather dashing and she felt Alice would have given him high marks for his regard to the ceremony of the occasion.

'I thought the occasion deserved it.' Eagerly she showed him into the living room, where the table was already laid with a lace tablecloth she had salvaged from the 'things to go' pile. 'We're having salamagundi, syllabub and fruit. OK? Oh, and there's mulligatawny soup too. All Alice's recipes. And the mulligatawny is Alice's version of a seventeenth-century recipe which is nothing like the tired old Indian version we're used to now.'

Adam surveyed the glorious plate of salamagundi, with its raised centrepiece of chopped chicken, shellfish, lemon, chives, endives and anchovies surrounded by hard-boiled eggs, duck slivers, cucumber, grapes and pickled red cabbage, in silence for a moment. 'Where's my usual ham sandwich?'

'Don't mention that word.'

'Which one?'

'I did four years' hard labour running a sandwich company.'

'What made you give it up?'

'My business partner left to get married, and Lunch-Bites was no fun at all after she left and . . .' She stopped. Her tongue was running away with her.

'What did I do to deserve all this spread?' he asked curiously, as they finished the soup, which had worked well, she thought. Adam's eyebrows hadn't shot up too much at the 'pepper water' – mulligatawny's translation into English. 'Not that I'm objecting, of course.'

'I'm not sure,' Rachel replied with a straight face. 'But you did force me into taking Alice Carter's script seriously.'

'To look at it,' he amended. 'I seem to have unleashed a tornado rather than the gentle breeze I was suggesting.'

'Really?' she paused. 'I could have sworn you had a deeper interest in it than that.'

Adam helped himself from the salamagundi plate. 'Never like to see a good thing go to waste.'

21

'Is that the script or a potential client, me?'

'Umph. Anchovies, I see. Good. I like them.'

'Alice preferred chicken apparently. That's what she listed first in her suggested ingredients. And,' Rachel added firmly, 'for your information, neither script nor potential client will go to waste.'

She needed to use her talents, and the cookery script was the spur. When she had first been introduced to cookery in her teens she had been seized by the sheer wonder of it, the increasingly available new ingredients and tastes, new approaches, new foods, old foods, every recipe was an adventure. Then had come the grim part, the sandwich business, which was an invaluable experience, but exciting it was not.

And now all her early enthusiasm was growing again.

'Do you have a food background?' she asked curiously.

'Certainly I do. I eat it.'

'No training in it?' she persisted.

'No.'

'So what did you do before you began the charity?' She was beginning to sense his reluctance to reply, and that made her all the more curious.

'Journalist.'

'Why did you give it up?'

He sighed. 'You really want to know? I'd much rather talk about Great-aunt Alice.'

'Yes, I do, please.' Journalists and charitable inclinations didn't seem to go hand in hand, so why the switch, she wondered.

'Because I grew tired of covering one story, then going on to the next without knowing the end. Without making a difference.'

'Is that why you set up your own charity?'

'Yes, this way I see the end, and *can* make a difference.'

'So that's why you want to know what I'm doing with the script. It's the ending?' She thought she understood – or did she? After all, for her it was a beginning. A brave new world.

His eyes glinted. 'Yes.'

She drew a deep breath, and plunged into what was in her mind. 'Did anything strike you as odd about the script?'

22

'Several things.'

'But the chief oddity?'

'The recipes are a typed carbon copy, but the illustrations are originals.'

Rachel was impressed. He had got it in one. 'And what does a carbon copy tell us?'

'Us?'

'It tells *us*,' she emphasized, 'there's an original somewhere. Or was at one time. Yet so far as I can trace, it hasn't been published. I've done some research,' she added.

'Me too.'

She stared at him in indignant amazement. 'Why should you?'

'I was interested. Remember, the script was briefly mine. Or rather my charity's.'

This didn't entirely answer Rachel's question, but she put it to one side. 'It isn't in the British Library catalogue, which is fairly conclusive. It might have been published locally and not been sent to the British Library, or it might have been a private publication by the family. The baron might have published it when he married Alice.'

'With the Crandene name on it, even a private publication would have reached the specialist second-hand booksellers by now, but it doesn't seem to have done.'

'How can you know?' She had the weirdest feeling the ground was being swept politely from under her feet.

'I told you I had contacts. I asked around. One's interested though. Her firm runs a cookery list.'

'Stop!' Rachel said clearly. 'Absolutely *stop*.'

'Eating or—'

'You know what I mean,' she said angrily. 'You're going too far too quickly.'

'Not at all. I'm clearing the ground of weeds so that you can begin to flower.'

She almost laughed, but managed to hold it back. 'Stop fencing with me, Adam.'

'OK. Suppose you tell me why you mind my being interested in this script.'

Rachel considered this, then had to admit, 'Because it's

mine, I suppose, and at the moment that's important.' Apart from Pops so relatively far away, there wasn't much else around to which she could lay claim. Then it struck her she was being completely illogical. She had informed Adam that the past affected nothing, but even though she saw this script as her future, it was undoubtedly also her past. She expected him to seize on this, for she was sure it wouldn't have escaped him, but to her relief, he didn't. In return, she should at least try to explain – if only for herself. 'I've had this wonderful idea, Adam, and publishing the script comes into it. It's second in importance though,' she added quickly.

'Tell me this wonderful idea, or will that spoil it?' When she did not immediately answer, he reached out across the table and took her hand. 'Try me, Rachel.'

His hand felt rather nice, and surely devoid of the professional counsellor who would sit objectively summing her up. Holding hands was personal. Anyway, she was so intent on her story, she realized she needed to share it, if only for a sounding board.

'I want to use the recipes professionally, published or not; perhaps self-published. Crandene—'

'Steady on a minute. Start from the beginning.'

She schooled herself to patience. 'I told you I had a sandwich business once. Now I want to start, in conjunction with the Crandene Foundation, to cook banquets in the old 1930s style there. I've looked it up, and they do fundraising events. It would be a wow. They have a restaurant already so it should be no problem to extend its range. I could self-publish the script, or get it published commercially, but I'd prefer to self-publish because if the book were a bestseller there'd be no need of my service.' The words were tumbling over one another now. 'Anyone could—'

'Problem!'

'Don't you like the idea?' Rachel was appalled to see a frown on Adam's face. Surely he must see this was the perfect way to use the script. Moreover it would provide a new life – and income – for her. Something his charity must approve of.

'Yes. It's a terrific idea.'

24

She relaxed, since he seemed to mean it. 'Then what's the snag?'

'The present Lord Beavers for a start.'

'I've already written to him. He's the chief executive of the foundation after all.'

'You don't let the grass grow under your feet.'

'You sound as if that's some kind of disadvantage.'

'Not at all. It's after my own heart. See what you want and go for it.'

'Then why the frown?'

'The publication side. If you publish it commercially, Crandene would benefit from the publicity it would undoubtedly get, but, as you say, their own staff could do what you are suggesting.'

'But they wouldn't have a relation of Alice Carter, dressed up in 1930s kit, to do the cooking.'

He roared with laughter. 'You'd look like a sausage in 1930s dress.'

'Thank you,' she retorted. 'As it happens, Alice has a very good recipe for sausages, so that would be highly suitable.' She thought for a moment. 'I could broaden my approach. In fact I'd do that anyway. I'll make the book a biography of Alice as well, not just her cookery book, so the book would be under my authorship. Then I'd be an asset to Crandene.'

'You really don't hang around.'

'Why should I?' she asked surprised. Now she was even more certain she was on the right track. A family history – she had Pops to help there – and the Crandene end to follow up. With access to the archives, who knew what she might discover? She was glad now she hadn't thrown out any of those family papers and photos. A close shave.

'I can see a few hitches,' Adam said casually. 'It will be interesting to see what Lord Beavers replies. And I suggest you check Alice's will. Make sure you legally own both the script and the copyright.'

'I've sent off for a copy, in fact.' Ownership? Copyright? A tiny seed of doubt crossed her mind, but she dismissed it. It had been in her mother's belongings, and Rachel was her sole heir. No one else could be involved surely?

'I've written to Michael Hartshorn too,' she continued. 'If anyone knows about this cookbook and whether it's published, he will.' He was the well known historian who had documented, in a bestseller called *Countdown at Crandene*, the story of its importance as a meeting place for the military and political world in the run up to the war in the 1930s.

'You believe in mixing your stews, don't you? Do you need me as a fellow mixer?'

'You have a charity to run.'

'It's up and running now. I'm not needed all the time.'

'But the charity's your life.'

'It's part of my life. Now I'm looking for a new part. Just like you.'

It was tempting to say yes, but she had to be firm. 'Look, Adam, after Marjorie and the sandwich business, I don't do partners. Not yet anyway. But friendly hands are welcome.' Not too friendly, she thought. She didn't do lovers either at the moment.

She wondered whether what she'd said would make him retreat, but all he said was, 'Understood.'

Spring 1914

'We'd lose our jobs, if they knew,' Alice said with a laugh, for at this moment she cared about nothing save that she was with Harry.

'Not on your life,' Harry joked, taking her hand as they stole off. 'We're too valuable.'

'Go on with you,' she giggled. 'Us?'

'You know, for want of a nail the shoe was lost, and before they knew where they were, the whole kingdom was lost. So Crandene's doomed without us nails.'

They had arranged to meet as usual behind the vegetable garden by the compost heaps, where any passing gardeners would turn a blind eye, and Alice's dad would never appear, since he was safe inside his workshop. This half day a week was a luxury the staff had only recently been given, but the edict against male and female servants getting too fond of each other was still as strict. Daft really, Alice knew, for everyone

26

did it, and you just had to make sure you weren't caught. If Mrs Cheney found out she was in trouble.

She had hated leaving the kitchens, where she'd risen to underkitchenmaid. She loved watching Monsieur Trente cook, the way he could mix things and come up with some entirely new taste, the way he could speak – yes, he really did chatter away in French – to a leg of lamb about how tenderly he'd treat it, how he'd cover it in herbs and wines, so that it was a king among *gigots*. She'd learned such a lot from him and had been upset when Mrs Cheney had taken her away when there was a vacancy as housemaid. She didn't like that nearly as much as being in the kitchens, for Monsieur Trente was a kind old thing really. Funny how scared she'd been of him when she first arrived at Crandene two years earlier. Provided you dodged the flying utensils he was easy to handle.

This was a sort of anniversary for Harry and her. They'd met two years ago today and Harry had remembered. He'd suggested they went up to Crown Wood to sit on the hill. They could take a picnic and be by themselves; he could take his beloved flute and pipe away to his – and her – heart's content. It was worth the risk of Mrs Cheney or old Palmer finding out they were together. Monsieur Trente had turned a blind eye as usual when she crept into the kitchen and pinched a bit of the rabbit pie. With an apple or two and some beer they had a nice picnic with them.

They walked up this hillside together whenever they could – which wasn't often. They'd sit down where they could look down on Crandene Place in the valley and feel like the king and queen. Down there everyone was running around as if in a caucus race like in Lewis Carroll's story, trying to keep the wheels of Crandene turning. As Harry always said, 'Their motor car ain't going anywhere, Alice. It's driving round in circles, just thinking it is. But this is the twentieth century. Men are in the air and doing all sorts of things, but here at Crandene the wheels keep turning just as they always did, going nowhere.

'They want to stay as they always were and keep us with them,' Harry would go on. 'I'm not saying anything against

27

the family, mind you. I like them. I like England. But not everyone or every country feels that way.'

'What would you think if you were Lord Beavers, Harry?' Alice said today, as she sat down on Harry's coat. 'Fancy owning all that.' She spread her arms out to embrace the whole valley. As far as she could see was Crandene estate land.

'I'd remember he couldn't do anything without us.'

'That's right. Mind you,' Alice added, 'Mrs Cheney won't let her ladyship come to the kitchen. Perhaps they want to come and not be so apart. They came for the servants' ball, remember? I liked that. Lady Beavers looked lovely. She was nice. Nicer than . . .' She stopped as an unhappy memory came to her.

'Than who?' Harry asked.

'That high and mighty son,' Alice muttered.

'The young master?' Harry said mockingly. 'He's all right, Alice. A bit of a stuffed shirt, that's all.'

Alice didn't say anything. She didn't like the Honourable Robert Beavers. She was supposed to turn her back if the family passed while she was doing her work in the house, but wouldn't, not if it was Mr Robert. That's how he was always addressed even though he was heir to the title. He'd had an elder brother who died, so Harry said, four years ago, but somehow Mr Robert was still known as that, even though as heir to the title he should now be Mr Beavers.

Alice always felt uneasy when she saw him. Once he'd actually come up behind her, put his arms her round her where they shouldn't be, and when she'd wriggled round to protest, he'd seized her firmly and begun kissing her. His horrid hot breath had been all over her and she'd hated it. She'd never told Harry about that and never would, for there'd have been a row and she and he would both have lost their places and their character references. The rest of the family was all right, but not Mr Robert. He was at university now, but when he came down, as he called it, in the summer, she intended to keep out of his way as much as she could.

'What do you think's going to happen to us for the rest of our lives, Harry? There's all our twenties and our thirties and our forties and our fifties, maybe more. It's for ever. What do you want most, Harry?'

'Some of that pie!' He made a grab for it, and when she protested he wasn't being serious, he said he was. Very serious. 'I want to marry you, Alice. When I'm a proper footman, not just steward's footman, and can keep you properly.'

This was surely the most magical hill in the world. She'd never dared to hope so much. 'Harry, do you really?'

'You didn't doubt it, did you?'

'No, I suppose not, but it's the first time you've said it.' She'd always been with Harry ever since she first came. Harry made her laugh, Harry was wise, Harry knew about flowers and birds and butterflies, Harry's merry eyes danced in her dreams all night, even when Lily was snoring.

'I thought you knew it. There's always only been you.'

'I love you, Harry,' she said putting her arms round him and his closed around her. This was a bit awkward sitting on the grass, but when she felt his lips on hers she forgot the discomfort. 'Oh Harry, we'll be together for ever and ever,' she said fervently when at last he let her go.

'You're only sixteen, Alice. You might change your mind, some whippersnapper of a smart valet might come along and snap you up and take you off to London with him.'

'You don't think I'd go, do you? Leave Crandene and you?'

'Do you like Crandene, Alice, or just us being together?' Harry asked presently when they'd had their picnic and were idly picking daisies and late cowslips from the grass to make a garland.

'I like you best,' she replied immediately, 'but I do like Crandene too.'

'Why?'

'It's beautiful. All these gardens and the house. Mrs Cheney says there's been a house here for hundreds of years. You can feel it when you look at the walls, and when you walk on the grass and see the vegetable garden. They're saying, "We're old and valuable. Look after us."'

'The Beavers have only been here fifty years or so.'

'I thought they'd lived here for ever.'

'They'd like you to think that. But old man Beavers, the first baron, who died ten years back, he came here when it was a ruin in the 1870s and rebuilt it. He was a soldier. He got the VC in the Crimea.'

'I know,' Alice said. You couldn't help but know that in Crandene Place. There were army pictures and remembrances everywhere, all of which she had to dust. Paintings of Major-General Lord Beavers and his son, who'd won the VC too, and now Mr Robert would soon be going into the army. That was good news. He wasn't the same sort as his grandfather sounded, or even like his father. He wasn't so big as them, not so much presence. But he had to go because he was the heir. It was a great tradition, Harry had explained. There were relics of the Crimea, and of India, all sorts of places. Places she'd hardly heard of.

'They say that one day there'll be another war,' Harry said. 'Nearer home. Fighting that Kaiser maybe.'

'It won't affect us at Crandene though,' Alice said confidently.

'No. We'll be safe enough here.'

'I might be back in the kitchens by then. Perhaps a vegetable cook even.' Her imagination soared.

'You'll be telling me Lily's getting promoted next.'

Alice giggled. Poor Lily would never make a cook and everyone, including Lily, knew it. 'I'd really like to be a cook,' she said wistfully, 'but Mrs Cheney wants me to train for parlourmaid one day.'

'Wouldn't you like to cook instead for me?' Harry asked.

Alice couldn't think of anything she would rather do. Have her own range and kitchen table, and little vegetable garden. 'Yes, Harry.' She flung herself on him so suddenly that he was knocked off balance, since he'd been lying on his side perching on one elbow, and they rolled over and over on the hillside together.

She would never forget this hill, never. The hill where she and Harry kissed and loved one another. The hill where Harry had said they would get married some day. The day when she knew she was Harry's for life. He kissed her again. 'Let's lie together close, Alice. Let's be close,' he said, and they were,

30

quietly with the spring sunshine warming them. After a bit he rolled away from her.

'That's enough, Alice,' he said hoarsely. 'That's enough until we're wed.'

Then he played a folksong or two on his flute while she sat very still, listening. He played 'The Minstrel Boy to the Wars has Gone' so hauntingly she shivered, remembering his talk of war nearer home. Then she remembered they were safe in Crandene, and nothing could touch them. Harry had said so.

At last he took her hand and they walked back down the hillside together to Crandene. As she ran up to the house alone, her heart sank. Here she was, happier than she'd ever been, and she had to run into Mr Robert lounging outside the servants' entrance, pretending he'd been taking his spaniel Spot for a walk, but she knew that was an excuse. He'd been waiting for her, and Spot was tied up to the hook on the wall.

'Well if it isn't Miss Alice, the prettiest housemaid around.'

'Good evening, sir.' She tried in vain to dodge.

'Come here.' He pulled her into his arms. She struggled to get away as he tried to clamp his mouth over hers and she could feel his body right up against her. Sobbing, she wrenched herself away and ran through the kitchen door – right into Mrs Cheney. Her gaze went past Alice to Mr Robert, smirking outside.

'I hope, Alice,' she said severely as she closed the door firmly, 'you haven't been encouraging Mr Robert. The family think poorly of that sort of behaviour.'

'No, Mrs Cheney.'

'You're not setting your cap at him, I hope, Alice.'

'No, Mrs Cheney.'

'I couldn't keep you on, if you were.'

'No, Mrs Cheney.' Alice thought she would burst with the unfairness of it all and rushed to her room which she still shared with Lily. Her perfect day had had the shadow of dusk stamped on it.

~

31

Rachel ran to the door to pick up the post. Today there were two letters, one bearing the stamp of the Crandene Foundation, and her heart began to beat faster. The short reply inside was not even signed by Lord Beavers, but by someone calling himself the development officer. It was very short – and very much to the point: 'Thank you for your interesting suggestion about the possibility of holding banquets at Crandene Place. I have discussed this with my board, but we regret that we cannot see our way to financing it at the moment.'

Rachel stared unbelievingly at the letter. Didn't they realize what an opportunity they were throwing up? Surely they must see it was a golden opportunity for them? She struggled to overcome this slap in the face, but in vain, hardly able to believe that her plans were so quickly doomed. There surely had to be a way to get her project moving. And she would find it. Perhaps Lord Beavers hadn't even seen her proposal? It was a slim chance, and she knew she had to face the fact that for whatever reason Crandene was not going to co-operate.

Still seething, she opened her second letter. This one was *much* more hopeful. It was true that Michael Hartshorn was in a sense peripheral to her plans, but no one could stop her from writing a biography of her aunt and publishing the recipes, and in this he might be very helpful indeed.

'So far as I know,' she read happily, 'no such cookery book has ever been published, or indeed anything by or about Alice Beavers or her time at Crandene, before or after her marriage to the late baron. I would certainly have known about it had it been so.' The letter went on to suggest they met, and that she should ring to arrange a time.

No use moping about one closed door, she thought triumphantly. Her open door lay ahead. Mum would have approved.

Three

M ichael Hartshorn must earn a tidy sum from his books, Rachel decided, as she walked up from Maida Vale tube station towards the loftier heights of St John's Wood, London. In May, London looked its best, its trees at their greenest, with blossom everywhere, and the confidence it implied for the summer to come matched hers. The month was nearly over now. When she had called Michael, she had had to restrain herself from arranging to see him the very next day, suggesting that they meet in about ten days. She needed time for more homework; she had scoured Canterbury for his book on Crandene, and then devoured it, eager for every scrap of knowledge she could acquire. She now knew a great deal more about the military and political manoeuvring of the 1930s, and about the Beavers family.

What she didn't know was much more about Alice. Not in depth at least. The book covered the period up to the outbreak of war in September 1939, by which time Alice had been Lady Beavers for a year, but it was curiously silent about her. Or should the word be bland? There were some additional facts given about her, which were helpful. Born in 1898, she was the third child of seven born to Elsie and Edward Carter. The two before her were boys, the three after her were girls, and Pops (Henry) came last in 1917. Alice had come to Crandene in 1912, stayed through just over half of the First World War and then left to better herself in the household of Major Sir John Dene, Tolbury Hall in Lincolnshire.

Back she had come to Crandene as chef in 1930, thus coinciding with the major years of Crandene's fame, before marrying the third baron in 1938. The war then broke out in 1939 and the Crandene way of life vanished for ever. Michael's book only had a few brief paragraphs about Crandene after 1939. During the war the house had become an army HQ, and thereafter had been opened to the public. Nor was there much said about the marriage, save that Lord Beavers had recently lost his first wife to cancer, and that Alice's fame had increased during the decade because of her cooking. Alice had died in 1984, fifteen years after her husband.

Just facts, yet a lot might be deduced from them, if only that Alice had had no problem with retracing the steps of her own past, by returning to the job she had quit over ten years earlier. Risky, but Alice had clearly made good in a big way by doing so. Rachel caught at her thoughts impatiently, aware she had fallen into the trap of presuming that marriage to Lord Beavers was automatically 'better' than any other way of life. Fine biographer you'll be, she reprimanded herself in amusement as she pressed the buzzer on the door of Michael Hartshorn's apartment.

'First floor, Miss Field,' the disembodied voice informed her. When she was face to face with its owner, she decided that he fitted the image of well-known author exactly. He was no Adam. He was into his forties for a start, and bore the casual studied image of those who have made it into London society. Dark, good looks, sturdily built without being overweight, and well-dressed without having raided every top designer in town. Off-putting, Rachel thought as she instantly stiffened. The image changed, however, when he smiled at her, and he became human. She was nevertheless aware of being summed up, judged, and accepted all in a trice. He had the trick – if trick it was – of making her feel she'd passed the test with flying colours.

'Come in,' he invited her, ushering her into what he described as his working room at the end of a short hallway. 'Coffee?'

The formalities were observed, journeys discussed, the sunny day admired, while Rachel took note of her surroundings. This was a writer's room without a doubt, and it impressed her. There were bookcases everywhere, a practical-sized desk and computer. It was a large, full and somehow comfortable room that managed to be businesslike as well.

34

'So, you're on the family history trail.' Michael settled himself easily into his chair, once coffee had been dispensed. 'And a descendent of Alice Beavers.'

'Not in the straight line,' Rachel pointed out. 'In fact, I knew very little about her till I read your book. She was my grandfather's elder sister, and I've become interested in her, or rather in the recipes she left. I kicked myself for not asking the right questions when my mother was alive and now I doubt if I can get much further. I'd like to though.' She had told Michael on the telephone about the recipes without enlarging on her plans for it.

'I'm glad you learned something from my book. I have to confess, Alice was a somewhat mysterious figure to me. I asked a lot of questions but I got very little information.'

'You have the bare facts.'

'The lack of flesh is that obvious, is it?' He grinned ruefully and Rachel decided she liked him. Any fears that he might play the great historian were temporarily allayed.

'Only to me,' she answered, 'because I'm impatient to know a lot more about her. So far as you're concerned, Alice was a peripheral figure.' Odd, she immediately realized, because that's exactly what Alice had *not* been. She had played a crucial part in building up the Crandene image and then had married Lord Beavers. Who knew what her influence had been then? What's more, Michael Hartshorn must have been aware of this too.

She was relieved when he commented, 'You think so, do you?'

Honesty was the best card here. 'No,' she replied.

'That's better. Now we know where we are. Let's start again, Rachel. Tell me more about why you want to do this family history project. You said these recipes she left made you interested to find out more.'

That was an understatement, for Alice seemed to becoming part of her. Not only did she want to know, she *had* to learn more. Alice didn't represent the past to her, she was rapidly becoming her future. Caution was needed here, though. After all, Rachel reflected, Michael must be on good terms with the enemy, as she had mentally dubbed Lord Beavers.

'Yes. My mother died recently and I found the recipes amongst her papers.'

'That's interesting. Did you know I interviewed your grandfather for the book? Your mother was present too.'

'No. I didn't know that.' Mixed feelings battled within her. If he had seen Pops and still discovered little more than she'd read, it didn't bode well for the visit she was planning herself. Unless Pops had taken against him and clammed up – or perhaps Mum had. She couldn't quite believe that, for Michael seemed reasonable and tactful enough.

'My mother . . .' She cleared her throat, annoyed with herself for displaying emotion.

'I'm sorry. You mentioned she had died. Was it very recently?'

'Three months now.' As she had hoped, he was obviously classifying her as an instant family historian, who would have forgotten all about this sudden desire to meet the ancestors in a month or two, when she was over the worst of the grief. Well, she wasn't, and she wouldn't. 'Did you learn anything more than you've covered in your book?' she asked.

'It sounds crazy, but hardly anything. I didn't get a rounded picture of the woman. Alice died, as you know, in 1984 and I'd no reason to meet her then.'

'I gather my mother rarely saw her.'

'Oh, but she did. She might not have talked about it to you, but which of us does know what our parents' lives are when we're not demanding their attention ourselves?'

'True.' She was grateful to him for making her feel better, but felt guilty all the same. Surely Mum must have talked about visits to Alice with her? She must just have forgotten.

'Your mother was still in her thirties when Alice died, and you must have been a child. By the time I met your mother your father had just left, and I suppose her mind might not have been fully on deceased aunts. She told me very little.'

'You seem to know a lot about my family.' How dare he mention Dad? It hadn't been necessary, and it was forbidden territory even for Rachel, let alone a stranger.

'I have to.' He spread his hands apologetically. 'I made

notes. Information doesn't get etched into my mind. I looked them up when I knew you were coming.'

'Yes. Sorry.' Get back to the present, Rachel, she told herself. 'My mother must surely have described Alice to you though.'

'Reserved, I gather. Your mother got on well with her, but she said she seemed to be living in a different world. Alice was always interested in Margaret's life, but made little mention of her own. They used to talk food a lot, because Alice was a fanatic about English food and its history.'

'That's clear from the recipes I have, and from your book,' she added tactfully.

'Ah yes. Your grandfather wasn't much help to me either. By the time he was born in 1917, Alice must have left for Lincolnshire, and though the family followed her there, he didn't know her except for her visits from Tolbury Hall on her days off. When they all returned to Crandene in 1930, he got to know her rather better. She used to take him out on walks or trips. He was vague about it though. She was just an older sister, albeit a grand one. Ruling the roost at Crandene, and coming home to tea on Sunday afternoons, when she seemed very posh in her smart clothes. What he did remember clearly was Alice's wedding to Lord Beavers in 1938. He was twenty-one then, and expecting a grand occasion – which it wasn't, probably because it coincided with the Munich crisis.'

'I don't remember seeing a wedding photo in your book,' Rachel said, suddenly realizing this.

'That's because there were very few, all of poor quality, and wouldn't have added anything to the book.'

'Aren't there any amongst the photos on show at Crandene?'

'No.' He looked at her. 'Remember the Crandene display is monitored by the children of the first marriage. Alice never had children of her own.'

'You mean there was no love lost between them. But surely somewhere there'd be a wedding picture, if only to provide a complete archive.'

'Not if they didn't like her.'

'That would affect later snapshots, but her husband would

have arranged photographs of the wedding itself.' Rachel suddenly felt fiercely protective of Alice. Perhaps every descendant resents it if one of their forebears turns out to have been less than perfect.

'You must have talked to the Beavers family,' she said, 'and you talked to Alice's. What conclusion did you come to about her, even if you didn't have evidence enough to put it in the book?'

'What conclusion would you have come to, Rachel, if you looked at the facts and there was nothing to contradict them?'

She felt her eyes sting with anger. 'You tell me. If I'm to write her family history, I need to know.'

'The conclusion I came to was that she was driven with ambition for whatever reason and used her undoubted cooking skills to get to the top. Another Rosa Lewis of the Cavendish, if you like, except that Alice didn't have the cash to buy a hotel so she took advantage of a grieving widower and married him. Hey presto. Goodbye cook, hello society hostess. But war must have thrown her plans into disarray, to say the least.'

'You've said enough for me to get the picture.'

'Sorry, but that's a biographer's job. You're wanting to tell a family story. I have to be objective. In your position I—'

'In my position, as you call it,' she interrupted, 'I need to be objective too. I'm not just telling a family story. I want to publish it in conjunction with the recipes. That puts a different complexion on it.'

'Do you?' He looked taken aback, but quickly recovered. 'My apologies. I thought you were just after an interesting hobby. These recipes are interesting then? Did you bring them with you? I'd like to see them.'

She hadn't intended to get drawn so far, but after all there was no reason not to put her cards on the table, including the knave. It could do no harm, and might do some good, presuming that Michael was on good terms with the Crandene Foundation.

'Yes, they are interesting, but no, I haven't brought them with me. I can send you a copy of a page or two if you like. It is – or was – my plan to give practical demonstrations of the recipes based around Alice, and preferably in conjunction with Crandene. But that seems out because the foundation have turned the idea down.'

'The foundation or Lord Beavers?'

'Both, but I addressed the letter to Lord Beavers.'

'Ah.'

Rachel grinned. 'And yes the letter was literate. I dotted my *i*'s and crossed my *t*'s, and addressed him properly.'

'I'm sure you did. Did you, however, know that they're in the middle of fundraising at present?'

'That's precisely what I hoped my idea could fit into.'

'I mean major gift, or to be technical, principal gift fundraising. One big hit, in other words. It's my hunch that they don't want to muddy the waters.'

Rachel flushed. 'I've no idea of muddying any waters, *Mr* Hartshorn.' Be blowed if she'd call him Michael. 'In fact, if I were a donor considering a major gift of presumably the odd million or two, I'd want to ensure the cause I was giving it to was reasonably forward thinking and not a dinosaur. Also that they had plans for increasing their own income, and were not intending to rely merely on my money to live on.'

'Point taken. But there's also one other factor.'

'What's that?'

'Have you considered what Crandene is really about, which makes cooking a sideline?'

A sideline? Rachel was taken aback. For her, and, she had assumed from its role in the 1930s, for Crandene, cookery was central. 'Go on,' she said. 'Explain.'

'Crandene is about the Beavers.'

'What about them?'

'The fact that you have to ask that is fairly damning, Rachel. Sorry to say so, but that's the case.'

'Are you trying to put me off?'

'I'm beginning to think nothing will put you off. A chip off the old Alice block.'

Rachel stood up. 'Perhaps I'd better go. I'm sorry to have wasted your time.'

'Sit down and don't be huffy. Understand the battlefield before you send your troops in.'

Unwillingly Rachel did so. 'The sitting down I can manage,' she said stiffly. 'I can't guarantee the huffy.'

'If we're to work together, you'll have to. I don't do huffy. My ex-wife does that.'

Rachel glanced at the photograph on top of one of the bookcases. Presumably that was she, unless it was a current girlfriend. The place had the air of a competent bachelor pad, though. *Had* she said anything about working together? She didn't recall so. Nevertheless, it was worth pursuing. 'OK, no huffy,' she agreed, grinning.

'The Beavers family is the army and the government,' Michael continued.

'The mix of army and politics at Crandene. I knew that.'

'But do you realize how deep it goes? Look at the story. The first baron, Major-General Gerald Beavers, received a retrospective VC when the award was introduced after the Crimean War. His regiment was the 97th Foot, which amalgamated with the 50th in 1881 to become the Queen's Own (Royal West Kent) Regiment. The 97th became the second battalion. His son, Alfred, the second baron, went into the 1st Battalion of the Royal West Kents, and won himself, believe it or not, a VC at the Gate of Swat with the Malakand Field Force on the Indian border with Afghanistan in 1897, when a gentleman nicknamed by us the Mad Mullah of Swat incited a holy war. It was from this that the famous Crandene political connection sprang. Winston Churchill, then a young subaltern and accredited journalist to the *Daily Telegraph*, took part in the fighting after the storming of the gate, which in fact was a narrow causeway into the Swat valley from the Malakand Pass. Churchill never forgot it.

'Winston's influence was strong, whether in or out of power, and winning that VC did Alfred Beavers' future political career no harm at all. Two VCs in the family provided a role model and when the next baron, Robert, the one Alice eventually married in 1938, *also* won a VC in the First World War, the pattern was set. What kind of pressure do you imagine that set up for his descendants? Since then VCs have been scarcer. Robert's son reached a DSO in the Second World War, which left it to the current Lord Beavers to do his best in the Falklands. He didn't get too far in the awards stakes, but as he had a desk job that's understandable. So you see the military heritage is the very basis of Crandene's past and now the future – albeit in a different way.'

Rachel was beginning to see Michael was right; in her anxiety to learn Alice's story, she hadn't fully appreciated the issues.

'So you can see that set beside this military heritage,' Michael continued, 'cookery books are sidelined. You'd have to work hard to convince Crandene that Alice's recipes should be in the forefront of the Crandene tradition.'

Michael spoke so dispassionately that Rachel could not fault his argument.

'Can I ask you,' she said, 'what you would think of my idea if there were no such other pressures?'

'I can't judge it. It seems good enough to me, but I'm no expert in this field. Do you want me to dig a little deeper?' He paused, then said a little awkwardly, 'As it happens, I'm in the middle of a book about the Beavers' army links.'

Was he indeed? It instantly occurred to her that this was colouring his perspective, but she dismissed the suspicion. Her project would provide no threat to his own work. 'That would be good of you,' she answered. No harm could come of it, she reasoned, and a word at court from Michael Hartshorn might turn the tables. After all, if cookery was so unimportant, it might take little to persuade the foundation to change its mind.

'Would there be any chance of your getting permission for me to look at the Crandene archives?'

'I should think so. You can come with me if you like, I'll show you round.'

One step forward at last, she thought thankfully, as she returned home. She now had two helpers on the sidelines, both of which she intended to keep firmly there.

She had hardly got inside the cottage when the telephone rang.

'How's the great plan going?' Adam asked.

'Puttering along, thanks. Crandene turned me down flat, but—'

'Glad to hear there's a helpful but.'

'I went to see Michael Hartshorn today. He's going to help.' She recounted what had happened, slightly defensively, because the air waves were telling her Adam didn't think much of her confiding her plans to Michael. 'He's going to take me round Crandene,' she added.

'Why?'

'I want to see the archives.'

'No. I mean you've just told me that this chap reckons Alice was a cold self-advancing bitch. He doesn't like her. He also thinks that cookery is a sideline so far as Crandene is concerned, and this new book of his is confined to its military achievements. So why's he helping you?'

A silence. 'Perhaps because he just likes my bright eyes,' she replied carefully. Adam's words had made her think.

'So do I, but that doesn't mean I'd jump at the chance of involving you in the inner workings of Never Alone, unless it was to my advantage to do so.'

'The fraternity of us writers,' she quipped.

'From what little I know about the writing community, fraternal/sororal love doesn't play much part.'

'Don't be so suspicious,' she retorted inadequately. It was usually she who was ultra-cautious, and so she gave some thought to this after she hung up. *Was* Michael unduly anxious to help? She didn't think so. And, after all, the same could be said of Adam. She could feel herself instinctively retreating from his eagerness to know what was happening over the script. Unfair, but alone is best, she told herself, although in this instance she could think of no good reason to support this. All books needed sources, living or written, and preferably both. This was merely a cookery book, little to do with Crandene's main business, as Michael had pointed out. What logical reason could there possibly be, therefore, for Michael or Adam to be serving their own interests by helping her? Adam had brought the script to her in the first place, Michael was in the middle of another book about Crandene with which the story of Alice Carter could not possibly conflict.

After supper she looked at *Repasts of Delight* again, which delighted the eye almost as much as she was sure its recipes

42

would delight the palate: rose pottage, oyster loaf, sucket of lettuce, mawmenny of chicken, flummery, quaking pudding, potted lobsters with honey, spiced mackerel with orange. What was entrancing her so much, apart from the fact that the recipes were based on old English traditions? She remembered Adam's 'because love was in the air'. That watercolour of the Windy Hill certainly suggested it, as did the dedication to Sam. If Sam wasn't her later husband, who was he? She would find out, in order to understand the real Alice. Who was she: the reserved Alice; the self-advancing bitch; or was there another Alice waiting for her to find the key?

August 1914

'I don't understand, Harry. Why should we go to war, just because an Austrian duke was shot in Bosnia? That's part of their empire,' Alice was whispering to Harry in the servants' hall. Rumours about the European crisis had been flying around for days, but then at supper Mr Palmer and Mrs Cheney and the upper servants had filed in to the servants' hall to say it looked probable that England would be at war by midnight.

'It's because of alliances,' he said, half excited as she was, half nervous. 'England and France are just like old Cheney and Palmer, who stick together even though they don't like each other.'

'Oh, Harry, how can you joke about it?'

'It's no joke, Alice. Countries are what their governments make them and governments are made up of people. Just like the servants' hall. And the family.'

'Do you think,' she suddenly dared to hope, 'Mr Robert will go to war?'

'Bound to. He'll join the Royal West Kents like his lordship.'

Thank goodness, Alice thought. Robert would go into the army and she'd be safe. It was all she could think of.

Then another, terrible thought struck her. 'You won't have to go to fight, will you, Harry?'

'Fine soldier I'd make. I suppose I'd volunteer if they needed me.'

'Harry!' Alice was aghast. How would she live without Harry, here on her own? Her whole life was Harry.

'It would only be for a few weeks, after all, till we chuck the Germans out of Belgium.'

It was beyond Alice as to why the murder of a duke in Bosnia had led to Germany invading Belgium, so she was glad it would only be a short fight. All the same, she couldn't help worrying. Everyone was saying how the men were already leaving Cranbridge village – reservists, that is. And the war hadn't even begun yet.

'But why would you want to go, Harry?'

He looked very serious. 'Someone has to stand up to the Kaiser. We don't want him coming here, do we?'

'Here? To Crandene?'

'Everywhere if he invaded England.'

She remembered her mother telling her that her grandmother as a little girl was threatened with the fear of old Boney coming to get them from across the Channel, and now there might be another Napoleon coming. And then Mr Robert would come home here to fight.

Today she had seen him, and she was still trembling from the awfulness of it. He was down from university, and caught her in the passageway, barring the way with his arm. 'You don't get past me, young Alice.'

She turned and walked quickly the other way, but he came up behind, violently pulling her into one of the bedrooms, then slamming the door behind him. Then he pulled her roughly into his arms so that she could not move.

'You've got to be nice to me, Alice,' he said thickly. 'It's your duty to be nice to me.'

Then he pushed her backwards against the bed until she fell down with him on top of her, tugging her skirts up, and grasping her body. She fought back with her one free hand, but she was choking from his lips devouring her face, his tongue forcing itself into her mouth.

'Don't scream or you'll be sacked,' he said, as he at last withdrew it. She'd thought she would choke.

She fought back all the same, as he ripped her dress, knowing she was lost, no one would find her. As he turned to her again, however, her free hand clawed at a feather pillow open at one end, and grabbing a handful she pushed the feathers in his face, choking him, so that he released his hold for a moment. Then she was away, racing down the corridor to the back stairs, where he would not follow her. When she had composed herself, she went straight to the kitchens, and up to Monsieur Trente, who was lovingly stirring a hollandaise sauce on the stove.

'Monsieur Trente, could I come back to work for you?' she asked. 'If everyone volunteers, you'll need more help. I could be a . . .' She was going to say kitchenmaid again, but then she remembered what she *really* wanted to do, and drew breath to say boldly, 'A vegetable cook. Or pastry. I can do it. I can learn. I want to be able to cook. Oh, please, Monsieur Trente.'

He looked horrified and helpless – out of his depth at being taken by surprise.

'I do not work with women.'

'You could learn to, Monsieur Trente.' She was desperate. 'I'll be no trouble.'

He looked at her carefully, and his eye fell to her ripped skirt. 'Now tell me, Alice. Do you not want to be a housemaid or do you want to be a vegetable cook? Which is more important?'

She knew the answer to that. She wanted to be back in the kitchens. She wanted to take the lovely vegetables brought in by the gardeners each day and turn them into works of art.

'Both,' she answered honestly, 'but most of all I want to be a cook like you.'

'I will not be kind to you, Alice, and you will think not at all of Mr Robert, and less of Mr Rolfe, if you please. And Mrs Cheney must agree.'

She smiled at his understanding, and the dimple responded in his left cheek. 'Yes, Monsieur Trente,' she agreed.

She couldn't wait to tell Harry, though not the reason that had driven her to it, and then her great news had been spoiled because of this greater news of war. Late in the evening though, after they stopped talking of war by mutual consent, she did tell him, and he was full of admiration.

'You'll be too grand for me, Alice,' he kidded her. 'What about us getting married then?'

45

'That's the most important, Harry. You'll be a footman soon after all, and I should have learned how to cook by then.'

'Don't see why you can't do both if the family lets us. Till we have kiddies, eh?' He seized his flute which was never far away and played a bit of 'Here Comes the Bride' as she laughed in pride.

'Oh, Harry.' Such happiness, such fun they'd have.

'Let's go up the windy hill tomorrow on our half day.' The windy hill was their joking name for it. Harry had given her a book of poems for her birthday by a young poet called Rupert Brooke, and then read one out to her: 'Breathless, we flung us on the windy hill, Laughed in the sun, and kissed the lovely grass.'

This Rupert had written because he'd heard of them, Harry told her. She liked the poems, because he wrote about ordinary things as well as lofty ones, and his poetry made her feel . . . well, excited, just as being with Harry did. There was one called *Dining-Room Tea* that they didn't understand at all, but there was a lovely line in it: 'When you were there, and you, and you, Happiness crowned the night.'

She felt like that about Harry. And the next day, on their hill, Harry was here with her to blot out the memory of Robert Beavers, and she felt his arms around her. And you, and you . . . there were wild flowers and bees, and birds singing. Oh, it was a wonderful summer here with Harry, and even though war had now come, it would only last a short time. She clung tightly to Harry, until he moved away.

'Don't you like me, Harry?'

'Course I do. You know that. But we're not married. We can't get too loving.'

'Even if I wanted to, Harry?' she asked, greatly daring.

'We are loving, Alice. Loving close like this for ever.'

Four

'So, where next?' Adam leaned back on the bench, and surveyed the pub garden with all the satisfaction of the replete luncher. The ham ploughman's had been good. 'Odd, isn't it,' he remarked, 'that the better the ploughman's the further it gets away from its origins. I don't see salads, baguettes and pickles, or even ham, figuring on the average medieval labourer's menu.'

'You're wrong there,' Rachel replied idly. 'Baguettes, no, but pickles and salads, yes. Not your tomatoes and cucumber, of course, but they had their own self-sufficiency vegetable patches and there was a lot more wild stuff available than we have today.'

'Would you come apicking with me this afternoon?'

'I should get back. I've an estate agent coming at four.' Suddenly this sounded less than attractive, despite the fact that yesterday it had seemed an excellent step towards her brave new world. It was good therapy sitting here with Adam surrounded by early roses heralding the arrival of summer. He'd invited her in repayment of the Alice lunch, or so he had said, but she guessed it was more than that.

'Presumably because you're putting the house on the market. That doesn't mean you're giving up on the script, does it?'

'No.' Giving up hadn't even crossed her mind. She had hoped against hope that Michael Hartshorn might magically turn the situation round, despite his discouraging words, and was disappointed that she'd heard nothing more from him, not only because she'd been holding back on visiting Crandene in order to take up his offer, but because she had found herself thinking about him more than she liked.

'If his reputation as a businessman is reliable, any angle would have a hard time slipping by.'

'Perhaps, but Michael pointed out Crandene is based on military and political traditions, compared with which Alice's role would seem very small.'

Two eyebrows were raised. 'Michael Hartshorn *would* take that view. He helped create that image.'

'Do you know him?' she whipped back angrily.

'I once ran into him somewhere.'

'You seem to run into a lot of people,' she remarked. Adam seemed disconcerted by her question, but perhaps it was imagination for there could be no reason for it, unless he had taken an instant dislike to Michael.

'Charity people do. We're like little moles running along tunnels, blind, sniffing out the next fundraising prospect. We're not choosy whose garden we pop up in.' Then, as Rachel grinned, he added, 'Have you actually sent this appeal to his lordship?'

'I posted it on the way here.'

'OK. What's the angle you raised?'

It was a reasonable question, and she decided to bounce the idea off him. 'My banquet business could supply Crandene with a winter income, as well as summer. It could be combined with hosting small winter conferences which would help cover their overheads on heating and staff. I've checked it, and they don't advertise anything like that at present on their web page.'

'Is that all?'

'Yes – but I think it's a pretty good "all".'

'So do I. It was a good idea to concentrate just on one aspect instead of presenting a list of twenty reasons why Crandene needs you. I can see why you made a success of your sandwich business.'

'Success? You have to be joking.'

'Did it go bankrupt?'

'No. I even sold the company when I left for France.'

'There you are then. Success. So, I ask again, what shall you do next?'

'Wait for his lordship's reply.'

48

'Can't we take a step further now? Why don't we drive over to Crandene, pay up our seven quid or whatever, and have a look-see. You can sniff out the atmosphere of the place, like a little mole yourself.'

Rachel made up her mind. It would indeed be a good chance to sniff out the territory with an undemanding companion.

Driving around Kent's narrow lanes in Adam's old MG was an experience. No shabby Never Alone vans today, though the MG, too, looked in need of restoration.

'There!' Adam pointed below them as the lane began to descend into the valley where Crandene lay. All she could glimpse from this angle were clusters of chimneys and what looked like cupolas, but it was exciting and intriguing enough to make her wonder why on earth she had never been here before.

Adam glanced at her and grinned as if reading her mind. 'Dramatic, isn't it?'

The driveway through the Crandene estate led off the lane they were on. With rhododendron bushes on either side, she could see no sign of the house. The car park was only half full on this early June weekday, and after consulting the guidebook they chose to walk along a footpath to the house rather than use the long gravel drive.

'If we go this way, we can walk by a lake,' Rachel pointed out. 'And there's an ice house in the hill on the far side. Do you think Alice popped out there to fetch it?'

'As cook she'd have been far too grand. She probably sent her Samuel, whoever he was.'

'I'll find out. I need access to the archives though. Even if Lord Beavers falls over backwards to help me, he'd hardly know the name of his grandfather's wife's earlier sweetheart.'

'Especially since the word "remembering" in the dedication suggests Samuel was dead.'

'Not necessarily,' she objected. 'It could have been the date of their wedding day. Perhaps she was married before she hooked his lordship.'

Adam whistled his appreciation, as the house came into view. 'I'd forgotten how splendid it was.'

It was beautiful to the eye. Photographs did not do it

justice, Rachel decided. The soft red brick, the gently curved Dutch gables, the towers topped with cupolas, the central stone wedding-cake turret, the chimney clusters, added to the symmetry of the windows and gables, gave her a sense of vicarious pride. She, Rachel Field, had a stake in this. True, it was an infinitesimally small stake, but it existed in the form of Alice.

'There doesn't seem to be any mention of Alice in the guidebook,' she commented to Adam.

'Other side of the family,' he replied laconically. 'I doubt if the kids of his first marriage welcomed the idea of a cook in the family.'

They elected to take the guided tour, sinking into pleasant anonymity in the group of tourists, both old and young. Even though there was little mention of Alice, the tour was instructive. In the Second World War the house had been rejected by the authorities as a hospital or convalescent home and instead become a divisional HQ. After the war, the family moved back in and converted it back to a home and showplace to raise income. The family (the great Lord Beavers, who would tomorrow be studying her letter, first class post willing) still lived in part of the house. She had expected to see a military portrait of Alice's husband to match those of his ancestors who had also been awarded the VC, but could not see one. There was only a rather insipid portrait of him as a young cadet, with a spaniel at his side, in the dining room.

Rachel longed to ask more questions about Alice, but stuck to what had been agreed with Adam. They should not draw attention to themselves. She could not resist one question: 'Are the 1930s kitchens open to the public?'

'Ah, we have a food buff here,' quoth their jovial guide. 'The foundation is currently discussing opening up the kitchens and servants' quarters, but Crandene is not exactly a Petworth in this respect, so it's uncertain whether it will go ahead.'

'Were the 1930s kitchens the original seventeenth-century ones?'

Yes and no turned out to be the answer. Yes, there was an original separate kitchen block, which matched the stables on the far side of the house, and there was an underground tunnel linking the kitchens to the main house. No, because in the nineteenth century this block had been joined to the house, by roofing in for convenience's sake, providing a linking corridor and extra rooms. It spoiled the original symmetry of the house's facade, but was a great deal more practical.

'If,' Adam whispered as they went out of the house exit, 'they are really thinking about making a feature of the kitchens, it's curiouser and curiouser that they didn't want even to discuss your idea.'

'Maybe that's exactly why they didn't. They have their own plans. Do you,' she said despondently, 'observe my hopes being dashed to the ground and my spirits falling rapidly after them?'

'No, but if you feel that way, we'll make straight for the cream tea.'

'Done.'

'Good. It's in your interests.'

'You mean I need fattening up?'

'No. You're perfect as you are. But in my experience the hand that wields the teapot often has The Knowledge.'

'What about keeping a low profile?'

'What about taking any opportunity offered?'

The old stables had been converted into an attractive tea-house with each stall providing a shelter for two tables, and one end converted into a kitchen. What had been a hayloft had been converted into an open area with wooden stairs erected to it. Now it was used for more tables and as an art display area, though from one glance at its offerings, Rachel decided she would dispute the word art. If only Alice's paintings could be displayed, they would make the current exhibits look like mere doodles.

It was waitress service, and a gleam came into Adam's eye as he realized that theirs was a lady of mature years. 'Interesting house,' he remarked to her. 'Have you worked here long?'

Adam had met his match. 'Man and boy, nearly a year,' was the prompt reply. Rachel tried to hold back a snigger as the waitress amiably took the order and departed.

'Well done,' she said gravely. 'Clearly a fount of Crandene wisdom. She too believes in a low profile.'

'Is that a challenge?'

'Yes.'

Adam unwound his legs from the bench, and disappeared purposefully. Ten minutes later he arrived with the tea tray and a large grin on his face.

'I bet you didn't know that the third baron had a passion for Staffordshire china.'

'No. Where is it then?'

'Safely tucked away in their private quarters. Under consideration for cautious display.'

'Some hopes, I'd have said. What's this to do with me though?'

'The baron had one particularly valuable piece, a one-off late eighteenth-century commission. It was called *The Kitchenmaid*. You can't see it because it's one of two pieces that his second wife Alice took with her when her husband died. They were personal presents to her.'

'What was the other one?'

'A nineteenth-century piece, *The Minstrel Boy*.'

'He wasn't called Samuel, was he?' Rachel joked. 'How come Mrs Man and Boy knows all this?'

'Her mother cleaned for Lord and Lady Beavers in the fifties, and became interested in the china. It was a whole lot cheaper then, so she has quite a collection herself.'

Disappointingly after this, the tea had proved less than average; the cake was stale, and the tea itself feeble. 'The standard's slipped since Alice's day,' Rachel commented as they left the tearoom to explore the gardens. 'I spy opportunities for Rachel Field Enterprises here.'

'I hope his lordship does too.'

The formal gardens were behind the house, but it was the walled vegetable garden that attracted Rachel. It was one of the largest she had ever seen.

'You're right about Lord Beavers,' she commented, 'or at least the foundation. They're on the ball. This vegetable garden is kept up, or at least has been recently restored. Look at those greenhouses, they're in a good state of preservation.' Eagerly she went over to inspect them, and found them in full production, growing peaches and figs, as well as young vegetables and tomatoes.

'And, look, here's a pineapple pit on the side,' she pointed out when at last she emerged. 'Wow. They're really going it. I bet that shall-we-open-the-kitchens discussion is positive. No wonder Alice became such a good cook of English food, with this vegetable garden to support her. It would inspire me too.'

'Maybe it will yet.'

She groaned. 'Don't encourage me in daydreaming yet. I can grow false hopes all by myself.' She studied the plan of the gardens that they had been given. 'There's a pets' cemetery behind here somewhere. Let's find it.'

'Are you a pet lover?'

'Never had time, but pets' cemeteries are interesting places. The epitaphs can sometimes bring a family to life more than the "Good wife and beloved mother"'s in church cemeteries.'

The pets' cemetery was surprisingly well kept for a tucked-away corner. Most that Rachel had seen were neglected, but here the grass was cut and the stones cleaned. Moreover, it was still kept up. One – to Ralph, the Hunter Home from the Hill – was dated only five years earlier, and another was erected in the 1980s. If Rachel had been hoping to find a Beloved Samuel, however, she was disappointed. Then one caught her eye: 'My cat Jeoffrey who reigned over the household from 1950 to 1967'. Underneath was a Christopher Smart quotation: 'The servant of the Living God, duly and daily serving Him'. Either Alice or Lord Beavers had a nice turn of wit, and Rachel's money would be on Alice. This pleased her very much.

'"Spot",' Adam read out. '"Died September 1916. Faithful friend to Robert Beavers". There, that's Alice's husband. Dog lover as well as cats then.'

Spot might have been the spaniel in the painting of Beavers in the dining room, she thought. It seemed strange walking here, knowing that Alice must have used these paths often, and known each part of these vast gardens. The path skirting the vegetable garden would, if her geography was right, have been the quickest way to the village. On the far side of the garden was another little-used path with a small side gate in the boundary wall that could have led up to Crown Hill.

53

Perhaps that was Alice's Windy Hill? Maybe Samuel was a gardener, she surmised; they would meet here, then creep out of the gate and up the hill. Rachel tried to stop her mind leaping ahead again. Surely, oh surely, if Crandene was forward thinking enough to see the financial opportunities in kitchens and vegetable gardens, then they must also see that her plans dovetailed perfectly with theirs.

The reply to her letter came so quickly, she could hardly believe it. It came almost by return of post, and a week later she was once again at Crandene, this time alone. Lord Beavers' letter was, like the earlier one, brief and to the point, but at least it had a more positive point than its predecessor, suggesting he was certainly willing to discuss the matter with her, and proposing a day the following week. Her confidence was soaring again. He *had* seen sense.

This meeting was in his office on the top floor of the house, and she wondered whether Lord Beavers was deliberately underlining that this was a business not family matter, but decided she was getting paranoiac. After all, it *was* business that called her here. She had learned from *Who's Who* the bare facts about this fifth baron. He was married with three children, and had come into the title only two years previously, on the death of his father, George. John Beavers was fifty-eight, but he looked younger, she thought, as he ushered her into the modest office. Grey-haired certainly, but he had the figure and face of a man who was keenly interested in and in control of everything around him. He cut an imposing figure, she reluctantly acknowledged.

'So, Miss Field,' he began after the courtesies had been exchanged, 'we're related by marriage.'

'Remotely, of course.' Rachel made light of it, sure that this was the way to play it, now she had sized him up. This was not the genial, outgoing man she had hoped for. This man's vibes were strictly at his command to release or restrain. 'The grandchild of your father's stepmother's brother hardly qualifies for an entry in the family bible.'

He smiled. 'Your great-aunt lived through an interesting period at Crandene, and indeed played a part in it. Did you

54

bring the recipes with you? I should be interested to see this script you mentioned.'

'One or two photocopies to illustrate what I have in mind.' She produced them, and laid them on the desk before him. He looked at them carefully.

'I hope I will not have to disappoint you.' It was friendly enough, but the claws were intended to show.

'I hope so too.' She injected a note of earnest purpose into her voice. 'My idea does seem a natural one for Crandene, especially with my family connection to Alice.'

'Describe your scheme fully for me, would you? Incidentally, I apologize for the fact that I did not answer your earlier letter myself. It slipped through on to the wrong pile.'

She was aware that she was politely being informed he was a busy man, but she would not be thrown, and continued at her own speed. Enthusiasm without emotion was her aim. 'It seems to me,' she concluded after making what she considered a good case, 'that my plan, together with the proposed book, could only further Crandene's aims and extend the range of its activities throughout the year.'

'Tell me,' he replied, 'if you do not get our co-operation in this venture, what will you do about this script then?'

Her answer was a prompt one. 'I shall either publish a combined biography and cookery book myself or find a commercial publisher for it.'

'That might not be possible,' he frowned. The tone was pleasant but firm.

'Why not?' she asked blankly, staggered that this had come so early in the discussion. 'I realize that Crandene itself might not wish to publish it, but there's no reason that I shouldn't.'

'There's every reason.' His expression ceased bland interest and turned into cold objectivity. 'I realize you could not have appreciated this but such banquets and such a book do not fit in with the foundation's aims. We have non-profit trust status and are bound by our governing document.'

'Which states?' Rachel could do cold objectivity too.

'The foundation is to further an understanding of the history of the nineteenth and twentieth centuries as reflected by Crandene and its political and military connections, and to promote educational studies therein. Cooking banquets would be outside its scope.'

'Then why are you considering opening up the kitchens to the public?'

Lord Beavers' eyes narrowed slightly. 'The kitchens are part of the house tour. Crandene's earlier history is also admissible under our governing document of course. But cooking banquets does not fall under the history of the house.'

'And your tearoom does?' With a great struggle she held back on any suggestion their current arrangements were less than perfect.

He sighed. 'I could explain it to you at much greater legal length, but I trust you will spare us both that tedium. I assure you I have been into it fully, because I am answerable to my board of trustees. Now, Miss Field, you say you want to research your family history. I'm prepared to allow you access to the Crandene archives and for you to publish a biography of Alice Beavers, provided the foundation approves the text first. In return, I should personally be interested in seeing this cookery script, and I hope that will be possible.'

Be damned if it would. Right of veto over her book? Absolutely no way. Rachel was beginning to dislike the fifth baron intensely, and she could be as obstinate as he – especially as her banqueting idea seemed doomed, at least as far as Crandene was concerned. Not in other venues though . . . Her mind began to leap ahead. Furthermore there was no way she was going to let the cookery script out of her hands, or even let him see it. Not the original anyway.

'I'll consider what you've said about the archives and thank you for that suggestion,' she answered briskly. 'Meanwhile I'll send you one or two more photocopied pages. It's too fragile to copy it all. As you see, it's a carbon copy, however. Might the original perhaps be in your own archives?'

'No. I've checked.'

Had he indeed. Odd thing to do for the head of a family which implied it had little time for Alice or her cookery.

'I should also make it clear,' he continued, 'that though there is no problem about your writing a biography, subject to my conditions, the cookery book might be another matter.'

56

'And why is that?'

'I gather that this is an unpublished script, and even if it were not it would still be in copyright since Alice Beavers did not die until 1984. There might therefore be issues that would concern Crandene.'

Rachel relaxed. She knew where she was on this one. The copy of Alice's will had duly arrived, and she had read it through. 'You mean if Alice's estate was bequeathed to the Beavers' family not her own? It wasn't. I've checked the will. Apart from a few items specifically mentioned, the small residual estate went to my grandfather, who is still alive. The cookery script would be part of that.'

'Ownership of the script, yes, but the copyright does not always pass with the script itself. Alice Carter was in the employment of Crandene at the time she wrote the cookery book. Under the law, the copyright might now rest with the foundation or even with myself personally.'

Rachel's brain went into overdrive, and came up with the flaw in this argument. 'You haven't seen the script,' she said flatly. 'How do you know it wasn't written when she was married to your grandfather and not during her time as cook?'

'Quite obviously the recipes date from the 1930s,' he snapped.

'I agree that's probable, but their actual writing down is more likely to have been in the 1940s or 1950s when she had time to compile them.'

'The legal presumption would be—'

'The presumption is that you are arguing two different cases, Lord Beavers. You have said you and Crandene are not interested in the recipes except on a personal basis, and don't wish to exploit them for the financial benefit of the foundation. On the other hand, you are interested enough to stop *me* doing so. Furthermore, you're developing the gardens and kitchens here for just such a purpose. I'm willing to discuss the whole matter at greater length with you. Are you and your board interested or not?' Rachel somewhat surprised herself, but she was glad it was out on the table.

'I have stated Crandene's position. Good day, Miss Field.'

He stood up. 'I should advise you that you are unlikely to find a publisher interested without a clear copyright situation and without your using the Crandene name, and if you do use it, we shall take legal advice.'

'I hate him, Adam,' she exploded over the telephone that evening. Alone certainly wasn't best tonight.

'He turned you down.' Adam didn't seem surprised.

'Not just turned. I'm down and out to the count of ten. I can't understand why though. He's banging on about the foundation's governing document, and my plan not being in line with that, whatever it is. Then he says he will dispute the copyright in the script. Then he switches tactics and says he'll use the Crandene trading name excuse to stop me publishing. Yet they're developing those gardens and the kitchens.'

'Well done, Rachel,' Adam said softly.

'What on earth do you mean? Please don't make fun of me, I can't bear it tonight.'

'I'm serious. You've got him on the run. He doesn't just make one threat. He makes several, where one would have done. How *very* interesting.'

'So it may be. But why?'

'Could just be old ways dying hard, as he's dragged kicking and screaming into the new fundraising age.'

'No way. He's right on the ball, Adam. He says he's no interest in the script except a personal one, yet he's trotting out copyright laws as though he looked them up yesterday. As I suspect he did.'

'Ah. Even more interesting. So what next? Giving up?'

'No, I'm not. I'm going right on, beginning with a visit to my grandfather.'

'Be careful, Rachel.'

'Of what? What I might find out about Alice?'

'Perhaps. There's something at Crandene I don't understand, and it's a powerful force to mess with. Just take care.'

Late August 1914

Nothing made sense anymore. She and Harry had thought Crandene would never change, but it had, ever since war was

58

declared on the fourth. The reservists had left first, and that took two of the footmen and two gardeners from Crandene. Then recruiting posters had gone up, even at Crandene itself, and off went most of the young male population of Cranbridge village. Eddie, her elder brother, had volunteered and his lordship had kindly let her go home to say goodbye. War, it seemed, meant the usual rules didn't apply. There was nothing but talk of war in the servants' hall this morning, and what a wonderful success the British had just had in France at a place called Mons three days ago. If it was so wonderful, Alice wondered why there was no talk of the army coming home? Instead more and more men were going off to fight.

The good news was that Mr Robert was one of them. He was sailing to France tomorrow to join the Royal West Kents' 1st Battalion. He'd be back soon of course, because everyone said the war must be over in a few months, and now there had been this victory she supposed it must be much closer than that. Meanwhile, her ladyship had organized a circle from the village to knit socks for the soldiers, and Miss Beavers had gone to help at a canteen for the troops at Dover. They'd had a giggle over that in the servants' hall, because Miss Beavers didn't even know how to make a cup of tea.

And then there was poor Monsieur Trente. 'Will you have to go back to France?' she'd asked him. What would happen if he did? He'd taught her so much, and they worked so well together; he told her how to cook things and how food should be respected and studied, not just thrown in a pot, and vegetables in particular. He said there was a French proverb: *Point de légumes, point de cuisinière.* The cook could therefore be judged by the respect he paid his vegetables. She didn't understand much French, although she was beginning to learn quite a lot from Monsieur Trente, but she said this proverb over and over again to herself, to memorize it.

'I would go to fight for France, but I am too old,' Monsieur Trente replied.

She was relieved, not just for selfish reasons, but because Monsieur Trente was a family man. He lived in, but, unusually for servants, he had a wife and son in Cranbridge village, and was privileged, for he was allowed to see them once a week by special arrangement. The sad thing was that his son had left to fight with the French army and Monsieur Trente didn't have the spirit even to be cross anymore. Not even when she curdled the hollandaise. She almost longed for him to flash his eyes and cry that she was an imbecile, so she would know things were normal again.

'Now the Germans come again, *petite* Alice. They came in 1870, and my grandfather and my father were killed at Sedan. I never knew either of them.'

'Oh, Monsieur Trente, how sad.' Suppose she had never known her father – it was a sobering thought.

'My mother told me if the Germans come again, I must fight for France, but now I am too old. I must fight on here in an English kitchen, and send my son to die for me.'

Furiously he attacked the escalopes with his mallet. Bang for Sedan. Bang for Paris. Bang for Belgium. Then suddenly he stopped and roared, 'And you, little Alice, what will you do for the war?'

'Me?' Alice was surprised. 'What can I do? I'm a kitchenmaid.'

'You will be sending your Harry. And, you will see, you too must fight Germans, they will not be beaten quickly.'

She blushed; Harry was a big secret between her and Monsieur Trente, in case Mrs Cheney found out.

'He isn't going to war, Monsieur Trente.'

'He will. His lordship says all big households have been told to encourage their bootboys, their lampboys, their footmen, their gardeners, all their young men, to volunteer. It is happening everywhere, and it will happen here.'

Alice thought of that dreadful poster she had seen in the village. Lord Kitchener's finger pointing out accusingly. Now that finger pointed at Harry, and Monsieur Trente seemed to be saying she should volunteer too. But women couldn't fight. All they could do was serve in the big houses. She had to earn money to support her parents and the little ones, so how could she do anything but stay here? Where would she go?

Perplexed, she forgot her usual caution, and took the rubbish to the outside bins herself. Once there she found her way back barred by Mr Robert and her heart jumped in fear.

60

'Good morning, Mr Robert,' she said woodenly, knowing full well he had waited deliberately for her, hoping she would emerge from the kitchens. She was usually safe inside and rarely saw him now except when he manufactured an excuse to come to the kitchens – usually that dreadful dog Spot wanted feeding – where there were always other people around.

'I came to say goodbye, Alice. You'll miss me, won't you?' It was a feeble attempt at his usual mockery.

'It's a grand thing to serve your country.' She trotted out the generally held statement, keeping the dustbin clasped before her, as a sort of weapon if needed. She could always drop it over his head.

'It's only grand if you're not going,' he said bitterly.

Alice stared at him in amazement. What a thing to say, especially in this household, where there was so much importance laid on armies and fighting and medals.

'Kiss me, Alice, kiss me goodbye. Just once.'

'No, Mr Robert.' She began to edge away, frightened.

'It's not much to ask when a chap has to leave to fight for his bloody country.'

'It wouldn't be proper. I wish you well, Mr Robert.'

'Then kiss me.' He lunged at her, and tore the bin away. 'Just one kiss.' Surprisingly, that's all it was, then he let her go. 'I don't want to go to France, Alice, but I've got to. Everyone has to. Even your precious Harry,' he sneered.

Her heart jumped in sudden fear. How did he find out about Harry? They had kept it such a secret; he couldn't have known long unless he had spied on them. But why hadn't he had Harry sacked if so? It would be just like him. Then she unwillingly realized the reason. He knew she would leave too. Normally they wouldn't get another job if they left without a character, but in wartime now it would be different. There'd be plenty of jobs. She wondered why Robert had this ridiculous interest in her. She couldn't understand it, when that nice lady, Miss Cecilia, was so much in love with him. Everyone said they'd marry, and Alice prayed for that day.

Never would she forget once when Mr Robert came to the kitchen and, finding her alone, whispered in her ear, 'You'll never escape me, Alice, never. It doesn't matter where you hide, I'll find you.' It had been just talk, of course, but she'd been scared.

She didn't get a chance to talk to Harry until they met for their usual ten-minute chat in one of the larders. This had been Monsieur Trente's suggestion, and it worked wonderfully well.

'You're not going to war, are you, Harry? Tell me you're not,' she pleaded.

'His lordship said us unmarried men could choose whether we went or stayed. I'm going to do it, Alice,' he told her gently. 'I know it's the right thing to do. All the chaps are going.'

'Right thing?' she echoed blankly. Once upon a time Mr Asquith and Parliament had been as remote as Buckingham Palace and His Majesty himself. They were represented by pictures in magazines and talk in the kitchen. But now they had come closer. She'd thought war was only to stop people like Napoleon from invading, or to settle disputes in far-off foreign countries, but now it had come to Crandene.

'Oh Harry.' Alice was cradled in his arms. 'You'll come back safe, won't you?'

'Of course I will. You'll see. They'll train us to be soldiers for a few weeks and then we'll be off to shove those Germans back home sharpish. It won't be for long. I don't want to leave, Alice, but a chap has to do what's right. What would I say to our kids if all the other dads had done their bit for England and I hadn't?'

Alice had no answer for this.

'Cheer up,' he comforted her. 'I'll take my flute and whistle you all my love from over there. We'll be married as soon as I'm back. I'll get paid for being a soldier, you'll see. We'll be rich.'

Five

So much for gentle breezes stirring the leaves on Alice's windy hill. Rachel grimaced as the wind whipped at her face, mocking the sun that was doing its best to persuade her it was summer. Its strength was hardly surprising here. Cap Blanc-Nez jutted out into the Channel, only twenty miles or so from England, but at such a distance in atmosphere and lifestyle it could have been a continent away. As it was a weekday, there were only two other cars parked on the stony chalk parking area. She'd chosen to walk the last hundred yards or so up to the tall stone monument on the Cap's peak, the wind against her all the way. It had been erected as a testament to British and French unity after the First World War, with memorials to Marshal Foch, the Dover Patrol, and to the British and French seamen for whom the Cap was a landmark, as was its near neighbour Cap Gris-Nez. Twenty years later war had broken out again, but there was no monument to that here, for it was the first war that was still etched into local folk memory. Dunkerque, with its bitter fighting, atrocities and final evacuation was a wound seared into the British psyche, not the French.

Not for the first time she wondered why Pops had chosen to live in France for about the last twenty years, the last five of them in a retirement home. He'd sold his business for a good sum, after his wife, her grandma, had died, and come to live in a village in the Pas de Calais, down towards the Somme. Mum had just said that he liked the place, and Rachel had supposed that was sufficient reason. Pops had been in the second war though, not the first. He'd fought in North Africa, and then again in the Normandy invasion and through to the last north European battles of 1945. She'd visited him

63

in Varville frequently, especially when she'd lived in France, and she knew this area like the back of her hand. Sometimes it occurred to her, however, that one didn't actually *study* the back of one's hands, and now it seemed to her she was seeing it for the first time – perhaps because she was seeing Pops not as her grandfather, but as her link with the generation he represented. She was interested in *his* youth, not coming as a representative of her own.

Adam, she had sensed, would have accompanied her here at the drop of a hat, but she wanted to see Pops alone. She – if she faced the truth – had an uneasy relationship with him, though she was never sure why this should be. She often had the impression that he disapproved of her, that he expected something of her that was never defined, and that while sometimes he was clearly glad to see her, more often he only tolerated her presence. Mum had always robustly told her this was nonsense, and that Pops felt awkward with the younger generation. Perhaps, but Rachel wasn't convinced.

She threw her head back and let the wind do its worst for a few moments; it was now surprisingly gentle on her face, and she closed her eyes and let her thoughts wander. These settled on lunch, and she laughed at herself. What else in France? The past was yesterday's food, the future tomorrow's, and what better tribute to Alice's memory than to enjoy the present's?

She drove down to the nearest restaurant, and ordered soup and salad, waving away tempting talk of local fish and *frites*. She would save her appetite for the evening. The farm where she regularly stayed was after her own heart, excellent home-produced ingredients, cooked with supreme flair. As she continued on her way to Varville, she decided that distancing herself from Crandene had been a good idea. She needed to step back to judge her next step after the slap in the face. Did she now publish and possibly be damned? Well, there was a simple answer to that: yes. No way was she going to sit down under Beavers' bullying. This was *her* family, *her* book. It was more than a project which she wanted to see succeed. It was part of her.

The farm was some way away from the coast, in the hinterland between the autoroute to Le Touquet and the Route

Nationale 1, and lay in a quiet green valley, which was remarkable so close to the thundering main roads. She decided to go along to see Pops immediately, so that she had time for a second visit if need be. The farm dog greeted her as an old friend, and showed every sign of wishing to accompany her, but then turned his attention to a passing duck on its hitherto peaceful route to the duck pond.

Rachel strolled along the road to the retirement home. L'Abri des Roses was converted from a former courtyard farmhouse and outbuildings, and was now a low rambling building with a series of self-contained rooms which meant the residents were able to have some privacy from each other, as well as company if they so wished. Nevertheless they were isolated, since even those who could walk had nowhere much to go. The village had only a small *mairie*, with not even a shop or café. A farm offered coffee and glasses of milk, but for a man like Pops who liked his whisky, this was hardly an inducement.

'*Bonjour madame,*' she greeted the manager, Madame Lefèvre, who opened the main door.

She was a brisk, efficient woman, not unfriendly but, conscious of her responsibilities, she took life very seriously. One did not jest with Madame Lefèvre, but after the courtesies were observed and Rachel had established that her grandfather was well enough to see her, she was allowed to proceed on her way to his room.

'Pops.' A rush of affection swept over her as she saw him there. He was seated in his chair by the window, stiff backed, hands on the arms of the chair, his eyes alert but watchful. On bad days they were vacant. The army junior officer was to the fore today, however. His still thick shock of white hair wore an invisible cap.

'So there you are, Rachel.' His grumpy voice suggested that she should have come ages ago. And so she should. Guilt immediately consumed her. She had come immediately after Mum's death to break the news personally to him, and then again after the funeral. That had been nearly four months ago. How could she explain that Mum's death had knocked her sideways, and that, still in shock at what had happened,

65

speaking to him on the telephone was the most she could manage for anyone, even for him. She was undoubtedly at fault. *But she was here now.*

'I'm sorry, Pops. Life's been tough.'

'It always is.'

'No, it's not, Pops. Not always.' She had to stand up to him or she would be lost in a guilt that was not of her making.

'It's time you realized—'

'No, Pops. It's time I kissed you,' she interrupted him firmly and proceeded gently to do so. 'I'm glad to see you, I really am.'

Taken by surprise, he looked more human, but his full age. 'You said you wanted to talk to me about Alice. Too much to expect you'd be interested in me, of course,' he added, to keep the guilt going.

She managed a grin. 'You first then. Tell me the latest gossip.'

She listened while he talked of the latest arrival in the home and of his deceased predecessor – the latter with particular relish. 'No stamina,' he announced. 'French, of course.' And finally, when he drew to a close, she raised the matter of Alice again.

'Can you bear to talk of her, Pops?'

'Oh, I can bear it, Rachel. I've been waiting long enough, you know.' He glanced wickedly at her, waiting for her reaction.

She didn't understand what he meant. Waiting for her – or waiting to talk about Alice?

'That's why,' he continued with malicious glee, 'I was surprised when that man came.'

'What man?' she asked sharply.

'Said he was a historian. Wanted to know about Alice.'

A cold hand clutched at her. *Adam*? Surely he wouldn't have done. What was this? A fantasy dreamed up by Pops to annoy her? 'What was his name?'

'Michael something, Michael Heartthrob?'

Rachel's head spun. What on earth was going on? 'Hartshorn is his name. Did you talk to him? What did he want to know?

What did you tell him?' The words came tumbling out. There was something weird here.

'Almost nothing,' he replied with relish. 'I had one of my bad days.'

'Deliberately? Oh Pops, how clever of you.'

'Glad you're pleased,' he said drily. 'I don't think he was. I did a pretty good job. I even managed the odd recollection for him. She liked the colour blue, I said, or was that the old song 'Alice Blue Gown'. Perhaps, I quavered, I was getting mixed up.'

Rachel laughed. She'd have this out with Michael the moment she was back, but she had to concentrate on Alice now. 'Are you mixed up now, Pops?'

'I'm not in my dotage yet. I'm only in my eighties. Tell me how you've been now.'

He wasn't going to talk about Alice until he was good and ready, so Rachel proceeded to give him an edited account of what had been happening, and what she proposed to do. 'I'm at a crossroads,' she concluded. 'I don't know whether to sell the house, or stay and—'

'And what?' he prompted her as she broke off.

'This brings me to Alice. Pops, among Mum's possessions were some papers of Alice's, including a script with some recipes in. Did you pass them on to her, or did Alice give them to Mum herself?'

'Recipes. That's what that fellow Heartthrob was talking about. I've just remembered.'

'What did he want to know?' Why should Michael be interested in *recipes*? Alice, yes, but the details of her cooking? Unless he'd just mentioned it because she, Rachel, had discussed it with him, and later sent a couple of copied pages – as she had to his Beavership. That must be it, she decided, though it left a nasty question mark in her mind.

'I've no idea. I just did my sweet old man bit. But it did ring a bell, so I've been mulling it over. Alice offered me a lot of family papers, when she was getting on a bit. I was just moving over here to France and said I could remember my family without a load of papers to wade through. She gave that smile of hers, and said no more, except that some of her

67

recipes were amongst them, so I suggested Margaret should have them.'

'Did she say anything about the recipes?'

'You're asking a lot, Rachel. This was twenty years ago. I suppose she either gave them to your mother or Margaret took them when she cleared the house after Alice died. That wasn't long after I last saw her.'

He was getting into irascible mode again, so she hastily switched subjects.

'Can you tell me something about Alice? I know it's a long time ago, but anything you can remember about her early life.'

He fixed her with his gimlet stare. Army officer interrogating naughty private. 'What do *you* remember?'

'Me? I never met her.'

'Oh, yes, you did. I've a photo of you with her somewhere. I took it myself, and I'm fairly certain it was that same day.'

'You mean I was *there* when all this was discussed?' Alice had died in 1984 when she was about eleven but she had no recollection at all of having met her. Why would she? Alice was her mother's aunt, and had played no obvious part in Rachel's life. Of all the bad luck, she'd probably been present when Alice was talking about the recipes, and she couldn't remember a blind thing about it.

Her grandfather hauled himself to his feet and went over to his desk. After fishing around for a few moments, he took out a black and white photograph and handed it to her.

'I fancied myself as a photographer, hence black and white. The effects are more striking.'

The photo was just of an ordinary group in a garden, with an old lady in a chair, and someone whom Rachel dimly recognized as her younger self at her side, standing awkwardly in the way she remembered doing when she was bored out of her mind. Perhaps she still did. And there was a younger Mum behind the chair grinning for the camera. It caught at Rachel's heart. Happier days, darling Mum, and she couldn't even remember this one. Or could she? She tried hard, looking at Alice, grey-haired, slender and smart despite her years, but not near enough to see the emotions on her face

68

or even to guess what they would be when the camera smile died. But she was catching a memory now. A hot day, she, Rachel, protesting because she would rather have been in the swimming pool with her friends. How did they get to where Alice had lived? Car, public transport? And indeed where had Alice been living then? Had she moved away? All she remembered was the general shape of the garden and – yes, a wonderful tea. Then the memory faded obstinately, and refused to reveal more. She could have wept with frustration.

'Where was she living then?'

'In Cranbridge – a mile or two from Crandene.'

Now she could place Alice in Cranbridge, the past had become personal. Alice was no longer just an ancestor, but someone she had met. Someone who had had a cat Jeoffrey whom she'd loved. The generations had touched fingertips.

'It was the last time I saw Alice.' Pops glanced at the photo again.

'She looks,' Rachel said, hesitantly, 'a reserved person. But you said she had a sweet smile.'

'Yes. She used it' – he concentrated for a moment – 'when she wanted to retreat into herself, but wanted you to know she loved you.' He coughed hastily, as though embarrassed at coming out with this flight of fancy.

'You knew her well then, even though she was big sister rather than sibling to you.'

'She was much older than me. I hardly knew her as I was growing up, even though we were all living in Lincolnshire when I was a child.'

This tied in with what she'd read in Michael's book, and she was impatient to know more.

'Alice was working at Tolbury Hall,' Pops continued, 'and Dad as a carpenter there, off and on, because he wasn't well. Alice lived in, of course, so we didn't see much of her. She came home once a month for a day, and every Wednesday she had a half day off.'

'And then she moved back to Crandene. Why?'

'I haven't the faintest idea.' He glared at her. 'I was a child. There'd been bad times, I gathered. At one time the family had been split up and put in the workhouse. What do you think of that? Husband, wife, children, all living separately, but somehow we all got together again. Looking back, I imagine Alice managed to get her job at Tolbury Hall, and then to haul the family up there with a house on the estate to go with it. Then we all came back to Crandene together. I remember that all right.'

There were huge gaps in this terrible story. Why had they left Crandene, and when were they in the workhouse, and why did they return to Kent? Michael hadn't mentioned the workhouse in his book, which had implied that Alice went straight to Tolbury Hall from Crandene. Had Pops not told him, or had he just not thought it important enough to include? Rachel stared at the face in the photograph; it was a strong one, and one that had known trouble. And yet that sweet smile.

'Tell me about Alice herself.'

'Well, let me see, what do you want to know? I was her pet, being the baby of the family. Last child in the family, born when my mother was forty-three. Still am the last one; the others have all gone now. The two eldest boys were killed in the war, and of the girls, Rosie, the nearest to me, was seven years older than me. So Alice would pet me, and bring me titbits from the kitchens. I remember that. She'd take me for walks on her afternoon off, and so on, and then she'd disappear again. I never thought anything of it. It seemed she was living in a different country, but it was only in the house less than a mile away. Things were easier in service after the war, but not that easy. She couldn't just come home when she liked, even though she was assistant chef then, and chef herself before she left. We saw more of her once we were back at Crandene.'

'That was nineteen thirty, wasn't it?'

'Was it? I was thirteen then. It was all very sudden. I hated it, Rachel.' For all the use of her name, he seemed to have forgotten her presence, taken back to a sudden remembrance of how it felt to be a teenager. 'I had my pals at school, I was going to be learning classics the next year, and playing in the first eleven, and then I was uprooted. All because Alice said so, according to what my mother told me. Mind you, Alice had changed by then.'

'Changed? In what way?'

70

'I can't be precise.' He frowned. 'She was more remote, and didn't take me out so often. Mind you, I was growing up, and didn't want to go around with my big sister so much, but everyone seemed to notice she'd changed. My mother said Alice was working too hard once she became chef, but I recall she'd been like it some while. Then Alice announced she'd got this job back at Crandene and she'd made it a condition we all went too. My parents didn't like it, but Alice ruled the roost by then, and she found them a really nice cottage in the village, all mod cons. It was rented at first, but later she bought it for them. My mother would never have to slave away again, she said. Indoor bath and water, even a boiler for the washing, and gas and electricity laid on. Mum was getting on for sixty by then and still had me living at home, so she was pleased about that. But it meant leaving Rosie behind, for she'd just married a local lad in Lincolnshire. Emmy too. Betty was older, born in 1901, and she was still living in Kent with her young family. That was a plus for coming back.'

So there might be other surviving descendants. She'd have to look into that. 'Did you see any of the life that went on at Crandene while Alice worked there?'

'Sometimes. She'd tell me if Churchill or Baldwin or any other famous names were coming and I'd go up there to watch them arrive. There were Germans too, sometimes. Von Ribbentrop was one of them. It was an interesting time. Wish I could remember more. But in 1935 I went to work in London, and lived away from home, so I didn't see so much of her. I remember the first time I went up to Crandene again when we returned. She showed me round and took me up Crown Hill. "This is The Windy Hill," she told me. "Don't forget it, darling." She'd never called me darling before, that's why I remember it. I was embarrassed.

'They were exciting days though, watching the Rolls-Royces and the Bentleys draw up, and the women, the dresses, the food. Now I wish I'd seen more of it. Then, I just took it for granted. One does at that age,' he said almost apologetically.

As she too had done, Rachel thought, glancing at herself as a bored eleven-year-old.

'Were you at her wedding to Lord Beavers?' she asked.

71

She had decided not to reveal the information she'd had from Michael. Let Pops tell it fresh.

'Of course. Well, that was a surprise. My parents were tickled pink. Us Carters at the wedding, with the posh folk. But it was a quiet wedding, just Lord Beavers, his children and us. Alice didn't wear white, and there were no bells or anything, just a nice lunch which she'd cooked herself. Strange really, for Crandene. I asked Alice if she didn't find it odd being in the Crandene dining room instead of behind the green baize door. "No," she said. I remember this clearly. "I'm where I should be."'

'So she planned to marry Lord Beavers? She must have been very ambitious.' Had Michael been right in his evaluation of Alice? It was a dismal thought.

'Funny thing that. My mother always said she wasn't, that she was a timid little thing as a girl. She never wanted to do anything much except to have a family, and that was the one thing she didn't have. Children.'

'But she landed up lady of the manor,' Rachel pointed out. There was a contradiction here, albeit one that gave her a better feeling about her great-aunt.

'Yes. She took it seriously from what I could see. Not visiting the sick and so forth, but administering the estate, and so on, especially during the war. Not the Alice I knew at all.'

'Did she have a difficult relationship with his children?'

'I wouldn't know. I was away at war, and afterwards I married your grandmother and set up house in London. They were just beginning to do First World War battlefield tours of France in the early 1970s, and though we didn't take a tour, Alice decided she wanted to go along. Robert had won a VC in 1916, which is what must have sparked it off. She wanted to go to the Somme; it didn't mean much to me, I was still too close to the second war, so this was old history to me. It was moving, I grant you. She even wanted to go round the graveyards. I didn't mind. If it had been the Bayeux cemetery from the second war I'd have felt differently, but there was no one here I knew. There was one grave she was looking for in particular – and she found it. "Someone you know?" I asked. "Yes," she said. "An old sweetheart?" I joked, never thinking she'd say yes. For me, Alice married Lord Beavers and that was that, but of course she was forty then, there must have been other men in her life. It was quite likely there would have been someone in the first war, for she'd have been a young girl then. She didn't answer; all she said was, "There," laying down some flowers she'd bought. "Remember this, Henry."'

'I did, though I forget the name. Harry something, I believe. Died at the Somme in 1916.'

'Are you sure it wasn't Samuel?' Rachel held her breath.

'Samuel? No, I'm pretty sure it wasn't. Who was he?'

'Alice's cookery book script was dedicated to Samuel.'

'The name rings no bells with me, but then that's hardly surprising. It could have been someone at Tolbury Hall, and if that affair had an unhappy ending it would explain why she left and came back to Crandene.'

'And you're quite sure the grave wasn't of a Samuel?'

'This, Rachel,' he said proudly, 'is one of my good days – and I do remember clearly. It wasn't. In fact, I seem to remember it was that visit made me think I'd like to live in France. Your grandmother and I came over here quite a lot after that.'

'There was a Staffordshire figure of a soldier,' Rachel suddenly remembered. 'One of a kitchenmaid and the other called *The Minstrel Boy*. Alice was very fond of them because Robert Beavers gave them to her. Do you know what became of them?'

'I wondered if you knew about them,' Pops said complacently. 'No need to worry. They'll be left to you.'

'I wasn't!' Rachel said indignantly.

'They're in that cupboard. I get them out now and then. Safer in there, and I know what they look like. No need to stare at them all day.'

She opened the door and saw Alice's treasures immediately. She squatted down until she was on the same level. *The Kitchenmaid* was an exquisite piece of art, probably earthenware rather than the porcelain of its companion, because it was an eighteenth-century work. The glaze was delicate and exquisite though. The kitchenmaid had cap, pink dress, and a bowl of vegetables in her hands, but was far from prettied up.

She had a lost look about her, as though recognizing her station in life, and wondering what it was all about. It was simple, tender and moving. The minstrel boy was clearly Victorian porcelain, but he too was a simple figure. He was playing a flute, dressed in a soldier's red jacket, and his whole bearing seemed to be saying: it is not war that's glory, but music. His eyes too bore a lost look as though he thought of home as he played.

'Thanks, Pops,' she said quietly, as she closed the door.

Despite several glasses of wine, a good meal and travel weariness, Rachel took a while to fall asleep that night, turning over in her mind just how much she now knew about Alice. She felt nearer to her but not near enough. The essential Alice was still eluding her. And who *was* Samuel? She would probe further tomorrow morning. Adam, she suddenly thought with no reason at all, would like this place. She could see him on this farm, feeding the donkey, lazing in the garden.

Thought of Adam, however, brought her to Michael, which postponed sleep a while longer as she fumed. He'd been dismissive about the chances of success at Crandene, and yet he felt interested enough to dash over here to see her grandfather again. *And* to raise the question of the script. Somewhere there was a trick she was missing.

When she returned to L'Abri des Roses the next morning, Madame was adamant. Mademoiselle Field would be welcome to sit with her grandfather, but it was not one of his good days. Rachel's heart sank; this sounded for real. She was right. The eyes that looked at her today were vacant, and though the pleased smile on his face as she walked in made her think he knew who she was, he didn't.

'Alice,' he said in a slightly puzzled way, 'I'm glad you've come at last.'

'I'm Rachel, not Alice,' she said quietly.

It made no difference. 'I keep meaning to ask you, Alice, who is Samuel? Crikey, those cakes you brought last week were good. All the chaps wanted some.' He rambled on until eventually she had to leave to drive back to Calais.

'I'll be back soon, Pops.' She kissed his forehead.

'Margaret?' he asked sharply and she had to steel herself to leave. This would pass, she knew it would, though it always shook her how he could be lucid on one day, and not on another. It was a familiar routine for him to confuse her with her mother.

As she reached the door, Madame Lefèvre was standing there. 'He thinks of the past,' she said matter of factly. 'It always upsets him.'

'Usually with elderly people it does the opposite,' Rachel pointed out, determined not to let Madame have the last word.

'Your grandpapa is himself.'

As if to prove her point, Pops' eyes suddenly became lucid again. 'Going so soon, Rachel?' he asked, sounding like a disappointed child.

'I have to, Pops. I'm booked on the three o'clock Seacat.'

'I remembered something about that script,' he announced triumphantly. 'Something Alice said. She didn't want it published. I think that was it,' he added uncertainly.

Rachel stared at him in disbelief. Why on earth wouldn't Alice want it published? Surely Pops must have made a mistake.

Madame Lefèvre saw the doubt in Rachel's eyes. 'He is perfectly clear, madame. It will not last, but *pour le moment, il vive encore.*'

She would ring Michael as soon as she got home. Rachel waited impatiently for every line of cars to disembark from the Seacat other than hers. Although she saw it as sneaky for him to have visited her grandfather at all without telling her, he might not see it that way, of course. And with the spanner Pops had just tossed into the works over publication, perhaps she would be better sleeping on it. She might even ring Adam first. Yes, she liked that idea.

This didn't prove necessary. As she drove up, she saw him, lounging against the side of the familiar van. It clearly wasn't there for him to drop off a plastic bag for donations, and she illogically felt crowded. Adam obviously recognized the car, for he strolled up to her as she parked.

'I wondered when you'd be back.'

75

'Did you indeed.' *Please* move out of my space.

'I could make you a cup of tea. You look as if you need one.'

Her first impulse was to turn him away, then she realized how touchy she was getting. She had things to discuss with Adam. Why not do it now? 'You're on. You might have waited till I called you though,' she couldn't resist adding.

'Impatient to see you again.'

'And to hear how the trip went?' she added drily.

'Yes.'

'You and Michael Hartshorn both.'

'What on earth do you mean?' The thought of being lumped together with Michael was clearly not welcome to him.

'He preceded me in a visit to my grandpa.'

Adam gave a satisfying whistle of surprise. 'Did he get anything out of him?'

'Not much, I gather. My grandfather had a conveniently bad day.'

'All the same, it's odd, if he didn't tell you he was going. How did he know where your grandfather was?'

'It could just be eagerness to get to know more about Alice. He interviewed him once, and as the home is in the same village, it can't have taken long to track him down. Eagerness,' she added pointedly, 'is not restricted to you.'

'I'm no Hartshorn.'

'How do I know that?'

'I hope you do,' he said seriously. 'I don't like what I hear about the gent. He's writing a book about the best of the military Beavers. So why should he dash over to see your grandfather if Alice Beavers has nothing to do with his subject? Something doesn't smell very sweet.'

She hesitated. 'Pops said – but it may not be reliable – that he was asking about the recipe script.'

'Ah. You weren't going to tell me that, were you?'

'Not yet,' she said truthfully.

'You should. Anything else you'd like to 'fess up to?' He spoke lightly, but he was looking very keenly at her, as though he knew perfectly well she had more on her mind. 'I'll make the tea while you think about it.' He busied himself with

76

tea, but it was only delaying the vital moment, and she knew it.

'Pops said,' she announced loudly, 'that Alice told him the recipes were not to be published. It wasn't one of his good days though.'

He said nothing, but she could see a hammering nerve in his cheek going like the clappers.

'It's an odd thing to be confused about,' he said at last. He leaned towards her over the small conservatory table. 'Rachel, I *really* don't like this.'

'Define "this" please.' Her voice didn't sound her own. She felt as if she were diving forward into a quicksand that might only be inches deep or . . .

'The script. Beavers turns you down but wants to see the script. Hartshorn wants to see it even though it's not in his current remit. He dashes over to see your grandfather. And Alice probably didn't want it published.'

'It's *recipes*, Adam. We must be drawing false conclusions here. They didn't like Alice, that's all.'

'Rachel, how keen are you on discovering Alice's story, if push comes to shove? Could you give it up?'

'No.' She grinned at him despairingly. 'That's my problem. I see a path marked Problems and I go right on, wondering what they are.' Like my life with François . . . She dragged her thoughts away. Road closed.

'Then tell them you're going ahead and publishing both the biog *and* the recipes. Tell Hartshorn. Tell Crandene. You don't have to *do* it. Just let them think you are.'

'I like it, Adam. Oh, *yes*.'

'Hey, don't say yes too quickly. You're not going to get a rosy reception from them. Not from Beavers, anyway.'

'So? I haven't exactly been welcomed into the family.'

'True . . .' he hesitated. 'Look, none of my business, but where is the script?'

'Here, of course.' Then she saw the look on his face. 'You don't think they'll try and pinch it, do you?'

'It's a possibility that crossed my mind. This cottage isn't exactly Fort Knox. Would you – probably not – like me to take it for a while?'

She instinctively reacted, firewall in place, and he saw it.

'Better not, I suppose. After all, you could still be burgled even if I've taken the script.'

'I'm sorry, Adam,' she apologized. 'I'm just used to dealing with things myself. I'll get it all copied in case.'

'Come over tomorrow. Copy it in my office.'

'I'll call you.'

Nothing more tonight. Nothing. She needed sleep. Just one more hurdle after he'd gone, but at least she knew now what line to take with Michael.

She rang him, carefully keeping her voice neutral, and even managed to pop a note of cheerfulness into it. 'Hi. It's Rachel. Just got back from seeing my grandfather. He mentioned you'd been to see him. Why on earth didn't you tell me, we could have gone together?'

'I'd no idea you were going so soon,' the answer came back swiftly. 'Anyway, I went on the spur of the moment. I'm glad you rang, though.'

Was he indeed. She was inwardly seething.

'Your grandfather wasn't able to give me much help,' he continued.

'On what?'

'A man called Harry Rolfe. That's whom I went to ask him about.'

August 1915

'*Non, non*, you are murdering that *pauvre filet, petite Alice*. How many times must I tell you, work with the ingredients, do not fight them. Only a bad cook does that. True cuisine improves on what nature has provided, it does not demolish it and begin again. Now, let us take this undercut, and slice it tenderly and so thinly to fry in its butter. Then ask yourself what it would like to wear this evening? Should it be horse-radish, or redcurrant jelly? Or a purée of fruit, as in olden days? *Think*, Alice, think of the *filet*, not of your Harry.'

Harry had been gone ten months now, and each day would have dragged if it had not been for Monsieur Trente. Even Lily was to leave tomorrow, her friend and confidante. She'd found a job in a munitions factory, which she said would not be such hard work as Crandene, and much better paid. Alice had been envious, thinking she should go too now Harry had left, but Monsieur Trente had been very angry. 'Everything I teach you you throw away? You are an *imbécile*, Alice. You are a good cook. You could do well, so why wish to leave?'

'It's the money,' she said, the first thing she thought of. 'I could give Mum and Dad much more.'

'Think of your Harry first. He wants to picture you at Crandene, not in a factory. Pah!'

And there it had ended. To take her mind off Harry, she threw herself into learning all she could about how to cook *and* about the ingredients. The harder she worked the less she worried about Harry. After all, he was only training so far in England, though soon he would be going to war.

'Wotcher, Monsieur Trente. Keeping her busy are you?'

'Harry!' she shrieked in delight at the shout from the doorway, making everyone look up. He was dressed in his khaki, looking so mature now, so confident, but was still her Harry all the same.

She threw herself into his arms to the great interest of Lily, who was just passing with a heavy plate carrier.

'I've got a twenty-four-hour pass, Alice,' he said huskily. 'And it's only eleven o'clock.'

A day! A whole day – nearly. 'But your parents,' she faltered, not wishing to be selfish. Harry's parents lived in Sissingbourne, which was further away than Cranbridge.

'I'll go home tonight. But today . . . ?' He raised a hopeful face to Monsieur Trente, who glared.

'Very well. You leave, little Alice. But take care Mrs Cheney does not discover this.'

Even Mrs Cheney wasn't so harsh nowadays, however. She had lost a nephew at somewhere called Hill 60 in France in the spring, and since then she had been much kinder. The war hadn't ended when they thought it would, and Harry had volunteered last October, and joined a new battalion of the Royal West Kents, the 8th. He'd been training and his coming here must mean the battalion was leaving. And only today was left.

'Shall we walk up the hill, Harry, like we used to?' she asked as they walked through the gardens.

'I'd like that. It's what I dreamed of, being here with you, Alice. And now I'm here, I dunno what to say to you.'

'I'll say it for you, Harry. You're off, aren't you? Going to France?'

'On Friday,' he said. 'At last. Don't know whether I'm glad or sorry. It had to come.'

'Glad?' she asked in astonishment. What is there to be glad about?

'It's what I've been training for. They need us, sweetheart. Besides, it's not so bad. Mr Robert – well, shouldn't call him that – Lieutenant Beavers was at the depot.'

'I thought he was in France.' Her heart sank. It had been so good without him.

'No. They needed officers at the depot to train us Tommies. He's due to go out to join 1st Battalion again – and, guess what, Alice, he says he'll try and get me a transfer so we can stick together like the old days.'

Her heart sank. She didn't like the sound of that at all. 'He never liked you, Harry,' she said slowly.

'That was before the war,' he reassured her. 'It's different now.'

She said nothing, but the joy of the day had been clouded, even on their hill. As they reached the top, she did her best to cheer up.

'If I stand on tiptoe I might see France from here,' she joked. 'I'll wave at you.'

'I'll fire my rifle – we actually got some last week – so you'll know I've seen you.'

Rifles. It brought war very close. 'Oh, Harry, you'll be back, won't you?'

'Of course I'll be back. I might be back before the apples on our tree fall. Listen, Alice, this is *our* hill, see.' He kissed her. 'So whenever I think of you over in France, I'll think of you standing on this hill. Promise me you'll wave, just as you said, every time you come here. It'll seem like I'm still with you then. Promise me, darling.'

Six

S omething, Rachel told herself, as she attacked a particularly vicious thistle, had to be done. Her capital was not going to last for ever and a future income had to be earned by hook or by crook. The hook she had planned so carefully was on temporary hold, and what the crook might be she hadn't as yet the faintest idea. If by a miracle her planned business materialized she'd need this house as a base; if not, she might as well sell up and be footloose and fancy free. That, at the moment, did not seem the appealing prospect it had before Alice Carter had re-entered her life. It would seem like failure and she wasn't prepared to throw the towel in yet.

Today, she had decided to work in the garden and contemplate Lord Beavers' reactions when he read her letter. It had been a carefully composed, nonchalant little note, announcing that she was going ahead with her biography and publication of the recipes. She also planned to start a catering business which would be based on British cuisine, using local produce, in which she could use the recipes. As for concerns about copyright, she wrote, discussion with Alice's surviving family had reassured her that they were recorded after her marriage to Lord Beavers, not before. (A white lie this, but she'd decided to risk it.) In the absence of evidence to the contrary, this was in any case the obvious conclusion since marriage to Lord Beavers would have given her the time to record the recipes, which as chef she would have lacked. In the circumstances, therefore, she was sure that he would understand why she was not enclosing a copy of the script, but here were an additional copy page or two.

'Take that and that and *that!*' She hoicked another nettle out from its lair with great pleasure, nicknaming it Bully Beavers.

Tomorrow, in order to cock a snook at his lordship she would be meeting Michael for the delayed visit to Crandene. She was longing to know how Harry Rolfe fitted into the picture, especially since Alice had taken the trouble to show Pops his grave. It wasn't so good a lead as one to Samuel would have been, but at the very least it was interesting. Michael's visit to Pops still left an aftertaste which was not pleasant, even though it had been in search of a legitimate target.

Alice's dictum (assuming she had in fact given it) that the recipes were not to be published was an even worse conundrum. Had it been a casual 'I'd rather keep them to myself for the moment' remark, or was it an order banning publication for all time? If so, why? It didn't make sense. Rachel thought of the Victorian lady traveller who had stipulated that her diaries be kept under lock and key for a hundred years – and no wonder, considering the delightful shenanigans she'd got up to with her escorting dragomen. But recipes were surely a different matter. Perhaps the mighty Lord Beavers had forbidden Alice to publish them, though why on earth he should do so was yet another question. That was over fifty years ago, and it was twenty since Alice had died. Whatever the reason had been, it couldn't matter now.

She had told Michael that she was still going ahead with the project, and that she would send him the promised copy pages. As for Adam's fears about the script itself, it was safe, and Rachel was pleased with her hiding place. She had taken the plunge, and soon would be feeling the temperature of the water.

'I couldn't resist coming here again,' she told Michael the next day, as he strolled up to her in the Crandene car park. She locked up her car and grinned at him. 'It's like poking my head in a lion's den.' Since Michael had reissued his invitation, she had accepted, deciding she might as well draw his fire. There might be something to learn here. For a start, why did he want to see her, as she had told him on the telephone that his professed interest, Harry Rolfe, was as much a mystery to her as to him. He'd asked hopefully whether there was any mention of a Rolfe in the script, but she had told him there was not.

'Not even indirectly?' he had asked.

'No. It's dedicated to a man called Samuel.'

'Perhaps that was her pet name for Rolfe.'

'Possibly.' But Rachel had not been convinced. It didn't sound very 'pet' to her ear. She tried to flatter herself that the invitation here was solely for her own wonderful company, but was not convinced by this either.

Today Michael looked less the important historian, and far more casual in short-sleeved shirt and linen trousers. She too had gone for casual, which seemed to set a mood for the day. Suspicion will be suspended, she told herself lightly, until further notice. On a sunny summer's day she was out to enjoy herself, even if she mentally wore her researcher's hat, and was provided with pen, paper and electronic notepad. She had assumed that Michael would have carte blanche at Crandene, and simply be waved through the gate, but it seemed not, for he insisted on forking up for both their entrance fees. At her demurral he pointed out that her company was 'research' so far as he was concerned. She was a descendant of Alice Beavers.

'But Alice plays no part in your new book.'

'Not her recipes. But Alice herself might have a minor role, because of Harry Rolfe. Want to hear more?'

'Of course.'

'I told you my book was centred on the military tradition of Crandene. While researching Robert Beavers and the VC he won in the First World War, I came across the name of Harry Rolfe, also from Crandene, in the 1st Battalion Royal West Kents, as was Robert, though Robert was a lieutenant and Rolfe a corporal. I then discovered that Rolfe had been in service at Crandene, and thought that it would make an interesting variation to have the servants' military careers as well as the Beavers family. When you mentioned your grandfather was still alive I thought the name might possibly mean something to him, as Alice might have known this Rolfe.'

'Why?' she argued, as they began to walk towards the house. 'She was a kitchenmaid and the servants were very hierarchical. It hardly seems worth a special dash to France.'

He laughed and put an arm round her shoulders, where it

83

felt very good, just right for a summer day. Nevertheless, she wanted to clear this question up once and for all.

'Playing Poirot, are you, Rachel? Sorry to disappoint you. I didn't go just to see your grandfather. Far from it. I had a tour of the battlefields planned, including the Somme, remembered your grandfather lived somewhere near my route back, and I tracked down the village and then by the phone directory his present whereabouts. I asked him if he knew the name Rolfe and he told me about the World War I cemetery and his visit to it with Alice.'

This wasn't good. 'So you might have put the name in his mind,' Rachel reasoned. And that meant Pops' story couldn't be relied upon. 'Did you mention the name first or did he?'

Michael hesitated. 'I can't be sure now.'

Oh damn. Was nothing ever going to be cut and dried where Alice was concerned? 'So it might even have been Samuel Pepys or whatever on the gravestone for all we know, since Pops could have become confused.'

'It's possible.' Michael looked somewhat crestfallen.

'Haven't you come across a single Samuel in your research?' she asked.

'Only the Samuel Hoare who came to Crandene in the 1930s. He was the British ambassador to Spain in World War II, Foreign Secretary in the early 1930s, negotiator of a secret plan with the French to appease Mussolini when he began flexing his muscles over Abyssinia. There was a public uproar and Anthony Eden took over his job pretty promptly in 1935. He wasn't exactly popular in the 1930s, though he went on to a distinguished career after that. I doubt if Alice would have dedicated her book to him though.'

'So who do you think her Samuel could have been?'

'My money would be on someone she met at Tolbury Hall.'

'Good thinking. I'll have to follow that up.' Michael was stating the obvious, she realized. Alice had been a young woman when she went to Lincolnshire, and had returned to Crandene a mature woman of over thirty. Why, she wondered, had she concentrated so much on Crandene as being the root of Alice's life? So much for her researching skills.

She drew a deep breath to tackle the next hurdle. 'Did Pops mention Alice's cooking at all?'

'I remember asking him about the recipe script, as you had mentioned it to me, simply because it might have jogged further memories. After all, he knew Robert Beavers and I didn't. I drew a blank though, just as you seem to have done.'

Was there a slight query at the end of that sentence? 'Yes, I did.'

'Is that the end of my interrogation then, ma'am?'

Rachel laughed, feeling somewhat shamefaced. 'The trouble with mysteries is that one sees bears instead of bushes.' She had a sinking feeling that for her they were still there, but at least they could temporarily retreat back into the undergrowth.

'Why are you so fascinated by this ancestor of yours? What's the mystery?'

Rachel thought about this. 'I suppose it's because she doesn't yet add up as a person. Pops' mother described her as a timid self-effacing girl; to Pops she was always kind, but remote and self-confident. I agree with you that to get where she eventually did she must have been very self-assured, and even self-promoting. Robert Beavers doesn't seem to me to have been the King Cophetua type, hunting for beggar maids. Yet by the end of her life she is described as reserved and self-effacing again.'

'Events shape personalities as well as genes.'

'Or bring different genes to the fore.'

'O wise young Solomon.'

'Thank you,' she answered demurely. It was hard to imagine that this banter was a façade hiding some ulterior motive on Michael's part for courting her company. She wasn't being badgered or being fed the Beavers' propaganda line, as she'd half suspected might happen. So far, she reminded herself. Anyway, he was too attractive a companion to consider as 'the enemy'. In fact, if Alice were not still lying between them like a sword of proxy, she could really fall for him, she decided. Away, Cupid, away, she hastily ordered. Any spare darts around should be thrown at the bullseye of Lord Beavers' co-operation.

'I take it you still want to go round the house again?' he

asked. 'You said you'd already done the tour once.' He hesitated. 'I've an apology to make. The bad news is that the Crandene archives are temporarily closed for research.'

'Why,' she replied carefully, 'does that not surprise me?' She'd put it to the back of her mind, hoping that his lordship wouldn't be so quick off the mark in throwing obstacles in her way. Some hopes. 'Closed, I take it, to me.'

'I'm afraid so. Look,' he added quickly, 'how about we have a private arrangement. *Very* private. I take notes on Alice not only for myself, but anything that might help you. Don't attribute any source.'

She thought fast, considering this from all angles. Co-operation should work both ways. Is that what Michael was counting on? She couldn't believe it, but she wasn't going to take the risk. Not yet anyway.

'I appreciate that, Michael, but it's too risky for you. Why don't we leave it as a compromise? If I have a puzzle about Alice I think you might be able to help with, I'll ring you.'

She couldn't tell from his expression what he was thinking, but she suspected he guessed just why she was turning down his offer. Then he said, 'And I could ring you if there are any titbits. I'd hate to find a Samuel, and be forbidden to let you know.'

'It's a deal,' she whipped back promptly and amity was restored. She wanted to ask why, if the archives were closed, he still wanted her to come today. The words hovered but remained unspoken. 'And to answer your original question, yes, I'd like to see the house again.'

'That sounds very formal.'

'It wasn't meant to be. This is partly a day off.'

'From what?'

'Recipes, of course.' She had nothing to lose by merely talking about them. 'I'm beginning to convert them into today's ingredients and methods, editing them as necessary, so that I can cook them myself. The ingredients are changing quite a lot. Butters and oils, rennet, pints of cream, and dozens of scallops won't go down well today. Nor are lobsters, cherries and samphire quite so readily available. And Alice's recipes were for elite consumption, of course, so I also have to consider the market I need to aim for.'

'Those aspiring to be Crandeners, I suspect, rather than today's version of them. Businessmen in grey suits.'

'It's my experience,' she replied mildly, 'that even business-men are human under the suits.'

'Reproof received. Now, suppose we go round the house while I give you the benefit of my military expertise. I've given you the bad news, so here's the good news. I've wangled the key to the kitchens.'

'Hey, Michael, now you're talking!' In her excitement, she gave him a hug, which he returned with much enthusiasm.

'I'll bring good news again,' he remarked.

'Any time,' she announced happily, wondering whether she was sending out wrong signals – and then wondering if they *were* wrong.

Going round Crandene with Michael was a totally different experience to her visit with Adam. Where Adam had looked, Michael talked. He explained the background and relevance of all the military portraits and mementoes in the house, especially in the formal dining room, which was laid with twenty place settings. The martinets with the monocles glared down at her once again, as though indignant at her temerity in staring at them for a second time.

'They did away with the old scarlet uniforms at the end of the nineteenth century in favour of khaki,' he explained, as she admired – if that was the word – the stunning portrait of the first Lord Beavers, clad in full dress uniform of scarlet tunic, sash, and dark blue trousers, sword at his side, opposite that of his son, who looked almost identical save that the glare was less pronounced.

'Quite something,' she observed.

'As I told you, Gerald won his VC for the storming of the Redan in the Crimea in 1855. He was in the ladder party from what was then the 97th Regiment of Foot, which spearheaded the attack on the fortress. His son Alfred won his VC when the 1st Battalion Royal West Kents stormed the gateway to the Swat Valley. They managed to capture a spur so that the artillery could take over to finish the job. Alfred led the final dash, having saved some of his wounded men from the less than desirable clutches of the enemy single-handed.'

'And Robert, the third baron?' she asked. 'There doesn't seem to be so much in the house about the First World War, even though he too won a VC.'

'No. My theory is that that war was so much closer to home and so fearful in its cost, that many chose to avoid remembrances. After all, it's still time *in* mind, rather than out of it, if you consider that through family memory we're still most of us in touch with the generation that was lost in it. It's when one loses that contact that it ceases to become real. The Victorian wars, fought far away without TV and only newspapers to transmit news, lent themselves to mementoes of deeds of derring-do, but the Great War was a different kettle of fish. As I told you, Robert Beavers won his VC at the battle for High Wood at the Somme in July 1916. After that he had a desk job at HQ till the end of the war.'

'What about *his* son?'

'This is George here.' Michael pointed out a head and shoulders portrait over the doorway. He was in khaki and the face did not look in the same mould as his ancestors. He had mild blue eyes, gazing not at the viewer but to his left, as if anxious to escape the limelight.

'I suppose,' Rachel said thoughtfully, 'that after World War II the era of portraits was really over, which accounts for the dutiful expression rather than the Up, Boys, and At 'Em of the earlier ones.'

'He did OK in fact,' Michael replied. 'He went through the second war with the West Kents. Unlike most of his fellow officers he came through it. He was captured in the desert, escaped and made his way back to a DSO. Rejoined the 4th Battalion then in Burma, and went through the Siege of Kohima – and survived that to get a bar to the DSO. Heard of the Dirty Half Hundred? That was them. Held the Kohima garrison regardless. He stayed in the army until his father died. He was a grand chap. I met him several times in his old age. By then he had grown into almost a caricature of the great British soldier, moustache, stern of eye, erect figure. His son went through Sandhurst, did ten years including the Falklands, and came out to go into business.'

'Surely there must be more portraits of Robert around somewhere?' Rachel commented. 'I've only seen the youth with the dog in the dining room.'

'You missed it. There is one painted after he got his VC – not a very good portrait. It's in the morning room, but not well hung. And on the stairs there's a splendid one painted in his old age. I don't know why it's not with the others.'

The portrait in the morning room was so unremarkable Rachel wasn't surprised she had missed it. There was little personality developed in that face, despite his achievement. Or perhaps he was deliberately hiding it. When they reached the stairs, however, she was amazed at the difference. Here was a good-looking, calm and confident man. Was it just chance or was it the result of marriage to Alice?

'He looks like the life and the soul of the community,' she said.

'Apparently he was. He did a good job and was generally popular around here in the fifties. Son George beat him hands down in charisma, but Robert worked his socks off to get the place up and running for him. But . . .' Michael stopped, caught her eye and laughed.

'And the current one?' she persisted, grinning. 'Does he take after father and grandfather?'

'You won't draw me on that, Rachel. You can make your own mind up. You deal with him on your business. I shall on mine.'

'I didn't take to him.' Why not be frank about it? she thought.

'Perhaps he didn't take to what you were saying. He's OK when you get to know him.'

'The lion of business tamed?'

'Something like that. Shall we attack the kitchens now I've got the magic key?'

It was fun to walk beyond the regular tour, out of the grand household and through the door into the corridor leading to the old kitchens. Rachel imagined herself in Alice's shoes, traversing this great divide day in, day out.

'This is the original kitchen block,' Michael explained, as he unlocked the door, 'which, I gather, is the one that Alice would have worked in, even though by her time they'd added the corridor and extra rooms in the interests of hotter food and fewer servants dying of pneumonia. The old tunnel still exists, but we weren't encouraged to visit it.'

'She worked *here* in the 1930s?' Rachel stared incredulously at the admittedly atmospheric, but dark, primitive kitchens. Old black ranges, a scullery with washboards, washing dollies, and one tap in the stone sink, piles of decaying copper saucepans and utensils, and general detritus of disuse. It was a paradise for the kitchen historian, but for cooking those 1930s recipes? Surely not.

'No,' he replied. 'I think you were misled on that. According to the curator, they were closed in 1932, and new kitchens converted at the rear of the main house. So Alice would have worked here when she first came, and for two years on her return. Do you suspect Alice's hand behind the conversion?'

'Could be. The dates suggest it.' She was still busy seeing Alice as a kitchenmaid here, as she walked slowly round the nest of rooms that made up the rest of this large kitchen block. 'That must have been the servants' hall.' She peered into one large room, and then into another the other side of the corridor. 'And this could have been Pug's Parlour.'

'What?'

'That got you. The name given to the butler or steward's private sanctum. He had his own personal boy to look after him.'

'I should rephrase that in your biography.'

She laughed. It was easy to fall back into the language of those times, and she'd been reading so much about life in service in Alice's youth that it came all too easily. 'Point taken.'

A pause. 'So you're determined to go ahead with this combined biography and cookbook then?'

'Of course,' she replied promptly. Crunch time had arrived.

'Is that wise if Lord Beavers is against it? He rang me when he got your last letter. He thought I'd be interested.'

'Did he say why he isn't?' she asked. *She* hadn't heard

from his lordship yet, so the speed with which he contacted Michael was strange. On the other hand, Michael seemed to have no qualms about telling her, so perhaps she was again seeing mountains where only molehills existed.

'I thought I'd explained that the emphasis at Crandene is increasingly on military and political associations, and that's where my book comes in.'

'Whereas mine goes out,' she managed to quip, aware of the sharp edge creeping into their voices. Trying to be fair, she had to acknowledge it wasn't Michael's fault if Beavers was blocking her path. Or was she being blinded by the sunshine of a July day?

'Crandene is planning a big military exhibition here next year in the grounds,' he told her casually. 'Big time stuff. I'm hoping to have my book out for it.'

'Is that commercial in the present attitude to war?'

'This is history, and it's based on the Crandene heroes. All four of them. The men rather than war itself.'

'What happens to the political connections of Crandene? Do they get a look in?'

'They'll be represented, but they're hardly a crowd-puller. Kids can't try their hands at a spot of political outmanoeuvring as they can with a plastic sword and red coat, or interactive computer battles.'

There was no answer to that, so Rachel switched back to safer ground. 'Can we see the later kitchen too?'

'No. That's still in use for the private quarters. It wouldn't tell you much anyway, since I gather it's been radically overhauled several times since Alice's day. Shall we get some tea and you can think up anything else you want to ask?'

It was odd walking into the same tearoom-cum-restaurant as she had with Adam so relatively recently. It was even the same waitress, though she gave no sign of recognition. Just as well, Rachel suddenly caught herself thinking, then wondered why she had this reaction. Michael was clearly working closely with the foundation and Lord Beavers himself. He might therefore have his hands tied as regards helping her, but that didn't mean he was out to obstruct her. Why should he? Adam seemed to be highly suspicious of Michael's intentions, but so far as Rachel could see there was nothing to justify this. She had had her own reservations about Michael, but they were disappearing.

The tea and walnut cake were just as bad as before, and she couldn't help thinking that Alice's cake recipes could only be a marked improvement. She told Michael this as a joke, but he laid his hand briefly over hers. 'Are you sure you're doing the right thing in pursuing this recipe book plan?'

'Why do you ask that?' Take this slowly, she decided. This is going to be the pro-Beavers line. To her surprise she was wrong.

'You're delving back into the past. I don't know you well, Rachel, but it seems to me that anyone suffering bereavement should at some point be looking to the future. Starting again. Has it not occurred to you that this sudden interest in Alice is only a form of grieving and will pass?'

'Yes it has, but I dismissed it as invalid. To me this *is* starting again. The past can strengthen you *for* the future. You must feel that in your historical work.'

'I do.' The hand over hers again – it felt very good indeed. Comfortable. Maybe even a pointer to the future. She reminded herself that work came first, and asked for the bill to put an end to this line of thinking. Casual companionship was one thing, looking beyond that was not on the cards.

'Mine,' Michael insisted.

'No way. You paid the entrance fees. Food is my pitch.'

'Your friend was here the other day,' the waitress observed chattily as she returned with the change.

'Adam?' she asked, caught off balance.

'Tall, thin. Very interested in Crandene.'

'Adam who?' Michael asked when they were walking back to the car park.

'Paynter. He runs a charity in Canterbury called Never Alone.' She silently cursed the waitress. Why couldn't she have kept quiet? It was tactless, to say the least. For all she knew, Rachel could be juggling husband and lover. As it was, it was still a nuisance. She wanted to keep independent of both men. This was *her* project.

'What's his interest in Crandene?'

'I don't know.' Another unanswered question. 'Perhaps,' she said in exasperation, 'he just likes me.'

92

'That's not impossible, I suppose. Why do you think I'm here?'

She managed to laugh at that.

'Are you spoken for, by the way?' he enquired.

'I love that phrase. Spoken for. No. Nor planning to be,' she added quickly.

'Good. Nor am I. Nor planning to be. So you'll come to dinner with me?'

'I'd like that.'

As she drove home, she realized to her surprise that it was still Crandene she was churning over in her mind, rather than the prospect of dinner with Michael. Something had made her uneasy about the afternoon but she couldn't pinpoint what it was. Perhaps it might have been what Michael said about her delving back into the past. She had always refused to do that, and had implied to Michael that Alice was part of her future. Did that not mean she was embracing the past in order to find the future, just as Adam had suggested? She'd never taken any interest in her ancestors before this, yet Mum and Pops represented the past too, and had made every effort to involve her. Was *that* why Pops so often seemed to disapprove of her? Because he sensed in her a rejection of what he stemmed from? The fault then lay in her, not Pops, but if so she had most surely dispelled it now by her interest in Crandene and Alice.

Then another possible reason for her unease came to her. The afternoon had reinforced her feeling that she was blithely prancing along her own path, but on either side of her both Michael and Adam seemed to be running independent enquiries while keeping tabs on her. Nonsense, she told herself. You, Rachel, have an ego the size of a hot air balloon – and probably just as full of gas.

Cheered up by this latter thought, though still not convinced she had reached the heart of her unease, she arrived home to find a letter on the mat. Letters were beginning to take on their former significance in life, now that e-mails took care of the everyday toing and froing. This one bore a red company stamp, but it was not Crandene's. It was from a firm of London solicitors, and the message inside was that they understood Miss Field was about to publish a script by

93

the late Lady Beavers and that Lord Beavers reserved all his rights in the matter.

It was a preliminary shot, but it glanced off the armour she was rapidly acquiring. Whether Crandene liked it or not, she was going over the top and into battle.

1916

There were no severe shortages of food yet, but the fact that prices were going up and up implied that if the war did not end soon times would get much harder. Mrs Cheney now went over the accounts with an eagle eye, saying it was their patriotic duty not to waste bread and milk, sugar or eggs. She herself was setting an example, she informed the servants' hall, by cutting – with the family's permission – the amount of jam and marmalade made in her stillroom.

'So what am I to do with all the strawberries?' Monsieur Trente lamented to Alice. 'We must grow more fruit, grow more vegetables, but cannot preserve them. Is this sensible? *Non*.'

It was a sad kitchen now. She and Monsieur Trente worked silently, each bearing their own grief. His son had been killed in battle at Verdun in France in April, and Alice often visited his wife in the village, a sad lady clad in black. But many people were now in black or wore black armbands. It had become commonplace in the last year. Young men left for the services, and were often not seen again. A memorial roll was kept in the church, and each Sunday Lord Beavers would solemnly read out all the names at the service. Everyone knew he was thinking of his own son Robert, out there with the Royal West Kents, and each family was thinking of its own sacrifice.

Alice was thinking of Harry. She no longer believed his comforting words about coming home soon. There'd been a big battle at Loos last autumn only a week or two after he had sailed for France, and Mr Robert had been in it, describing every terrible detail to her when he came home on leave. She was sure he did it deliberately to frighten her about Harry, and when he saw her white face he told her he'd managed to get a transfer to 1st Battalion for him. She should have

94

been comforted, everyone told her, but she wasn't. There was something about the look on his face that made her tremble all the time he was telling her how men's arms, legs and heads were blown off, about the corpses left to rot. That this would happen to Harry was her greatest fear. She had nightmares for weeks until a bunch of letters all arrived together from him, and he sounded just the same dear old chap.

It was nearly Christmas when they had arrived, and he told her that even if he was on duty in a trench it would be quite jolly. It didn't sound as if it would be jolly to Alice, and she instantly suspected the letters weren't telling her the truth. At least he could sound cheerful, though, and that must mean he wasn't too badly off.

15th December 1915

My darling Alice,

Here's hoping you have my last letter and keep it close so you know how much I love you, dear. Life isn't too bad here. When we're in the Rest Village, as we call it, this is quite a jolly place with cafés and wine. The food isn't up to much, not like Crandene. How I wish I was going to be with you this Christmas, eating the jolly Christmas pudding and finding the threepenny bit like I did last year, laughing at Mr P. Only don't show him this will you, he'll come right out here and yell out Rolfe! Worse than old Fritz in the trenches opposite. So far Fritz isn't taking much notice of us. We're in the line but all is quiet. Mr Robert is arranging for me to transfer to his battalion, it's a cracker, so I'll be all right. Us Crandene folk will stick together. Now write to me, Alice, about yourself, so I can think of what you're doing. Tell me about Christmas Day, and are you having the servants ball this year? And what are you cooking there with Mr Trente? We'll be all right here as the regiment is sending out money for gifts from a special Christmas Cheer Fund raised by their ladies back home. I'd rather have a picture of you, dear Alice.

Your loving Harry

Since then over six months had passed. She'd learned not to worry too much now if she didn't hear from him. If he was in the trenches he couldn't always write and it depended where they were as to when the letters came. He'd sent her some funny postcards too, cartoons of soldiers in a trench. She'd sent him a photograph of herself in the garden at home, and he'd written back to say he'd had it done up posh in a painted frame.

'What's on for dinner today, Monsieur Trente?' she asked as they began the luncheon preparations.

'A celebration. Monsieur le lieutenant Robert comes on leave. We shall have three courses today, not two, her ladyship tells me. We shall have the first of the strawberries and the asparagus. And broad beans. As if there were no war.'

His voice broke, and Alice saw there were tears in his eyes. She forced herself to make the anchovy and cucumber stuffing for Mr Robert's favourite mutton to help Monsieur Trente, but it brought unwelcome thoughts. She knew Mr Robert would seek her out. She was an assistant chef now and he could legitimately demand her presence in the house. He had never touched her again, but she knew all too well he had not forgotten her. His eyes raked her over from top to toe as though he would devour her as greedily as the mutton. The last time he came home on leave was in February, and he'd caught her up on her afternoon off, as she set off to see her family. She'd heard Spot barking and turned round in terror to see Mr Robert running after her.

'You're growing up, Alice. Time you were married.'

She had pulled her coat around her, for she knew what he meant. Her figure was filling out.

'Yes, sir, when the war's over.'

He had given an odd laugh. 'You'll wait a long time for that. Any time you fancy a bit of the *droit de seigneur* let me know.'

She knew what he meant by that too. She stopped short on the path. 'I'm engaged to Harry Rolfe, Mr Robert. We're as good as married. And if you touch me ever again, I'll go straight to your father. No matter if he does sack me, there are plenty of jobs now for girls.'

He went silent, and then said in a completely different tone of voice, 'You've no idea what it's like out there, Alice. It's hell every day, every night. It's hell when it happens, the guns, the screaming, the "got to do your duty, lead your men". And it's even worse hell waiting for it to come. And it will. You and Spot – you're all I have.'

'Harry—'

'And to hell with Harry,' he said so quietly, he didn't even sound angry anymore. 'You're mine, Alice. I'll have you one way or another.'

She'd run then, and looked over her shoulder to see him not running after her as she expected but sobbing his eyes out like a child. She didn't understand him, and he terrified her.

Now he was coming home again. Everyone said that the British would be making a big push soon, but it couldn't be that soon if Mr Robert was coming on leave. It was June already, and oh how she wished for Harry to be with her. She decided she would slip up to the hill this afternoon after she had finished the dinner preparations.

Poor Monsieur Trente, so grey, so sad, he didn't even shout at her anymore. He even said thank you, Alice, or thank you, *ma petite*, and she knew why. He needed her, he said. There was no Lily anymore for her to giggle with. She had gone long ago to the munitions factory and the newcomer Gladys wasn't a patch on her. It wouldn't be long before she left too, Alice reckoned. The servant numbers had fallen dramatically, but there was less to do, for there wasn't so much entertaining. Dad worked all the time at his carpentry and helping out in the gardens now they were short of men, and so did the little ones at home. Not so little now of course. Betty was fifteen now, and a housemaid, and Emmy was eight; she helped with the vegetables sometimes. The very idea of a eight-year-old being entrusted with preparing vegetables would not have been possible before this war started. Little Rosie was still only six, but Mum was hoping she'd be in the family way just once more, and have another baby. She was over forty now, but she wanted one last chance, she said.

Through force of habit Alice slipped past the vegetable gardens trying not to be noticed, and out of the side gate to climb the hill. Sometimes she would pause on the grass footpath up the hillside, and pretend Harry was here beside her, his hand in hers. Sometimes it almost felt as though she could feel it; she could hear the wind whistling like his flute, 'I'm here, Alice. Isn't it jolly?' But when she opened her eyes, the illusion was shattered, and there she was alone again.

Today as she climbed the hill, rich in its wild flowers and bird life, she wondered how mankind could have gone so astray as to ignore this beauty and tear it up with war. When she reached the top, she sat on the grass for some time until at last she stood up and as the breeze whipped round her skirts, she lifted her arm to wave as she always did.

'I'm here, Harry,' she called out loudly.

As her arm fell back to her side, she felt his hand slip into hers. But it was not the wind this time. It was Harry himself.

Seven

'A whole day,' Alice breathed. 'I can't believe it. And another half day as well before you go back.'

'Mr Robert fixed it for me to have leave too. First Battalion's up near Arras at present, quiet part of the line, you see. They can do without us for a couple of days. He's put me up for corporal as well. What do you think of that, eh?' He whirled her round the apple tree.

'It sounds very grand, Harry.' That's what she replied, but it didn't mean anything to her. All she could think of was that Mr Robert had had a hand in this glorious moment. Why? Her stomach lurched in fear. It wasn't like him to be generous where Harry and she were concerned. Perhaps, she comforted herself, he really had got fond of Harry and had forgotten all that silly nonsense about her being 'his'. Even if that wasn't likely, she struggled to forget it so that this precious time should not be wasted.

'Being corporal means I can do all sorts of things.'

'Be careful, won't you?' It was a stupid thing to say, when he was fighting in a war, but Harry must know what she meant.

She sat down on the grass under their apple tree, and Harry followed suit, cuddling up to her. It was unusual to find a tree like this at the top of a hill. There must have been an orchard here once, she supposed, or it seeded itself and grew and grew in spite of all the other wild saplings and grasses fighting for existence. On it went, year after year, leaves, blossom, fruit, bare branches, just as she and Harry would. He put his arm round her. 'You bet I'll be careful. After all, we'll be married

99

just as soon as we've licked old Fritz. Now, look here, you'll be able to get tomorrow off, won't you, Alice?'

'The whole day? Oh, but I couldn't. Mrs Cheney . . .'

'She'll listen to what Mr Robert says, pet. And he won't stop you.' He grinned at her. 'He knows all about it, see?'

'Knows about what?' She didn't like the sound of this at all.

'We, my lady, are off!'

'Off where?'

'Not telling you. It's a surprise. You just pack us the best picnic ever' – he paused – 'in one of the family picnic baskets!'

'*What!*' Had Harry gone mad? She couldn't do that, and he knew it. He was laughing his head off.

'And then we'll put it in the Rolls-Royce,' he continued triumphantly.

Now she knew he was going off his trolley. 'You and your jokes,' she said fondly, nestling up to him.

'No joke, Alice. Mr Robert suggested it when I said I wanted something special for tomorrow. Now that all the horses have gone for the army, the motor cars are all Crandene has, he says. The family won't need the Rolls tomorrow, so he says we're to have it. I can drive, see. I learned in France. So, future Mrs Rolfe, tomorrow we are off *to the seaside!*' he ended with a triumphant shout.

'The seaside?' Visions of sun and sand and picnics and Harry all blended into one glorious whole. She'd only been to the seaside once in her entire life, on a Sunday school outing years ago, but she'd never forgotten its marvels.

'There'll be pierrots and slot machines and funny hats to wear and jolly things to do. Won't it be fun?'

A whole day, she thought, at the seaside with Harry. More than fun. It would be a sort of summer Christmas. All she could ever want given to her tomorrow.

'*Un peu de jambon persillée, and pâté de gésiers*, and Alice, *ma petite*, so you think of me just a little, my smoked fillets of trout. And some of the garden strawberries would not be missed from his lordship's table, I think.'

100

Alice couldn't speak for happiness. She just watched Monsieur Trente fill the baskets with the best produce of his kitchen. All she could find to say, when at last he closed the lid and did up the straps, was, 'Thank you, Monsieur Trente.'

He beamed at her. 'It is for me also. Through you, I live just a little.'

On an impulse, since they were momentarily alone in the kitchen, she flung her arms round his neck and kissed him on the cheek, and then, fearing the results of such temerity, seized the picnic basket and ran.

Harry was waiting outside, spic and span in his uniform, and she felt like Queen Mary herself in her best Sunday cotton lawn dress, as she handed him the basket. She felt so proud as they walked round to the far side of the house where the stables were. They were rundown and home only to the motor cars now, and even they were polished more than used owing to the petrol restrictions.

The first thing she saw, or rather heard, was Spot, who came racing towards them, barking. Instantly she realized that where Spot was Mr Robert would be nearby, and a terrible foreboding came over her. As they walked up to the Rolls-Royce, Mr Robert himself appeared deep in conversation with old Charlie. The chauffeur had gone into the army a year ago, and Charlie, his predecessor, had leaped at the chance of returning to his beloved motor car even though he was over seventy now.

From the smirk on Mr Robert's face, Alice knew something was wrong.

'Ah, morning, Rolfe.' Robert's expression immediately turned to one of concern. 'Alice' – he nodded at her – 'bad news, I'm afraid.'

'Her ladyship?' Alice was instantly alarmed knowing that Lady Beavers had not been well, though surely Monsieur Trente would have said.

'No. It's my father. Apparently there are posters all over the place telling one not to drive for pleasure. I wouldn't have known, of course, but now my father's put his foot down.'

Harry's face was stiff with disappointment, and Alice boiled with rage on his behalf. This was planned, it had to be.

'I've another idea, though,' Robert continued earnestly.

101

'Don't like letting people down, especially one of my men, eh, Harry?'

'Yes, sir,' he muttered.

'I've got to run over to Groombridge Place on army business, so you could hop in the dicky seat of my Riley. It'll give you a drive out.'

Harry's face lit up again. 'That's good of you, sir.'

Alice took a deep breath. Spend the day with Mr Robert? Never. 'Thank you, sir,' she said, ever so gratefully, 'but that wouldn't suit.'

Robert stared at her. 'Why not?' he asked flatly.

'It's silly of me, sir.' She put on her best act, with her voice breaking. 'It's just that Groombridge Place has sad memories. I had a sister in service there, and I went to see her once – and then she died. You see, sir, both you and me want Harry to have a happy day, but if we went there, I couldn't be happy, could I? And that would make Harry sad. So we'd best stay here,' she said firmly.

'Alice, you were fibbing,' Harry said, puzzled, after Robert, his face black with anger, climbed up into the Riley and drove off without a word. 'You never had a sister in service there.'

Alice hesitated. Should she tell the truth? No. She didn't want bad blood between Mr Robert and Harry. She decided to tell part of the truth. 'I want to spend the day with you, Harry. I won't share you. Not with anyone.'

'But I wanted to make today so special for you.' Harry looked the picture of misery.

'You have, by being here. And now,' Alice said with determination, quite surprising herself, 'I'll tell you what we're going to do. We're going to walk up our hill and have our picnic there. Where else?'

Their hill. Always their hill. She knew this place as well as she knew Harry. She knew it in all its moods, sun and storm: she knew it in the bare beauty of winter, when the gaunt branches were laden with snow; she knew it in spring, covered in celandines and new growing grass; she knew it in autumn lit by the red richness of the leaves; and she knew it in glorious summer. As it was today.

'This is good, Alice.' Harry sighed. The picnic was unpacked under the apple tree and he tasted all Monsieur Trente's marvels one by one. 'You were right.'

'What's it like over there, Harry?' she asked hesitantly when at last they'd finished and were lying back on the grass.

'Not so bad. Don't let's talk of it now though.'

But she had to put her mind at rest. 'They keep saying there might be a big push forward before the summer's out.'

'We're in the back lines though,' he said reassuringly.

'You might be moved.'

'Some time or other, I suppose. Not yet. Anyway, I came through the last show at Loos, didn't I? And there was another one in April when Fritz got lively. Came through that, too.'

'You didn't tell me.' What else wasn't he telling her?

'I want to think of you here, of the jolly life we're going to have when this lot is over, not about over there. I want to think of when we're married, of what'll be like to hold you in my arms – and I don't want to wait much longer.'

He'd never spoken so outrightly, so passionately before, and Alice went very quiet. All she could hear were the bees humming around the clover and the occasional chirp of birdsong. And Harry breathing.

'I'm coming back, do you hear, Alice?' he continued matter of factly. 'Never think otherwise. You and me, we'll be together for ever. Understand?'

She rolled over towards him, and threw her arms round him. 'Yes,' she cried. 'I know.' She could hear his breathing deepen, then he half sat up, and as she took her arm away he put his round her. Both of them. Then somehow they were lying down again close, their arms wrapped round each other.

'There's no one around, Alice, no one. Do you mind if I . . . ?' His hands were trembling as he unbuttoned her frock, then he was pushing up her skirt. 'I won't go far, I promise. It wouldn't be right. But just to feel close. Oh I need that. I do.'

'I want you to, Harry.' It felt wonderful to be here so close to him, and to feel his hands on her. It was like a summer's day itself what was going on right inside her. She didn't want him to stop, she wanted him to go on and on, to make this summer's day complete.

*

'You're really my wife now, aren't you?' Harry laughed shakily some time later. 'You believe it? Not sure I do.'

'Yes.' Everything seemed different now to Alice. She wanted to laugh, to cry, to kiss Harry, to leap up and dance around, all at the same time. It had hurt a bit, but then not at all, and Harry and she had been together in their own little world which would never vanish. Is this, she wondered, what happened to everyone? This bliss?

'You're not sorry, are you?' he asked doubtfully.

'*Sorry?* Oh I'm glad, so glad.' Alice burst into tears and he rocked her gently from side to side.

'Hello, what are these tears for?'

'Happiness.'

'That's what we'll always have. Just you see. No sunsets on that.'

Seeing him at the Never Alone HQ revealed a different Adam to Rachel. The professional distance he had kept so far (or so she explained it to herself) had given place to professional expertise. One moment he was in the shop, rearranging or pronouncing on donated china, the next he was on the phone in the offices upstairs discussing Gift Aid implications with Inland Revenue.

Rachel chuckled to herself at his comings and goings as she made use of the copier. It had been bad enough copying just the three pages earlier, but copying the whole script was even more daunting. Her heart was in her mouth as she handled the script page by page, every moment expecting something to go wrong, and her precious script to disintegrate into dust. Stupid, but that's how she felt. She wanted no one's eyes on it but her own, and Adam seemed intuitively to guess how she might feel. He did not, as she had half expected, loom over her to peer again at Alice's work. She was very conscious of using the charity's colour cartridges up at a high rate of knots, but Adam insisted she carry on.

'You can make a contribution to the charity box, if you like,' he suggested, and she pushed several ten-pound notes into the box. She needed at least one full colour copy for safety, another to work on, and two black and white ones.

The Never Alone premises were in a medieval house, just off the main street of Canterbury. 'If you strip the paper off,' Adam had joked, 'the walls will fall down.'

She didn't believe it. It could do with a lick of fresh paint, but she was beginning to realize that no death-watch beetle would dare to linger anywhere near Adam.

'It's in need of restoration then?' she asked.

'No. Of leaving alone. It's good old wattle and daub behind that thin covering of plaster. Just think, Chaucer probably galloped past this window.'

'He was hardly Never Alone material. He'd have had a merry band of pilgrims with him.'

'Not so hard to imagine, is it?'

She leaned out of the window. Only a hundred yards or so away was the cathedral itself, and it seemed fitting that Adam's charity should be based here.

'All the people coming and going to Never Alone must make it a sort of modern pilgrimage.'

Adam seemed pleased at this notion. 'We always need more volunteers.'

'You seem to have plenty already.'

'We try. That's the mistake a lot of charities can make, not treating their volunteers well. They're not paid so why should they be ordered around? We have a Christmas party for ours – and the ball of course.'

'What ball? That sounds very grand.'

'Our annual summer event at Medlar House. It's fun – want to come? It's on Saturday night. I'll treat you.'

'And you run a charity?' she mocked. 'No. I'll come, but buy a ticket. Do you need volunteers to serve the food?'

'Thanks, but we go grand on this one. Caterers are brought in – and you can suspend your professional eye for the evening. They're good.' He paused, then changed tack. 'How did you get on with the great Hartshorn at Crandene? An aphrodisiacal experience?'

105

'What on earth do you mean?' Rachel was aware she was blushing.

'Isn't that what Hartshorn means? A sort of poor man's unicorn,' Adam said innocently.

She played it his way. 'I got more insight into the military side of the house – *and* I saw the old kitchens.' She couldn't resist adding, 'The waitress in the tearoom told me you'd returned too.'

'I did. I confess it, oh great detective. Does that make you feel crowded too?'

She laughed. 'Why do you always sweep the ground from under my feet?'

'It's my Walter Raleigh role, only I prefer sweeping the ground to ruining my best cloak.'

'Don't be daft.'

'Very well. I went for the same reason as you. We were so full of Alice and cookery when we went, that I didn't pay much attention to anything else. Finding myself near Crandene, I popped back. That do?'

He seemed on the level – so she apologized, somewhat unwillingly. Amazing the way both he and Michael always had a simple explanation for anything that affected Crandene. Then she was ashamed of herself for being so sensitive.

'Now I'll tell you something to rile you,' Adam continued cheerfully. 'Be careful with your chum Unicornhorn.'

'Are you warning me off?'

'Delete the off and the answer's yes. You told me on the phone that his lordship has given you his thumbs-down answer via his solicitors. What's Unicorn's position?'

'He doesn't have one. He's merely interested in Alice's script.' She was beginning to think she shouldn't have come here. It put her in Adam's debt. 'Michael was in France on a battlefield tour and thought my grandfather might know the name Harry Rolfe. Only it might not be Harry Rolfe.'

'Very clear so far.'

She lost patience. 'Look, Adam, I don't understand what this is all about. Are you warning me that Michael is in cahoots with Lord Beavers?'

Then the *real* reason for her unease when she was last with

106

Michael dawned on her at last. He had made an odd reply to her. She'd mentioned Adam to him. The normal reaction to that would be: 'Who's Adam?', but Michael hadn't asked that. Instead he'd replied with: 'Adam who?' A small thing, but with her heightened sense of awareness it might not be so small. Why should Michael care what Adam's surname was?

She moved back in front of the copier to start work again, and Adam shifted to its side, one hand resting on the pile of copied sheets. Instead of the machine her eyes were caught by that hand. Hands could be expressive, both in their movement and in their stillness, revealing more about their owner than mere words. Adam's hand was tanned, slender, long fingered – and vulnerable. What a damned stupid thing to think about a hand, she instantly reacted. But she looked again – and then fleetingly up at his face, and for a moment caught his glance. Vulnerable. Guard down. Only for a moment, then he looked away, but it had been enough. The effect had her almost physically swaying.

'Adam?'

'All yours.' He indicated the copier, but there was an uncertainty in his voice that suggested he'd been as shaken as she. 'Anything else you want?'

She shook her head, but inside she was crying out: 'Only you.'

When she reached home, she sent the promised copied recipe pages to Michael. Then she tucked the script back into its secure hiding place, feeling like a latterday Indiana Jones setting out on another adventure.

In a way it was a kind of adventure, or at least a mission. She still felt dazed, and it was an effort to force herself back on to the next step of her Alice Carter strategy. The solicitors' letter went unanswered, for she had no answer to give, since she could not publish the recipes anyway, now she knew Alice had embargoed it. The biography was a different matter. For this she could make a plan of attack, for there were other sources of research than Crandene. Tolbury Hall was the most important. There might be records of the Carters in Cranbridge, there might even be some of Alice's siblings' descendants around. She could study parish records, and begin building a picture of the Carter family. There might be people still alive to whom Alice might have talked about her early life. Even carers perhaps, Alice must have been close to someone. There might be staff members from Crandene during the period of her marriage to Lord Beavers and people who remembered Crandene during the war. Once this framework was in place, she could begin to think how she could use those recipes without breaching Alice's publication ban.

Meanwhile there was Adam's ball, but far from groaning at the prospect of sorting out something to wear, it now became a pleasurable challenge. She had been told that it was semi-formal, and she hadn't worn even semi-formal for some time. Nothing in her practical wardrobe managed to pass this test, so she splashed out on a new floaty dress; it was cream and slim fitting, and its purchase made her excited at the thought of an evening out – and even more excited because it was with Adam.

He had announced his intention of driving to pick her up, and she had agreed with no hesitation at all. 'So that you can drink yourself into a stupor,' he explained. 'No point in us both remaining teetotal for the evening.'

She was conscious of his eyes on her legs as she slid into the MG when it turned up promptly at seven. Not the van today thankfully. 'Nice,' he said.

'You haven't seen my legs for some time, have you?'

'I treasured the memory, though.'

Light, but it seemed to her that spring was in the air, July or not.

There must have been at least a hundred and fifty people at the ball, and Medlar, a magnificent nineteenth-century house outside Canterbury set in large grounds, looked an ideal venue for a magical summer night. Adam immediately threw himself into his MC role, but still assumed he was her partner – and for once she had no problem with this. Everyone seemed to be in a couple, and she slipped back into the role with ease. Just for this evening, she told herself. Adam proved to be a good dancer, better than she was, but far from finding this annoying, she realized that she was enjoying herself more than she had done since François . . . Forget him, Rachel ordered herself. Right *now*. And she did.

'Your eyes are sparkling,' Adam observed. 'It suits you.' He was holding her very close, and she didn't mind at all. Then as the rhythm changed he shot her whirling away, then pulled her back to him. Typical, she wondered hazily. Would he be that kind of lover? *Lover?* Rachel, where are you going?

'It's the champagne,' she answered to herself, as well as to him.

'Sparkling Saumur actually, but not bad. And in case you're wondering whether all those folk who need our charity are missing out on benefits because of the cost of this, we have a separate sponsor for this event.'

'Sounds very organized, as usual.'

From what she gathered from the volunteers, Adam was a hands-on CEO. It was Adam this and Adam that, and Adam aren't you wonderful – and yet Adam had told her he was ready to move on from Never Alone, which seemed odd. Back to journalism? That didn't seem likely either.

Adam disappeared for a while, but reappeared half an hour later. 'The supper dance, I do believe,' He held out his arm and she placed hers solemnly upon it. 'I had to sort out a problem with the hi-fi for when the band goes home. Sorry to be elusive.'

The wine had loosened her tongue. 'You often are.'

'Am I?' He looked startled.

'Let's say Never Alone Adam is usually present.'

'I keep forgetting to take my charity hat off.'

'Because you're bald underneath?'

'Why don't you find out?'

It was all very bland, very polished banter, but underneath it her stomach was churning in its effort to discipline her feelings into some kind of order.

Supper was a buffet, and from her position at the end of a longish queue, it looked good. She couldn't have done better herself, from its appearance at least. There was something familiar about the presentation of the tomato mousse – and, now she came to think of it, about the whole display. She and Marjorie . . .

It *was* Marjorie!

Rachel could hardly believe it. Four years or so older, but the same hair, the same grin, the same air of zesty determination. What, she asked herself in astonishment, could she be doing here? It had to be very unlikely indeed that Marjorie was here just by chance. Once over the shock, however, she realized how delighted she was to see her again. Marjorie's marriage and move to Dorset had been a personal blow as well as a business one. Dorset and Kevin were a long way from Kent, however, so what in the world was happening?

'Afterwards, lady!' Rachel said in mock severity when she got near enough. 'In my office in five.'

'Give me sixty.' Marjorie looked pleased, though hardly flabbergasted to see her, Rachel noted.

'Done deal.'

Rachel set out purposefully with her tray, and waited for Adam to join her, so that she could track this 'coincidence' down to its only possible source.

'I see by your face that you're wondering whether it's entirely by chance that Marjorie is here,' he commented, placing a bottle on the table, and pouring her a glass of wine.

'Wouldn't you?'

'Of course. The answer is no and yes. It was coincidence that I ran into Marjorie last month at another do. You'd mentioned a Marjorie that you'd worked with, and it isn't that common a name amongst our generation, so I merely asked whether she was *your* Marjorie. Since we needed a caterer for the ball, it went on from there.'

'You didn't tell me.'

'Life has to hold some happy surprises. She's working from Rye incidentally.'

'With Kevin?' Rachel was very doubtful about that. Kevin had not only disliked Rachel, but Marjorie's involvement in anything so demeaning as a sandwich business. He had grand ideas, did Kevin.

'She'll tell you.'

The music was getting louder and the dancing wilder, so after the meal Rachel remained in the now almost deserted dining room, until Marjorie at last came to join her. 'I know that look on your face, Rachel,' she said calmly, pouring herself a drink. 'It reads: why didn't you get in touch? Answer: I didn't know you were back, and I didn't know where you were in France. You forgot to let me know.'

'I split up from François,' Rachel explained guiltily, aware she'd been so full of misery that she had let life slip by her. 'After I came back, there was my mother to nurse. She died in February.'

'Oh Rachel. How bloody unfair. I loved your mother.'

Just like Marjorie. 'My words exactly,' Rachel replied. 'And how about you? Where's Kevin?'

'In Australia with a blonde backpacker. Divorce is pending.'

'They're backpacking together? I don't see Kevin . . . ?'

They caught each other's eye and roared with laughter. Kevin was, or had been, a prim and proper bore (in Rachel's opinion), jealous of everything in Marjorie's life but himself. A blonde bimbo sounded just up his street in one way, but a backpacking one was a million miles away.

'No. She's given it up for a life of luxury.' There was a hint of bitterness here so Rachel quickly changed the subject.

'Adam told me how he met you.'

'Right. I'm working for this outfit called Let's Party. I set the company up with a chum of Kevin's – the human variety. As it happens though,' she eyed Rachel thoughtfully, 'he wants out.'

One door closes, but the next one doesn't necessarily slam in your face. 'Hey, is that an offer?'

'Why not? There's time to mull it over. Nevil, that's my business partner, doesn't want to go till the end of the year. He just has a hankering to cater his way round the world and I don't.'

'No sandwiches,' Rachel decreed. 'I couldn't do that again.'

'You have to be joking. We only do baguettes.'

'And ciabatta, I bet, Ria.' Her pet name for Marjorie slipped out of the past. 'Did Adam tell you how he met me?'

'Not a word. Do tell.'

'I took some old stuff of Mum's into his Never Alone shop in Canterbury, and he came to return something he thought

I should keep.' There would be time to tell her more. The knowledge that Marjorie was back in her life sent the evening, already on Cloud Nine, right up to Cloud Eighteen.

On the way home in the car, she chattered to Adam about Marjorie, including the opportunity the reunion had offered. She suddenly wondered if Adam had had that in mind too. So what if he did plan it? She was grateful.

'Would you consider taking it up?' he asked.

'It would be a way out for the recipes, wouldn't it? We could at least cook from Alice's work. No copyright in that.' Already she was remembering Marjorie staggering around their kitchen moaning She Never Minced Words, Only Chicken, at yet another order for their special curried chicken mayonnaise. She had been fun to work with.

Rachel was filled with happiness as Adam cut through the lanes, the headlights picking up the occasional late-partying squirrel or vole. As they skirted Canterbury, the lights of the city sent a glow up into the sky. Once the first sight of journey's end for the pilgrims would have been the spire of the cathedral from Hambledon Hill on their approach to Canterbury, the light that shone in the darkness of medieval life. Rachel could not quite believe that something good had happened tonight. Yet it had. Adam would come into the cottage with her for – what – coffee? Drink? And what then? She was turning this round in her mind in a pleasant haze as the car turned into the lane to Chilford.

'Good to see streets lights again,' Adam remarked idly, seeing the sky lit up ahead.

'We only have one,' she replied sleepily. Then she paid quick, alarmed attention. 'That's not streetlights,' she said sharply. 'It's *red*, Adam. It's a fire.'

At the tone in her voice he accelerated, and now she could see the road blocked ahead by fire engines. Her stomach heaved as they drove towards the figures silhouetted in the red glow. She knew. She didn't need Adam's appalled 'Rachel!' to tell her the inevitable. It was *her* row of cottages that the fire hoses were playing on.

She could hear Adam draw in his breath as he parked for there was no room ahead. Her eyes were fixed on the glow.

It was next door – no, of course it wasn't. It was *her* cottage from which flames leaped from roof and first-floor windows. The hoses of two fire engines were playing on them, but the flames were merely laughing at them.

It was another three hours before the fire was out and at last the fire engines and police had departed, their work complete for the moment. Neighbours returned to their beds, but smoke was in the air, in Rachel's clothes and in her nostrils, and within her the heavy choking smoke of shock. Unable to contribute, she listened as Adam talked to her about what would happen next. Insurance, police, fire reports; they all passed over her.

Was she insured? he asked. Yes, she was. The supervisor had declared the building safe. New locks would be put on first thing tomorrow. Locks? When all that was valuable to her inside was gone? And still Adam talked. She was glad, for she was incapable of thinking straight.

'The fire people are pretty sure it was started deliberately. We'll know more tomorrow.' His words didn't make sense at first and then they came home to her with full force.

'I have to go in there *now*.' She was suddenly awake and aware.

'No. You need sleep.' Adam spoke as though this was the most obvious thing in the world. Not to her. Where was she to sleep? She supposed someone must have asked her, and she given some sort of answer. What had it been? Could she sleep here in this wreckage, with piles of furniture still in the garden? *And what of the script?*

'You're coming home with me, Rachel.'

That too seemed the most obvious thing in the world as he led her back to his car, and it slid its way back through the lanes to his home.

Eight

Rachel dreamed that the black night around her and within her was lit up with mocking flames she couldn't control. Long tenuous fingers stretched out for her and receded, she was being sucked closer and closer to the heart of the furnace. Faces appeared and disappeared out of the flames. She turned to flee, only to find her legs leaden, and the hounds of hell after her, greedily following her, gaining on her . . .

'Rachel!'

Another face, set against the grey of the room, made the flames recede. It was Adam, and he sat down at her bedside while she recovered herself from nightmare into waking nightmare.

'You were crying out,' he said matter-of-factly. 'Can I get you something? Hot milk? Cocoa?'

Cocoa for this? She went straight back into the horror of what had happened, coupled with the impossibility of coping while night fears ruled. But perhaps . . . ?

'Yes, yes, please.'

She was aware of his padding down the stairs, leaving her alone. She wouldn't go back into it, she couldn't. Instead she struggled to sit up, propping herself against pillows, reaching out to put the light on, and then changing her mind. She could face no light until tomorrow, and first she had to get through the night. It seemed only a minute before Adam reappeared with hot milk. She grimaced at the whiteness of it.

'Better than cocoa at the moment,' he said.

She usually never drank it straight, but a cautious sip at it made her wonder why not. 'It's good.'

'Perhaps that's the brandy I threw in it.'

Of course it was. Stupid of her. She drank her way through

114

it, aware of Adam, who was sitting watching her. Finally she finished.

'Thanks. That's much better. I'll know next time I can fight demons with hot milk.' Any moment now he would leave her, and she'd have to start the battle again. When she closed her eyes, would they still be there? She shivered, and Adam slithered further towards her to put his arm round her.

'Would a cuddle protect you?'

'Yes, please.' It seemed the natural thing, and he crept into the bed beside her. 'Best turn over,' he whispered practically, and then held her in his arms. It felt odd at first, asexual, but then through the thin bathrobe he was wearing, she was aware that it wasn't. But he made no move, and eventually she fell asleep, lulled by both the comfort of his presence and the hot milk. In the morning he had gone, and she wondered if he had been part of her dream. Opening her eyes more fully, she saw the empty mug on the bedside table and knew it had been the real Adam.

But now there was the day to face.

Adam's house was in Littleford, five miles from Canterbury on the far side from Chilford. It looked a comfortable rambling solid thirties-type house, with a 'settled-in' feel to it. She peered out of the window at the fields opposite, and then padded in one of his bathrobes into the bathroom. He'd fished out a new toothbrush and the toothpaste, not to mention clean towels and soap. She carefully showered and brushed her teeth, then turned to the next problem. She had no choice but to put on yesterday's underwear, but she shuddered at the cream dress. It was only when she was halfway into it that she noticed two neat piles of blouses and some trousers. Women's. She tried to get her mind round this, but failed. Clearly they were meant as try-ons for her. She managed to find some light cotton trousers, which were baggy but at least stayed on her, plus a rather nice white overblouse.

'Hey.' Adam looked up as she came into the kitchen.

'I feel like Charley's Aunt. Do you keep these spare clothes for stray women who drop in?'

'If I used that as a seduction technique, believe me I'd choose better than your current outfit.'

115

Then the obvious belatedly occurred to her. 'Of course. Charity bags.'

'You got it.'

A sudden silence as they caught each other's eye and memory of the night returned. Something was different between them. There was a bond between them now, acknowledged on that day in his office, cemented by their closeness in the night. It could either go on or be ignored, but she knew which path she wanted to take. She put her arms round him and kissed him on the cheek. 'Thank you, Adam.'

In a moment the situation was reversed, and she was in his arms, his lips on hers. When at last he released her, he said shakily, 'It could have been you in there, Rachel.'

'But it wasn't. I'm here.'

'I can feel that.' Then he kissed her again, holding her so close she could hear the thudding of his chest. 'God, I was scared by that fire. It was arson; they found the petrol can.'

'Yes.' She'd realized it probably was, but now that it was out in the open, the shock hit her, and she sat down, trembling. 'An insecure way of killing someone,' she pointed out. 'Do you think it was the script they were after?' She could think of nothing else to explain it.

'No. The seat of the fire was at the back. A window had been forced and the fire must have swept through your living room, up your stairs and into the room above. The neighbours noticed it about one o'clock, when it was blazing away. If you'd been asleep . . . It's all my damn fault, too.'

'How do you make that out?' Rachel was grappling with the implications of what he'd told her. Even with the help of morning light, they raised demons that made her glad she was not alone.

'I was the one who persuaded you to tell Beavers and Hartshorn you were going ahead regardless.'

'I have a mind of my own, you know, and I agreed with you. It was the only thing to do. To smoke them out—' Rachel broke off as the phrase hit her, and Adam held her again, rocking her gently to and fro. She couldn't get her mind round the fact that Adam was suggesting Crandene in whatever form was behind this attack. And was he really implying that she was the target, not the script? She couldn't cope with that – not yet.

'Have some breakfast,' he said at last.

'I'm not hungry.'

'Everything looks better after morning coffee and toast. You can have even have the full English if you like.'

She shuddered. 'Toast, please. I can do it, though.'

'And have yoghurt or cheese, or an egg. Fortify yourself.'

'I am fortified.' Silly thing to say, really, since she was aware she was trembling. 'You're providing splendid armour, Adam. Are you . . . ?' She broke off, knowing she couldn't trespass on more of Adam's time.

'Busy today?' he supplied for her.

'For all I know you might be entertaining your entire family tree for lunch today,' she explained, hoping against hope that he wasn't and despising herself at the same time for being wimpish about coping alone.

'As it happens, my family tree lives in Berkshire, and I've emailed my entire harem to cancel all arrangements until further notice.'

'What a relief. I really don't think I could cope with too much competition.'

'You won't have to. I'm the faithful type.'

Sometime, somewhere, somehow, she'd have to think about that. But not now. Toast was enough. And the glorious tea.

She fell very silent as they approached Chilford. Adam had brought the van, so that she could rescue anything she wished. If there was anything left.

Not much could be done today about insurance, she supposed, as it was a Sunday. She'd have to find the policy, but with a sudden pang she knew it had probably gone. it occurred to her that Adam had not even mentioned Alice's script. He must assume it had gone for ever, whereas, having had time to think rationally about it, she was fairly sure it would be safe. Nevertheless the sickening thought of what might have been lost, including all those other family papers and photographs, came to her. Any moment now she'd have to face it. Find out what had escaped and what had vanished for ever.

117

Which brought her back to the implications of what Adam had told her. He had assumed – and what other explanation could there be, if the fire had been started deliberately – that Crandene was somehow involved, which must mean it was instigated by Lord Beavers. Her head began to spin. If Adam's other suspicions about Michael were correct, it could only be that he was in cahoots with Beavers because of the Crandene connection. And she couldn't believe that.

That's what logic said, but then logic also said how on earth could she, Rachel Field, represent such a threat to the mighty Lord Beavers or to the Crandene Foundation that her attempted murder was the only way out, in order to rid themselves, not only of her, but with luck any mention of Alice Beavers with her? But her first. They must surely know that the fire could be proven as arson, and yet they took that risk. Why not, she reasoned. There would be no proof whatsoever that they were connected. She spent a brief moment considering the picture of Lord Beavers himself driving over to pop petrol – if that's what it was – through her back window, and dismissed it as rubbish. He'd have had a contract with someone to do it, yet this had an unreality about it, as though she were taking part in a TV film.

What was real enough was the sight of her home as they drove up, and the smell of smoke in the air. Her car was still where she had left it on the hard standing of her front garden, though it bore evidence of the night's events. She bled for it, charred soot, dust and litter. Cars were not important, but the house was. Here Mum and she had spent happy times, and tragic times, and she had cared so little for it that she had been proposing to sell it without good reason. Fate had certainly knocked that on the head. Rachel was filled with a great anger that anyone could dare to do this to her home. There were charred, boarded-up windows where the fire, water and salvage had demolished them, and she dreaded what she might find at the rear.

Adam took her hand, as they approached the house, after she began to fish for her keys – then she remembered what he had said about locks last night. Of course, the door would have been forced by the firemen. Her neighbours, a retired couple,

118

with whom she'd always maintained a polite distance, now came out, full of concern and, realizing it was genuine, she did her best to cope with discussing insurance, going to the police station tomorrow, house security, the locksmith's bill, storing anything she wished in their attic. Tomorrow was a working day, tomorrow all these things must be faced in earnest, but meanwhile the trauma of today must be endured.

'I told the police I saw someone early last evening,' Shirley Bond, her neighbour, was saying. 'A fish man.'

'Fish man?' she echoed. 'I don't have a fish man.'

'He looked like a fish man,' Shirley replied. 'He said he had a special delivery parcel. That would have been about eightish. He said he'd left it round the back. Thinking you'd be home later, I didn't worry, and then, well, we went to bed and I forgot all about it. There was nothing there this morning, so unless the firemen took it, that was peculiar. I told the police.'

Rachel took a deep breath. 'Thanks,' she said, genuinely grateful. After all, she told herself, even if the Bonds had gone round to investigate and found no fish – did fish come in parcels? – they'd hardly be looking for traces of arson. The fish man must have returned later, and merely been scouting out his entry point when she saw him.

Rachel took the new key and they went in. At first sight it didn't look too bad, obviously because the fire had begun at the back. She peered into the front area of the house, where water damage was evident. Beyond that, in the dining area, was a mass of black-charred furniture, ashes. She forced herself to look at it calmly, then went on to the kitchen.

This was more or less intact, but she could see where the fire had swept up the stairs like a tornado. 'Can we walk up the stairs?' she asked Adam steadily.

'Yes. The supervisor said they're basically safe though they don't look it. Do you want to go up?'

'I'd like to see if I've any clothes left.'

A stupid thing to say, really, she thought. Anything salvageable would take weeks of washing to get the stench out.

'Bring whatever you like to my place and we'll do our best with it.'

That reminded her. 'I'll have to find a B and B or guest house nearby to stay in while this is sorted. I suppose Canterbury would be best.'

'Stay with me tonight at any rate. There's already been one attempt on your life. I'd rather there wasn't a second for which I can blame myself. And wherever you choose to go, keep an official address with your neighbours, your solicitors, or a friend, but don't let *anyone* else know where you're staying.'

Their eyes met, and then she looked round at the black horror of what had once been her bedroom. Reluctantly she saw the sense of what he was saying. Even now it seemed melodramatic, but the slight chance that he was right made it the logical thing to do. Tonight, he'd said. Was she disappointed he hadn't invited her to stay on? No. She'd have felt crowded, in his debt. He must have sensed she would need her own space, and that was good of him.

'Tell you what,' she said. 'I'll cook you dinner.'

'An Alice dinner? Done.'

'Adam—'

'You don't have to tell me,' he cut in. 'I realize the script must be burned. Have you checked?'

'I don't have to. I know it's all right.'

'What?' His face lit up.

'Come and see.' She led him downstairs and unlocked the back door, averting her eyes from the area marked off in the living room by the police, and went out into the fresh air of her back garden. Reasonably fresh. Furniture that had been tossed out here still had its aura of smoke.

'Are we walking up that hill again?' he enquired.

'Not so far as that. Here. The garden shed.' She turned the handle, and went in.

'Is that where it is?' he asked incredulously. 'It's not even locked.'

'Why should it be. No one would expect the script to be in here, would they?'

'True.' Adam gazed at the rusty paint tins, and assortment of garden pots and garden tools. 'Where is it?'

'Here.' She went to her mother's old bike, and undid the straps of its ancient basket, taking out a stout brown paper bag, so that he could peer inside at the script.

120

She withdrew it for his closer inspection. 'No deception, ladies and gentlemen. Here it is, the one and only original script.'

It fell open at the page with the illustration of the two pies at the seaside and Rachel was once more overcome at the care that had gone into its composition. The recipes she typed out nowadays would never last as long.

'Let's go and see whether the copies have survived. They were in the living room.'

It was her excuse to tackle the worst problem. Nothing that had been on the table could have escaped, Rachel realized. It had been reduced to charred ash and bits of wood. In trepidation she went back to the garden, where the desk had been salvaged. Although it was barely recognizable as a desk, she found to her pleasure that some papers had survived, albeit singed, in the top part, though nothing had in the drawers.

'Where were your family papers?'

'The guest room.' Of course. Everything had seemed so unimportant beside the enormity of her mother's death, and she had bundled things up and shoved them in there. Her own bedroom had been virtually demolished, but the gloryhole of the small guest room might just have escaped in part.

She dashed inside and upstairs, again followed by Adam. 'Take care,' he called. 'Some of these floorboards are badly charred, so the firemen said.'

The door to the guest room had gone, but a few things remained unscathed inside, including an old leather suitcase. She opened it cautiously – not difficult since the lid was half burned off anyway. Most of the items were charred beyond repair. Maybe a forensic lab could do something with them, but for her purposes they were gone. But a photograph album had escaped. She hugged it to her fiercely. This was all she had left. A few papers and this one album. She found herself crying with relief in Adam's arms.

'How could they *do* this? Everything's gone.'

'Except you . . .'

'And this album.'

'The script, Rachel,' he said quietly. 'Don't let anyone know that it's still OK. *No one*. Not Marjorie, not—'

121

'Michael?'

'Yes.'

Rather to his surprise, she suspected, she immediately agreed. 'I've already decided what to do. I'll write to Lord Bloody Beavers and his solicitors informing them of the fire (since they seem to think they might own the copyright in the script) and that family papers were destroyed and copies of Alice's script. I'll word it so that they conclude the original has gone too. Then they can't possibly think I am any danger to them. Is that OK?'

'Very good.'

'There's one problem.' She frowned. 'Since it can't be me personally that they've taken a dislike to, it has to be my connection with Alice. Why? Is it because they don't want me nosing around into her life? Or is it that I represent some other threat to them?'

'Such as?'

'Well,' she scrabbled around for ideas, 'perhaps some priceless relic has gone down through Alice's side of the family and would come to me. The Staffordshire figures, for example.'

'Weak.'

'Perhaps I am the true and only heir to Crandene.'

'Nice one, but Alice had no kids.'

'Perhaps Alice was actually the legitimate daughter of Robert Beavers' father and could prove it, so Crandene would belong to Pops and when he dies would come to me.'

'The smoke has affected your brain, sweetheart. The Beavers family would have known about this threat and therefore Robert would hardly have married his step-sister. Anyway, she was a mere female so wouldn't have inherited any-way.'

'Adam, is that sweetheart as in sweetheart or as in casual chum?'

'Do you want the answer here and now?'

'Yes.'

'The floorboards won't stand it. Nor that bed. Would a kiss on account do?'

'I think I'd like that.' It was the most wonderful kiss she'd ever had; it began a tingle that went all down her body and back again to the sweet taste of his lips.

'I wish you had that cream dress on, not these thick old trousers.'

'I wish I had them off.'

'Later, lover. Later – unfortunately.'

For the first time she felt lifted away from the desolation around her. Sex had played no significant part in her life since François had left. There had been one or two rebound mistakes, but then nothing. To have it suddenly come upon her was – even in the midst of this carnage of her former life – something to be savoured, a revelation that she could still be lifted out of the treadmill of sorting out her life into unexpected pleasures.

Perhaps more than pleasure, she thought. Perhaps love was once again rearing its beguiling head in her life. Her mind more on this than on what she was doing, she began to pack as many salvageable clothes as she could find, together with a few forlorn other necessities, and it took Adam to draw her back into the reality of what lay around them.

'What are you going to do about Alice, Rachel, besides writing to Crandene? Put a hold on all plans?'

She was amazed that he could even think that. 'No way. I'm going right ahead. I'm going to write Alice's biography, and, though she doesn't know it yet, Marjorie and I are going to try out Alice's recipes.'

June 1916

'Alice?' Mr Palmer said with the air of one conferring an honour. 'Mr Robert wishes to see you in the morning room.'

Her heart sank. Harry had left only yesterday to go back to France, but Mr Robert had stayed on for a few more days. Now this. Her parting with Harry had been awful, and today she was still full of misery. How could she cope in his absence? He always talked about when the war was over, but it never was. She'd won his agreement, however, that they need not wait any longer if the war went on into next year. If he got wind of another leave, they would get married, and be blowed to old Fritz.

123

Now she had to go to see Mr Robert. True, he would hardly molest her in the morning room, but even so she didn't trust him an inch. She hated him.

She had to go, however, and she gathered her strength as she marched along the corridor to the morning room, and went in. He was sitting in one of the armchairs, not at the desk, and got up as she came in, an unexpected courtesy from him.

'Sit down, Alice.'

'I'll stand if you don't mind, sir.'

'Sit, please.'

'I'd rather stand.'

'Oh, please yourself. I'll sit though. Has Rolfe gone?'

'Yes, sir.' Where was this leading?

'You're going to marry him, aren't you?'

Her heart sank. Back to that again. 'Yes, sir. We're pledged.' Despite herself a glow came into her cheeks, as she remembered what had happened between them, and then she blushed as if Mr Robert could read her thoughts.

He was clearly in a stew about something, because he changed his mind and stood up again. 'I'll be going back tomorrow, Alice. Do you mind at all?'

She was at a loss how to deal with this. 'Harry's told me it's quiet where you are now, sir. There's an occasional bit of bother but mostly they go to the café and—' She broke off because Mr Robert was laughing. Not real laughing, as though he were happy, but nasty and bitter.

'He's keeping the truth from you. Certainly it's like that sometimes. But most of the time he's in a trench, in the wet and the mud, and the rats to listen to his blasted flute. There's going to be a big push, and it's my belief our battalion will be in it. Everyone will; the French are too busy at Verdun to come to fight Fritz in our sector. So everyone will be there at this great big party at the Somme. That's where we're heading shortly, I'm sure of that. So think of us, Alice, Harry and me, both loving you.'

'Sir—'

'Damn you.' He glared at her. 'What *is* it about you? You're only a bloody kitchenmaid but I can't get you out of my mind.'

124

'Sir—'

'Your damned eyes, the way you look down, the way you blush, the way your breasts . . .'

Alice began to back out of the room, but he barked at her, 'Come back, I'm sorry. I'm not going to hurt you. I just want to say goodbye, that's all.'

Cautiously she ventured nearer again. 'I don't know why you think about me either, sir,' she replied truthfully. 'I'm not clever, not like Miss Cecilia, and I'm not very pretty.'

'Don't talk about Miss Cecilia. I hear enough about her from my father.'

Alice disregarded him. 'It's a shame, sir. She's ever so fond of you. Everyone says so. And you going off to the war again, she's very sad.'

He gave a short bark of laughter. 'She adores me and you won't look at me. Yet it's your face I see every blasted where I go. It's you I want to hold in my arms.' He swallowed and his face flushed. 'I don't mean to upset you, Alice. I really don't. I'm upset myself, as a matter of fact. Spot's not too good. I doubt if I'll see the old fellow again.'

'I'm sorry, sir. I know how fond you are of him.'

'Will you kiss me goodbye, Alice? Not much to ask.'

'No, sir!' Alice was alarmed.

'Just one kiss.' He came towards her, and she backed away. 'Good God, girl, I'm not going to rape you. Just a kiss.'

She quickly made up her mind. 'I'll kiss you on your cheek, sir, just the once, because you're off to war and I wish you well for your parents' sake and Miss Cecilia's. But my heart's Harry's. It always will be, and my love's all for him and him alone.'

She was nervous, for Mr Robert was working himself up, eyes bright. 'Kiss me then,' he said hoarsely.

He wasn't in his right mind, surely, but she'd said she'd do it, so she must. Nervously she approached him and he held his arms out. She drew close to him and they closed around her, as she kissed him on the cheek, then tried in vain to pull away.

'I won't harm you,' he said huskily. 'I just want to feel you close for a moment. I know you're going to be mine, Alice, even if you don't.'

'Harry's, sir.' She pulled herself away desperately, and this time managed it, running for the door.

She glanced back, to see him standing there with a sort of smile on his face, whispering, 'Mine,' to himself. 'Mine.'

Nine

Rachel opened her eyes, not quite sure if she was still dreaming, and put her arms round the rolled-up figure in the duvet next to her.

'Adam?'

The duvet promptly unwound itself, and he was looking up at her, grinning. So was she. In fact she had the biggest grin on her face she could remember for a long time.

'Clever of us, yes?' He reached for her.

'I suppose it has been done before.'

'Millions of years of history suggests it has.'

'But not as happily as us.'

'Shall we prove it to them again?'

The proving took some time, and it was only after the sun had been streaming in for some considerable while that Rachel remembered it was Monday, and pointed out to Adam that there were things to be done. He wasn't impressed, but grudgingly departed for the shower ten minutes later. Should she get up too and pad along to the other bathroom? she pondered, or should she allow herself the luxury of waiting in state here in bed? Duty won, even the kind she had to face today, though grappling with police and insurance didn't seem nearly so bad now there was Adam.

Now there was Adam, she repeated to herself. Was there? Had the distance between them finally been crossed in all respects, or only in the physical? Yet the one, she decided, must surely be the path to the other. Oh, the glory of last night, of this morning, and oh, the even greater glory of the days to come. She sprang out of bed, and looked out of Adam's bedroom window into the garden. She'd never have thought of Adam as a gardener, and perhaps her rose-tinted spectacles were firmly in place, but it had the tended sprawl that she liked, halfway between the extremes of wilderness and regimentation. An empty bag of nuts hung from a tree, roses bloomed on ramblers, and the borders were full of lilies, marguerites and snapdragons. A whole new world, with Adam in it.

Despite all this, today she knew she had to leave. Today she must find herself a B and B, and then set about finding more permanent rented accommodation. She couldn't move far from Chilford, since she'd need to be at hand to supervise rebuilding work. Her heart sank. So many hurdles. So many decisions, and she had to tackle them alone. Adam's presence yesterday and today was a bonus, she told herself, not a fixture, even though they were lovers. She'd made that mistake with François, sharing bed and board too soon, until the stars in her eyes gradually lost their brightness and had to be constantly repolished.

'You look very gloomy.' Adam had come back into the bedroom, and come up behind her, putting his arms round her.

'Not now.'

He nuzzled her neck. 'Good.'

Breakfast twenty minutes later at the round pine table in the kitchen was beginning to take on an uncomfortable air of familiarity, as did the marmalade pot, and the willow pattern bowls for the grapefruit Adam produced.

'Why don't you stay here till you've found a B and B? Don't rush it.'

Oh, the temptation. 'The sooner I face it the better, perhaps. But thank you.' She managed a bracing smile.

'Up to you. Didn't . . . ?' He broke off, busying himself with making coffee, his back to her.

'Go on,' she said.

'Last night make a difference?'

In a moment she was in his arms again, rushing to him in horrified apology. 'I'm a fool. I'm out of practice in relationships,' she murmured.

'Me too.'

'Have you ever been married?' Amazing she'd known him this long and never asked.

'Live-in partner for four years. The lady left when I announced my intention of departing the journalistic way of life.'

'Related facts?'

'Oh yes.'

'She wasn't worthy of you.'

'She's the past, and you know how I deal with that.'

'As the way to the future?'

'Ah. You remember my words. But you should see what I do, not listen to what I say.'

'You mean that was your professional baloney,' Rachel said indignantly. 'I've been trying to follow that advice ever since.'

'Quite right. For me, though, it's physician, heal thyself.' He kissed her again. 'It seems we're two of a kind, Rachel. Is that good?'

'I can't answer that,' she answered steadily. 'All I know is, *we're* good together. Isn't that enough?' For the moment, she thought, it is, and wondered if Adam was thinking the same.

May 1929

Lilies. Always lilies for dear Monsieur Trente. Alice laid the bunch reverently on the grave. She had let Madame Trente come alone on this first anniversary of his death, but now she too could be here to mourn. What would her life – and that of her family – have been if it had not been for him? It was he who had, unbeknown to the Beavers family, taken her in when she was thrown out of Crandene without home or money. Even he, however, had been unable to do anything for her family, who had simultaneously been ousted from their cottage and reduced to going into the workhouse.

There they would have remained if it had not been for Monsieur Trente. It was he who had insisted when late in 1918 he was offered a job in Lincolnshire at Tolbury Hall that Alice must come with him as his sous-chef-de-cuisine. And that had paved the way for her getting a job for Dad on the estate together with a cottage for the family. During their two years in the workhouse Dad had been classed as able-bodied

129

and forced to work at stone-breaking for the roads. It had aged him and he looked like an old man, though he was scarcely fifty. As for Mum, separated from Dad and for most of the time from her children too, she had crept around like a mouse for the first month or two in Lincolnshire in case she should be noticed by Them and dragged back to misery.

Workhouses might save you from physical starvation, but they condemned your soul to death. Mum – and all the family – had had to cope not only with her elder brother Edward's death at Passchendaele while she was in the workhouse, but also with that of Frank, the second eldest, who had been killed just before the Armistice. War had dealt cruelly by Alice. Not content with taking Harry, it had stolen her beloved brothers too.

She owed everything to Monsieur Trente. Tolbury Hall was smaller but much freer than Crandene, and she could see much more of her family. At first Alice had found it hard to adjust to the flat, more open landscape of Lincolnshire, but now she loved it. The Great North Road snaking by, redolent of adventure, the stone cottages, the rivers running through miles of open farmland, were all so different from Kent.

Alice told herself she must not think of Kent. Not of the hills, its valleys, its red roofs, its woodland, or its lush flowers and fruit. There were few hills in Lincolnshire to remind her of what she must forget. She had a new life, and what was gone before lived only deep in her heart, where it would never be forgotten. She no longer had so many obligations. Rosie was nineteen now and to Alice's pleasure a teacher in the local infant school; Emmy was a typist in a Stamford office, and to be married next year. Betty had stayed in Kent, married to her George. Even little Henry was twelve now and not so little. She'd taken up painting, and tried to interest him with her landscapes. When this didn't work, she tried animals and birds, and finally funny cartoon-like characters, which at last caught his attention, and he too began to draw.

'I like *bridges* and things,' he explained. 'Like Isambard Brunel. I'm going to design the biggest and best bridge in the world.'

Perhaps he would, who knew?

Alice strolled back to Tolbury Hall, reflecting on how lucky

130

she was. She was thirty-one, and though Dad was ageing, the family had been able to stay on in the cottage. Sir John Dene, the major, was good that way, not like the Beavers family, and anyway Alice had power now she was chef. She hadn't expected this promotion when Monsieur Trente died. She thought they'd bring in a new chef over her, but they didn't; Major Dene liked her cooking. She'd had to do a lot while Monsieur Trente was ill, and had daringly experimented with dishes of her own, which found favour with the family. Tolbury Hall gardens were full of wonderful produce, and she had been well taught by Monsieur Trente how to use it. Work in harmony with the food *comme ça, petite Alice*. She had thought she had no tears left to spill after Harry's death, but she was wrong. Monsieur Trente's death was another blow.

Fancy her, Alice Carter, chef of Tolbury Hall, with a sous-chef of her own. She'd come a long way, and any happiness she had now was due to Tolbury Hall, as well as Monsieur Trente. It had given her a job and it gave her back her beloved family, which now included Henry. My youngest, Mum always proudly announced, the one she'd always wanted.

As she walked into the kitchen, Alice felt her usual glow of pride as she saw everything neatly laid out, as Monsieur Trente had always demanded. She had a staff of three, far fewer than even Tolbury Hall would have had before the war, let alone Crandene, but the war had changed everything. It had taken most of the menfolk for ever, and insidiously the young women, for they now knew there was more money and less slavery outside service. Catch the modern young miss working the hours Alice had at Crandene. Now there were charlestons and bobbed hair and short skirts, replacing the formal servants' ball, mobcapped hair and long dresses sweeping the floor. Oh, it was a different world all right. It was on fire with music and energy, and for all Major Dene said darkly it wouldn't be long before there was another war, Alice couldn't see it happening. The one that had passed had been too terrible, too ghastly. It would be as if Harry had died for nothing.

'Afternoon, Miss Carter.'

She went over to the stove and sniffed approvingly at the

asparagus soup, tasting a spoonful. 'Not so bad, Toby. Well done. Glad you remembered to add the spinach for colour.'

She hadn't been sure how young Toby Williams would respond either to working for a woman or to trying to develop into a chef. He had begun his Tolbury life as butler's boy which naturally endeared him to her, but he tended to be scatterbrained, despite his intelligence. Monsieur Trente had said he had the makings of a chef, however, and that was good enough for Alice. It was turning out well, once she'd established who was giving the orders – and that they had to be obeyed. He had sulked a bit, but after a year he settled down to learn, and was becoming interested in food himself. He could barely read when he had first come, but after a little gentle teaching from her now immersed himself in recipe books – and particularly old English ones, as did she.

Lady Dene, the major's wife, had a collection of old books in the library, some quite valuable, such as Sir Kenelm Digbie's seventeenth-century *The Closet Opened*, and Richard Dolby's book about the Thatched Tavern in St James's. In addition to the books, her ladyship tended to collect recipes from each country house in which she stayed, and then bind them into books. She'd often show them to Alice first. 'What do you think, Alice? Could you manage this?'

The remarkable thing was that she trusted Alice. If Alice pointed out Tolbury Hall wouldn't have the quality of game available for such a recipe, or that the cost of such a fish dish in Lincolnshire would be exorbitant, or that the flavours would not mix, or even that Alice thought the recipe too time-consuming for the Tolbury kitchens, then it was never mentioned again.

'The major wants to see you, Miss Carter.'

Alice glanced at the dinner preparations. 'Can you manage the roast duck and cucumbers, Toby?'

His eyes lit up. 'Yes, Miss Carter. I've already put the cucs and onions in to soak with the wine.'

'Marinate, Toby. Not soak.'

The major was at his desk when she went in to his study.

'How's young Henry?' he asked. Henry was a great favourite of his.

132

'Driving Mum mad, sir, as always, but he's good at heart.'

She saw that the major was having one of his tired days, not physically weary, but mentally. She could always recognize this for she had such days. There were times when the past was just too much to cope with, however hard you tried. The major had come through the war well, so everybody said, but she knew he hadn't. Not mentally, anyway.

After she had told him that Harry had died at the Somme, he would sometimes talk to her, while she tried to steel herself not to think about Harry, but to concentrate on what he said. He talked of the nightmares, the endless march of death that took men haphazardly, the brave, the cowardly, rich or poor, officer or private. He spoke of the anguish of the padres and of the dedication of the stretcher bearers and nurses, and he spoke of the responsibilities of the officers. That was the worst. He had had to lead men to their death realizing that it was all for nothing, that the commanders at the top were nonplussed as to how to end this new static form of warfare, too old to change, but unable to call on a new generation, the bravest and wisest of which were already dead, lost in the slaughter of the war's early years. The Somme had been the turning point for the major. He had fought there, and gone on through Ypres and right through to the bitter end, by which time there was hardly a tree standing in the battlefields. Like the army itself, the major said. All gone, but the stumps of the gaunt few.

Everyone said the major had been a real fire-eater before the war, but that since its end he had been as gentle as a lamb. She thought she could understand why. After you'd seen such horrors there would be nothing in England's countryside with the power to move you. She had listened to his outpourings horrified at the tale they told, so different from the bright hopes to end tyranny with which men had volunteered in 1914. Hopes that Harry had shared – and now it all seemed to have been for nothing. Thank God Harry had not known that. Or had he? Had he realized it already and not shared it with her? Did he not think her strong enough to bear it? Perhaps then she would not have been, but now she was.

Sometimes old war pals would come to visit the major, but they never talked of war. She would never have entered the dining room at Crandene, but here at Tolbury Hall where there were fewer staff and less formality she'd quite often serve a dish or two herself, or come in to talk about the food with the guests. She heard enough to recognize that though war linked these men, it was a silent bond, for the conversation was all light-hearted.

'Alice, Lady Dene and I shall be entertaining next weekend.'

She was pleased to hear that. She liked such chances to expand her repertoire. 'How many for dinner, sir. Four extra?'

The major smiled. 'I'm going to astound you, Alice. Sixteen – and they are here for the whole weekend.'

'Oh, sir.'

'You look worried, Alice. Can't you manage that?'

'I can, sir. I'll love it. It's just that Mrs Haythrop . . .' Mrs Haythrop was the housekeeper, but she was no Mrs Cheney. She was nearing the age when she would have to hand over her keys to a younger woman, but the major was too softhearted to say so, until really necessary. 'It would mean her opening up more bedrooms and finding the linen,' Alice explained.

He understood the problem perfectly. 'Lady Dene has already spoken to Mrs Haythrop. I wonder if one of your sisters, Rose or Emmy, might like to come in to lend a hand for the weekend and, if possible, a day or two in advance as well.'

'They couldn't manage except at the weekend, sir. But Mum might come. Leave it with me.'

'Thank you, Alice.'

'And the menus, sir?'

'Lady Dene will leave them to you, as always.' He thought for a moment. 'However, my friends are all former war colleagues and they are coming here to discuss a permanent memorial to my regiment to be erected in France. I am being ridiculous, no doubt, but it seems to me that an English meal, rather than French-inspired, would remind us all of how fortunate we have been to live here, and at the same time be a tribute to our fallen friends' courage.'

'Yes, sir.' Alice vowed that she'd do the best menu she could for the major and his friends. 'Lincolnshire lamb and cheeses, sir, perhaps. I'll have a good think about the rest.' Then she remembered. 'What about the wine, sir? That would have to be French.'

'Don't tell me you can't whip up a good English claret to rival Bordeaux, Alice. You disappoint me.'

She laughed. 'No, sir, but I might manage something just to show that France doesn't have it all its own way. My Dad's got really keen on making sloe gin. That would make a change from American cocktails.'

'And no doubt have us under the table before your meal is even tasted.'

She left the major happily, remembering that tomorrow was her afternoon off. She'd see Henry and they'd take a walk together. He probably hated them, but he would remember later in life all he learned about English hedgerows and flowers and birds. Just as she had learned so much from Harry. Quickly she switched her thoughts. Think about the menu. It was beginning to form in her head already. Syllabubs perhaps. Now they were something she hadn't done for a time. There'd be apricots if she was lucky, perhaps even a few early strawberries. She'd have a word with Albert. He was Tolbury's magnificent head gardener and always enjoyed a challenge. And she'd serve lemon cheese, so much more exciting than cream. The new season's peas might be ready. Soup – nothing more English than that. *Real* soup, made from a stock of which Monsieur Trente would have approved. Stock before the war took three or four days to make. Not today. No tammy cloths for straining now. No time, no time, the world rushed by to its future, oblivious to its today, let alone its past. And there was no choice. One had to rush with it, or be trampled into dust.

By the next day she had it all planned in her mind and looked forward to her visit home even more happily. Henry, not greatly to her surprise, showed little enthusiasm at the suggestion of a walk, but they had a lovely day all the same.

'Miss Carter, there's been a tramp looking for you,' Toby suddenly recalled, on her return.

'For me? I don't know any tramps. You mean a tramp asked to see the chef?'

135

'No, he asked for Miss Alice Carter.'

A clever tramp, she thought wryly. Better to know the name if you want to make an impression. One didn't see so many tramps around now. Before the war they had been a part of the year's cycle in a village such as Cranbridge. Tramps would turn up at hoppicking time and other harvesting periods in the hope of casual work They tended to be regular visitors every year however, and so became known to the village. Then there was the other sort who travelled the length and breadth of the country, and called not to any time pattern but irregularly in the hope of odd jobs in return for food. Monsieur Trente had taught his staff to be generous to tramps, but had to stop after this was discovered by his lordship. No food unless they worked for it was the rule after that.

After the war there seemed to be fewer of the old tramps, but a new kind sprang up. When the 'land fit for heroes to live in' failed to materialize, many destitute soldiers were reduced to begging or selling matches in cities or tramping from village to village as pedlars with whatever wares they could obtain. The expected land of plenty as regards jobs and houses was still a pipedream.

Alice was puzzled that this tramp had asked for her by name. He could, it is true, easily have discovered her name on his way through the grounds, but few would bother to do so.

'He said he'd come again tomorrow afternoon,' Toby said helpfully.

Alice thought no more about it, and returned to the delights of her cooking.

But the next afternoon he did come again. She saw him coming up the path towards the back entrance to the house. Something made her stop what she was doing to watch him. He was shabby, but he had an upright bearing for a tramp, and she put him down as a former soldier. An inexplicable fear took hold of her as she found herself going to the door to meet him.

He swept off his battered bowler. 'I seek Miss Alice Carter, ma'am.'

'I'm Alice Carter.'

'Ma'am, Corporal Peasbody at your service. Late of The Queen's Own Royal West Kent Regiment, 1st Battalion.'

What he then told her changed Alice's life for ever.

Rachel looked at the letter in her hand in horror. In the turmoil of the last few days, she had completely forgotten Michael's dinner invitation which they'd arranged on the telephone the day before the ball. The date had come and gone. Hence his plaintive letter which had been held at the post office for her. She'd stood him up without meaning to. Would she please ring him, the letter requested, and tell him what the hell was going on. Why was her phone disconnected? She hastily rang him from her mobile, explaining what had happened, and apologizing time and time again. She exercised economy with the truth over the fire.

'I don't know how it happened,' she ended. 'Fortunately I was out.'

After his suitably horrified sympathy, he said, 'Do you want to make another date for dinner, or postpone it till you're more sorted?'

Rachel forced herself to think as clearly as she could. She was continuing her investigations into Alice's life, and if she accepted Marjorie's half-offer of a partnership, that could be a perfect way to use the recipes. For both, it might be as well to have a friend in the Beavers camp. True, he wasn't completely in it, at least she hoped he wasn't, but at least he was on speaking terms with the enemy and involved with next year's Crandene venture.

'Yes, I would,' she told Michael. 'It's generous of you to forgive me.'

'Shall we meet in London?'

'Yes please,' she replied promptly. Her turf down here was well and truly occupied, firstly by the B and B where she was living and secondly, though not in order of importance, with Adam. 'I'll treat myself courtesy of the insurance accommodation allowance to a night in a hotel.'

A pause. 'Good. Tuesday then? Give me your mobile number and I can at least keep in touch.'

'You won't lose me again, I promise.'

Adam didn't seem too delighted at this news when she broke

it to him, which amused and flattered her. She explained her reasons for accepting Michael's invitation to the point where he laughed. 'You think I'm jealous?'

'Well, no, of course not.'

'Wrong. I am.'

'Good. No need though.' Indeed there wasn't. She looked back with faint surprise on the Rachel who had been mildly attracted by Michael, to the point where hugs had seemed a really good idea. That was in another life, a life pre-Adam.

'I got the impression from your earlier description that Unicornhorn was the sexiest man in London bar none.'

'What on earth could I have said to give you that idea?' she asked crossly, quite certain she had said nothing at all to indicate that.

'Body language. Your eyes shiftily switched away from me when you talked about him, lover mine.'

'Now I can do the same to him when I talk about you.'

'Have you?' he asked casually. 'I mean, talked about me?'

'I mentioned you once.'

'Are you going to tell him more now?'

'No. This is a business dinner and you're strictly private.'

He hugged her. 'Private, I like that.' His hands moved over her. 'Talking of which . . .'

She checked into a hotel in South Kensington on the following Tuesday – suitably far away from St John's Wood to avoid being walked home or possible complications. She decided this was arrogance on her part, but on further contemplation, thought that it was fully justified. Michael took her to a French restaurant in Hampstead, which was good and she told him so.

'I'm relieved,' he answered. 'It's not easy choosing a restaurant when you're dining with a chef.'

'I'm broad-stomached,' she explained gravely. 'Especially when they do a cassoulet like this. Not usually my first choice for an August dish, but I'm glad I made it.'

Inevitably the subject of the fire kept recurring in the conversation. Rachel skirted round any mention that it might have been deliberate but she sensed he was fishing, so perhaps she wasn't doing a very good job of vague mentions of faulty wires.

'What about the script?' Eventually he asked the inevitable. 'I hope that Great-aunt Alice hasn't perished?'

'Gone, I'm afraid. I've a few notes left.' It was true in a way, since the script had indeed gone. It had gone to Adam's back shed, complete with the bike which he had hoicked into his van. 'I can't think of a better hiding place,' he'd admitted.

Michael looked aghast. 'I'm really sorry about that. I know how much it meant to you.'

She tried to look suitably doleful, feeling extremely guilty at the need (and reason) for deception. 'I can manage to reconstruct a few of the recipes at least.'

'And the biography?'

'I've lost most of my family papers. It doesn't look good.'

'So poor old Samuel is doomed to lie in his anonymous grave.'

She laughed (just). 'I can't help thinking about him though. My best guess is that Samuel was someone she met while she was at Tolbury Hall. Your Harry Rolfe might have been her early sweetheart, or someone she just worked with at Crandene, but Samuel was her real flame. She might even have left Tolbury because it didn't work out. Perhaps he left her for someone else, or perhaps he died too. Anyway, I've told Lord Beavers he doesn't have to worry his pretty head about my affairs any longer,' she concluded brightly.

'In what way?' Michael was busily attacking his duck *aux petits pois* but she sensed he was deeply interested.

'I can't publish the cookery book, so I shan't be swanning around the countryside boasting that I'm cooking from Crandene recipes. Crandene is safe from me.'

'Is that what you think he fears?'

'What else? You explained he didn't want any distractions from the military legacy of Crandene. Fair enough. How's your book going, by the way?'

'I'm pushing ahead. I should be finished on schedule. My deadline for handing it in is the end of October, that's nearly three months. It'll be published next June to coincide with the big summer show.'

'Which will consist of what? Any further forward yet?'

'Yes, I've become a consultant on the historical side, so it's moving ahead. There are going to be detailed exhibitions of the battles the Beaverses won the awards in, and they'll be the whole focus of the show. We're working on possible re-enactments too, or at least videos of the battlefields and how it all happened. The battle for High Wood on the Somme will be one of them, of course. That's why I thought that Harry Rolfe might be an interesting inclusion. Master and servant fight together, that sort of thing. But without more information about him, I can't do it.'

'What did Robert win the VC for? General valour?'

'No. It was very specific. High Wood was a ghastly show, and no one was quite sure whether the Germans were still holding the corner of the wood that night. The 1st Battalion Royal West Kents were part of 13th Brigade, which was ordered to make an assault to take Switch Trench to the east of the wood. First Battalion, which had only just arrived after a day and night march in sweltering heat, was detailed to make the vital first step, which was to get control of a trench four hundred yards away from them. They called it Wood Lane, and it ran south-easterly down from the corner of the wood in the Longueval direction. The problem was that the trench lay beyond the crest of a slight hill, so no one knew whether there were still any Germans in the trench or not. Nor whether there were any Germans in the corner of High Wood they'd be passing en route to Wood Lane. Well, there were Germans both in the trench and in the wood. The CO was convinced there were, but was told by HQ that the wood was either clear or it would be cleared before 1st Battalion set off.

'Robert was ordered by the CO to detach a platoon from the attacking battalion force to double-check the situation in that corner of the wood, but nearly every man was mown down by machine-gun fire, and the Germans turned their attention on the rest of the battalion. Though some of the battalion managed to occupy the Wood Lane trench for an hour or two, they had

140

to be withdrawn. Robert got his VC because when one man from the platoon sent to High Wood managed to report back to him, Robert insisted on going under artillery fire to help get the wounded men to safety. Brave – and in a sense stupid – because Robert's orders were to hold the trench. But it was an enormous morale booster to his men to see him charge into the fire to save non-officers. Even so, the battalion took four hundred casualties that night.'

'He doesn't look capable of that sort of heroism in his portraits.'

'Which of us does till the testing time comes? In a way that's what the Crandene show will be about. It'll be called For Valour, like the VC motto, but it will be *about* valour too. It's a kind of proving ground that heroes really do exist, and anyone can be one. Lord Beavers feels strongly about that.'

'Perhaps because he hasn't got a VC himself.'

She meant it straightforwardly, but Michael took it amiss. 'He's a straight guy, Rachel. I know he's thwarted your plans, but that doesn't mean he hasn't had good reason to, from his viewpoint. He had the future of Crandene to think about, and he's pinning all his hopes on next year. No detours.'

She gave him as good as she got, suppressing any thought of how 'thwarting' might have included trying to murder her. 'Is pinning all one's hopes on one throw of the dice good business though?'

He grinned at her, friction over. 'OK, you win. Of course not *all* his hopes. Crandene is a big operation.'

'You said something about his need for funding.'

'All non-profits need funding, but this kind of exhibition needs a lot of lovely dosh in sponsorship. That way, the costs are paid for them, but the revenue all goes into the Crandene coffers. If we have a rotten summer next year though, who knows whether it will be a success or not? The Gate of Swat in the rain could prove a very soggy non-event.'

She laughed and the atmosphere lightened between them, as he paid the bill. 'That was very good. Thank you.'

'Where are you staying?

No reason not to tell him. 'South Kensington.'

'No, I meant while your home is being rebuilt.'

'I'm finding rented accommodation, but at the moment I'm with a friend.' Not true anymore, but avoided handing over the address. She had found a bed and breakfast halfway between Littleford and Chilford, and the arrangement suited them both well. She had stayed overnight with Adam several times, but the knowledge that her base was elsewhere relaxed her. As it did Adam, perhaps, and if at the breakfast table that morning she had found herself hoping he would suggest she stayed for ever, she reprimanded herself for illogicality. 'I'm not sure where I'll be after tomorrow,' she continued, 'so for the moment my mobile or care of Chilford post office is best.' She wondered whether he'd press her further. He didn't.

'Is the friend Adam Paynter, by any chance?'

The very thing she didn't want to come up. 'Yes, as a matter of fact,' she replied stiffly, cursing herself for drinking too much wine, with its inevitable loosening of her tongue.

'How did that come about?'

'It just did. Does it matter?'

'Oh it does, Rachel. Do you know *who* he is – unless there's more than one Adam Paynter running a charity in Canterbury?'

'I get the feeling you want to tell me.' Prickles were beginning to run up and down her spine.

'Want to? Wrong. I *should* tell you. Do you know who his uncle is?'

'No.' She wanted to shut her ears to this, to rush out of the restaurant and leap into a taxi to safety, but she couldn't.

'His full name is Adam Paynter Foster. The Paynter comes from his mother's side of the family. His father is John Foster's brother.'

The name rang a faint bell. 'Who's he?'

'An American billionaire philanthropist, particularly interested in non-profit organizations and charities connected with military matters, which the Foster Foundation supports. John Foster takes a personal interest in all its activities and particularly over Crandene, owing to the fact that Foster's grandfather, whom he adored, went through the First World War, and spent the last twenty years of his life stuffing his grandson's head full of facts and figures.'

'So?' Rachel asked cautiously. 'I can't see what this has to do with Adam and me.'

'Can't you?' He looked at her pityingly. 'John Foster spent many years trying to inculcate his nephew Adam – who incidentally was then his heir – with his own pet projects. Adam didn't take to it and marched out to do his own thing.'

'I don't know how you know all this, and I can't see how it links—'

'I gather he remains in touch with his uncle, however, and in case this is not yet clear to you, John Foster is the great white hope for sponsorship for the Crandene exhibition, on which I suspect that the future of Crandene depends. You can see why I have a vested interest in Adam Paynter. And I know about all this, as you put it, because John Foster told me personally.'

Rachel struggled to sort this out, aware that she was shaking. If Michael knew about Adam then surely Adam must have known more about Michael than he was letting on. 'Adam's interested in Crandene, of course, but he's never mentioned his uncle.'

'Of course not. But he visited Crandene twice to your knowledge. It displays a certain interest, wouldn't you agree? And now you're staying with him. At his suggestion?'

'I was at his charity ball the night of the fire . . .' The ground was being cut from under her feet.

'So Adam Paynter knew you were out that night. Did anyone else?'

This roused her. 'What the hell are you suggesting?' she asked angrily. 'That Adam deliberately set fire to my house?'

Michael looked taken aback. 'I hadn't got quite that far, I admit. But it's a possibility. *Was* it arson?'

She ignored the latter question. 'What you're implying is nonsense. Adam was with me.'

'He could have paid someone to do it.'

That did it. This was an action replay of Adam's scenario about Lord Beavers. 'I'm sorry, Michael. I should go.'

'No, it's me who should apologize.' He rose to leave with her. 'I didn't realize you'd take it so hard. You're clearly involved with Adam, and I should have been more tactful. But you need to be aware of what you might be getting into.'

'Not now that I'm no longer any concern to Crandene,' Rachel pointed out coldly. 'I shan't be publishing my biography because there are no recipes to go with it. Anyway, all I wanted was to write a family history and cook a few recipes,' she ended angrily. 'What on earth is so world-shattering about that?'

'It depends whose world it shatters.'

Ten

Adam hadn't told her the full story about Crandene and himself. However much she wrestled with this fact, she couldn't ignore it. What Michael had revealed might not, she reminded herself, be correct, but so far it had all the dismal ring of truth. She didn't believe – how could she? – that Adam had had anything to do with the fire, and the very idea was ridiculous. Nevertheless the fact that she had been kept in the dark about his reason for interest in Crandene was enough for her to cope with. Every moment the train was taking her nearer to Canterbury and the moment when she would have to face Adam. It would be hypocritical to ignore this bombshell, merely in order to choose her own time to tackle him. How could she share his bed with this on her mind?

It occurred to her that he might have been sworn to secrecy by his uncle over Crandene, and she clung to this straw of hope until she realized that Adam had also kept quiet about his real name. Why should he do that, since it was hardly likely she would have connected him with his uncle since Foster was a common name? This brought her back to the heart of the matter: how could she reconcile Adam the lover with Adam of the possible ulterior motives for cultivating her friendship? It was he who had brought her the script in the first place, and why should he have done so if he were prepared to go to such lengths – the fire – to keep her quiet about it. Thankfully she realized that this at least simply did not add up.

Nevertheless, the sooner she had this out with him the better. Conflict churned inside her. She wanted to get this anger out of her system and yet to bury it for ever. The former had to win, and she knew it. To do that, she had to lay any suspicions to rest, however stupid they might seem. There was too much she didn't understand.

The Never Alone shop was busy when she arrived, and there was no sign of Adam. Fortunately she was recognized before she had to battle to the counter, and was waved upstairs. Her resolve almost failed her, but there was no turning back. Adam was on the phone as she walked in, and the instant smile that lit up his eyes as he motioned her to sit down almost broke her nerve again. When he put the phone down, however, he frowned.

'I see from your set face that the Unicornhorn has given you my entire family history,' he commented. 'I wondered if he knew it.'

'Not your entire history, but enough to have kept me awake most of the night. Adam—'

'Not here,' he interrupted. 'If it's confession time we should talk privately. We could go into the cathedral grounds. Open air is best. We don't want another bloody murder in the cathedral.'

'Don't joke, Adam, please.'

'You have got worked up about it, haven't you?' He looked at her curiously.

'Wouldn't you, if I suddenly turned out to be someone you didn't know?'

He gave a twisted smile. 'I rather thought you did know me. However, let's get it over with.'

She followed him downstairs and waited outside while he spoke to the two shop volunteers, then came out to join her. The cathedral grounds were as crowded as could be expected on a sunny afternoon in the holiday season, so with one accord they decided to walk on to the Dane John park, which was equally packed. Children were playing, the world and his wife were strolling – it all seemed so normal that Rachel had to convince herself of the need for this discussion at all.

'So tell me what Mr Unicornhorn revealed.' Adam carefully peeled the paper off the ice-cream he'd insisted on buying. She had refused one. How could she be serious whilst licking a choc-ice? Nevertheless she regretted it.

'No, Adam. You tell me who *you* are and what your interest

in Crandene really is. And why you didn't come clean with me from the start. Please,' she added belatedly.

'A tall order. Would you like me to recite the whole of Chaucer's *Canterbury Tales* as well?'

'Crandene will do.' She was determined not to get riled.

'Very well. My American uncle John Foster, my father's brother, runs a philanthropic foundation with the emphasis on non-profits with military interests. My father is involved in its British branch. Any questions so far?'

'Yes. What kind of non-profits? Educational military academies and museums, or benevolent associations for old soldiers and dependants, or for the victims of war?'

'Chiefly the first.'

'Hence Crandene and next year's show.'

'My word, the unicorn's tongue has been busy. Yes, though that fact, Rachel, is not public knowledge, and I'd be glad if you didn't pass it on. Interesting that Mr Unicornhorn knows about it.'

'You do too and Mr Uni— Michael' – she quickly amended – 'said you had differed with your uncle and had walked out of the family business, so to speak.'

A flush of anger crossed his face, and one which for a change he wasn't bothering to hide. 'My personal affairs are nothing to do with anyone but me and my uncle.'

'Perhaps also me, just a little,' she replied sharply. 'After all, you have been very interested in Crandene. Why's that, if you're estranged from your uncle?'

'We had a difference of opinion. That doesn't wipe out the past though. Knowing of his possible connection with Crandene I was naturally interested in the script when I found it. I brought it back to you in accordance with Never Alone's code of conduct, but lingered till you'd looked at it, since I'd been intrigued when I first saw it. That all seems fairly straightforward to me.'

'But the script is about cookery not war.'

'I said *I* was intrigued, not my uncle.' He sighed. 'Look, Rachel, let's stop this cross-examination right now. I'll explain everything about my uncle – but I want not a word of this to go back to Hartshorn, is that clear?'

'Yes, unless—'

'Unless what?' The muscle in his cheek was hammering to and fro.

Every fear had to be out in the open. 'Unless I need to tell someone for my own protection.' It was out, yet she wanted to recall those words at any price, as she saw the look on his face.

He just stared at her, looking completely nonplussed. 'That could be the worst thing that anyone's ever said to me. Are you really implying that I'd ever hurt you, or merely that I might gabble away and reveal something that could lead to another attack on you. Either way, you're crazy.'

'I don't know, Adam. I just don't know. All I know is that someone apparently wants me dead, and I have to understand why by examining every possibility. I need to get away. Adam, I love you . . .' The words that should have been a triumphant declaration sounded tinny and false, even to her.

'Pity you don't trust me then.' He had retreated. The lover had vanished into the Adam she had first met.

'I don't trust anyone at present. I've had enough shocks to last me a lifetime – which might not be very long unless I get a whole lot smarter. Discovering that you'd been holding out on me was the last straw.' It was the truth, and what else could she say?

'Hardly holding out. I only talk on a need to know basis, and we hadn't reached that point. So that's why you wanted to move out. Bed was fine, but all the time you've had these suspicions as to ulterior motives on my part. Thanks a bunch.' He continued licking that damned ice cream.

'No.' But even as she vehemently denied it, she realized there might be a grain of truth in what he said.

'Are you going to move in with the unicorn?'

'No,' she repeated listlessly. 'He hasn't even suggested it. Anyway, alone is best at present.'

'I've always found it so.'

His words had no edge to them, but they wounded her, for all she had chosen that path herself. It was over, his words implied, and moreover that it was probably not there in the first place.

'Will you stay at your B and B?' he asked casually.

Tell no one, he had told her earlier. No one, and that should include him. She'd offer him one small repentance, however. 'Yes, for the moment. And long-term I might see whether Marjorie wants me as a partner, and I might lodge there, at least until my own house is ready again.'

'Good idea. You're not giving up on Great-aunt Alice though, are you?'

'No, and *I'd* be glad if you didn't pass that on.'

To her surprise he demurred at this. 'Not sure about that. Let's say I'll come to you first?'

'And if I say no?'

'We'll talk it over like civilized folks.' He gave her a sudden smile. 'It would only be in dire necessity.'

'To do with your uncle?'

'Yes. I suppose having made that reservation I'll have to put you in the picture. You want to know why I quarrelled with him? OK. Crandene wasn't even a twinkle in his sponsoring eye when I gaily waved away his millions. I thought war should include its victims, which includes the dependants of both sides and the innocent bystanders who've suffered by being dragged into it. He disagreed, though he's far from being a right-wing hawk, glorifying war for its own sake. He has his own hobby horse. He believes the world needs heroes in the military field, not just footballers and pop stars, and that there is such a thing as courage. The fashion now is to debunk all heroes, and his pet hobby is to prove the military debunkers wrong – or rather to show that not all heroes can necessarily be debunked. That's why he's interested in Crandene.

'It's the nature of courage that interests him. Don't ask me why, and I don't think he's wrong either. I merely think his view is too limited. I told him I thought the nature of courage belonged to other people than those in the public eye, and though I respected his views, if he made me his heir I'd seek to broaden the foundation's remit. He told me to get lost, and get lost I have. We still converse, but we don't *talk*, and that's how it's going to remain.'

Rachel remembered Adam's 'physician, heal thyself'. It was beginning to fit. He too had turned his back on the past

149

– and she, she realized, was now part of it. No question. It was over.

'My uncle likes England,' Adam continued, 'and spends several months here every year. He owns a house near my parents in Berkshire. Next year he'll come over for the entire summer while the Crandene show is on. If it goes ahead. I won't be playing any part, in case you were wondering.'

'*If* ? You mean it isn't certain?' Rachel was shaken. Surely Michael had been talking in terms of an event that was actually going to take place?

'Ah, didn't Unicorn tell you that bit? My uncle's not known for speedy decisions and he's been delaying his final decision. Nothing sinister about that except that he's a fussy fellow and likes all the Ts and Is neatly crossed and dotted before he puts trembling hand to cheque.'

'But it's getting late, isn't it? It's less than a year away.'

'It is. Particularly since I suspect his Beavership has already committed himself heavily to the project.'

'Is there any danger your uncle will back out?'

'I doubt it. Crandene's his favourite subject at present. He's buried in books about the Crimea, about the First World War and the Gate of Swat, a real regimental bore. You'd never think he's not held a rifle in his hands in his life. It's all heroes – and their lives thereafter. He likes to link the two, you see, to show there's nothing for debunkers to fasten on with their usual glee. So as well as the military side of the show, there'll be lots of smiling family pics, if my uncle comes in on the deal. He wouldn't back out, unless something came up that invalidated the whole bang shoot.'

'Such as?' Rachel asked warily.

'I've no idea. Maybe your Samuel is the key to why his Beavership isn't too keen on your delving too far into Alice's life. Maybe Samuel was her illegitimate son by one of the Beavers. Who knows?'

The implications of this struck home immediately and Rachel began to feel sick. She'd been thinking in terms of Samuel as a lover, but of course Adam was right. Who knew what she might turn up if she dug deep enough? If she continued to investigate Alice's story, a sword of Damocles

150

would accompany her wherever she went, in case the news got back to Crandene. And there would be no Adam to help. If she didn't continue, however, she would be betraying not only her family, but herself.

'I won't say anything about this to Michael, I promise.'

If she expected Adam to comment, she was disappointed. He merely offered to bring over her mother's bike with its precious contents, and try as she would, she still couldn't help registering the fact that he seemed eager to keep tabs on that script.

Spring 1930

'Of course I remember you, Miss Carter.' Lady Beavers smiled warmly at her. 'Your face, anyway. You were a housemaid when I first began to visit Crandene. Indeed, I recall you acted as my personal maid on one occasion. There was a ball, and I had the most fearful accident with my gown. You were on duty in the ladies' withdrawing room and you helped me so much. You calmed me down, and repaired my dress, and when I sallied forth, I felt quite myself again.'

This room looked just the same. The same curtains, the same wallpaper, the same writing desk. Alice noticed it bore a few different photographs, however. There was one of the wedding of Miss Cecilia and Mr Robert, or rather Lord Beavers as he now was. His father had died two years ago, so she'd read in *The Times*. There was even, against tradition, a photograph of their two children, a son, George, born in 1921 and a daughter, Gwendolen, born in 1924. She had read of their births in *The Times* too. Alice was glad the new Lady Beavers was letting a glimmer of life into Crandene. It needed it.

'I was pleased to hear of your ladyship's marriage to Lord Beavers,' Alice replied. 'And I was sorry for your bereavement. His old lordship was very good to me.' Not always, he hadn't stood up for her when they'd been turned from the house, but she knew that wasn't all his fault.

'A great loss. Her ladyship now lives in the dower house, so we have her with us still. Now, you tell me in your letter of application that you have always wished to return to Crandene,

Miss Carter. Why was that? I am told by Sir John that you are highly valued at Tolbury. Does the situation there not suit you?'

'Indeed it does, your ladyship. I shall be sorry indeed to leave. My heart is in Kent, though, and when I saw the advertisement for a chef de cuisine at Crandene I knew I should apply for it. My family misses Kent, and one of my sisters who lives here still has great need of her mother.' The words came out just as she had planned, earnest and sincere – as indeed they were.

'Sir John speaks highly of your competence as a chef. However, there is a great deal more entertaining at Crandene now that my husband is heavily involved in government. Should you be able to cope with that?'

'Yes, your ladyship. I should enjoy it above all things. I am always adding to my repertoire of English recipes and—'

'*English* dishes? Oh dear, I had thought that since you were trained by Monsieur Trente you would be able to cook in the French manner.'

'As you may require, your ladyship. I am trained in French cuisine also. Nevertheless all great houses are used to French dishes. Crandene might provide something different. Now that his lordship is in government, perhaps his kitchens should reflect not only the glory of Crandene's produce, but the glories of the cuisine of the country he represents: England – and not only England. There are Scottish, Irish and Welsh dishes too.'

Lady Cecilia looked doubtful. 'My dear Miss Carter, that is indeed an idea. However, what are these glories of English cuisine? Roast beef, no doubt, and Windsor soup. But Lancashire hotpot and roly poly pudding are not quite Crandene, are they?'

'Oh, there is a much greater range than that, my lady. Perhaps I might show you some sample recipes.'

She opened her handbag and produced a neatly written menu card: sorrel soup with fried bread cubes, crayfish with watercress, steamed samphire, goose pudding, jugged celery, apple tansy, lemon cheese, devon junket, stilton cheese, fresh fruit, hop tops with toast, cold sideboard: Hindle Wakes – Salamagundi.

152

'If I might be permitted to cook such a dinner for you . . .' Alice suggested humbly.

Two days later, Alice waited outside the Crandene dining room. The verdict was inevitable of course. She had no fear that she would be rejected. She knew Mr Robert's tastes, she knew how to adapt them for her ladyship. It had been difficult to work with the current Crandene staff, but she had managed.

'By heaven,' Alice heard the familiar voice through the door of the dining room, 'I don't know who this new cook is, but she's a cracker. Take her on. Well done, Cecilia.'

'So you approve, Robert?'

Alice smiled slightly, as she heard his confirmation: 'I should say I do.'

She was sitting on the bench in the entrance hall, hands neatly in lap, as befitted the perfect servant, when the footman came out to call her in.

As she entered she saw the puzzled look on his lordship's face, and then, 'Don't I know you?' came simultaneously with recognition. 'Good God.' Fear, anger, outrage and something else passed over Robert's face. 'It's Alice Carter, Cecilia. We can't have her.'

'My dear Robert, why ever not? She has superb references. I kept it as a surprise for you. She is used to Crandene's ways, after all.'

'Leave us, Cecilia.'

The tone of her husband's voice made her ladyship gasp in amazement, but casting a thoughtful look at Alice, she obediently departed.

'I'm glad to be at Crandene again, sir,' Alice observed in her colourless voice.

'I thought never to set eyes on you again, Alice,' Robert repeated huskily. 'What the blazes are you doing here?'

'I'm going to be Crandene's chef, your lordship.'

'You can't.'

'Why not, sir?'

'You know bloody well why not.'

'That was all long ago, sir. Long forgotten.'

'By you, perhaps. Not by me.'

153

'You're married now sir, with children. And I'm no longer a kitchenmaid. I'm middle-aged.'

'It isn't possible.'

'Oh, but it is, sir.' Alice was completely calm.

'Damn you, girl, you think you can contradict me in my own house and tell me who's going to work here and who isn't?'

'I'm going to be Crandene's cook and I'll be a good one. I'm the best there is. I'll make Crandene's cuisine famous, so that the King and Queen themselves will beg to come here. And the Prime Minister too, sir. You won't ever see me. I'll be in the kitchens working for Crandene, as though nothing had ever happened. And that includes forgetting the past.'

'And what do you expect in return, little Alice?' he asked sneeringly, but his attention was caught.

'A good salary, sir, but we can fix that between us. I'm not greedy. I need enough to pay the rent on a cottage for my family. It doesn't have to be on the estate and it won't be tied to any job that I or any of them might have here. That's fair, isn't it, after what happened?'

'Fair?' He looked at her as if she were mad.

'You just agree to that,' she continued, 'and you need not set eyes on me anymore. I'll do my share, you do yours. Think about it, sir, you with your military reputation and your new career in Parliament. Crandene could be the meeting place for the most powerful in the land when they want to confer privately. What with the stock market crash last year and Germany in a dangerously unstable state, they'll need places like Crandene where people can talk in private. A good cuisine is what draws people together. So I'll put Crandene on the map in that respect.'

'Other chefs could do that. Give me one good reason why I don't send you packing now, Alice.' He peered at her. 'I'd be crazy to employ you. Yet you're still a beauty, you know, even more than you were. Those cheekbones and your eyes, and what's more you're a mature woman now. Is that why you're here?'

'No. I'm not for you. Ever. I'm your cook, so you can forget all that.' She kept back a shudder of repugnance.

'You've changed Alice,' he continued, still staring at her.

154

'You're harder now. What did bring you here then? Revenge for turning you out?'

'No, sir.'

'What then?'

'The Somme.'

She'd done it. She had had no doubt about the outcome, but even so she treated her triumph with quiet satisfaction, as she returned to the kitchens, where the staff were busy clearing away after dinner. How surprised they'd be when she rolled up her sleeves and helped wash up. At least they'd got more than one tap now. The house had been modernized with hot water throughout, even some electricity, though she noted there were still gas lamps upstairs.

The kitchens too had an antiquated air about them. There were the old cast iron ranges she'd slaved over in her youth, first cleaning, then cooking on them. Not what she was used to now at all. She'd have at least two Radiation gas stoves installed. And a modern Frigidaire. In fact, a whole new kitchen was required if she was to put Crandene on the map. And the new kitchen would be in the main house, not attached by corridors as at present. That had been for another age. As for the kitchen staff, they needed discipline and they'd get it from her. Not too much, but enough so that they knew what was what. And she'd train them too. No use her being a devotee of good cuisine unless her staff were too.

Rachel looked around her room in the B and B. It was large, bright and airy, and overlooked the farm garden. It was welcoming, it was comfortable. But it was lonely, and at times she felt it would choke her. What on earth was happening to her life? How could she have gone from the depths of despair to the dizzy heights of happiness and back again in such a short time? She knew there was no use wallowing in self pity, no use even to wonder if she had been right to mistrust Adam. Trust me, he had said, when he hadn't trusted her. Trust me, said Michael, when he had given her no reason to.

And yet she did wonder. She had lost Adam, when the horizon had seemed so bright. Sex was a great betrayer. It lulled you into thinking there could be no potholes ahead in the path before you, and she had run straight into major roadworks. He had said he had turned his back on his own past, yet his interest in Crandene could only stem from his uncle's involvement.

Nothing added up. Somebody, she had to keep reminding herself, had tried to kill her. It had been no accident. The police, the firemen, and the insurance people were all agreed on that. Either Adam, the only person who would have known she was out, arranged the fire but didn't want her killed, or she had to assume the Beavers foundation had done so, and, not knowing she was out, *did* want her killed. Or perhaps someone else, as yet nameless, arranged it. It was a bleak prospect, but one she had to face.

Worse, if someone had wanted her dead, did they still? She hadn't discovered anything more about Alice that could be a threat to anyone, and she had now yelled out to the whole world (save Adam) that she was out of the picture so far as Crandene was concerned. Great-aunt Alice could go hang, was her public message. In theory, therefore, no one should now want her dead, and it was tempting to leave it that way.

The problem was that although she had believed that the past did not matter, she'd changed her mind. If her pursuit of more information about Alice had stirred up so much angst, then there had to be more to discover – and only her to do it. But this time she'd go it alone.

Tolbury would have to be her next stop to see if she could track down the mysterious Samuel, whether lover or baby, or anything about Alice that would give her some clues as to her life. With any luck Tolbury Hall still existed and maybe still had records of its staff. Anyone who had worked with her or known her in the nearest village would have to be in their eighties at least, but there might be a chance. There might even be descendants of Alice's two sisters who had married locally in Lincolnshire. Pops had said that he was the only survivor of the family, but why on earth hadn't she asked him about any of his nephews and

156

nieces who might still be living there? Or anywhere, come to that?

She telephoned Pops, hoping to catch him on a good day, and had to try three times before she was successful. Good was qualified.

'Emmy who?'

'Your youngest sister.'

'That was Rosie. Died young did Rosie. That husband of hers didn't treat her right.'

'Did she have a family?'

Long pause. 'Had a son. Killed in the war, he was.'

'Married?'

'Who?'

'Rosie's son.'

Deep scorn now. 'Poor lad was only twelve when he died. Bombing raid it was. All went together. The whole family.'

'And Emmy? She was your other—'

'I know who Emmy was, young woman. My sister. Went to Australia.'

So much for descendants in Lincolnshire. She'd have to pin her faith on Tolbury Hall. She decided to leave her pursuit of the third sister, Betty, until she'd returned from Lincolnshire. A little often was best so far as Pops was concerned.

Her mother's old bicycle was currently parked in the farm barn, but beside her on the bed lay the carrier bag with Alice's script.

'What am I to do with you, my lovely?' Rachel extracted it from the bag, and again marvelled at the colourful pages, shouting out at her for recognition. The waste of it, she thought. Forbidden to publish by Alice herself (Rachel had to assume) and she was unable to boast the recipes as being Alice's own if she ever used them, since the majority were presumed lost. The script was a testament not only to Alice's recipes but to those times, since Alice had often attributed names to the recipes clearly in honour of Crandene's guests: Sir Osbert Sitwell's Syllabub, Mr Chamberlain's Chicken Pudding, Mr Dawson's Damson Cheese, and of course Mr Slippery Sam's Eel Pie. This might be the Sir Samuel Hoare to whom Michael had referred. But to call him Slippery Sam hardly suggested Alice

157

had a secret liaison with him unless he'd dumped her. Or if this were a public nickname for him, maybe using it was to pull the wool over her readers' eyes as to the real state of the relationship between them. No. It didn't add up, and Rachel's frustration grew. *Nothing* added up.

She raked her memory in vain for a famous politician called Dawson, but failed. Then it occurred to her this might be Geoffrey Dawson, editor of *The Times*. Wasn't he the editor at the time of Edward VIII's abdication? Perhaps it had been at Crandene that the Abdication Crisis had been thrashed out between the Prime Minister, the press, and the Archbishop of Canterbury. It was an intriguing thought, and had the merit of standing up to scrutiny, unlike Slippery Sam.

First things first, Rachel decided. That meant Tolbury and contacting Marjorie to tell her she'd like to begin working with her again when her current partner left at the end of the year. Keep busy, she told herself. The more she occupied the front of her mind that way, the less she would heed the ache in her heart.

Alice, did you ever feel this way? Did you throw yourself into civey sauces and cinnamon baked onions in the hope of forgetting your Samuel? Perhaps some things never changed. If she couldn't solve her own problems, at least she could do her best for Alice's.

Eleven

A pub was always a good place to start sizing up a village, and the Golden Lion at Canterworth, the nearest to Tolbury Hall, was no exception. Rachel collapsed thankfully into a comfortable red plush corner seat, with a shandy, and awaited her ploughman's. The queues on the northbound A1 and the soul-destroying never-ending stream of lorries had exhausted her, and she had been relieved to turn off into the country roads.

The countryside here was amazingly quiet considering the proximity of the old Great North Road thundering by, and the local people in the pub eyed her with faint surprise, as though strangers were still a novelty. An illusion of course, but a pleasant one. On balance she had decided against writing to the owners of Tolbury Hall before her visit, partly because so far she'd been able to find out very little about the house. Seeing the hall itself might help her focus on the right questions, and secondly, well, perhaps she was paranoiac, but suppose there were some vast network amongst the establishment which would enable a murderously inclined Lord Beavers to be in touch with Tolbury Hall, and find out she was still hell-bent on discovering more about Alice Carter. Rachel was somewhat ashamed of this theory, but she didn't regret allowing it into her thinking. Tolbury Hall was open to Joe Public from 2 p.m. this afternoon, so this Joe was going to munch her way through her ploughman's, which proved to have a good hunk of local Stilton and some interesting plum chutney, and be on the Tolbury doorstep on the dot.

From the size of the car park inside the iron gates of the Tolbury estate, she quickly realized that the hall was no Crandene. It covered a comfortable number of cars, rather than

159

enormous coach parties she had feared, and this boded well for
the house itself. She bought her ticket at the gatehouse ticket
office, went into the courtyard, and immediately fell in love
with the warm red brick of the seventeenth-century building,
the regular-shaped windows with their stone facings, and the
irregular towers. There were gardens here too, so her guide
book made clear. Moreover, one of the two walled vegetable
gardens had been restored to the exact plan and contents of
the 1920s garden, which was exciting. It might not help her
much with reconstructing Alice's life, but it would be a good
indicator to how Alice had worked. As Rachel skipped through
the guide, the only let-down was that the Dene family, who
had lived here since the house was built, had died out only ten
years previously, and the present owners were only distantly
related. No scope for resurrecting old memories there, alas.

Once inside the entrance hall, she discovered that one could
see the house only by guided tour, which was both a blessing
and a nuisance. It meant she couldn't go round in her own
time, lingering where she chose, but on the other hand there
would be someone on the spot at whom to shoot questions.
It all depended what sort of guide turned up. The moment
she spotted her group's escort, however, Rachel thought she
might be in luck. The guide had all the look of the genuinely
involved professional. She was in her fifties, had bright lively
eyes, and a gleam of fanaticism when she talked of the house.
The longcase clock with the repeat mechanism for the hard
of hearing, the Reynolds masterpiece of an eighteenth-century
Mrs Dene (later a baronetcy had come the family's way), the
mahogany-seated water-closet used by King Edward VII and
George V, the exquisite Greuze head of a girl, all were spoken
of with personal love.

'Were all these in the house when the Denes lived here,'
Rachel asked, enchanted, 'or are they the new owners' collection?'

'Everything was here then. It's remarkable really.' The guide
leaped on this chance to expand on her usual patter. 'The last
baronet died unmarried, but the new owners decided to keep
the house intact to open to the public. They have their own
rooms but maintain the rest of the house more or less as it was

before the Second World War, which in effect means little has been changed since Edwardian times. Sir John Dene and his wife Susannah were conservative to say the least.'

So this, Rachel realized, was more or less as Alice had known the house. It was here that Alice must have made the transition from kitchenmaid to chef. A big jump. How on earth had it happened? She must have been very lucky or very determined even to get the chance of improving her skills so greatly.

Disappointingly, once again the tour did not include the kitchens. Rachel had seen the morning room where Alice must have come to receive her orders for the day, seen the dining room with which Alice must have been well acquainted, together with the drawing room, bedrooms, nursery, and count-less other rooms. Tantalizingly she had also seen the door that must surely lead to the kitchens. She could always ask whether it was possible to see them, of course, and at the end of the tour she did.

'They're not open, I'm afraid,' was the answer. 'They're still in use.'

'My great-aunt was the chef here in the 1920s' – Rachel put on her most earnest pleading expression – 'I'd love to have seen where she worked.'

'Really?' The light of the fanatic kicked into play. 'Now who would that have been? Toby Williams was the famous chef here in the nineteen thirties, but I expect you know about him. And I think there was a Charles Trente here before that.'

'I don't know where my great-aunt fits in,' Rachel admitted. 'I do know she left in 1930 to work as head chef at Crandene in Kent.'

'I've heard of Crandene. That's impressive. Are you sure it was here that she worked?'

'Quite certain. My grandfather, who is still alive and her brother, was living here with the family and remembers it quite clearly.'

'I could try to get you permission to see the kitchens for another day, but I doubt if they'd tell you much. They've been extensively modernized.'

So that was that. 'Would there be any early photographs

161

of the house or staff that I could see?' Rachel tried another tack.

'Now there I can help you.' The guide checked her watch. 'I've half an hour before my next group. We take it in turns, you see. The library has some archives and there are photograph albums amongst them. I could take you in before the next group hits it.'

She led the way to the library, seeming almost as eager as Rachel herself. Probably she was. She would take the fact she hadn't known about Alice as a personal challenge. 'There's a mass of archive material, of course, but most of it's in the County Archive office now. What was your great-aunt's name?'

'Alice Carter.'

'Yes, of course. The name rings several bells now.' Obviously relieved, the guide hauled out a leatherbound photograph album from a low cupboard beneath the shelving and spread it on a reading desk. 'Here we are, this is the 1920s album. I seem to remember there's at least one very good one of Alice Carter. Unique for that era in my experience.' She riffled through the pages and finally pointed to a large photo of a middle-aged man and woman with an apron-clad figure between them, standing on what Rachel recognized as the front steps to the Tolbury Hall entrance.

'It's of Sir John Dene and his wife with Alice.'

Alice was a beautiful woman, Rachel thought. Why had she not realized this before? Her expression was severe in this photo, but it only served to emphasize the perfect oval face, cheekbones and eyes.

'And there's another one, too,' the guide continued. 'One of my favourites. Here it is.'

Rachel peered at it. Alice was standing with an elderly man in the gardens, laughing, and holding between them an enormous birthday cake. 'Who is the man?'

'Charles Trente, the chef I mentioned.' She checked the caption. 'It says here he was chef from January 1919 to 1928, and if your Alice left in 1930 that would suggest she was chef from Trente's exit to the time she left. A maximum of two years. She was clearly popular, wouldn't you say?'

Rachel would. Not many employers would bother to be photographed with the cook in those days. She compared the two photos of Alice and thought they could almost have been two different people from the change of atmosphere. Was Alice having a bad hair day in the photo with her employers, or was she just ill at ease? That didn't seem likely, as she must have been on good terms with them for them to want to be photographed with her.

'It says here,' the guide continued, showing her an indexed volume named Servant Records 1920–1950, 'that Charles Trente died in 1928. He didn't just retire or switch jobs. Then after Alice left in 1930 there were three chefs in quick succession, after which Toby Williams took over in 1934. He stayed with the family right through the war up to the 1960s when Sir John died and the son took over.'

'Does it say when Alice arrived at Tolbury?'

The guide hunted, but without success. 'No mention of her, which would indicate she was already here in 1920, and there's no earlier volume, I'm afraid. The war, of course.'

Of course. No easy answers where Alice was concerned. Still, she was a little further forward at least.

'Is there anyone still alive who might remember my great-aunt?'

'Toby Williams would have been the man you needed. I think he began work in the kitchens earlier than his period as chef.' She consulted the records again. 'Yes, he came here in 1927, so he would have known Alice. I'm afraid he died several years ago, though.'

'So Tolbury Hall kept in touch with him?'

'Oh yes. He was local you see. He lived in Canterworth and his son still does. Peter Williams used to run a restaurant in Stamford, and now he and his wife run a B and B.'

'Not,' Rachel asked, her hopes rising rapidly, 'Cale Farm by any chance?'

'That's right. You know it?'

'I'm staying there tonight,' Rachel told her, highly amused at the blissful ways of serendipity, since her booking of a B and B on the internet had been entirely at random.

The Williams lived in the former farmhouse, and had

163

converted its outbuildings into comfortable rooms, and Rachel congratulated herself on her forethought in booking her evening meal here rather than opting for the pub. It wasn't until after the first-class meal however that she had a chance to tackle her host since he had been doing the cooking. Lincolnshire lamb with marrow and tomatoes had been right up her street, and she was impatient to meet the man behind the meal. So much for his retirement. He looked well into his seventies, but his wife was quite a lot younger, about sixty perhaps. Just as well, since it had fallen to her to do the serving.

At last Rachel was able to launch into family history mode. 'I'm here to do some research into the life of my great-aunt,' she told him casually, after congratulating him on the excellent meal.

'Ah, the family history bloodhound. You look young for that.'

'That's because it's history with a purpose in my case,' she admitted. 'I want to cook my great-aunt's recipes. She was chef at the hall for a while.'

'Oh yes?' She had caught his interest at least. 'Who was that then?'

'Alice Carter.'

He gave a bark of laughter. 'Not our Alice! It drove us all mad at home. Dad used to rabbit on about Alice always told him to do this or that, and Alice thought and Alice said.'

'So your father was actually trained by Alice?' She had struck gold.

'Indeed he was. That started him off and then when she left he was still too young to be chef, so he stayed on for a while till they had a vacancy and reckoned he was old enough. And that was it. He never left till he was forced to. Went through the war and all. The services didn't want him because of his eyesight – he was all but blind in one eye was poor old Dad. But the hall was an officers' HQ during the war, and the major wangled him a job on the staff so he could do his bit for the war by cooking for His Majesty's army. You could say your old aunt started the whole family off with its cooking, Dad, me and now Marty.'

'Marty?' Of course. 'You don't mean *the* Marty Williams?'

Marty Williams was a TV darling of the masses. She hadn't connected the names.

'That's him. English food for ever, à la Carter.'

'Do you remember anything else your father said about Alice or why she left Tolbury?'

She was on a roll now, but was disappointed when he looked doubtful.

'I've got one or two snaps somewhere, maybe, but I don't remember any anecdotes. I suppose Dad used to tell them but they went in one ear and out the other. I was only a kid when she left Tolbury.' He disappeared for five minutes and triumphantly came back with an old album. Inside ancient photo hinges had peeled off leaving many photos loose. 'This is the best one,' he said, pointing out a snap of Alice being handed some kind of tray by a young man, with other staff grouped around. 'That's Dad presenting her with a silver tureen when she left.'

'That must have cost a lot.'

'She was popular was Alice.'

'She looks dour here though,' Rachel observed.

'Now that,' Mr Williams suddenly said, 'does remind me of something. The last year or so she was there, so Dad used to say, she got very grim. She left to go south again, back to where she lived as a girl, and Dad heard that she became quite famous as a cook at Crandene.' He squinted at the photo again. 'It's beginning to come back to me now. Dad thought she changed after the tramp came.'

'A *tramp*?'

'Yes. This fellow came to ask for her one day, and she wasn't there, so my Dad spoke to him. He saw him come back next day and talk to Alice.'

'Who was he?' At last. A lead of some sort.

'Dad never found out, but he said Alice was never the same afterwards, and though she was there for another year or so, he had a hunch it was all to do with this tramp that she went back to Kent.'

'You don't remember the name? It wasn't Samuel, was it?' Rachel's stomach felt knotted with excitement.

'No idea.'

'Or were there any Samuels on the staff?'

'Again, no idea. You can look through this book if you like. Dad photographed well nigh everyone. Might be a Samuel there.'

There wasn't, and, frustrated, Rachel left Cale Farm the next morning no whit the wiser as to who Samuel had been. It must, it surely *must* have been this tramp. Although Peter Williams had informed her there was no one else in the village who'd be able to help, she nevertheless wandered round it before the drive home. At least Alice had been here. Her family might even have lived here rather than actually on the estate. Again, Peter hadn't been able to help. Alice had known this place, she told herself, known the church. The *churchyard*. Of course. That might yield something. A Samuel perhaps? After all, the tramp's visit and Alice's grim period might not have been simultaneous. Suppose he was a long lost love of hers with only weeks to live . . .

Her mind fantasized as she walked round the churchyard glancing at the gravestones. Many of them were unreadable, and there was no one to ask if there was a plan of the graves. She found two Samuels, one who died in 1934, and another who died aged 84 in 1925. Neither of them had any date of 15 November attached to them as in the dedication, which was hardly surprising since she had no idea of the date's significance, and neither of them seemed likely candidates anyway. What she did find, however, was the grave of Charles Trente, with his widow's name added underneath in 1930. That was the chef for whom Alice had worked, who became chef at Tolbury in 1919, about the same time as Alice arrived. Was that a clue? Was Alice in love with Charles and felt an obligation to his widow to stay on till her death? But if so, where did Samuel fit in? Not to mention Harry Rolfe.

June 1935

Alice looked with satisfaction on the remains of the dinner just concluding in the main dining room. The fruit fools and tansies had gone well, as had the beef. The Duke of Wellington's favourite recipe was always a favourite at Crandene too, even

166

if it was rumoured that the famous Iron Duke had only liked it because it looked like his army boots. Her ladyship had just popped in specially to say how good the dinner was.

'You've excelled yourself, Alice. Well done. That beef was superb. And Alice, my husband has asked if you could join the gentlemen in the dining room for a few moments. They are at their port – and oh, Alice, that marvellous Stilton. Where do you obtain such splendid cheese? I gather Mr Baldwin was particularly enthusiastic over your achievement this evening. Don't let him lure you away from us, will you?' she laughed.

Alice had smiled. 'No, your ladyship. Nothing would take me away from Crandene.'

'That is a relief. I can't think what Crandene would be without you.'

Alice took her time as she walked towards the dining room from which came the sounds of loud laughter, born of bellies well filled with her food. She had learned that food could give you power as well as being one's private enthusiasm. Yes, everything was going well. Part of her plan was to read the newspapers carefully, particularly *The Times*, and she could guess the reason that this weekend above all others was such an important occasion. Her ladyship had murmured that it was in honour of His Majesty's Silver Jubilee celebrations, and Alice had looked suitably impressed. She was quite sure it was nothing of the kind, however. This was a political meeting, away from London and – obviously – from Chequers. Tonight, she guessed, was the Dividing of Spoils discussion.

She opened the door, as always amused to see the power at the table. There was Mr Baldwin, Sir Robert Vansittart, Mr Churchill, and many other government ministers – excepting of course the Prime Minister whose removal they were here to discuss.

These were dangerous times. It was obvious Hitler and Mussolini were watching lynx-eyed to know which way Britain would jump over their respective gambles for conquest of more territory. Ramsay MacDonald, the Prime Minister, was in no fit state to run the coalition National Government any longer, and Mr Baldwin panted in the wings to be called on stage. Alice's

167

sharp eyes noticed Geoffrey Dawson here; *The Times* had to be kept informed and consulted. There were other problems too. The king's health was worrying and all the more so since there were more rumours about the Prince of Wales's liaison with an American divorcée, Mrs Simpson, who was still married to her second husband. What concerned the government even more was that the Prince of Wales appeared to have as little political judgement as social, and that his appetite both for the trappings of monarchy and his private life might not be matched by his diligence in its everyday routine.

Alice maintained her demure demeanour at the door until Robert should summon her. Their eyes met. There was less tension between them now. She had kept her word; she remained in her kitchens and caused no trouble. Instead she worked for Crandene and Robert appreciated this. He had relaxed, as she had intended. Her cuisine here was now well-known, and provided a magnet for Crandene to be adopted as a meeting place. Robert's position was now established. A VC holder, with political acumen, he could hope for an improved place in government. If MacDonald went, there would be an election, and thereafter Robert would not be forgotten.

'Gentlemen.' Robert inclined his head to his guests. 'May I present Miss Alice Carter, to whom our stomachs are greatly indebted.'

Alice bowed to the assembled company whose approval was loud and enthusiastic.

'I wonder you keep Miss Carter at Crandene, Robert,' Baldwin said jovially. 'When might we entice you to the bright lights of London, Miss Carter?'

'Crandene is world enough for me, sir.'

She retired, blushing her gratitude. The brandy would now flow before they joined the ladies, for they had a lot to talk about. The main discussions on strategy would take place here, while the ladies were safely occupied elsewhere, then the rest of the weekend would see the company break up into small groups to dissect the situation further. What might this mean? What might that? What if? No doubt Mr Hitler was having similar discussions in Germany, and Signor Mussolini in Italy. Such discussions would decide the life and possible death of millions of human beings. Did they ever take that into consideration? Alice wondered.

She couldn't influence the world's future. Her path lay here in Kent. Mum and Dad were old and needed some financial help. Her sisters were all married with families of their own, but there was still Henry. He was eighteen now, and clever. She had considered asking Lord Beavers to help get him into parliament in some low position where he could work himself up, but Henry didn't want that. He still wanted to build bridges, so he had finished at technical college, and was working with an engineering company, still bridge mad.

Now she was clear of major family obligations, she could look with satisfaction at what she was creating here. Who would have come to Crandene if it hadn't been for her? There were plenty of large country houses with hosts more amenable than Robert. True, his VC helped, since it gave him military standing as well as political, but there needed to be a social draw as well, and her cooking provided it, just as she had predicted. All things considered, she was playing her hand well, and soon – in another two or three years – it would be time for Robert himself to step upon her prepared stage.

Alice returned to the kitchens to oversee the clearing-up, and to preside at servants' supper. Usually this would be taken before they served dinner, but on big occasions such as this she needed their help for that precious hour, and had explained the reasons to her staff, who on the whole enjoyed the change. After all, there might be leftover delicacies from the main house to eat up. When she had first returned to Crandene five years earlier, the servants still followed the archaic rules of hierarchy, even going so far as to stick to the upper servants entering the hall in procession to join the lower servants for one course and processing solemnly out again for dessert in the butler's parlour. It was outdated nonsense, but no one had dared take the outrageous step of changing it. She had. She had flatly refused to be considered an upper servant and sat with the rest of the staff. Mrs Cheney and Mr Palmer had long since retired, and their successors fell easily into her ways.

She listened and joined in with the chatter over supper, then,

169

excusing herself, retired to her room up on the top floor. She liked it up here, she could gaze out in the last of the evening light over the parkland of Crandene, and see right up to their windy hill, where Harry still lived on.

She was tired, but could not resist looking at her manuscript. She unlocked her desk, and took out her paints and pen nibs to begin another page of her precious work. The planning and typing of each page had been done, and now she was in the midst of the illustrations. Today should be the seaside, which she and Harry had never seen together, but which lived as vividly in her imagination as if they strolled the piers and promenades together. It would accompany the recipes for fried John Dory, and for scallops with bacon she would paint an elegant-hatted lobster strolling hand in hand with a pretty skirted scallop. And underneath there would be a sunset over the calm sea with two dark silhouetted figures against it, or should it be two pies, again hand in hand?

After she had returned from Tolbury Hall she had visited Harry's parents, but there was no bond to find between them. They had lost another son in the war too, just as Mum and Dad had. Both Alice's elder brothers had gone in the end, Edward first, and Frank later. The Rolfes had also lost a daughter to scarlet fever. To them Harry was but one of the loved ones who had vanished. It was commonplace even now, seventeen years after the war had ended, to find families still struggling to close the gap over the missing. Her visit to the Rolfes had made Alice all the more determined never to forget. For her the gap would for ever remain open.

Once back from Tolbury, Rachel decided to tackle the next stage. It was the beginning of September now and the approach of autumn made the end of the year suddenly seem much nearer. There was no use unravelling the secrets of Alice's life, if she could not in some way make recompense by using her recipes, even if they could not be acknowledged. Anyway, taking action was one way to stop wishing she could talk about Tolbury Hall to Adam. Adam is past, she told herself. Over.

But the words had no meaning, for he was obstinately hanging on in her heart, just as Samuel had obviously done in Alice's.

Marjorie was working out of her own home, a rambling old house near, but not in, Rye. Kevin hadn't (for once) been mean when it came to getting rid of her, Marjorie had joked. The house was a fair size, with room for Marjorie and – somewhat to Rachel's surprise – her mother, to spread themselves, plus room to build purpose-built kitchens at the rear. Rachel was impressed. In their sandwich days they'd worked out of Rachel's Bromley flat, always falling over each other, never enough room to store stuff, and with office administration situated in Rachel's bedroom.

Rachel had always had an uneasy relationship with Marjorie's mother – which was not difficult, Marjorie always reassured her. Julia Thomas was the opposite to Marjorie; where her daughter was relaxed, she was like a coiled spring, where her daughter was happy-go-lucky, her mother took life hard, even though if she chose she could be good company. Yeah, like a wasp, Marjorie always joked. Today was clearly not a good company day.

'Marjorie told me you were back, Rachel.' The gimlet eyes looked her up and down, and silently informed her she had been found wanting.

'I'm so glad Marjorie and I met again,' Rachel offered, well used to this treatment.

The silence that greeted this conveyed the information that Julia was not of the same opinion. Then: 'Well, I have things to do. Perhaps I'll see you later.'

'I hope so,' Rachel murmured politely, and tried not to laugh as Marjorie led the way to her working room.

She needn't have bothered as Marjorie remarked cheerfully, 'The old bat never changes, does she? Pity it's again the law to force bats to switch residence.'

Once settled in Marjorie's office – also in the purpose-built block – things settled down to their old basis remarkably quickly.

'You talked about having a vacancy at the end of the year,' Rachel jumped right in. 'What do you think? Could it work if I joined you again?'

'Why not?' came the prompt answer. Marjorie had obviously been mulling it over, since the answer came pat. 'We made a good team before. This company's scope is broader though. Are you up for it in theory? I can fill in the broad picture if so.'

'I am. My great-aunt stalks grimly before me, you see.'

'Does she indeed. Her ghost I take it? Otherwise she'd be rather aged to be stalking anywhere.'

'I'll explain later about her. You first.' Rachel curbed her desire to burst straight into her Alice Carter story. Best to find out whether there was room for her work on the recipes here or not.

As Marjorie talked, it became clear there was. Marjorie was a great waver of arms and they were enthusiastically flailing while she talked of catering for large events, from balls to formal dinners, and of the casual staff they'd need. 'Not too keen on weddings,' Marjorie added. 'Too samey. Too much chicken tikka and prawn cocktail unless you choose carefully.'

'I'm with you there.' Rachel was relieved. 'It might get like the sandwich business.'

'Never again, fun though that was for the first thirteen million offerings. Now tell me about your great-aunt.'

'Strictly private at present. OK?'

Marjorie understood perfectly. 'My mother can prise out my toenails in vain.'

Rachel took a deep breath and launched forth with an edited account of Alice Carter, her own wish to discover more about her family and the cookery script with its tempting recipes. She held back on telling Marjorie the whole story about the script, giving her to understand she had copies of most of the recipes. Which indeed she had. She'd been preparing new ones. Instead she concentrated on tempting her with roast turkey with honey, maumenny, tansies, almond sauce, green chicken fricassée, and whim whams.

'English food, yes. I can see that working.' Marjorie's eyes lit up, to Rachel's pleasure and relief. 'But you mentioned Crandene. That's really odd.'

'Why?'

172

'Coincidence that's all. I've just been asked to put in a tender for catering there next year.'

The long arm of coincidence again. Strange the way it kept reaching out. Or was it so strange? Rachel swallowed. Had Adam once again been stirring pots? Surely not. It must be pure coincidence this time. 'Tell me more,' she said evenly.

'They're putting on some do and they want something special to go with it. I'm one of the chosen few and I'm going there with sample menus next week. It's a big undertaking and I'd need more staff, something I've always fought shy of.'

'How did Crandene hear of you?' This was *too* close for coincidence.

'Word of mouth, I suppose. They're not on my mailing list.'

'You don't think that mouth might be Adam's, do you?'

'Could well be, I suppose. Does he have a connection with Crandene. Why?' Marjorie glanced at her. 'Does it matter how they got my name?'

Oh yes, it mattered. Although Adam was the most likely instigator of this new angle, it might possibly be Lord Beavers himself, who might have had Rachel's past investigated. How could he know she was thinking of working with Marjorie again, however? No, it had to be Adam – or, it occurred to her, Adam in collusion with Beavers – determined to keep a hand on the tiller of Alice Carter. Thoughts – rational and irrational – raced round her head, and she saw Marjorie looking at her enquiringly.

'Adam and I have split up,' Rachel forced herself to explain.

'I didn't know there was anything to split,' Marjorie pointed out.

'There was for a brief time but not now. We're on perfectly good terms,' she lied.

'Really?'

'Yes,' Rachel answered defiantly. 'But if it is Adam who has set up this—'

'Thank him for me. Could mean big dosh.'

'There's a problem, Marjorie. There's rather more to this story than I told you.' Rachel decided she'd no option but to come clean about the full story of the script. 'No one must know about it though,' she finished. 'So far as most people know, the script went in the arson attack on my house – which could have done for me too.'

'Ah.' Marjorie looked at her for a moment. 'You're usually level-headed, Rachel, but you do have your moments of screwiness. This isn't one of them, is it?'

'Definitely not. That fire was very real arson.'

'In that case, I shouldn't put in my tender for this commission if you think Crandene's connected with the attack.'

'Yes, do quote for it, Marjorie. I've assured everyone that I'm giving up the quest to discover more about Alice Carter, so there should be no more risk. But I have to find out more about Alice, and Crandene is the only place to do it. If you get the commission and I'm working with you, that would be ideal. Even if his lordship wouldn't agree with the word ideal.'

'Better to have the enemy in your sights than hidden in the long grass?'

'You got it.' The die was cast. Crandene had unwittingly opened another tentative door to her. Was it Alice or Adam calling to her this time? Perhaps she was having another moment of 'screwiness', but she hoped it might be both.

Twelve

If anything was going to stiffen her resolve to discover what had been so remarkable about the life of Alice Carter, the smell of smoke did. Never, never again did she want to have to think about fire and arson. All fragments of clothes and papers had now been sorted out and anything that was salvageable had been moved next door to her neighbour's attic. Only the remaining family papers accompanied Rachel to her new cottage near Challock.

She had moved from her B and B at the farm as soon as she had sorted out her future with Marjorie. The new cottage was next to a pub which gave her reassurance of a kind, since its friendly hum (and good food) suggested a community tight around her. The police, hardly surprisingly, were getting nowhere with the mysterious 'fish man' arsonist, but her life was resuming some sort of normality, even if collecting mail from the post office and using only her mobile phone would not be her usual chosen path. Laughing at herself for doing so, she devised yet another hiding place for Alice's script, changed her mind, copied the script again, then took the original to her solicitors in Canterbury for safe keeping.

There had been no word from Adam, and her reasoning that if he had been behind Crandene's approach to Marjorie it must mean he still had some feeling for her was promptly squashed by his silence. He had not trusted her over his interest in Crandene; she had not trusted him over the fire at her home. Although she had not told him of her move to this cottage, he had her mobile number, but still the silence continued. One way or another the fog of Alice Carter had fallen between them and until she had groped her way into the clear air there was no hope that they could come together again.

Adam was like a terrier. He wouldn't let go of his interest in Crandene, with his uncle on the brink of his decision, and nor could she blame him. He, as did she, scented a mystery and she didn't own Alice Carter, related to her or not. Nor did she own Crandene. He and Michael were free agents on opposing sides of the Crandene fence: Michael, in whose interests it must surely be to let any sleeping dog of doubt over the Crandene story lie; and Adam in whose interest the reverse applied. And both were concerned with Alice on the slight chance it affected their various interests. Rachel merely wanted to know the truth about her great-aunt. It seemed stupid that they might all three be working on the Carter/Crandene trail, but none of them was communicating.

There were times when she felt like hauling up the white flag, forgetting Alice and throwing herself wholeheartedly into her new partnership with Marjorie, but she refrained. Instead, she gritted her teeth and got down to some serious paperwork. First she plodded through what papers and photos remained in order to make up as complete a family tree as she probably needed, and spent a long time on the telephone to Pops, trying to track down the fourth sister, Betty, who had married in Kent. At first he denied all knowledge of her, then he agreed that when he returned to Kent there was a yet another sister for him to reckon with whom he'd never met before. And yes, her name was Betty, he agreed, now he came to think about it.

'What was her married surname?'

'How would I remember that?'

'Your address book?' Rachel tried hopefully.

'She's long gone. She wasn't much younger than Alice.'

'Did she have a family?'

It transpired there was a Cousin Joe, who was years younger than Pops, and spoiled, according to him. But again, no name, though he'd think about it, he informed her. She had little confidence that he'd remember.

She recalled Pops' casual mention of a workhouse. Where, she wondered, Kent or Lincolnshire? And how and why did Alice go to Lincolnshire at all? The workhouse records for Cranbridge proved to be in the Maidstone archive office, where she spent an exhausting day, but found entries, to her delight, for Elsie, Betty, Emmy and Rosie Carter, inmates, and Edward Carter, outworker, registered from November 1916. No mention of Alice. Odd. They were there for just over two years and all discharged themselves in December 1918. That fitted with the Lincolnshire dates. At last! One tiny piece of the jigsaw in place.

Rachel had also sent for a copy of the third Lord Beavers' will, which proved to have been dated not long before he died in 1969, and bequeathed to 'my beloved wife Alice' the freehold of Church Cottage, Cranbridge, and a sum of £8,000 a year from the estate revenue, a respectable amount in those days, though not enough to cause resentment from his children, Rachel guessed. When Alice wrote her own will she had been still living at Church Cottage, which she had then bequeathed to Pops. What did that tell her? So far as Rachel could see, only that Lord Beavers had no quarrel with his wife.

The only positive step forward was that Marjorie telephoned to tell her that she had been asked to go to Crandene for a discussion over the catering contract, together with rival bidders. Greatly daring, Rachel promptly suggested that she met her there.

'My pet,' Marjorie pointed out, 'from what I gather you would hardly be an asset at the interview.'

Rachel had laughed. 'Correct. That's your turf. I'll meet you in the pub afterwards.'

Having arrived early, she spent some time wandering round the churchyard. She knew Alice herself had been cremated, but had hoped to find something of relevance. The Beavers' family memorials in the church told her little she did not know already. She toyed with the idea that Alice had held the key to some dark secret about Crandene, but discarded it. If Alice had been an emotional blackmailer, she would have awarded herself more in the will than the freehold of one cottage and, by the time she died, a barely adequate income. Nor had there been anything in the will to suggest that she had done anything to annoy her husband or any of the Beavers family. On the contrary, her will specified various objects to be returned to Crandene.

Rachel gave up searching this churchyard, having found nothing, let alone Alice's Samuel. On a damp late September day it had been an unrewarding task. Somewhere there must be a clue to who Samuel was. There wasn't even a Harry Rolfe mentioned here – or any Rolfes come to that. She strolled back up the slope of the green to the pub, stopping to look at the war memorial. If under the First World War she hoped to see the name of Harry Rolfe appear, or, by some miracle, a Samuel, once again she had no luck. She did see the two Carter brothers though: Edward and Frank. She gazed at them transfixed, as suddenly all her poring over records sprang into life. And then she spotted an even more evocative name, Guy Trente.

Could he have been related to Charles Trente, the Tolbury chef? If so, perhaps Charles and Alice had gone from here together to Tolbury. Could Guy possibly be his son – Trente wasn't a common name. Rachel felt a rising excitement. A memorial implied he probably wasn't buried here, and that Guy died overseas. As was Charles, Guy was a French name as well as British. If he was Charles's son, it must be a strong presumption that Charles had also been chef at Crandene, which would explain a lot. Now there was a thought, and if only she had access to the Crandene archives it could have been confirmed in a flash. Her frustration grew. One step forward, one step back.

She settled herself in the White Hart and waited impatiently for Marjorie's arrival from her interview. She jumped up as soon as she entered, waving furiously to attract her attention.

'How did you get on?' she hurled at her, before she'd even sat down.

'Pretty well.' Marjorie smirked. 'You can buy me a drink – shandy, please.' When Rachel still lingered, she put her out of her misery by adding, 'I'll hear next week. I felt a fraud for not telling them my current partner was leaving though.'

'Believe me, it's a whole lot better than announcing you were teaming up with me.' Rachel went off to get Marjorie's drink, but when she returned, put to her the other question she had been longing to ask. 'Did you get any clue as to whether the interview was fixed through Adam?'

'I prefer to think it's my own charm and my own cooking.'

'Of course.' Rachel apologized to her. 'I've got Adam on the brain,' she concluded ruefully.

'Not the brain, if I read the situation aright. What happened to split you up?'

'We blew it together.'

'Maybe it'll blow back again.'

'I hope so.' Rachel realized what she'd instinctively replied, and grinned. 'Where did that come from, I wonder?'

'Your heart?'

'Don't have one at the moment.'

'Join the club. Cooking or cats are the answer. Now what's this cottage you want to drag me to?'

'It's where Alice lived after her husband died. She left it in her will to my grandfather.'

'I take it that it isn't now yours?'

'No. He sold it a couple of years later to a Mrs Joan Parsons, and according to the electoral roll he still lives there, so I wrote to her.'

'Asking what?'

'Just if I could see the house, explaining who I am.'

'What's that going to tell you?'

'I haven't the faintest idea.'

'I see.' Marjorie looked resigned. 'One of your serendipity hunts. How I remember them. Oh, let's try out something new. Hey, what about some deadly nightshade sandwiches, or arsenic and apple?'

'That's not fair,' Rachel protested, hurt by this unfair joke. 'There's not a mention of the slightest touch of food poisoning in my record.'

'Not for want of trying,' Marjorie goaded her. 'Remember the cheese and chilli tryout?'

'It'll be good to be back, Marjorie, I'm looking forward to it.'

'Me too.' A pause. 'So's my mother. She hasn't had any good bait to gnash her teeth on for a long time.'

After lunch they strolled along the road to the cottage, which was set back from the roadway with a garden in front of it. A brick path led up to the front door and, hardly surprisingly, it was close to the church. More surprisingly, it was far from large; two bedrooms, or three at the most, Rachel guessed. There was a gravel driveway at the side of the house, so obviously Alice had had a car, unless Joan Parsons had radically altered the grounds.

The door was opened promptly and Joan Parsons – older than Rachel had expected – greeted them. She seemed in her early to mid seventies, with the weather-beaten face that suggested she was wearing mental gardening boots.

'Mrs Parsons? My business partner Marjorie Thomas and I'm Rachel Field.'

'What business is that?'

'Catering, like my great-aunt.'

'Yes. You said she was chef at Crandene.' Joan Parsons led the way into the living room, still divided off from the dining area by an inner wall with a door through.

'And later Lady Beavers,' Rachel added. 'She lived here after her husband died until 1984. I even came here once when I was about ten.'

The house didn't look familiar, but then why should it? Rachel still only had a vague memory of the back garden as shown in the photograph she'd seen.

'Go through the house and have a look if you like. I've changed quite a lot, of course. Go upstairs too.'

Rachel took her up on this offer, though Marjorie had been right. The small rooms upstairs, one of which was now a bathroom, told her nothing. Nothing struck her in the immaculately kept garden either – until she turned and looked up at the back of the house. At last something caught at her memory. The dormer window, the paved patio, the steps, and woman with a tray coming down towards them. Waiting for her in her mental image were herself, Mum, and that third figure, Great-aunt Alice, sitting in that chair, clad in – yes – a red-flowered dress.

'So what can I do for you, apart from letting you see this house?' Joan asked.

'Can you tell me if this is how the house was when you bought it? I don't think my grandfather would have changed anything in the brief time he owned it. And did you buy it with any furniture in it?'

'I haven't done a good deal. Modernized the bathroom and done a little in the kitchen. It's the garden changed mostly. It was run-down when I bought it, of course. And yes, most of the furniture was still here.'

'Did you live in Cranbridge before?'

Joan hesitated slightly. 'Nearby.'

'Did you know my great-aunt?' Rachel held her breath.

Again a pause. 'She died in 1984, and I didn't come here till two years later.'

'There must be someone in the village who remembers her? It's only twenty-odd years ago.'

'You could ask around. I can't think of anyone offhand.' Joan Parsons was friendly enough, but Rachel left with a feeling, not of disappointment, but of irritation. There must surely have been more to find out here, and she was missing something. Alice had lived here for fifteen years and yet Rachel seemed no nearer to her here than she had been at Tolbury.

'Where next?' Marjorie asked plaintively, as they left. 'Or am I permitted to return to work?'

'Permission granted. Oh, I can bounce the workhouse off you.'

'Bounce away. I've a broad back.'

'So far as I can make out, Alice was still working at Crandene when her family was in the workhouse, because she's not listed as an inmate. Doesn't that strike you as odd?'

'She wouldn't have earned much as a kitchenmaid here. Not enough to pay for a whole family to be rehoused.'

'But this was wartime. If it were simply a question of cash, Alice could have left to get another better paid job. Perhaps she did. Michael said she only worked for part of the war at Crandene.'

'Rachel, take my advice, and leave it alone. The answer will come in the middle of the night.'

'I'll try,' Rachel replied gloomily, 'I haven't much else to do with my nights at present.'

September 1937

'Alice?' The head on the pillow moved slightly.

'Your ladyship?' She moved closer.

'Some barley water, if you please.'

181

Alice poured out a glass, and held it to Lady Beavers' mouth. Please, please don't die, she willed her. But she knew it was useless her pleading with fate this time. Lady Beavers would never recover.

This illness had come out of the blue. It must surely be cancer, for the pain was so great. How unfair it was, with her ladyship so young. What would happen to this house if she died? To her children too? They were growing up now. George was sixteen, but that was no age to lose a mother, and Gwendolen was only thirteen.

Alice willed her ladyship to live with all the strength she had, and sat at the bedside for another hour before Lady Beavers fell asleep. Then she quietly left the room, handing over the vigil to Robert's sister, Mrs Janes. That this sadness should come upon the family was so unexpected, and so hard with Robert's career riding high in government and Crandene itself so prominent in the affairs of the country. And, worst, her ladyship had done nothing to call down this affliction upon her.

Alice returned to the kitchens to prepare a supper that no one would feel like eating, and later that evening came the terrible news that her ladyship had died. To her surprise and gratitude, Mrs Janes came in to ask her whether she would like to pay her last respects to Cecilia Beavers, and summoning up her strength Alice went up to the bedroom.

Finding herself alone, she placed a kiss upon the still-warm forehead. 'Goodbye, dearest Miss Cecilia,' she whispered.

But then she realized she wasn't alone.

'Alice,' came a hoarse whisper from the gloom of the darkened room. Robert was sitting on the far side of the bedroom quite still, half hidden in an armchair.

Alice hesitated. 'Your lordship?'

For once she did not know what to do. Should she retreat? Should she offer words of condolence. Then it was solved for her, for he burst into harsh retching sobs, and instinctively she ran towards him.

'Alice!' He reached for her from his chair, grasped her round her body and drew her close to him. 'For God's sake, what shall I do without her?'

She kneeled down and held him while he sobbed on her

shoulder. 'You understand, don't you?' he choked. 'She was the best of me.'

Alice stayed silent, until at last he calmed down, and she made as if to move. He clutched her near to him again. 'Don't go, Alice. Don't leave me.'

'I must, sir, and you should be with your children.'

He misunderstood – or she had. 'Don't leave Crandene. I couldn't bear that too.'

'Sir,' she whispered, 'save your strength. You will need it in the days to come.'

'I have no strength, Alice. She was my strength. Don't you understand? Help me.'

'You'll recover, sir. It's the shock. The terrible shock. There are those that need you.' Meaningless words, but what others were there?

'I haven't always done right by you, Alice. You know why.'

She grew cold. 'Perhaps, sir.'

Alice went back to her room, shaken. She genuinely mourned her late ladyship, and now she must help Crandene with the funeral arrangements as well as the catering, working as she had always done from behind the scenes.

First she went to her desk, and looked at her precious work, *Repasts of Delight*. It was nearly finished, but her plans had now been thrown into disarray. She had not bargained for this, and for once she could not think what to do. Man proposes, God disposes. This was not her way forward, not after the death of her ladyship. It was too cruel. She felt tears come to her eyes. Death took the best from her: Harry, Monsieur Trente, her mother, and now her ladyship, the best of Crandene.

Robert avoided her as the weeks went by, and she administered more and more of Crandene on his behalf. Christmas was a quiet time that year, yet Robert suddenly roused himself to insist on the old traditions being maintained. The servants filed in for their presents as usual and Robert, clad all in black, handed them out. Alice had chosen them all for him, including her own, which was a cross on a chain. As he handed her the small box, however, she realized that she had been wrong.

183

Nothing had changed for her. She might have pity for Robert, but the hatred was still there.

As the new year came, she glanced at her work again, and suddenly saw her way ahead. The plan was so simple that she almost laughed. She wondered only when the right time might be. Soon, she thought. It would be when Lady Beavers had been dead for at least six months.

~

'Rachel Field?' The voice was slightly familiar but Rachel could not place it. Ten o'clock in the morning was an unusual time for a private call, and she'd assumed it was a call centre doing the spec rounds.

'Speaking.'

'Marty Williams. I'm Toby Williams' grandson. You talked to my father at Canterworth.'

'So I did. This is good of you to call.' No wonder the voice sounded familiar. She'd heard it on TV often enough.

'Dad said you were interested in Alice Carter but he couldn't tell you much.'

'He was very helpful.' She held her breath, wondering what was coming her way. Could it by any chance be Samuel cropping up at last?

'He knew I was close to my grandfather, see. I was always badgering him to tell me about Tolbury. Odd in a kid, isn't it? Even more in a teenager, though by then I guess I had my boots on the food table. Anyway my granddad talked a lot about your Alice.'

'You remember what he said?' she asked eagerly.

'Not everything, of course, but a fair amount. Dad said you were interested not so much in the cooking – I could bend your ear for hours over that – but in what he told you about a tramp calling to see Alice one day.'

'Both the cooking and the tramp actually.' She wasn't going to let anything slip by. 'But the tramp first and foremost. Your father didn't know who he was.'

'Ah, but I do. Gramps used to tell me about him, because he reckoned it was all due to this tramp that Alice left, and he had

184

to go through three years of crap chefs above him before he got his chance. Mind you, it gave him the opportunity to practise what she'd taught him, and make sure the veggie gardens were kept going.'

The tramp, the tramp was all Rachel could think of.

'So Gramps asked Alice who this tramp was since Alice looked so shattered after his visit,' Marty continued. 'And he always remembered what little she said, because she clammed up tight as an oyster after that.'

'What was it?'

'Just an old soldier, Alice told him. He'd said his name was Corporal Peasbody.'

'Samuel Peasbody?' she hardly dared ask.

'Can't help you there.'

Thirteen

At least she had a name to follow up, and Rachel's excitement began to bubble up once more. Surely, oh surely Corporal Peasbody must be Samuel. She had a sudden doubt, as Alice had reportedly become more reserved after meeting this Samuel, which didn't seem to fit. And why should his appearance have influenced her to return to Crandene? Perhaps there was no connection between the two events, or perhaps Kent was where Peasbody lived. If, Rachel fumed once again, she had access to Crandene's records, she might so easily have found out. She fantasized that Peasbody might himself have worked at Crandene and had told Alice of the vacancy there. Perhaps Alice had returned to Crandene on his account, only to lose him for whatever reason in the years that followed. Maybe even she dumped him for Lord Beavers – but that would hardly fit in with the dedication of the script: *To Samuel, remembering November 15th.*

So where next in the great search for Samuel Peasbody? National Archives at Kew might give her some clues as to his military service, but as it was after the war that Alice had met him, his wartime service might not be relevant. Still, she had to begin somewhere, and for this Michael was her most obvious source of possible information. He had been researching the Royal West Kent Regiment for his book, and had come up with a probable connection between Robert Beavers and Harry Rolfe. She could at least eliminate the possibility that Peasbody had a similar connection. With luck Michael would put her continuing interest in Alice's affairs down to nothing more than curiosity. Moreover contacting him might take her mind off Adam.

She had still heard nothing from Adam, which she supposed

was hardly surprising. She had tried to dismiss him from her mind by convincing herself that their quarrel had merely proved how poles apart they were, but obstinately he clung on, both by day and more persistently by night.

'We're two of a kind, Rachel,' he'd said. 'Is that good?' And she hadn't been able to answer. They were each captive in a pit they had dug for themselves out of distrust born of their past experiences. Turning your back on the past, she was realizing too late, only meant it would come along and kick you from behind.

Her days were overbusy with the rebuilding of her home, but the darker October evenings were harder to fill. She spent many of them with the copy of Alice's script, working out the suitable recipes to adapt for modern use and how the ingredients would have to alter. There were still two months to go before she would be joining Marjorie, however, and during them she had determined to lick this puzzle of Alice once and for all.

Michael obviously recognized her voice when she rang him, because he immediately came back with: 'Good to hear from you, Rachel.' Remembering their last meeting, however, she wondered if she was being over sensitive in detecting a lukewarm tone in his voice.

Nonsense, she told herself. 'I've got a name to throw at you,' she announced cheerfully.

'An Alice Carter name?'

'Very much so.'

'Fire straight ahead.'

'Corporal Peasbody.'

She could almost hear the silence. Then: 'Not him again.'

'That sounds bad,' she observed brightly. 'But at least you've heard of him.'

'I've tripped over his name often enough.'

'Tripped? So what's wrong with this Peasbody?' This wasn't sounding good.

'He was a nutter par excellence.'

'In what way?' Here we go again. Two steps forward, two steps back.

'Have you time to come up here? I'll show you what I have on the poor old corporal.'

187

Two days later Rachel was once more ringing the doorbell of Michael's flat. She had debated whether it was even worth coming, since it seemed quite clear the Peasbody trail was a dead end. Nevertheless it was forward action of a kind, although she realized with some astonishment that once she'd have been eager to come if only for the sake of seeing Michael again. Not now. The sight of his dark good looks as he greeted her and produced coffee with his usual flourish left her unmoved.

'So tell me the worst,' she said.

'OK. Background first. Your Corporal Peasbody was indeed with the Royal West Kents and in the 1st Battalion, as was Robert Beavers. Robert was an officer, of course, but Peasbody was in the same show at the Somme as the one in which Robert won his VC, one of the battles for High Wood, on 22nd July 1916. He was in the platoon ordered to check the wood out. Only one or two, including Peasbody, got out of it alive, and, as I told you, the whole of the battalion attack was a disaster. Peasbody reported back to Robert and they both did a great job in fetching some of the wounded back to the lines under fire. The difference between him and Robert, however, was that he was never the same man thereafter. He was severely wounded, and ended up with a grudge that though Robert got the VC he only received a Military Medal. He reckoned it was because Robert was an officer, of course, which was nonsense, because the awarding of the VC doesn't work that way. He stirred up a fuss after the war, and got various steward jobs in the military clubs of London before he shot his mouth off once too often and they got wise to him. No one would employ him and he landed up tramping the countryside, talking to anyone who would listen to him.' Michael looked at her. 'Would I be right in thinking one of them was Alice?'

'Apparently so.' It was even worse than she'd feared. This didn't fit in at all with her theories.

'Thereafter he ended up in an asylum. So tell me how he connects with Alice Carter.'

'He went to see her in Lincolnshire in 1929, and according to a chef who used to work with Alice she was never the same after that. It wasn't long after that she returned to Crandene.'

Michael toyed with a second cup of coffee but did not

comment. Rachel's mind then began to click into gear. 'Did he rave about anything else or just the awards? That doesn't seem enough to get him shut up in an asylum. Do you know?'

'No.'

It was an unusually short reply for Michael, she thought, since he enjoyed expounding and speculating. 'You seem to know quite a lot about him, so can't you even hazard a guess?'

'I can only go by what I've been told.' Michael's cheeks were beginning to look flushed.

'And do you always believe it?' she asked quietly.

'I'm a historian,' he snapped back at her. 'I gather all the evidence I can, decide whether it makes a convincing case that a jury of my peers would agree with, and present it.'

'With all the pros and cons?'

He was getting angry now. 'That's what being a historian means.'

'Then what about Peasbody? You've passed judgement on him, giving the cons without telling me the pros.'

'There aren't any for heaven's sake. The 1920s are a long time ago now. There's no other evidence to gather.'

Pretty weak for a historian. 'Then you're dismissing him as a witness out of hand?'

'A witness to what? You're hardly making yourself clear, Rachel. You have a line of your own to pursue, I suppose, and I'm sorry I can't give you more help. I can only supply facts, not rumours.'

She pounced. 'What rumours? About Peasbody?'

'I repeat I have no idea and nor has anyone else what Peasbody used to rave about apart from his Military Medal, which incidentally was given for bravery in the field and was a reasonably high-ranking award.'

'For a non-officer,' she goaded him.

'You're getting bloody rude, Rachel. Are you suggesting I'm biased?'

'I don't know. We're going round in circles, Michael. I'm sure that you know something more about this Peasbody than you're telling me.'

He was really angry now, but she wasn't going to be put off. After all, she'd little enough to lose. 'I might tell a fellow

189

historian, but not you. What you're seeking is some dramatic story about Alice Carter, but there isn't one. As I politely told you, she was a kitchenmaid with ambitions, who leaped for the main chance when the lady of the house died and stepped in smartly, taking advantage of a bereaved man's loneliness.'

'Perhaps you withheld evidence from yourself as well as from me,' she fought back. 'Perhaps that's due to the same fault you're accusing me of. It doesn't fit in with your theory. What's more, you wouldn't be getting so annoyed with me if your book weren't somehow affected by this. Not to mention next year's Crandene show with which you're tied in.'

'Rubbish.'

'Remember the words you once used to me, Michael? "It depends whose world it shatters." Whose world would Peasbody have shattered? Alice Carter's?'

He'd expected her to finish with something else. She could see that immediately from his face. It had relaxed. Fear had been followed by relief that she'd taken a wrong turn. Well, she could quickly reverse that.

'I'm wrong, aren't I?' she hurled at him. 'It's the Beavers world that would be shattered. What did Robert Beavers do to poor old Peasbody? After all, he was the Samuel of Alice's life, wasn't he? The man she loved?'

His mouth quivered in amusement. 'Rachel, you're out of your depth. If it matters a damn, Peasbody's name was Jacob, not Samuel, and nothing you can say can alter the fact that he was a lunatic.'

'But he still might have had the power to shake Robert Beavers.' She'd put her foot in it now. She might as well go further. 'Perhaps you have to decide whether you're a historian or a writer of authorized biographies. Is that the problem?'

He stared at her, no longer amused. Far from it. 'You're barking up the wrong tree, Rachel.'

'I'll bark longer if I have to, and bark at the whole Beavers family, until I know the truth about Alice and Peasbody, Jacob or Samuel.'

He sighed in exasperation. 'My book's nearly finished. Do you seriously expect me to put in a lot of rumours and hearsay without proof?'

'But suppose there were proof. What would you do then?'

'Judge its quality when I saw it.'

'Convenient.'

'Perhaps it would be better if you left now.' Michael rose abruptly to his feet, and picked up her coat to hand to her. 'I've tried to help—'

'But not to the point where your historian's mind is forced to question what you've already written.'

'If I spelled out a lot of rumours to you, you'd believe them, and go haring after false trails. And they aren't true, it's as simple as that.'

'Then as you're a historian,' she whipped back smartly with her exit line, 'Lord Beavers has nothing to fear.'

Rachel was more shaken than she had realized by this encounter and mulled it over on her way home in the train. Had she gone too far? It was clear Michael hadn't told her all he knew, though he must be torn about it, since he'd agreed to see her in the first place. That at least suggested a tug of historian's conscience. And that in turn confirmed that Peasbody must have something to do with Michael's current buddy Lord Beavers and the Crandene show.

That led her to three conclusions. First, she might have gone too far for her own safety if she wished to preserve the fiction that she was only mildly interested in Alice now. Secondly, she needed to find out more about Peasbody and his connection – if any – with Robert Beavers. And thirdly, if she was right that there were rumours that might reflect on Robert Beavers she might be duty bound to tell Adam, since his uncle was at least on the point of his decision about the show, if it was not already made. She tried to distinguish the logic of needing to contact Adam from her longing to do just that, but gave up the struggle.

When she left the train at Canterbury, she found herself once more walking – quickly – towards Never Alone, although she had little idea what she would say to Adam when she got there. Never Alone was still open, although it was five thirty, but nevertheless she was unlucky. Adam wasn't there.

'Out fundraising?' she asked, trying to sound as though her visit were completely casual.

191

'Probably. Aren't we always? Can I give him a message?' the volunteer asked. 'He should be in tomorrow.'

'Just say I called.'

So much for great reconciliations. Disappointed, she made her way back to the car park, though the thought of returning to her silent cottage was a dismal one. To take her mind off Adam she ran mentally through the gamut of the ready meals in the freezer. Even professional cooks were allowed nights off, but none of the freezer contents appealed. The pub did.

Her heart did a somersault as she saw an MG parked outside her cottage. Adam? *Here?* Quickly, she parked behind it, but there was no sign of its driver. Then she found a note stuck in the windscreen wiper: 'In the pub'.

The day miraculously transformed itself as she tried to reduce her mental gallop into the pub into a stroll. She saw him immediately, sitting at a bench with what looked like coffee or tea before him. She disciplined herself into caution – after all, she had no idea what brought him here. Whatever the reason, he hadn't noticed her yet.

'Never Alone with a cup of tea?' she asked, taking him by surprise. Test the water. Don't rush it, she tried to tell herself.

It didn't need testing, as Adam simply stood up, took her in his arms and kissed her.

'It was my fault,' she said at last.

'Mine.'

'Ours then. I called at Never Alone just now. They'll tell you tomorrow so I might as well confess now.'

'Nice one.'

'You look very smug. It's been too long, Adam.'

'My thoughts exactly. Tea or—'

'Tea can wait.'

'Again my thoughts exactly.' He went to the bar to settle up and returned to take her firmly by the hand, out of the pub and into her cottage.

'I thought,' she remarked innocently some hours later, 'that my whereabouts were a secret after I moved from the B and B.'

'To the great detective all things are possible. I followed you home from the post office one day.'

'That simple?'

'Yes. Just as well no one else thought of it.'

'Don't, Adam.' She shivered. 'It's a forbidden subject in bed.'

'Sorry. Let's consider dinner instead.'

'Pub or ready meal?'

'What happened to the great cook? Alice must be looking down in horror. I only came to enjoy one of your feasts. Let's choose ready meal, because we can have it here. I've a bottle of pop in the car.'

The Indian proved not to be too bad, and the bottle of pop turned out to be a good claret and mixed surprisingly well with the curries. The drowsy afterglow of both Adam and the claret made it easier to broach the first subject on her mind.

'Where now, Adam?'

'Together. Somehow.'

'I thought we agreed that two of a kind weren't good together.'

'Sometimes too much thinking isn't good either.'

'Nor is heading for the same ending twice.' How ridiculous, she thought hazily, to be here with Adam again, trying to talk dispassionately about something so fragile as their relationship.

'I've been working on it,' he answered.

'On what?' She was lost.

'Facing up to the past, I suppose. Putting Annie in her rightful place.'

So that was her name. 'And has she gone?'

He hesitated. 'Lingering. How about you?'

He wasn't looking at her and now it was her turn. Over François she could take a chance to say she'd banished his legacy for good. But there was more to it. She wanted to reach out to Adam with one hand and Marjorie with the other, but Alice was in the way. Ridiculous, but how could she step forward with this ghost from the past at her heels? And moreover there was another question.

'Do you still love Annie?' An old-fashioned question for a

problem as old as time, and as relevant today as the common cold. No cure available yet.

'No.'

She laughed in sheer relief. 'So what lingers? Commitment?'

'In a way. I walked away from the situation last time, just like I did from John, my uncle.'

'And as I've always done. Two of a kind. You were right. So what's the road back – or forward?' She was quite muddled now. All she could think of was Adam, the afternoon, and his return to her.

'It might be Alice,' he answered.

'*Alice?*'

'I see her as a debt I owe my uncle. I need to know as much as you why the name of Alice Beavers arouses such emotion at Crandene.'

'And I do too,' Rachel replied, almost weeping with relief as this crystallized in her mind. Alice was her debt to the past as well.

'Good.' He grinned, as he poured another glass of wine. 'So tell me what's been happening, Sherlock. And do you need a Watson?'

'A Mycroft.'

'You flatter me. On second thoughts, you don't.'

She kissed him, and then began to talk about Tolbury, about the Williams family, and finally of Peasbody and Michael's contribution, ending with her theory of some link between Peasbody and Crandene. 'And I'm convinced there must be some link between Peasbody and Alice's Samuel.'

'I've been doing some work in the Crandene archives,' Adam told her casually. 'I don't recall any mention of a Peasbody there.'

Had he indeed. Perhaps that was how Crandene had got Marjorie's name. She managed to refrain from asking him direct. Time enough for that. 'I doubt if there would be. It doesn't sound as though Peasbody was a great fan of Robert Beavers.'

'So the great unicorn's mouth proclaims.'

'A somewhat tight-lipped mouth.'

194

'Ah. A falling out of bosom colleagues by any chance? Is this to what I owe the honour of your visit?'

She looked at him, aghast that the wound was still tender. 'The visit served as an excuse to see you. A valid one. Michael admitted by his silence that though Peasbody was a lunatic what he was saying must have relevance to Beavers.'

'Difficult for him.'

'I told him to decide whether he was a historian or a biased biographer.'

He laughed out loud. 'Good for you. You don't mince your words, do you?'

'My mince is of very high quality. Very little fat. I left him thinking about it.'

'So you think our Mike knows more about Peasbody than he's saying?'

'Not necessarily. I had the impression that Peasbody's story might rebound on Robert Beavers, but it might embarrass Michael if there was something to support that, so he's avoiding probing any further.'

'I can help there.'

'*You* can?'

'One of the reasons I was coming to see you. As well as peering at the Crandene archives – fixed through my highly curious uncle incidentally – I did some scurrying round my old journalist haunts.'

'But there wouldn't be anything detrimental to the Beavers in print, surely. Rumours can be libellous.'

'Sure, but I had human contacts too. Robert Beavers died in 1969 and there were many fulsome obituaries. I know an old chap who was a regular obituarist for military folk at that time and he's still busy taking tours round the First World War battlefields. I managed to catch him between trips last week, and though naturally enough he didn't remember precisely what he'd said about Robert, he did remember writing the obit. In 1969 there were plenty of people around who'd fought in the first war, some of whom had known Robert Beavers. One or two of them told him there had been some nasty rumours flying around—'

'About Peasbody?'

195

'Forget Peasbody, dearest. This is Robert Beavers we're talking about.'

'That he didn't deserve his VC?' This was her prize theory and she was impatient to air it.

'Wrong. There's no evidence on that score. No, these rumours were that he'd made a fearful cock-up and lost or not acted on a message from the Brigade HQ that there was indeed a German strongpoint in that corner of High Wood and that the Gordon Highlanders platoon had just been wiped out. Although they'd still have had to attack the strongpoint, if the battalion were ever to reach its objective, the Wood Lane Trench, more men could have been sent in than just the one platoon. As it was, the Royal West Kents' platoon was decimated too.'

'The platoon with Corporal Peasbody in it. If the rumours were true, no wonder old Peasbody was ranting and raving afterwards, and no wonder Michael was pretty quiet about it. The problem is,' Rachel remembered desolately, 'that Michael says he isn't a Samuel, he was Jacob.'

'Maybe Jacob was his first official name, but he didn't use it. It often happens.'

'Perhaps.' Her doubt remained.

'How about forgetting Peasbody and thinking about Harry Rolfe?'

'How can we? Michael could accidentally have sent Pops in the wrong direction over that by mentioning Rolfe to him first. Suppose it *was* Samuel Peasbody on that tombstone to which Alice took him?'

'Possible – if it wasn't for two things.'

'What are they?'

'Firstly, the obvious – sorry. Peasbody was alive and kicking in 1929 and even if he'd dropped dead the day after he met Alice, he wouldn't be buried in a war cemetery.'

'Ah. I make a great researcher, don't I?' Rachel was furious with herself. It had to be the red wine, surely.

'First-class lover though.'

'Second reason?' she asked, highly pleased.

'Thanks to my endeavours during our absence from each other, I've discovered that Harry Rolfe was first lampboy, then butler's boy, then a footman at Crandene. He was killed at High Wood on 22nd July 1916. Buried in the Caterpillar Valley cemetery near Longueval.'

April 1938

'Do come in, Alice. You said you wished to see me. Not that young daughter of mine creating havoc in the servants' quarters, I suppose?'

'No, your lordship, Miss Gwendolen hasn't been near us.' Alice stood blank-faced before Robert, who was busy writing at his desk.

'What then? A raise in wages?' He laughed heartily. 'We can certainly talk about that. You deserve it.'

'Not in wages, sir.'

The tone of her voice did not alter, yet Robert laid down his pen and glanced at her sharply. Alice had put on her Sunday best dress, as a symbol of the day's importance, and was holding her carrier bag in one hand. It was the anniversary of the first time she and Harry had climbed their hill together, and so it was fitting that she should choose today. To Robert it must seem just another day in the life of Crandene, but she knew that it would change everything here. She wasn't even nervous now that the time had come at last.

'You're not going to leave us, are you, Alice?' Sudden fear entered his lordship's eyes, but she reassured him on that.

'Oh no, sir. I wouldn't do that. I'm part of Crandene, aren't I?'

He agreed, but he looked away. She supposed he was thinking how unlike her it was to blow her own trumpet. She'd be blowing it so hard in a minute the walls of Jericho would surely come tumbling down for her, so she could march in victorious. Not that she'd get pleasure out of it. It was just what she had to do.

'I thought you'd like to see what I've been doing in my spare time,' she continued, 'not that there's much of it what with my job and my family, but every now and then I add a bit.' She put her carrier bag on his desk, and saw his eyes bulge with amazement at her temerity. Then she took out its precious contents.

197

'Look, sir.'

She opened up one spread before him, and he blinked at it.

'These are recipes,' he said, perhaps relieved, 'and most artistic drawings. I do congratulate you.' He peered at one. 'Very quaint. Two pies, I see, walking hand in hand, at the seaside. Most amusing. Do all these pages have recipes on them?'

'They do. I thought I might publish them,' she replied.

'But my dear Alice, cooks don't—' Robert broke off, but she knew exactly what he was going to say. That female cooks don't publish cookery books, only the occasional male chef such as Escoffier and ladies like the Countess Morphy, who published collections. Alice was neither.

'I think it might go well, since they're recipes I use here at Crandene when all your famous visitors come. Look, there's Mr Slippery Sam's Eel Pie—'

'Sir Samuel does not visit Crandene anymore,' he cut in swiftly, and somewhat coldly.

'Perhaps I'll omit that one then. In the circumstances, his being what you might call unpopular now.' More than unpopular. Everyone knew him as Slippery Sam since he'd had to resign after discussing a pact with the French foreign minister Laval that would effectively let Mussolini take over most of Abyssinia unopposed by Britain and France. There'd been outrage in Parliament and the country and Sam was dropped like a hot potato. Perhaps that was fair or perhaps it wasn't, since she had a shrewd suspicion he was being made the scapegoat. In any case, Mussolini had duly marched into Abyssinia and Hitler was now busy annexing Austria. But she, Alice Carter, wasn't expected to have an opinion on such things. She was the cook. She didn't care, though.

'It might be wiser. So did you wish to ask my permission to publish these, Alice?'

'No, sir, not your permission. I shall publish them. I've written them in my own time, you see, and although I cook them here at Crandene they're all based on recipes I created at Tolbury Hall, so there's no question that you as my employer might own copyright. I've taken care of that. I've a letter from Sir John Dene confirming it.'

He looked puzzled. 'I should be delighted to write a fore-word, Alice. You know I'd do that for you.'

'I don't think you'd approve of my book, sir. Not really. Not in the circumstances.' Alice calmly proceeded to explain exactly why this was as Robert's face grew paler and paler.

By the time she had finished explaining, he was choking so much she thought he might have a fit or a stroke. And that wouldn't do at all.

'Publish and be damned,' he finally spluttered. 'No one will notice anything like that.'

'Very well, sir. If that's your last word.' Alice calmly packed her script back into the carrier bag, and walked towards the door, then she turned back, as if a sudden thought had struck her. 'They might pick it up, sir. Someone will realize the significance, and think of the fun then. Even if they don't I might spread the word. You see, I really should have to leave Crandene then, and both that nice Mr Chamberlain and that funny Mr Churchill have asked me to join their households. Of course I'd prefer to stay here.'

Robert gaped at her. 'What do you want, damn you, woman. Money? Isn't it enough you've tortured me all these years without this blackmail?'

'No.'

'Why, Alice, why?'

'It's easy, sir. I suppose you could define it as hatred.'

'How much do you want?'

'It's not money I'm after. I'm going to marry you, Robert. I'm going to be the next Lady Beavers.'

'Good God, Alice . . .' Robert struggled incoherently with this. 'You know how I feel about you, but you're the cook.'

'Nowadays that isn't so important. Not so important as when you turned me out of Crandene and put my family into the workhouse. There's going to be another war soon. That's obvious now Hitler's taken over Austria. You might be glad you married a cook and someone who can work beside you at Crandene. Someone who knows her political onions as well as you do, Robert.'

He eyed her up and down. She could almost see him calculating whether she meant what she said and what the risks might be. 'What about my children?'

'I'll treat them respectfully. They won't like me for marrying you and I don't blame them, but I'll take nothing from their future. You can leave to them in your will what you'd have left them anyway. Just allow me enough to keep me going. I'll trust you on that.' The pause after she had finished made him relax.

'Oh,' she added, 'and the cottage in the village where my dad lives, I'd want the freehold of that now. That's not much to ask, is it? I'll sign to everything before we're wed, and so will you.'

'You've thought all this out, haven't you?' Robert eyed her with a certain respect, she noticed. The bastard. 'I suppose it might work,' he admitted grudgingly.

'It might indeed, sir.'

'But I want that script – and anything that goes with it.'

'I understand. I'm lodging it all with my solicitors with instructions to release it to you after we are wed. The very day if you like.'

'I'll destroy everything, Alice. You realize that?'

'I do indeed, sir.'

'There's some lovely work in the script.'

'It's all in my head too, sir.'

'You mean you'd do another one?' The horror of realizing she would always keep her power over him brought terror to his eyes.

'No, sir. You know I always keep my word. I'll not publish or speak of anything if you keep your word to me. It's closed.'

'We could be happy, Alice.' Now the terror was leaving him, he was thinking it through.

'I doubt that, sir.'

'Why ever not? You've made me wait long enough for you. Now you've come to me of your free choice.'

'I forgot to mention, your lordship, there's one other condition,' she said politely. 'I'll work at your side, I'll keep you company and support you by day and by evening. But not by night. I'll not share your bed. Ever.'

200

She'd done it. The stone in her heart had achieved all it wanted when she saw the look on his face. Alice clutched her carrier bag to her and left the room. She would take it right now to Hargreaves & Seaton, for safekeeping. Just in case Robert thought to forestall her. She doubted it, he was too stunned to think so clearly.

'I've done it, Harry,' she whispered. 'Our hill, for ever.'

Alice returned from Tonbridge, having deposited the script and its attachments safely. She had taken care that Robert should know she had left it there by asking them to telephone him to confirm it, and that it would be released the day they were wed.

She returned to her kitchen to prepare dinner as though nothing had changed. But it had. She was in power at last. Her original plan had been to leave Crandene with the script, publish it and then tell him so that he would live the rest of his life with the knowledge that at any moment the sword of Damocles might fall. But this plan was better, so much better. This way she could stay close to Harry for ever. If Robert did not trust her, he would realize there was nothing he could do to prevent her telling anyone she chose and at any time, apart from murdering her. If he murdered her, so what? Now that Henry was nearly twenty-one her life would be her own once more, for soon he would marry and begin a new family. But she knew Robert would never harm her. Oddly enough, they trusted each other. She knew his promise now given would not be broken, and he would know that hers also would be kept. Oh yes, they would make a handsome couple. Tongues would wag about the lord who married his cook, but let them. They would soon tire.

Her script, her lovely script, her testament to the past would in due course be destroyed, but she could let it go, despite all the work. After all, locked in her desk was the carbon copy she'd made in case Robert had gone berserk and destroyed the script there and then. This one she would always keep, but never use. The illustrations in it were even better than the top copy. It was her own secret love. Her work had been more than an instrument of revenge. It was a testament to a love that was past so that it could live for ever elsewhere than in her heart.

Relief and tension that her plan was now in motion made her suddenly weak. She felt tears in her eyes, and was surprised for she had not cried since the death of her ladyship. But now she cried for Harry and for the life with him she had never had.

~

'Pops?' Rachel whispered gently, but he didn't stir. She motioned Adam to sit well back in case Pops got a shock at waking up and seeing a stranger.

Suddenly, after a few minutes, Pops' eyes flew open. 'Another of 'em, eh?' He was looking at Adam.

'Another what?' Rachel grinned at him.

'How should I know?' he muttered. 'Lover, is it? I don't know what things are coming to. Your mother and I possessed the ability to make up our minds.'

'I'm your granddaughter, Pops, not Margaret.'

'You look like her. Behave like her too. Divorce indeed.'

'She was happier that way,' Rachel said defensively, aware of Adam listening in amusement.

'Well, what do you want?'

'More family history please. I've become interested in it, and so has Adam.'

'What's he interested in our family history for? Thinking of joining it, young man, and want to check us out first?'

'That's it in a nutshell,' Adam replied promptly. Maybe he had his own Pops in the background, Rachel thought, or more likely he'd sat with so many Never Alone clients that he was well versed in how to bat back conversational surprises.

'You remember you told me about that gravestone you visited with Alice?' Rachel asked.

'Alice? She's my sister. Haven't seen her for ages.'

This was getting worse. 'Pops, do you remember whose gravestone it was?'

'I told you. I remember quite clearly. I wish you wouldn't treat me like some kind of imbecile. I might speak more Russian than Czech nowadays, but I still have my marbles.'

She saw Adam's eyebrows shoot fractionally up and she shook her head to indicate all wasn't yet lost.

'Now look, young Rachel,' Pops continued, 'I told you that gravestone was Harry Rolfe's and that's whose it was, see?'

She would get no further with that. 'Have you ever heard of a Samuel Peasbody?'

He stared at her. 'Now that name rings a bell. Let me think.'

He thought for so long that she was beginning to think they should tiptoe out, but then out came one triumphant blast: 'Thought so, that was the feller Alice was so fond of.' Rachel's hopes suddenly rose, and then sank, as he continued, 'But his name wasn't Samuel. It was Jacob.'

Here we go again, she thought. 'Perhaps that was his second name,' she tried hopefully.

'No. "This is Uncle Jacob," Alice told me. He wasn't a real uncle of course, everyone was uncle in those days. "Corporal Peasbody, young sir," he said, saluting me. I was only a boy so that impressed me. Now why should she introduce him as Jacob if his name was Samuel, you tell me that.'

She couldn't. But why put the name Samuel in her script if Alice knew him as Jacob? Oh hell. Why did it have to be so complicated?

'Was he,' Rachel sought for the right word, 'soft in the head?'

'It's you who's off your trolley, young woman,' Pops retorted with great disdain. 'Of course he wasn't. Not then anyway. He was simple, but he knew his Ps and Qs and his goldfinches and skylarks. He came with us on walks.'

'In Lincolnshire?'

'Look, I said my memory was clear but it was over seventy years ago. How should I know? I remember she brought him to the cottage, that's all: it could have been Cranbridge, it could have been Lincolnshire.'

'So you knew him in Kent too?' This was more hopeful.

He thought for a while. 'Yes, he came every so often, but then after a while Alice would talk about going to see him. He's not too well, she told us. She told me later he was in a hospital, maybe it was a workhouse, I wouldn't know. Well,

203

fancy that, I haven't thought of Uncle Jacob Peasbody for many a long year.'

'So he wasn't off his head?'

'Not a bit of it. He liked different things to most people but his mind was as clear as a bell. Don't know where you got such rubbish from.'

'Did he talk to you about the war at all?' Adam asked.

'Not that I recall. Might have done with Alice.'

'So what do you make of that?' Rachel asked as she and Adam strolled back to the hotel. They'd had a bad crossing over the Channel in a force eight, and the dry land – even in November – was welcome. 'Two different versions. One from a boy in his teens, now a rambling old man, the other from a presumably mature man based on hearsay.'

'And related by a biased historian.'

'Um.'

'My money's on Harry Rolfe,' Adam said plaintively. 'You keep avoiding him. He seems to be an elusive character.'

'He must have come from somewhere in the Cranbridge area. It would be worth finding out where, if that would satisfy you.'

'There might be some descendants.'

'It's possible.' Rachel sighed. Out there somewhere was Alice's story, and leading to it were a hundred and one trails, only a few of which would bear fruit. This was supposed to be the fun of family history, but there was more at stake for her than just fun. By tacit agreement, Adam might stay overnight with her, or she with him, but both knew they were marking time. In a few weeks it would be Christmas and then New Year. The new year meant she would be working with Marjorie in Rye and by then Adam's uncle would have signed on the dotted line for his sponsorship of the Crandene show. And still they were no nearer knowing whether or not Alice's story had any bearing on that. 'I don't know where to go next though,' she said.

'I do.' Adam took her hand. 'Just time before dinner.'

Fourteen

A friend had once told her that a happy New Year's Eve was a sign of a good year to come. Rachel hoped so, for so far it was going brilliantly, albeit that only two weeks of it had passed. The world, if not at her feet, was certainly dancing around somewhere. As Marjorie and she worked from Rye, which was far to commute to each day, Adam had suggested she live with Marjorie while they were working and on days off – such as they were – with him. A splendid solution. Goodbye lonely cottage. She was either on her way to the man she loved or returning to the work she loved, and what was the occasional snowstorm or frosty road compared with that? The rebuilding of her own cottage had been almost complete by the time the bad weather had arrived in late November, and the builders were now working on the inside. What happened when it was finished was open. It would bring a commitment of some sort, but for the moment she lived for the day – and for Alice Carter.

Yesterday Adam had discovered that his uncle had signed the contract for his sponsorship of the Crandene exhibition, formally entitled: For Valour.

'That should make Lord Beavers very happy,' she had observed.

'I gather it did.'

She had hesitated, reluctant to open up a wasps' nest best left alone. 'It must have been hard for you. Did you tell him anything about the rumours about Robert Beavers?'

'So much for my facing up to the past and getting involved with John again.' He made a face. 'I made my dissenting noises, but he glared at me and said I'd always been a debunker of heroes, and when I had got any hard evidence of a nasty smell at Crandene I could come back.'

205

'So he's signed and that's that.'

'More or less. He was sufficiently interested in what I had to say to be canny, though; he's only handed fifty per cent of the money over. The other fifty per cent will come on his approval of the exhibition when the real work starts on putting it together in mid April.'

'If he doesn't give it, where would that leave his lordship?'

'Up the creek is my guess. Fifty per cent is good, but the other fifty is a mighty lot to have to fork out from Crandene's general revenue.'

'Maybe we're barking up the wrong tree to think that Alice's story rebounds on the Beavers' reputation. Even though his Beavership thinks I've abandoned the quest, he'd still be concerned if there were any truth to the rumours.'

'Especially if the unicorn has told him you're still tinkering with Alice's life story.'

'He would also be able to tell him that I was getting precisely nowhere.'

'Has the unicorn been in touch?'

'Yes, he has. I had a Christmas card waiting for me at the post office with a nice little olive branch drawn on it.'

'Sweet.'

'He must mean it, Adam. He hasn't exactly been pursuing me to find out what I'm up to. You seem to imagine he's hand in hand with his Beavership, but I'm sure you're wrong.'

'They must see themselves as safe now. They're not bothered about ancient rumours surfacing – even if there's any truth in them.'

'If some scandal erupted as the show itself was launched, the press would be on to it like a flash,' Rachel pointed out.

'But it would be small beer compared with having received John Foster's lovely dosh.'

'We don't know how small the beer might be. It might be very large indeed – good as publicity in the short run, but bad for Crandene overall.'

'You're arrived at the same time as good news,' Marjorie greeted her, as she reached the Rye office.

'Great. What is it?'

'I've got the job, or rather we have.'

For a moment it didn't click, and then it did. 'The job at Crandene? That's terrific.' Or was it, Rachel wondered? All sorts of problems might lie ahead now. It didn't matter, she decided. It was an opportunity – if she played it right. The difficulty would be sorting out which way *was* right.

'I assumed it had all fallen through, because it was so long since I did that sample meal for the board. All that remains is to agree menus with them. I've a date next week.'

'Not,' Rachel asked hopefully, 'with his lordship? Of course he might revoke the offer once he knows I'm on board.'

'Let's take a step at a time. Let's make his big mouth water so much he'll swallow you whole.'

Rachel would still dearly love a chance to see the Crandene archives herself. So far she had had once piece of luck, and another dead end. The luck was that she'd discovered that Harry Rolfe had been born in Sissingbrooke, a nearby village to Cranbridge, and by dint of long (and expensive) tracing through birth and marriage certificates, followed by investigation of the electoral roll, she'd found out that there was still a descendant living in the village. Harry and his brothers had been killed in the war, but his sister had married and had a family. One of her children still lived in Sissingbrooke, and a visit to her with Adam had produced a little fruit at last. All she had was a family photo album, which showed several pictures of Harry, one of which was taken in uniform in 1916. He looked a nice lad, with bright eyes and a cheeky smile, but Rachel had thought there was little else here for her. Then the owner had pointed out a bad snapshot taken in a garden; written underneath was: 'My mum with Harry and his fiancée Alice'.

So Alice had loved Harry who had died on the Somme. That began to take shape now. But where did the shape go after that? Where did Samuel (whoever he was) and Peasbody fit in? Maybe Samuel was Alice's pet name for him – but why should it be? Peasbody's second name was Thomas, and Harry's was Albert. Nothing added up. Even the significance of the 15th November had eluded them. Obviously Harry was Alice's early sweetheart but he seemed to have no relevance to the script. That must have come from a later affair and so far they hadn't the slightest idea of who it might have been with.

She had been hopeful of another breakthrough, when Pops, during the course of a Christmas telephone conversation, suddenly came up with Cousin Joe's name.

'Vickers,' he'd said triumphantly. 'That was it.'

But neither certificates nor electoral roll had so far turned up any line in Cousin Joe, and Rachel clung to the hope that somehow she could tackle those archives, just in case any of Alice's private papers were there.

'Do you mind if I tell Beavers myself that I've joined you?'

'Go ahead.'

'If you lose the contract as a result, I'll resign,' Rachel promised.

It took only a few days for a reply to Rachel's letter, and she read it with astonishment. 'It's OK,' she said, re-reading the letter. 'At least I think it is.'

'*Think?*'

'Have a look for yourself.' She handed it over to Marjorie. 'In principle that's fine and he appreciates my telling him. He'd like to see me too when you go.'

'Nothing like putting one's head in the den to find out what the lions would like for dinner,' Marjorie replied lightly.

Rachel wasn't so sure. Boiling oil could still be poured over her head. A nasty accident perhaps? No, he wouldn't risk that in Crandene itself.

'Let's discuss menus,' Rachel said firmly. 'Much more interesting. What does he want?'

'Ideas that are linked to the exhibition.'

'Curries for the Gate of Swat? That sort of thing? Borscht for the Crimea?'

'Yes, but not too close or we'd be on starvation rations for the two world wars. He also wants to lay on special dinners in the evenings with lecturers on the campaigns and so on. Pukka, but not too exorbitant in price. He's aiming for a broad market.'

'I don't see why we shouldn't slip one or two of Alice's recipes in somehow, do you?' Rachel asked. 'After all, she learned the trade during World War I and must have overseen cooking here during the Second World War. We won't reveal they're hers, unless his Beavership has a change of heart and wants to highlight them.'

As they drove through the gates of Crandene, the less it seemed probable that someone here could have been responsible for that fire. It was surely too grand for dirty tricks. Too risky too, with John Foster taking a keen interest in the preparations for the For Valour exhibition. By winter, Crandene seemed a different place, more atmospheric, even if desolate, with a sense of waiting for the next season. It was a cold day with the frost still lying on the grass, and they were glad to get inside.

Marjorie had decided to send in her suggested menus before their visit, and so this meeting was with Lord Beavers alone to hear the results. Was that worse or better? Rachel wondered. As they marched across the carpet to the two chairs placed by the huge desk, she thought of how Hitler used this psychological ploy in his power game with visitors. The thought didn't encourage her.

Rachel had disciplined herself to treat this purely as a business meeting, and banished any temptation to mention Alice Carter. She needed all her concentration for any subtext that might be emanating from his lordship. She was still suspicious of his ready acceptance of her as part of Marjorie's team.

'Good morning, Miss Thomas, Miss Field.'

So much for the opening gambit. All smiles and formal welcome. Rachel could cope with that, as she could with the pleasantries that followed over Lord Beavers' surprise that she and Marjorie knew each other.

'We're former business partners,' Marjorie explained. 'My meeting Rachel again was coincidence.'

Rachel couldn't resist it. 'At the time I was, as you know, looking for such an opportunity.'

'Indeed, yes. I'm sorry we could not have co-operated in that way, Miss Field. However, it's all turned out for the best perhaps, since undoubtedly from these menus before me it seems you will both be using your skills and your formidable knowledge, I am sure, of the English cooking tradition. No

209

doubt you now understand why I could not encourage you at that time, Miss Field. Our plans for the exhibition were not sufficiently formulated and we needed a broader scope and different approach than your proposal offered.'

Oh clever, very clever, to bring up the past, Rachel noted, and even more to suggest that it was all his doing that she could work here after all. Dead or alive, she wondered cynically, although looking at him she had to admit it was hard to imagine him as an assassin creeping at dead of night to burn down the house. Yet someone had done it, someone who answered to the description of 'fish man'. Lord Beavers was no beauty, but he certainly didn't appear to have any resemblance either to a fish or the possible bearer of them.

'In principle,' Lord Beavers was saying, 'the menus are approved but there are one or two details you might like to discuss with Mrs Tomkins, our cook here, after we've finished talking, and the board would like to add something to suggest the Falklands front.

'That's a good idea,' Rachel said honestly, even though it was obvious why the Falklands should be included. That's where he'd served in the army. 'And something with a South American flavour?'

'Possible. Unfortunately,' he paused, 'the 1930s period doesn't fit into the mould of the Crandene show, since we are emphasizing different aspects.' Another pause. 'I was sorry to hear from Michael Hartshorn about the fire at your home.'

'Thank you.' She felt a fierce anger at this farce, realizing he'd deliberately angled the conversation this way. 'It was very painful. I lost a great deal.'

'I understand you are still researching into the life of Alice Carter, Miss Field.' It came so softly out of the blue, but she caught herself in time.

'Do you?' she replied politely. Michael, she wondered angrily. He had probably guessed her interest was still greater than she pretended. It wouldn't have been hard from what she recalled of that conversation. 'Yes, I am for my own interest now that I know more about her. A private family history for my grandchildren, if any.' Make a joke of it.

210

'A splendid idea. I could return the copy pages of the script that you so kindly sent me, if you wish.'

A splendid idea? 'That's good of you, but I'd lent a few pages to another friend, and managed to get them back, thank you.' It came out so pat Rachel decided she must be a natural liar.

'By all means use the Crandene archives while you are working here, if they can be of help.'

'That's very good of you.' What the hell was going on here? Pit-pat, pit-pat. Patting the ball to and fro. She hadn't even had to ask, and here he was presenting her with her wish on a plate. Did he want to keep the enemy under his eye? Then why didn't he take that view before? Was he looking for another opportunity to bump her off?

'I gather from Marty Williams that you managed to find a link to a gentleman called Peasbody,' he continued.

Her first thought was that her ideas about conspiracy weren't so far-fetched. Then she realized Lord Beavers could well be a regular diner at Marty's London restaurant. No point blaming Marty, though. How could he have known what was at stake here?

'Yes,' she replied brightly. 'Does that name mean anything to you?'

'Nothing, I'm afraid. Of course, I knew Alice Beavers, since I saw her at family events up to the time my grandfather died, and I kept in touch with her after that. She was a wonderful old bird.'

Was she indeed, Rachel fumed, but she kept a smiling face. 'So the two families did get on. I had the impression that the Beavers family didn't like her, and who could blame you? From your point of view she stepped very quickly into your grandmother's shoes.'

'I don't think they was close, but there was no antipathy, I assure you. Alice didn't chatter to me about her past, nor would I have been much interested at my age then.'

'Was her marriage to your grandfather a happy one?' Rachel threw down her gauntlet very casually.

'Who really knows whether any marriage is happy save the two involved. Judging from what I saw, I would say yes.'

And what did that tell her? Nothing. More chatter and then they were shaking hands all on the best of terms, and she and Marjorie were marching back across the carpet again.

'Shaking hands with one's potential assassin,' she exploded to Adam on the phone later.

'Interesting experience.'

'And, Adam, he knows I've been doing my research, and he doesn't mind – he doesn't even seem to care. He's even offered to help. It doesn't make sense.'

'Now that is *very* interesting. Think about it.'

She did, and she thought about something else too, something about which she was still not sufficiently certain to discuss with Adam. Perhaps she had villains on the mind at Crandene, but as she and Marjorie walked into the car park they had passed the attendant, standing looking upwards into the trees at the far end, his face sideways to them. He was hatless, hair sleeked back, pointed nose and, as he turned to look at them, she saw his cold starey eyes.

'Nasty fishy sort of face,' Marjorie had remarked casually. 'Glad we paid up.'

Rachel didn't answer as the shock hit her. The fish man. Now she knew what her neighbour meant.

November 1942

'Alice.'

She looked up in surprise from making the dough for her bacon turnover. It was unusual to see Robert in the kitchens. Usually they kept to their own routines, Robert's in Whitehall or in his office here, she administering the grounds and the Crandene kitchens. They usually met for dinner unless Robert were staying overnight in London, and would discuss what had happened during the day in each of their lives. Increasingly Robert had come to talk to her about the war situation now he was in the Cabinet, however, and so she knew more than the public how perilous the situation was. More and more convoys lost at sea, the Russians struggling at Stalingrad, and the situation in North Africa critical. If Rommel broke through the Alamein line to Egypt, then the war might be lost for good.

In return she talked to Robert of the situation at Crandene, on which she kept a close and active eye. Most of the house was occupied by the military now, and even though she and Robert had their own apartment, brown uniforms dominated. Reluctant to yield her kitchens, she controlled the food at Crandene as well as hers and Robert's. Much of the grounds had been dug up for growing vegetables and this again she controlled. She had given a wry smile when Robert had hesitantly suggested she play a role in the village too, but reluctantly agreed. She would be no Lady of the Manor though. She was not a Miss Cecilia, with her kind heart and ever-open door. Alice had no heart left to give, but she could see grief and need, and when she saw it, she tried to help. Practical help, not bowls of gruel.

Sometimes to her surprise Robert would want to come with her to see what was happening in the Crandene grounds, asking her detailed questions of output and prices. She had not given him credit for a deep interest in Crandene itself, but he seemed genuinely determined that Crandene's contribution to the war effort should be as great as possible. There were even secret chambers dug in the grounds, which she was not officially supposed to know. They had been built for resistance in the invasion that had never happened, and still remained there in case need arose. After all, if there were to be another attempt to liberate Europe (although the recent disaster at Dieppe made that unlikely for some while), Kent would be in the forefront of preparations, yet would not want to be seen to be so.

Alice spent much of her time in the kitchens, and whereas in the first year of her marriage this had been looked on with awkward surprise by visitors, it was now taken for granted. It was wartime after all. In 1939 she had played both hostess and cook, overseeing both duties, and once guests grew accustomed to this they accepted it as normal. Robert had been nervous of her inclusion at such large dinners at first, but then, she realized, he was surprised at how well she could keep her end up in political conversation, and how knowledgeable she was. After a while the old tradition of the women retiring while the gentlemen talked was quietly forgotten. It was a good partnership they had – on that level.

213

'Yes, Robert?' She was so used to seeing him as she did the butcher, or the baker, as a part of her life, that it took her a moment or two to realize that something was wrong. He looked distraught.

'Can you spare time, please?'

'Of course.'

'Is it the African offensive?' she asked, when they were alone. It was cold outside, raw for early November, but Robert said he needed the air, so she seized one of her gardening jackets for warmth. She could see now how upset he was. She knew that the battle currently being waged on the El Alamein front was vital if Rommel were to be stopped, and this new Commander-in-Chief Montgomery certainly seemed determined to push him out of Africa. It was going well from the reports, but how could one really tell? Perhaps there had been a setback.

'That continues well,' he told her. 'The news is that Rommel is retreating.'

'Robert, that is splendid news. If Montgomery can keep up the pressure . . .' Alice stopped, realizing that this was not what Robert had to tell her. 'It's bad news, isn't it? I can see from your face.'

'George is missing.'

He was staring straight ahead, lost in his own world.

'I am very sorry to hear that, Robert. He could be a POW, of course. Let us hope so. I do most sincerely.'

'Or he could be dead.' he said harshly. 'I know.'

Alice grieved for George; she liked him and they had formed a reasonably good friendship. He would be twenty-one this year; how hard if war took him too, as it had taken Harry. Robert had lost Cecilia too young, to lose George too would be even worse. She did not want that kind of vengeance to fall on him. That wasn't her plan either. Her vengeance had been set in motion on the day they had married, and she had watched as he destroyed the script, both knowing that meant nothing. Every time he looked at her, he would remember. He had turned one despairing look on her and then left the room for his solitary bed. Since then they had a working relationship, partners who had a job to do together. When it was finished for the day, they separated. Neither had ever crossed the boundary. She had never wished to, nor ever would. If Robert did, he did not mention it. For sexual companionship he had a mistress in London; Alice had stipulated that it should not be at Crandene, and he had agreed – for Crandene's sake. Today, now that his son was missing, Robert had to endure something of what she had suffered when Harry died, but she would not have wished this upon him.

He began to speak, not looking at her, not really talking to her either, just with her.

'This war thing, Alice, it changes you. My God it does. You grow up thinking you know the world around you, how to treat it, what lies ahead, what's good and what's bad in it, you're given the lessons that can help you survive it. Rules. Play up, play up and play the game. That's what they tell you. Shoot when you see the whites of their eyes, and you'll be a man, my son. Courage comes easy if you're trained to be an English gentleman. There's a tradition, a duty. And in this family, well, you know how it was. Grandfather Beavers in the Crimea, Father at the Gate of Swat. You're shown the pictures, told how brave they were, how they won their VCs in every detail. It was going to be easy if you were a Beavers, that's the impression I got. You only had to go into battle and the enemy would fall dead on either side, and a gong awaited you at the triumphal end.

'If my brother had lived, it would all have fallen on him. I had it relatively easy until he died. I was going into politics, not the army. But as soon as he went, that was that. I had to go to Sandhurst, no question of it. Someone had to stand up for the tradition of the Beavers. Someone had to win a medal to join the two VCs, and it had damned well better be a good one. They told you how glory could be won in war, and a medal was its proof.

'It's what they don't tell you that matters though. They don't tell you how war changes you. The dead and the dying, and the pointlessness of it. Putting orders into effect, knowing you've got to lead the fellows into battle – for what? A bit of barbed wire if you're lucky. You can't even count the runs in that damned cricket match. There aren't any. You just count the number of empty places on the roster. They don't tell you the fear that guts you when you open your eyes and it's dawn, and you have to start. They don't tell you what you can do when the guns are blazing, the ground's opening up in holes beneath your feet, and the smoke blinds you so you don't blasted know whether you're going forwards or backwards. You're English, you'll cope. But what if you can't?'

Alice listened as he rambled on. Was this an attempt to make her understand – or make himself understand? Neither perhaps, just the misery pouring out at the loss of his son. She wondered if he were asking for her sympathy, but he did not seem to be, or even seeking her understanding. He just wanted her there. That far she could go to help him.

They had reached the front door now, and he gave her a twisted smile. 'Thank you for listening, Alice. I appreciate it.'

'Robert, I am truly sad for George.'

He stopped and looked at her. 'I know.'

'Tell me if there's any news. *Any.*'

He gave a kind of nod. 'Yes.'

At Christmas, Alice was battling with a real turkey – given to her by the butcher to thank her for her help over something she could hardly remember. It had seemed trivial to her, but the turkey was the result. She was grateful because Robert's sister and her husband were coming to spend the holiday with them, and Robert's daughter Gwendolen might get leave from the WAAF if she was lucky. Alice was just about to put it in the range to cook slowly overnight when Robert appeared, beaming all over his face.

'Splendid news. The best,' he carolled. 'The best Christmas ever. George is safe. He was a POW but managed to escape. He'll be back with his unit any moment. How's that for Beavers bravery, eh?'

'Robert, I'm delighted,' Alice said sincerely.

'He's been recommended for an immediate DSO. He managed to wipe a column or two of Jerries out at Alamein. Howzat, eh? Another one for the record books.'

How's that indeed, thought Alice. She was truly glad for

George – and for Robert. And, she supposed, for Crandene. The tradition would go on. However much Robert might have his weak moments nothing would affect the great tradition. He was as much a victim of it as ever. Victim? She surprised herself. Odd, she'd never thought before in terms of Robert being a victim. A victim like Harry. Only no one but she remembered Harry. She would look at her script just once tonight. She rarely did now, but Christmas was special.

~

Rachel nestled in Adam's arms. He still had an open fire at his home and on this cold winter day it was welcome. Hot chestnuts and real toast, she thought lazily. I could do some toasted marshmallow too perhaps, and be really childish.

'So why do you think I need not worry about the fish man?' She had finally decided she'd tell Adam about her suspicion.

'Firstly, the chap doesn't have be your arsonist, just because you don't like his face. Secondly, even if he is, the very fact that Lord Beavers seems actively to be encouraging you to carry on with the research seems to suggest we haven't much to worry about.'

'Yes, but you said *think* about it on the phone. What did you mean?'

'There has to be some reason Beavers no longer seems to care about you. What's changed?'

'I've given up the idea of publication.'

'Sure, but if you are still researching, anything you discover about Alice will remain in your mind, published or not. It still would pose a danger if it's adverse to the Beavers. Beavers must know by now, thanks to Unicorn, that you and I are an item. He also knows who I am, and yet he doesn't seem worried.'

'There's one other thing that's changed, I suppose.'

'What's that?'

'He thinks the script is destroyed, although I don't see how that affects anything. It doesn't give any clues to Alice's life.'

He stared at her. 'You, Rachel, are a genius. You're the Mycroft Holmes, not me.'

'Many thanks. Why?'

'That's it. Don't you see?'

'I can see you're getting excited. Why?'

'It's the *script* itself. There must be something in it that Beavers is worried about. It must – or he thinks it must – have something damaging to the family in it. It was never *you* he wanted dead, just that script burned. The evidence. I bet you anything you like fish man was sitting waiting for you to go out that night. He probably sat there night after night waiting for his chance.'

'The script,' Rachel repeated, trying to take all this in. And then she realized he was right. Because she and Adam had seen nothing in it other than the recipes and the beauty of the illustrations didn't necessarily mean there wasn't anything more.

'*Repasts of Delight*,' she exclaimed. 'Of course. How could I have been so dumb? Re pasts, two words. About her happy past.'

'And there must be more. The dedication, probably.'

'Forget about Samuel. There must be something in the script itself, just waiting till we have the sense to see it.'

Fifteen

The script lay spread out between them on the hearthrug in his living room. Adam was propped up against one armchair, legs sprawled before him, she against the opposite one. It was a comfortable position, especially with the fire glowing warm next to them. Even though what they were looking at was only a colour photocopy, the stunning versatility and invention of Alice's work shone through.

'First question,' Adam began.

'Yes, m'lud?'

'Why do you only have the carbon copy of the original?'

'Something happened to the top copy. Perhaps it was lost by a prospective publisher.'

'Or the Beavers family still has it.'

'No. They wouldn't have asked me for the copy pages. Unless they'd destroyed the original, of course.'

'Ha! The game's afoot. I bet that's exactly what happened. The script was thought to have been long destroyed, until you tripped along in your sweetly pretty way—'

'I am *not* sweetly pretty.'

'Very well. Along you came in your ugly blundering way, shouting to the Beavers family, "Look what I've got here."'

Rachel considered this. 'I agree it's a feasible argument. But it assumes there's some deep dark secret hidden in it – and I don't see where.'

'So,' Adam picked up another page, 'let's make a start with this little beauty.'

'There are three possibilities, aren't there?' Rachel said slowly, a frown forming as she did so. 'One: the clue is Samuel; two, the secret is hidden in the drawings; or, three, in the recipes themselves.'

219

Though the patchy typing did little for the recipes, the illustrations glowed with life: the cook bending down to offer a sprig of mint to a bright green cartoon pea; the butler's pantry with just one or two dishes on the dresser, as if just put there after the washing up; the oil lamp hanging outside an open door, waiting for the viewer to step into the unknown; and the paintings of the Windy Hill itself.

'Or perhaps all three are right,' Adam commented.

'Or any combination of two of them.'

'Or none at all.'

Rachel laughed. 'What powers of deduction. What a team we make.'

'That's fortunate. The answer isn't going to be presented on a plate borne by Alice herself. She's making us work for it.'

'She must surely have confided in someone. Mum perhaps; but if so why didn't she pass the secret on to me? Even if she had no family left beside Pops and Mum, she'd have had some kind of carer.'

'There was no carer relationship in those days.'

'By 1984 there must have been, even if it was called Social Services. But all her possessions and every trace of her have vanished. Nothing but a book left.'

'"To prove your blood and mine".'

Rachel gave him a puzzled glance.

'Line by Yeats, longing for his lost love,' Adam explained. 'Do you think that's what this is?' He pointed to the script.

'Do you mean her love for Samuel is recorded in this book?' Rachel offered innocently, then ducked as a cushion came flying her way.

'Forget Samuel,' Adam howled.

'How can I? Suppose he was the footman at Tolbury Hall, and that's why she left.'

'Harry, think Harry. Concentrate, Rachel. Suppose it's the pictures the message is hidden in. The tree on the flyleaf for instance. The pies at the seaside. Let's look at them as a whole not just one by one.'

'You mean they illustrate the love affair or they're hiding some kind of code, but they can't be.'

'Why not?'

220

'Because they're not specific enough.' Rachel frowned as she thought this through. 'They might illustrate Alice's story, but if Alice had wanted to leave a definite message, then using the pictures would be hard because the meaning would be different to different people. Take this hill picture, for example. Is it the blossom or the tree or the hillside that's important? This one has a caption, but even so the meaning can't be certain. And the picture of the two pies at the seaside: is it the pie, the sea or the promenade that she wants us to concentrate on? And Uriah Heep's Humble Pie. Does that have a message? If so, it isn't a clear one.'

'Point taken. So let's consider the recipes. Is there anything odd about them?'

'Not that I can see. I've been working with them long enough, converting them, using them. They're not easy, but I didn't pick up anything strange about them.' Rachel paused. Or was there something she was missing? *Why* weren't they easy to deal with? Even if they weren't, she couldn't define anything unusual about them.

'Suppose there's a code worked in with the wording?' she suggested. It all seemed very *Boys' Own*ish, but then, she realized, the 1920s and 1930s had been the age of *Boys' Own*: children's adventure, secret inks, and spies with black hats pulled down over their eyes were the thrills of the day.

'Who do you know who's a codebreaker?'

'No one.'

He sighed. 'It seems to me I should see my other Mycroft Holmes.'

'Who he?'

'John Foster. My esteemed uncle adores spies and in particular codes and cipher messages. When the Ultra secret was broken to the world in the 1970s he was thirty-odd and found another passion in life.'

'The Enigma machine?'

'No. My Aunt Joyce. Her mother had worked at Bletchley Park, and passed her fascination with cryptography on to her daughter. Joyce died five years ago, so don't appear too knowledgeable about codes in his presence. He may get a gleam in his matrimonial eye.'

'Nowhere. That's how far we got. We studied quaking pudding, tansy of rice, stewed cucumbers, everything from soups to savouries. Not the glimpse of a secret anywhere,' Rachel reported gloomily to Marjorie the next day.

'At least we can make use of them.' (Rachel had left a copy of some of the recipes with Marjorie to see what she could make of them for the Crandene commission.) 'I love the Mutton Kibobed. And Sir Samuel's Salamawhatsit. That's a must.'

'We can't call it after Sir Samuel. He's 1930s and not military.'

'We'll call it Victorian Salamawhatsit then. Why not? Alice probably developed it from a Victorian recipe. So if the script doesn't reveal Alice's dirty secret, where next?'

'Again nowhere.' Rachel grimaced. 'We haven't found *our* Samuel or even a pointer to him, and we can't crack the secret because we don't know where it lies. There's only the Crandene archives left and Adam's been through them already. I'd still like to see them though. Did you say you were going to Crandene again this week?'

'*We* are. We need to sort out the kitchen requirements with the good Mrs Tomkins, bless her little stale quiches. The stuff needs to be ordered in good time. I gather mid April is D Day for it. Can you make tomorrow? You're staying tonight, aren't you?'

'Yes. By the way, you were always keen on crossword puzzles, weren't you? Adam thinks we need a code enthusiast to help us. His uncle is keen, but for various reasons he doesn't want to go to him yet.'

'Crossword puzzles, yes, but not codes.' Marjorie grinned. 'I can help you though. Guess who knows everything about codes and ciphers from hieroglyphs to Enigma?'

'Who?' Rachel was already suspicious.

'My mother. She was a WAAF once and did some kind of intelligence work.'

Rachel groaned. 'A joke?'

'Far from it. Come on, don't be shy. We'll see her now.'

*

'A pile of recipes?' Julia looked disdainfully upon such mundane items, as Rachel, resigned to her fate, placed copies of the recipes before her.

'We're sure there's some kind of secret hidden in the text,' Rachel explained doggedly ignoring her irritation, 'and since the recipes themselves don't provide the answer we can only think it's in code.'

Julia sighed. 'Code or cipher. There *is* a difference. Is it important?' she asked languidly.

Very.' Rachel tried to look meek and hopeful.

A gleam came into Julia's eye. 'Well, of course, Rachel, if I can help in any humble way, I'd be only too glad to offer my cryptographic services.'

Rachel swallowed back the instinct to hit back. 'I'd be very grateful.'

Julia didn't even notice her humility, she was already engrossed in studying the recipes. 'I need to know the purpose of this code or cipher. What did the encrypter intend? If it's a cipher there would have to be an independent key. How many people would this be known to? Just one or more?' When Rachel looked blank, Julia's voice grew impatient as well as imperious. '*Why* did she encrypt her message?'

'I don't know,' Rachel was forced to confess.

Julia heaved another deep sigh. 'Think, if you please.'

Rachel did her best to oblige. 'My great-aunt didn't want the script published,' she explained, 'so that would imply that it was meant for one other person only, but also that if it *were* published it's possible more than one person could spot the code – or cipher,' she quickly amended.

'That is reasonably logical.' Praise from Julia was praise indeed. 'Why go to all the trouble of encrypting something so loosely that any Tom, Dick or Harry might decrypt it?'

'I don't know,' Rachel repeated helplessly.

'I do,' Julia announced with relish. 'Blackmail, or the threat of it. Now we don't have the key, but it should be simple, given your reasoning, to work out what it is.'

Rachel edged out after Marjorie. No audience was required now. Her mother would be happy for days, Marjorie assured her.

'Even Crandene doesn't seem so much of a lions' den after your mother,' Rachel remarked.

'That's what's given me my fearless nature.'

At last the Crandene archives room. It sounded so grand, but in fact was little more than an overspill library on the top floor with cupboards and filing cabinets to hold the records. It was also provided with a zealous assistant who leaped to her feet to obey Rachel's slightest wish, and even though she would have preferred to poke around for herself, Rachel had no reason to think that anything was being withheld from her. On the contrary, she was beginning to feel a very small figure against the account books, files and books piled high on the table before her.

Adam had mentioned a servants' record book, and she had asked for that. Adam had been following up the Harry Rolfe story, she reasoned, and as she was concentrating on Alice, she might possibly pick up something new. There was even, to her surprise, an Alice Beavers file, offered willingly by the assistant. It was stuffed with papers to do with property coming back and forth from Church Cottage. There was also a copy of Alice's will, and the details of funeral expenses. She found it interesting that the Beavers family had paid for that. Obviously they were keen to be seen as dutiful. There was a clipping from a local paper about the funeral, a church service followed by the cremation, and a list of mourners was given. Amongst them Rachel was interested to see a Mrs J Parsons. *Joan* Parsons, she wondered? Odd, because she'd had the impression – no, had been *given* the impression that Joan Parsons didn't know Alice. She had bought the house two years after her death, she had told Rachel. There might be something to check out there. Perhaps she was missing something.

Rachel continued reading through the files and eventually found the servant record book that had so excited Adam. On the assumption he might have stopped at Harry's death, she continued further – and was rewarded. In late 1916 Alice Carter, kitchenmaid, was dismissed for immorality.

Immorality? All sorts of bells began to ring in Rachel's head then. Immorality probably only meant one thing. Alice had been pregnant. So simple; the answer had been there all the time. And surely, surely, it explained everything? She felt like dancing her way down the stairs out to the restaurant to share her glee with Marjorie. It explained why at last Alice had married Robert Beavers: to legitimize her son. Suppose George was actually Alice's son and not Cecilia's? It would all add up. No, it wouldn't, she reluctantly realized, because Alice went to work in Lincolnshire presumably with the son (or daughter). Or had she brought him back to Crandene and left him here, after Cecilia had married Robert? No, that was highly unlikely. All sorts of tongues would have wagged at the difference between a newborn baby and a five-year-old boy. Perhaps there had been an earlier wedding between Alice and Beavers? Was that what the Beaverses were worried about? Did Robert marry bigamously? She couldn't believe that. If he had, of course, any son borne by Alice would then have been the legitimate heir. That might indeed set his Beavership running about on hot bricks. More food for thought.

February 1950

It was one o'clock in the morning. Alice woke instantly at the tap on their locked adjacent door, seized her dressing gown and hurried to open it. This had never happened before, and must therefore be urgent.

'Robert?' She was aghast at his ashen face.

'Can I come in, Alice?'

'Of course. The result has come through then.'

'Another Labour government.'

'But that makes no difference to your position in the Lords.'

'Four and a half years of enduring Attlee, and now it looks as if he'll get in again. It's over for me, Alice. I can't wait five more years in the hope of another Cabinet position, and I've no interest in sitting on my hind quarters in the Lords yapping to brick walls.'

She hadn't expected this. At the 1945 election Winston Churchill had been thrown out of office, after all he had done for the nation during the war, and a Labour government under

Clement Attlee had taken over. The Bank Manager, Robert called him. Robert had decided to sit it out in the House of Lords for the one parliament, convinced that Labour would never stay the course of government. Now it appeared it had, and it would be a cruel blow to Robert.

'Sleep on it, Robert.'

'Very well, but I don't see much prospect for the future. My time is over.'

'You've many years of work before you yet, Robert. Look how long Gladstone went on, and Lord Salisbury. And you're only fifty-seven.'

'No, I'm finished in politics. If they don't want Churchill, they certainly don't want me.'

'We'll talk tomorrow, Robert. You might feel differently then.'

He left, reluctantly she felt. She took a step as if to follow him, but stopped herself. Better they talk tomorrow.

The next morning he confided in her. 'It's Crandene, Alice. I feel I've failed it.'

Strange how Robert seemed only truly relaxed when he was out in the Crandene grounds, no matter what the weather. In February even Crandene looked bleak, bedraggled by earlier snow and ice, and with no signs yet of spring to give life to the gardens.

'How can you say that? A politician's life is always up and down. Crandene remains here as your strength to help you through the bad times.'

'Ah, but one has to give to it, as well as take. And what have I done for Crandene?'

She was silent for a moment. 'You have loved it, Robert.'

'Coming from you, I can believe that,' he said gratefully. 'You wouldn't lie. Yet you've done more for it. You've tended it, kept it going throughout the war. You have loved it too.'

Have I, she wondered? Or have I done only what I had to as my duty? Or are duty and love the same? She thought not. She could never love Crandene so possessively as its owners had over the years. 'I'm only a caretaker,' she said truthfully.

'Is that all? Don't you love it? What *do* you love, Alice?

226

It's not me, it's not Crandene, you say. Nor your kitchens. So what is it?'

'I love my hill.' She was amazed and furious with herself for involuntarily speaking of it to Robert of all people.

'Hill? What hill?'

She had spoken now, and must force herself to continue. 'That hill, Robert.' She pointed to the horizon, where the hill peeped over the walls of the vegetable garden. 'Harry Rolfe's hill and mine.' Only the bare branches of the trees were visible on the hillside now, and they only faintly. 'We used to go there together. It was our hill.'

There was an awkward silence. 'I can do nothing about it, Alice,' he said at last. 'If I could, I would. For all you have done for me.'

She was jolted out of her past. 'For Crandene, Robert,' she whipped back. Never for him.

'For me,' he maintained. 'You've been at my side, Alice. A rock. Unyielding, hard, but there. Did you not realize that rocks have their place in life?'

'No,' she whispered. 'I did not.' How could she say she had not intended to help him in any way, save in keeping Crandene going? That she had intended to be a constant and painful thorn every day, but now he was saying he depended on her. How was it possible that the situation had become so turned around? How had this happened out of what had sprung from hatred? Surely she still hated him? She had not considered it for so long, she tried to welcome the idea as an old companion, but now it meant nothing.

'What will you do now?' The words fell from her lips. 'Will you not even sit in the House any more?'

'I shall leave politics.'

'For what? The business world?'

'I don't know. Crandene needs me. Crandene also needs money unfortunately. We are not rich, Alice. The war has taken our income in tax. I could sell, of course.'

'Sell Crandene?' Alice gazed at him in shock. 'Some of the houses and the grounds perhaps. But Crandene itself – Robert, you cannot.'

227

'Why not? Many such houses have been sold as hospitals or schools or hotels.'

'Not Crandene,' she repeated. 'Robert, you must fight for it. You love it, I know you do.'

'What use is love, Alice? It comes to nothing, it achieves nothing. I loved you. You know I did, albeit in my own bloody stupid way. I still do love you. But one has to face facts that love does not beget love, nor does it pay bills.'

Dear God, what should she say? Her emotions, even hatred, had, she now realized, died years ago. She was stuck on a flat plain from which she had no reply for him. For once, she could not deal with the situation, no longer mistress of her spider's web.

She could only express her emotions through Crandene. 'You can't sell Crandene itself,' she repeated. 'We'll fight for it. We have to. Together we can do it.'

'Together? A poor togetherness of a marriage.'

'Not poor,' she said shakily. 'A rich together. We have Crandene. We must make it work.'

'The estate, you mean. Make it pay for itself?' She saw a glimmer of response, a flicker of interest, even of hope. 'Alice, what would you think about opening the house to the public? I'd need your help. It wouldn't make a lot of money but if we sold off some of the land and houses and had a restaurant here as well – now that's an idea. You'd like that. It would mean hard work, though . . .'

'We could manage it, Robert, I'm sure.' Alice felt suddenly eager. It was something new. They would not, as so many of their friends were doing, merely be trying to pick up the pieces of their previous existence. But she realized there was another factor they must consider. 'There is George to think about. He is your heir . . .'

'George is too young to be tied here, and only recently married. He deserves a time apart from the burden of Crandene. Let's make a heritage for him here. What do you think, eh?'

'Robert, I believe . . .'

'What, Alice? Tell me it's yes.'

'I believe you are a truly brave man. Braver than your father.' She could see the instant doubt in his eyes. He didn't

228

believe her. He thought she was trying to please him, over this of all issues. Never. She spoke the truth.

'The Gate of Swat?' he reminded her ironically.

'That was a moment of instant bravery on your father's part. You're being brave for the rest of your life. Think about it.'

He fought his emotions for a moment. 'Do you think that if one moment is lost to evil, any bravery can ever wipe it out?'

'One can go on, Robert – and that takes courage.'

Some days later, he spoke to her after dinner in the drawing room. Again this was unusual. If they were both there together, usually they were each occupied with their own affairs. Life was changing, however, and now they had matters to discuss.

'I have a present for you, Alice,' Robert said diffidently.

'For me? But the cost—'

'Let us see it as a symbol of our going forward together.'

He placed a large cardboard box before her, in which she found two packages rolled up carefully in tissue paper. She unwrapped the first with care, and found a china figurine within it. It was a dainty figure of a girl in a mob cap with broom, pink print dress and black shawl.

'It's called *The Kitchenmaid*,' he said gruffly. 'Eighteenth century. From the Woods family; one of their early figures with enamel overglaze.'

'Robert, it's lovely. Staffordshire, isn't it?' Alice laughed. 'How amused Monsieur Trente would be to see this.'

'Who was he?'

'Don't you remember? He was the French cook here for many years. He was a good friend to me.'

'Yes, I think I do. Moustache and droopy eyes.'

'Thank you, Robert. This will remind me of those days.'

'The other one, Alice, open that.'

She unrolled it carefully to find another Staffordshire figure. A soldier, no, a mere boy, but in uniform and with a harp slung over one shoulder. *'The Minstrel Boy,'* she whispered. She looked up at him, realizing why he had chosen it.

Robert's lips quivered. 'Nineteenth century this one, but rare and first from the mould.' A silence, then: 'He was

229

always chirpy, Alice. Always singing, or playing that flute of his. Somehow it reminded me of him. You don't mind, do you? Bit of a risk.'

She held Harry in her hands. Robert had given him back to her, as best he could. She could not see the figure much longer for the tears that blurred her eyes. 'No, I don't mind,' she managed to say.

He sat down at her side. 'There, there, old girl,' he said awkwardly, putting his arm round her. She let it stay there, for she had not the strength – or the desire – to resist it.

~

'Joan Parsons,' Rachel exclaimed triumphantly, as she related the previous day's experience to Adam on her return to Kent. 'I'm sure there's more to be found out there. And I think Robert Beavers seduced her. Alice, I mean. Not Joan Parsons.'

'Proof. You've no proof,' Adam jeered.

'You need a thesis before proof,' Rachel pointed out.

'What happened to Alice's child if she were pregnant? Stillborn, miscarriage?'

'Pops!' she whispered, as it suddenly came to her that there had been another child born around that time. 'Suppose Pops is really the heir to Crandene, the child of Alice and Robert. That makes me, if I, no, they, were legitimate—'

'Rachel, sit down. Did I ever tell you your eyes are like the fishpools in Heshbon?'

'No, but—'

'Or "thy belly like a heap of wheat set about with lilies"?'

'No, but, Adam, you must—'

'Or that "thy breasts are like two young roes that are twins"?' He began to caress them.

'Tell me again later,' she murmured.

The later was several hours, but Rachel eventually asked lazily, 'What were you quoting from? Or were you making it up? It seemed familiar.'

'All quite proper. It's in the Bible. The Song of Solomon.'

'Well, Solomon, you did pretty well in making me feel like the Queen of Sheba.' Something familiar there too, she

230

suddenly thought. Sheba . . . ? 'Sheba!' she shouted, with the memory coming back.

'What about her, O Lady Queen?'

'She was in the script. At the end, there was a quotation from Ruskin. Don't you remember? Something about needing the knowledge of the Queen of Sheba to be a cook.'

'Bathsheba maybe. I don't see the Queen of Sheba muddying her hands with sheeps' eyes and kebabs.'

'Nor Bathsheba either. She was a floozie. *Adam!*'

She leaped out of bed, and rushed to his bookshelf.

'Rachel, what are you doing?'

'Looking for a Bible.'

'Have you repented of me?'

'A Bible, a Bible, I need a *Bible*,' she shouted.

'There should be one in the living-room bookcase. Third shelf, right-hand end.'

She ran into the living room, hunting for it, failing to find it, and tracking it down in the middle of the sixth shelf. She hurried back and perched on the bed at his side. 'Samuel,' she crowed.

'Samuel? Oh, *Samuel*.' Adam seized the Bible from her and began riffling through the pages. 'What was the reference?'

'To Samuel, remembering November 15th.'

'Well that's a problem for a start. No such calendar in those days. Even the Babylonians were only just thinking out time.'

'But it must be a cryptic reference. Like the Armistice, the eleventh day of the eleventh month.'

'That's not very cryptic. I see what you mean though. The eleventh chapter. Or the fifteenth chapter.'

'And the fifteenth verse, or the eleventh. Oh do hurry up, Adam.'

'There are two books of Samuel.'

'Try both. Probably the second book though. The "To" in the dedication would cover that.'

'Clever.'

'Sex sharpens the brain,' she laughed.

'Good, we'll do it again sometime.'

She grabbed the Bible from him again. 'You're taking much

too long. Look, here it is. The fifteenth verse of the eleventh chapter. Oh, Adam, just look. "And he wrote in the letter, saying, Set ye Uriah in the forefront of the hottest battle and retire ye from him that he may be smitten and die."'

'Uriah the Hittite, well well,' Adam said slowly. 'If I remember right, the lady Bathsheba was married to Uriah, who never left her alone with another man. So King David was never able to gratify his desires – except by getting rid of Uriah.'

'But who's Uriah?' Rachel asked. 'Surely not Peasbody.'

'Forget Peasbody, woman. This must be Harry Rolfe she's referring to. And suppose King David is none other than our friend Robert Beavers?'

Sixteen

'My dear Rachel, you can hardly blame me.' Julia's feathers were ruffled, but try as she might Rachel could see no way of unruffling them. She hadn't been blaming Julia, merely asking if there had been any progress. With the dedication at last understood, if there was a further message concealed in the recipes she was impatient to know what it was. Mid April, the date when John Foster would be completing his sponsorship payments, was only six weeks away. 'These things take time.'

'I realize it's a tough problem and of course there may be nothing hidden there at all . . .'

A sigh of exasperation. 'This lady seems to have gone to a great deal of trouble merely for the sake of a few recipes,' Julia remarked icily.

'I'm certain there is something else there.'

'Why?' The word whipped out challengingly. 'Because you want there to be? That, Rachel, is unsound logic.'

'No. Because everyone has gone to a great deal of trouble to prevent the contents of the script from becoming public.'

'No doubt from a mere motive of family rivalries.'

'There's no sign of that. And sometimes I think there is something odd about the script too, but I can't put my finger on just what it is.'

'Then I suggest you put it there immediately, Rachel.'

It was a command from the headmistress, and once more Rachel tried her best to track down just what had been unusual in Alice's work. 'It was while I was converting some of the recipes to modern use.'

'But *what* was odd? Just pursue your thoughts to the end. Take one of the recipes that you were studying and look at it.'

Rachel obediently thought of a recipe and turned to it. 'Apple mousse with orangeflower water,' she suggested.

'Does anything strike you as strange about it now? How do you go about converting these recipes?'

'First I look at the ingredients to ensure that they're all available today. Then I study the quantities and adapt them to modern tastes. Cream, for instance, is there an alternative? Or anything too laden with eggs. This recipe has three which isn't too bad, but—' Rachel stopped short. 'That's it,' she cried.

'Eggs? What's so strange about them?'

'Lists of ingredients tend to run in the order one uses them in the recipe. In other words one wouldn't begin a list with a pinch of cinnamon. Yet look at this recipe. It begins with the eggs, which are only used after the apples and sugar. And—' in curiosity Rachel turned to one of the other recipes – 'here, in the tomato soup recipe, the anchovies begin the list although only one or two are needed for deepening the flavour.'

'Could that not be put down to carelessness or the fact that this is a draft script?'

'I don't think anything Alice did over this was careless, nor was it a draft. The illustrations being originals prove that.'

Julia sniffed. 'Perhaps not. Nevertheless the moment an amateur sets out to encrypt something, confusion reigns. I do wish they would leave it to us professionals.'

'But how could eggs and anchovies be a code? You mean that perhaps the first letters of the first word in each list of ingredients add up to a message?' Eagerly Rachel seized a page of the script and read out, 'BBSHW. That doesn't work. Or perhaps the first letters of every ingredient in the list. No. That doesn't work either.'

'Amateurs,' Julia snorted. 'Leave it with me. I think you'll find the answer is something quite simple. Probably it is merely a code.'

Quite simple or not, it took three days before Marjorie rang in despair, demanding Rachel's and even Adam's presence if it brought Rachel over more speedily. Her mother had scarcely appeared from her room, save for silent meals, and Marjorie was, amazingly, feeling lonely.

'Is that Rachel?' Julia's stentorian tones rang out as soon as she walked through the door.

'Prepare to meet thy doom,' Rachel whispered to Adam, as she opened the door with a smile carefully arranged on her face.

Julia was surrounded by stacks of paper and card indexes, with her computer screen poised for instant action, and two large empty grids before her on an easel. 'I believe I have found the basis of this problem.'

'You have?' Rachel flung her arms round Julia's neck, who seemed somewhat flustered at this mode of thanks.

'I've hardly solved it, Rachel. There is no need for such emotion. I am, I believe, on the track. It is a substitution cipher, the simplest of all, but I had to admit for an amateur it is quite cleverly done. It's not the initial letters but the ingredients themselves that form the cipher.'

'How?' It sounded double Dutch to Rachel.

'I believe the encrypter, your great-aunt,' Julia added, as if Rachel might be in doubt, 'has taken the basic ingredients of the recipes, and that each recipe contributes one letter to the message she wished to convey. And, incidentally, who is this young man?'

'I'm sorry. Julia, this is Adam Paynter. Adam, Marjorie's mother, Julia Thomas.'

Adam obliged with a charming bow, which took Julia aback even more than Rachel's welcome, and impressed Rachel herself. No wonder he was a wow at Never Alone.

'What is the message then?' Adam asked eagerly.

'Do you play chess, Mr Paynter?' Julia asked in irritation. 'No.'

'I thought not. Patience is required for chess, and clearly you do not possess that quality. It is also required for cipher work, such as this. My initial cryptanalytic attack suggests each of the first ingredients stands for a letter of the alphabet, not for an entire word. The trick is to work out the key, in other words, which letters they represent. There are well over two hundred recipes here, and it might turn out that not all of them contribute to our puzzle.'

'So how might we proceed?' Rachel caught herself imitating

Julia's stately manner and tried not to look at Adam, in case she giggled.

'I suggest you list for me the first ingredients of each recipe; a hit and miss procedure, but it may suffice for the moment. Then let us assume that your ancestor's message follows the normal pattern of English, in other words, that E is the most common letter of the alphabet. From the ingredients you have listed, we can then work out provisionally what might stand for E.'

'What letter is most common after E?'

'Frequency tables show the vowels A, I and O will also be high. Also, T, N, S, R and H.'

Grateful that her task was at least straightforward, Rachel dictated with Adam doing the listings. 'Suppose the letters, once decrypted, aren't in consecutive order?' he asked.

'I believe they would be,' Julia announced loftily. 'Bear in mind Alice Carter was not a professional and that we are working on the assumption that she wanted it to be relatively simple to decrypt even without the key. It might be that it is the first two ingredients, of course, or even three, rather than the first one alone. However, let us begin with just one.'

'The majority of these recipes start with an odd ingredient.' Rachel had been checking. 'And of course some of them might start with the expected ingredient, and still contribute.'

'Now you're beginning to think logically,' Julia said approvingly.

'Hey,' Adam interrupted. 'I've got forty-nine recipes beginning with salt. Eggs come next, with thirty-three. Then cream with twenty-four.'

'Then let us consider that salt beginning a recipe represents E.' With great ceremony Julia pencilled 'salt' under the E in the first row of grid headings. 'Our first recipe with salt is the third in the soups section, carrot and orange. Does anything occur to you that we have not considered, however?'

Rachel froze inside, transported back to schooldays, but Adam shot to the rescue. 'Spaces. We're not allowing for those.'

Julia wore her knowing, superior smile. 'Quite. Either they have been ignored, or, if we are unlucky, an irrelevant recipe

236

has been put in to signify a space, or more probably salt represents a space.'

'You'd worked that out already, hadn't you?' Rachel said crossly.

'I merely use my eyes, Rachel. It might not be such a safe method as a nose for a cook, but for a cryptanalyst it most certainly is a help. As I was taught in my childhood, I looks and I looks, and then I sees. And do you know what I saw?'

Rachel looked at the first recipes again and this time it leaped out at her 'There's a typed asterisk underneath salt and pepper where they begin a list of ingredients.'

'Yes, indeed. Salt and pepper could stand for letters of the alphabet, but it is a fair assumption that they each mark a space. Some lists are headed salt and pepper, some pepper and salt. What would the difference between the two be? There are merely a few initial peppers, and far more salts.'

'Punctuation,' Adam chipped in. 'One of them represents the full stops, the other, presumably salt, the space between words.'

'We can at least march on with this as a thesis,' Julia said approvingly.

'What about the desserts?' asked Rachel innocently. 'Not much salt in the recipes.'

'Damnation.' Julia flushed as though guilty of major blasphemy. 'How very vexatious.'

'It might not be.' Rachel was flipping through the pudding recipes. 'Suppose one took another more or less staple ingredient; sugar, for example.' Excited, she whipped through them. 'There are quite a few here with sugar at the top *and* there's an asterisk under it.'

'And the full stop would be?'

'I don't know. There aren't that many puddings. Yes – how about isinglass? Another asterisk.'

'What?' Adam asked blankly.

'The Victorian form of gelatine, made from some part of a fish I've forgotten. It only went out in the twentieth century, and gelatine came in. So where do we go next, Julia?' Rachel was conscious of being pulled in two directions: eagerness to find out more now that they were on the point of getting so

237

near to Alice, combined with an odd reluctance. Alice was her great-aunt, her past; suppose the final revelation of her life story brought her not closer to Alice, but further away?

'We shall try eggs,' Julia announced, having busied herself with pencilling in crosses on the grid to indicate spaces, and a circle with a dot in it for a full stop. 'Which is the first recipe to use eggs as a first ingredient?'

'Recipe nineteen,' Adam said promptly. 'Game soup.'

'So we may tentatively place an E in square nineteen.' Julia moved purposefully to the grid. 'And the next?'

'Twenty-five. Fennel soup.'

'Splendid.' Julia worked her way through the remaining thirty-one possible Es. 'In the puddings section we have a word of one letter, for which the relevant recipe begins with butter, which now becomes another starting point.'

'Representing I,' said Adam. 'It has to be.'

'Or A,' Rachel pointed out.

'Well done, Rachel. A professional is nervous of certainties,' Julia said somewhat patronizingly. 'So butter equals I or A. Another space on our chart. Well done. Adam, now tell me the number of butters that begin lists of ingredients, if you please.'

'Twenty,' he announced.

'Mark them if you please on our chart. Pencil in both I and A, nothing more.' Julia was clearly in her element now. Rachel stole a glance at Marjorie, who had crept in to say that lunch was ready, not sure whether she'd be glad Julia was so involved, or furious at the disruption to work. She *looked* quite equable about it.

'Now let us take another cryptographic line of attack. Let us consider the remaining ingredients after deducting butter and eggs.'

Once they'd made a list of twenty-four letters, Rachel dared to propose the next stage: 'The first word could be as, at, am, an.'

'Or it, in, is, if,' Adam meanly pointed out.

Rachel groaned, and Julia intervened. 'Let us take the remaining two-letter words, of which there are a further eight. One of them, we are presuming, ends in E. What therefore might the other letter be?'

238

'M,' Rachel said promptly. 'Or H.'

'Or B. That is just possible, as is R. However let us plump for a provisional M or H. Now look at this second word according to our provisional space division. It has four letters, two of which we believe might be H or M, the first and the last. So this presumes the second letter must be a vowel, and the relevant recipe ingredient is butter, agreed to be I or A. With A we could therefore have hash or hath, or at a pinch marm, but the first word of our message has a different ingredient key. The first recipe begins with cheese. If butter represents A, then cheese is I. In hath, in hash, for instance. However, if butter is I, then—'

'I can tell you what the first two words are,' Rachel broke in quietly. 'At High, which we'll find is followed by Wood.' And as Julia looked blank, she added, 'The Somme.'

Today might crack it, Rachel thought hopefully; they had been hard at work on it for three days and her head was reeling. They were down to only a few letters still to sort out, and with each one their task became easier.

Julia called Marjorie in as she was about to write the last letters on to the grid. Rachel was touched by this. It showed a human side of Julia she had scarcely suspected, that she wanted her daughter to witness her triumph. And triumph it was as they all four stood round the grid and Julia slowly read Alice Carter's message.

> At High Wood on the Somme in July nineteen sixteen Robert Beavers knowingly sent Harry Rolfe to certain death by withholding information because Harry was my sweetheart. Discovering that Harry was still alive though wounded he went out to find him and shot him. Of this I have proof. Alice Carter. Nineteen twenty-nine.

'For which act of bravery Robert Beavers was awarded the VC,' said Adam quietly.

Why had she assumed the breaking of the cipher would solve everything? Rachel wondered. She, Marjorie, Adam – and as a courtesy Julia – had spent the entire evening discussing how this might affect the Crandene commission, but Rachel was well aware that the deeper problem was over the For Valour exhibition itself. Her work on Alice's own story would have to wait until that was settled.

'Evidence,' Adam said gloomily, as they went to bed that night. 'What real evidence do we have?'

'I knew you were going to ask that, and the answer's none.'

'Alice obviously had some. What do you imagine it was?'

'There was nothing else in the papers, nor that secret pocket. Alice must have destroyed it.'

'Then why not the script too? I can't go to John with what we have. It's not enough.'

'Not enough?' Rachel echoed. 'Surely it must cast more than doubt in his mind, and since the script confirmed the rumours you heard were flying around, that's some kind of proof in itself.'

She caught sight of his flushed face and realized this wasn't about Alice at all. 'It's about you, isn't it?' she asked quietly. 'You don't want to go back to argue the toss with your uncle. You'd rather walk away.'

'Not how I'd put it.'

'On to the next thing, never backwards. You admitted that much to me.'

'Did I?'

He had retreated into the distance again, but she wasn't having that. This was a bedroom, the room where above all others distance must play no part.

'Until you look back at Annie and say that's over, we can't go forward, Adam.'

'Leave Annie out of it, please.'

'I can't. You can't. Annie, your uncle, they're the same. Sort it out, understand it, and then go forward.'

'Now who's the physician in need of healing, who preferred being alone to committing?'

He didn't throw this at her in anger, but sadly. The barrier between them was put there by both of them, and Rachel had no answer for him. There had to be one, however, and she would find it, she vowed, as they lay silently – and apart – in bed.

*

'I can't do it, Rachel.' Adam was adamant that he wasn't going to tackle his uncle again. All Alice's careful work had gone for nothing. All this build-up, only to see Lord Beavers triumph after all. Rachel knew there'd be no point trying to persuade him. The most she could do was hope that even now, in the month before the mid April deadline on the second payment, something new would emerge. He was at least willing to talk that over. She was busy helping Marjorie organize a retirement party for a local businessman, and Adam decided to wait till the end of the day so that they could return together to Kent. Her actual role this morning was making coronation chicken, while Marjorie prepared other salads, but Adam still wanted to talk about Alice. A good sign? she wondered. Perhaps.

'Even though what we've got might shake my uncle,' Adam said, 'it's not sufficient to make him back out of the Crandene deal. Alice presumably was intending to publish it and then spread the word around that there was a nice little puzzle attached, so proof wasn't so important to her. It was the gossip factor she would have been after.'

'Can one blame her?'

'No. Revenge, they say, is a dish best eaten cold.'

'More than cold in this case. Icy.' Rachel had her own problems with Alice's script. It had lost some of its charm when its purpose became clear. She had been presented not just with a timid ex-kitchenmaid as an ancestor, but with a hard, self-serving blackmailer – for surely that is what it was. She must have held it over Robert's head as a threat if he did not marry her. Two Alices. Both her ancestors, yet they did not tie up. Nothing connected them either to each other, or to her.

'Remember Robert Beavers won his VC for going out to fetch the wounded,' Adam said. 'He had the option of turning the award down but he didn't, and so Alice must have intended he should remember his actions every day of his life. She planned to write too difficult a cipher to decrypt without a hint from its author that it existed, and yet there would always be the "suppose" in Beavers' mind if it were published. Clever. The interesting thing is why Alice wanted to marry him, though.'

241

'Michael Hartshorn thinks it was because she was an ambitious harpy.'

'So did she just give up the Harry script for him to destroy in return for a comfortable life?'

'That doesn't fit with Pops' image of her.' Rachel hesitated. 'Alice didn't know that Cecilia Beavers was going to die – but after her death, perhaps she saw a way of making Robert remember Harry at even closer quarters. She didn't care about the world knowing, she wanted him to know that she was aware of what he'd done. What better way of ensuring that than to marry him? They'd be in holy gridlock.'

'Good thesis, but think what it must have done to her life.'

'She must have discovered the truth through Corporal Peasbody, but the evidence . . .'

'Is gone with the wind. Or with her death. You're really sure there was nothing left amongst her papers?'

'If there was it has gone. But I really don't think so, because in all probability it would have been with the script. Adam, just think of it, her youth spent mourning Harry's loss, only to find out that he had deliberately been sent to his death.'

'Balance it with remembering it was wartime. Suppose Peasbody made a genuine mistake in the kerfuffle?'

'But Alice believed the evidence he showed her, and he must have given it to her.'

'What would Alice and Peasbody consider as evidence though, that's the question? I bet it's one your chum Unicorn would like to debate till kingdom come.'

Marjorie came rushing in with a bowl of rice salad. 'A Michael Hartshorn wants to see you, Rachel.'

'The strong arm of coincidence,' Adam called after her as an astonished Rachel hurried out to the main house to greet him.

'What on earth are you doing here?' she asked.

'I tracked down where you were – or rather where Adam Paynter was – through Never Alone. I gave up on trying to track you down, so I assumed that where he was there would be a good chance of finding you.'

'I haven't been answering my mobile recently. We've had a lot on our minds,' she said defensively. Should she tell him about the script? 'Come in,' she finished brightly.

He glanced round their working surfaces. 'Can I take you to lunch?'

'Fine. Adam's here too so we'll keep it dutch, but thanks anyway.'

'Adam ought to be in on this,' Michael said. 'He, or rather his uncle, is affected by what I've come to tell you.' Curiouser and curiouser.

Could this possibly be *evidence*? She watched impatiently as Adam and Michael mentally prowled round, sizing each other up. She nursed a fantasy that this mutual guardedness was because of her, but she sensed that Crandene was a more contentious subject than she was at present.

The village pub wasn't crowded and they were able to get a table where they could talk in relative privacy. While Adam bought drinks, Michael said to her awkwardly, 'This isn't easy. You'll remember your earlier comments on my being a historian or otherwise?'

'I'm afraid I do.'

'They stung me, to say the least. But they made me look again at what I was doing. I don't like having to admit that, but it's the truth.'

'Your Crandene book must be passed for press by now, and due for publication.' She had been going on to say that she realized how hard this was for him, but he interrupted.

'It'll be out in May. And I want to explain that my conscience is clear on the use of such material as I had when I wrote the book. But there was always a niggle at the back of my mind. There usually is, of course, it's the name of the game, but this one lingered.'

'A niggle over what? Robert's VC?'

'No. Not then at least. It was only about a line of enquiry I had never followed up. There had seemed no point, but after what you so expressively hurled at me I decided I would. It wasn't easy, believe me, with a book just passed for press. I went to the Imperial War Museum, and saw the keeper of the manuscripts department. My niggle was that someone had told me years ago that old Peasbody had written his memoirs while he was in the home or asylum, whatever it was. Knowing his mental state I'd discounted them, but I decided I should

243

have a quick look to check. Old soldiers who can't get their scripts published often bequeath them to the museum to store for historians to read. Some of them are invaluable, and most of them provide an interesting snippet or two.'

'So what did Peasbody's say?'

'I've got it verbatim for you on my laptop, and brought you a copy. Not the whole lot, of course, just what he had to say about the 22nd July 1916. Briefly his story was that he had brought a message to Robert Beavers from Battalion HQ that the Gordon Highlanders had been more or less wiped out in High Wood and that the German strongpoint was still intact there.'

'So what's new about that?' Adam plonked a drink before Michael and sat down to listen.

'Nothing. Except that it's gone down in history that whatever the battalion CO's suspicions might have been that there were German machine guns trained on them from that wood, higher authority said it was clear. It was a mere safety precaution that a platoon was sent to confirm it. According to Peasbody, Robert then got the information but didn't act on it. Our corporal couldn't believe it when only the platoon of C Company already detailed was sent in against it. And worse, it was his platoon. That meant his best mate Harry Rolfe would be in it too. They had precious little time to mull it over. Peasbody told Harry what was happening, and how he couldn't make out why the message wasn't acted on. There were, to be fair, a lot of crazy orders in those days, and there was nothing they could do about it. Harry went very white apparently, and then he said, making a joke of it to Peasbody, "Look here, Jacob. I shall be a goner you know." Peasbody replied, "Don't be so daft, don't talk that way. We'll both come through it." But Harry said, no he wouldn't. Robert Beavers wanted him dead because he was jealous of his girl back home, and this was his way of doing it. Peasbody pooh-poohed it, but Harry scribbled a few lines on the top of a page torn out of his pocket bible, and gave it to him. "There," he said, "give that to Alice if you get back, and make sure you do, old chap. You'll find her at Crandene." He gave Jacob his picture of Alice too, so she would know the message

244

was genuine. Well, the platoon did go in and most of it perished.

'A few survived the fire, including Peasbody – and Harry himself, though he was wounded. Peasbody managed to drag Harry into a shellhole for cover, then got back to his company front line. He said he wasn't waiting for the official stretcher bearers, he was going back for the wounded. Robert Beavers said he was coming too. Peasbody wrote that Beavers was like a madman. Crazy with fear, he said, yet he went out with him, telling Peasbody to bring in one wounded soldier while he would bring Harry. Peasbody glanced over his shoulder though and swears he saw Beavers with his gun pointing down into the shellhole. There was so much noise going on he wouldn't have heard the shot, he said, but when Beavers brought Harry back, he saw him then, and he was dead. What's more, he saw a fresh gunshot wound bleeding. Robert ordered him out again; they both went out to bring back more wounded but Peasbody was crazy with anger by this time and was taken away delirious to the first aid dressing station.'

'It's the word of a crazy man; one can't place trust in it,' Adam said.

'Alice did,' she said swiftly.

'What more evidence is there that this story's true?' Adam shot at Michael.

'Peabody wasn't altogether crazy when he wrote his memoirs. He listed sources at the back of the script.'

Rachel caught her breath. 'That's Alice's evidence?'

'It could be based on that list. He wrote that he spent ten years tracing Alice Carter and by the time he found her, he'd collected more evidence on Robert Beavers. Another soldier who swore Harry only had a slight injury in the shellhole, and another one who overheard Peasbody giving the message to Robert. He'd even managed to trace the officer who sent it.'

'Any bullet could have hit Harry in the shellhole though,' Adam pointed out, to Rachel's indignation. He seemed far too anxious to look at the flaws in the argument – and again she knew why.

'True,' Michael said. 'And as for the telephone message, there's no proof that Robert ever received it other than

245

Peasbody's. However, Peasbody also found out after the war that Robert Beavers was sent on leave for some months after that, and he never rose to the highest army ranks.'

'Circumstantial and hearsay evidence,' Adam countered.

'Added together,' Michael said, 'I think it sheds a question mark over the VC.'

'If we had the evidence, it might,' Adam agreed.

Rachel didn't look at him, unable to believe Adam still would not commit himself over Peasbody's story. Why did she mind so much, she asked herself? *She* believed Alice's story and that was surely the most important thing. Or was it? If the story of the Beavers VC was never questioned, the For Valour show would go ahead, sponsored by John Foster, and the legend would become unassailable. The truth was something she owed the past, and how could she pay this debt without Adam's help?

'We do have some evidence, Michael. I have a copy of the whole script. It survived the fire.'

'I guessed as much.'

'Have you told Lord Beavers that?'

'No.' He looked at her. 'Believe me?'

'Yes.' This was between her and Michael, not Adam.

Seventeen

July 1969

It was too cruel. After all Robert had done to save Crandene and now that it was at last beginning to thrive, illness had him in its grip. He had had test after test after test, and all they could say as a result was that nothing could be done. Six months they had estimated, or perhaps a little longer, and three of those had already passed.

He was patient about it, so accepting. It was Alice who raged against fate. They were sitting on the terrace in the afternoon sun, as they so often did now. In the mornings, she would work in the restaurant and on the Crandene management, the afternoons she spent here with Robert. Four days a week the public would come, and on the other three Crandene was theirs to enjoy.

'Is there anything you would like to do, Robert?'

He clung to her hand, looking out over the gardens. He did this even on the public days, for it pleased him to watch the visitors come in. It had been hard work to set Crandene up in the best way for visitors, but finally they had chosen to present it as a house that was loved and lived in.

She'd had an argument with him over the paintings, however. He had not wished any portraits of himself to be hung, but she had insisted.

'You know very well what I feel,' he'd protested. 'I don't deserve the medal. Why hang my bloody portraits up?'

Only a few years earlier she would have agreed with him but not now. 'You have done so much, Robert. Look on this as one last obligation to Crandene. You say you don't deserve

247

the medal,' she forced herself to add, 'but the family of the other two soldiers whose lives you saved would disagree.' Only Harry, my Harry . . .

'It doesn't compensate. You can have your way if you wish, but I'm damned if I'll let them hang beside my father's and grandfather's. They've cursed me all my life.'

'Cursed you?' she asked surprised at his vehemence over mere pictures.

'The pressure to achieve so-called glory in battle. Do you think if I hadn't had to watch their eyes sneering down at me I would have gone into the army at all? Even if I'd been forced into the services I'd have chosen the navy or the air force, or intelligence. Anything but army.'

'You've had a good political career in a time of national emergency, and now you have Crandene.'

'But the wasted years. The blot—'

'We won't talk about that.'

'We have to,' he said more gently. 'I'll be dead soon, and you'll be alone. Before I go I need to tell you what it was like. He was there, all the time, reminding me of you. I liked him, Alice. I did. I could see why you loved him. But I couldn't have the life I wanted, and I couldn't have you. I was only a coward, however brave you claim I am now. Sheer funking terror, every time I had to go back to the front. And there was Harry, chirpy, scared maybe, but hiding it. I couldn't. I felt everyone must see it. And then came the big push at the Somme. I knew what lay ahead. When we arrived on the 19th July after leaving Arras we were in reserve next day, when the division first went in to attack High Wood. But we heard all about it. Nothing achieved, but heroes, my God, there were heroes that day. Sergeant Traill, for instance, kept going all day long. I couldn't do that, I kept thinking, I can't. I knew the chances of our getting to the Wood Lane trench, let alone Switch Trench, were virtually nil. And what was it for? We'd only be a few yards further forward. I was right. The whole Somme achieved nothing, save death and destruction. All the so-called Great War achieved was to lead to another world war, in which my son had to fight. You know why I sent Harry out in that platoon, Alice? Because I was certain I would die too,

I couldn't bear the thought that I'd be dead, and he wouldn't. That he'd be coming home to you.'

'And later, Robert, as he lay wounded?' This was the heart of it, the truth she could not understand even now.

'I was like a man possessed. I was still convinced I'd be dead before the attack was over. I knew it. So I went out with Peasbody to bring the wounded in. I needed to see how badly wounded Harry was. That's all. I wanted him to die, as I would die myself. If I died, and he was only wounded, he would survive and he would come back to you. I was going to shoot him, and then myself, but I shot him before I meant to, just to get rid of that grin. He was scared, he could see I was out of my wits, but he still grinned. We'd both go together, I reasoned, though you can't call it reasoning on a battlefield. Peasbody caught at my arm. "I'll help you sir, I'll help you get Harry back." But when he did and saw the fresh blood, he knew. We got Harry back but he was dead when we got there. Peasbody looked at me queerly, as though he'd seen me do it, but he couldn't have. He guessed, and he guessed right.'

It was another world, another age. All these years the stone in her heart had lain there, and then it had dissolved, almost without her noticing.

'Is there such a thing as atonement Alice? Even for what I did?' Robert asked.

'You have made it, Robert. Long ago.'

'The day you came at last to my bed.'

'Yes.' She stroked his hand. She had thought about that so much. If she truly forgave Robert, she then had a duty as a wife, and more than that he needed the love of a wife. As a result the last ten years had been her happiest since Harry died. This mature love was so far away from that youthful dream that it seemed to be happening to a different person.

'Would you do something for me, Alice, before I go?'

'Anything I can.'

'Today is the 22nd. I've been thinking about it a lot.'

'I too.' She always did. The anniversary.

'I would like, but you may not wish this, Alice – you must be truthful – I would like to walk with you up your hill. Harry's hill.'

249

How could she? She had not expected this challenge. It was her last bastion. She never went there now, but the hill was waiting for her. And so was Harry. How could she share the hill, least of all with the man who had taken him from her, even though that had been in another life and she had made her peace with him. Would Harry have wanted her to take him with her? No, she had to decide herself, and she made her choice quickly.

'Yes, Robert. Shall we go now? Are you strong enough?'

He did not answer, but rose with difficulty out of his chair, and taking her arm they set off through the gardens, past the vegetable garden to which she had come as a kitchenmaid. He paused there. 'Alice, I'd like to see the pets once again.'

'If you feel strong enough, Robert.' She knew he meant the pets' cemetery tucked away behind the vegetable garden.

She had thought he would go to see Spot's grave first, but he didn't.

'"My cat Jeoffrey,"' he read out. '"Servant of the living God." Your first present to me, Alice. What made you think of it?'

'I wanted to give you something, Robert, in return for *The Minstrel Boy*. Something we could share.'

'And we did. Night after night he sat there on the hearthrug staring into that fire. Big and black and round. I never fancied another cat after him. Haven't been much of a servant to God myself, but you and Jeoffrey made up for it.'

'Jeoffrey did,' she corrected. 'Perhaps he showed us both the way. Shall we say hello to Spot now?'

He managed a laugh. 'You never liked old Spot, did you?'

'I'll apologize to him, shall I, Robert?' She stood in front of Spot's gravestone, half laughing, half sincere. 'Spot, I didn't understand. I thought love was for youth, for the sunshine, and for the joy. You knew it was for everyone and every mood and every time. You were wiser than me, dear Spot.'

Robert gently took her arm. 'I'm ready for the hill now. Shall we go?'

Alice opened the rarely used door in the lane, then with Robert climbed the overgrown footpath opposite, each footstep bringing its memories and its pain.

'It is quite a climb,' she said, worried for Robert.

'Not with you, Alice.'

She saw there were tears in his eyes. 'Don't cry, darling, don't cry. Let's be happy today.'

He looked lovingly at her, as they continued upwards, until at last they reached the top. He was panting now and she let him lean on her. The apple tree was still there but looked sad with age, still bearing leaves but without fruit. It looked near to its end, wilting as though it had only been waiting for her return.

'Sit down, my love,' she said, 'as Harry and I used to.'

She felt a wrench at her heart, as it opened up to memory once more. She remembered the girl she had once been, and the woman she had become. Had it been a betrayal to bring Robert here or a resolution? The latter surely. Out of the past is born the present, and love can live in both.

'Thank you for bringing me to your hill, Alice,' he said.

'Ours now, Robert. Because I love you so much.'

~

Mid April was swiftly approaching, and Rachel was deter-minedly throwing herself into the plans for the dinners and other catering that she and Marjorie were commissioned to provide for the For Valour exhibition. Nevertheless, it was a farce. Every day that passed she felt it more strongly, yet there was nothing she could do about it. She had seen nothing of Adam since she had at last persuaded him that even if he didn't want to talk to his uncle about Robert Beavers, she should be allowed to put the case to him. She had wrestled with herself over this, her loyalties divided. Her commitment to Alice fought against that to Marjorie. If the exhibition were cancelled, away would go her big summer commission. *Their* commission. John Foster had reluctantly agreed to come to Rye to discuss it, and arrived in a five-year-old Peugeot which warmed Rachel to him. She had expected a stretch limousine at the very least. He was not as she had expected either; an older version of Adam. He wore spectacles, was rounded rather than lean, and looked perhaps deceptively mild. Every lad's favourite uncle – with the exception that this uncle had worked his way up to be a billionaire.

To her relief, Adam turned up in his MG. Not having heard from him, she hadn't known what to expect – and nor did she now. It seemed clear from his affable but non-committal attitude that the professional Never Alone Adam was back with a vengeance.

Marjorie had declined to be present, saying she would get lunch, as she wasn't a major player, but Julia seized the opportunity to meet a fellow cryptography enthusiast. To do him justice, John Foster listened patiently while Rachel related the whole story, he admired the script, and lit up with enthusiasm when Julia took him through the ciphers. But in the end, as Adam had predicted, it got nowhere. It was the first time Rachel had seen him for over a month, for they had tacitly separated. It had taken courage for Rachel to ring him to suggest she talk to John Foster, and she hadn't expected him to agree. When he said he'd be present too, but it was her floor, she had been undecided how to take this. Was it an olive branch, a compromise, or sheer curiosity?

'This script is your evidence, Rachel?' John asked.

'No. There are Jacob Peasbody's memoirs and his list of evidence.'

'But the evidence itself isn't here.'

'No.'

John Foster rubbed his nose thoughtfully. 'War's an odd beast. How can you tell the difference between a moment's madness that wins the VC and the madness that succumbs to a quite different impulse? Seems to me there's a case to answer here, but until there's cast iron proof the fat lady ain't going to sing.'

'I beg your pardon, Mr Foster?' Julia asked, startled.

'Forgive me, ma'am. Just a turn of phrase. Let's get down to this script again,' he continued. 'Does Lord Beavers know about it?'

'Yes. He doesn't necessarily know about the cipher, and he also believes it's been destroyed. This copy anyway,' Rachel told him.

'Did he know about it before you approached him in the first place?'

'We think he might have done.'

'Not the kind of thing a grandfather would rush to tell his grandson, is it? Not something to be proud of, winning the VC in disputed circumstances. Nope. Yet I've seen or heard nothing yet that convinces me Robert didn't deserve it.'

'At the very least you must agree there's more to the story than the Crandene exhibition proposes to celebrate.' Adam decided to intervene.

Mistake, Rachel realized with horror. That wasn't the way to go about things with the John Fosters of this world. Adam hadn't been convinced in the first place, and they'd agreed that he'd keep out of it. But no, just when she didn't welcome it, he was coming in on her side.

'That's you all over, Adam. Always take the side of the debunkers.'

'And suppose, just suppose, we found the evidence?'

'That's different.'

'But suppose, just suppose,' Adam added softly, 'that the show goes forward and someone else then brings forth evidence.'

'No such thing as bad publicity,' Foster whipped back.

'Oh come on!' Adam raged. 'What kind of moral stance is that?'

'As moral as yours.' The retort was just as sharp. 'Ruining a man's reputation without proof.'

Julia coughed. 'Might I make a suggestion?'

'Please do, ma'am.'

'Why not allow, say, another week to see if a compromise can be found?'

'There is no compromise,' Adam said flatly.

'But there is. For a start, Robert Beavers seems to have rescued other men, which suggests his VC might not be entirely undeserved, even if Rachel's story is shown to be correct. You could perhaps consider extending Harry Rolfe's story into the show.'

'Now that's an idea, ma'am.' John Foster leaned warmly towards her, and Rachel could see Adam biting his lip to

253

refrain from pointing out that he had suggested something like this way back at the beginning.

'Perhaps,' Julia waxed enthusiastic, 'Rachel might even find more evidence to support her theory.'

Theory indeed. How could Julia even say that when she herself had decrypted the text? 'A week isn't long to find more evidence, with nothing moving at present,' Rachel pointed out.

'I have been listening very carefully to everything you have said. It is, of course, a cryptographer's task to do so. There is an angle you have mentioned but not yet followed up. I have. A trained mind, Mr Foster. It always wins in the end.'

'It does indeed, ma'am.'

'Rachel, you mentioned Joan Parsons possibly being at the funeral,' Julia continued, 'and who she was. I went to see her. Did you know she worked at Crandene during the war? She was only a teenager then, but she knew Alice well and the friendship continued. Indeed, in Alice's old age, Joan Parsons looked after her. She mentioned she would be willing to talk to you again when I explained what we had discovered,' Julia added airily.

'Joan Parsons was keeping all that back. Why?' Rachel fumed to Adam afterwards.

'I could hazard a guess. When are you going?'

'Tomorrow. She still didn't sound very chatty, though.' She looked at him suspiciously. 'How can you hazard a guess? Are you holding back on me?'

'Far from it. Didn't you wonder why I suddenly came round to your way of thinking and turned up here?'

'You've got more evidence?' she demanded, hope leaping up once more.

'No, but a line on some. I decided,' he flushed, 'to go for it, and stop making excuses about needing cast-iron proof before I tackled John. You were right. It was time I stopped walking away and walked *into* life instead. See where involvement got me. Flat on my face.'

'Adam, don't—' she broke off, not wanting to plead. Not wanting to cry out, 'Don't go away again.'

254

'Don't stop? Is that what you were going to say? I'm not.' He grinned. 'I'm in for the duration. As you are. You've made that quite clear.'

Her head spun. What had she made clear? Commitment to Alice, yes. But permanent commitment to Adam, to any man? She hadn't thought further than the fact she wanted to be with him. But the question could come marching down their road at any moment and demand an answer. What would hers be? She had blocked off the future in this dive into the past, yet, as Adam himself had said, they were linked.

'Tell me about this new line of evidence.' Oh, well done, Rachel. Kill off any talk of commitment.

'You'll love it. I've been playing around with birth certificates on your behalf. Remember Alice's sister Betty, whose child was Cousin Joe Vickers?'

Rachel was disappointed. 'I've checked all the local voters' lists – no luck. Nor the birth certificates. I decided Pops was rambling when he called to say the name was Vickers.'

'My guess is that he was. He remembered the name by association. Say it to yourself.'

Puzzled, she dutifully did so. Then: 'Oh, Pops,' she said softly. 'It was Parsons, wasn't it. So you think Joan Parsons is related to Cousin Joe—'

'Is Cousin Jo or Cousin Joan? Did Pops ever imply it was a male cousin?'

'Do come in, Miss Field,' Joan Parsons said welcomingly. 'Or perhaps I might call you Rachel. Mrs Thomas explained to me how important this is.'

'Yes, call me Rachel, please. After all, we are related. Some kind of second or third cousins.'

Joan roared with laughter. 'You've smoked me out, eh?'

'Why didn't you *tell* me?' Rachel asked, following Joan into the living room.

'That's a tough one. I suppose I assumed you'd know from Uncle Henry and when you obviously didn't, I decided to lie low. Alice was a cagey old lady, and though she never said a word against the Beavers' family, I always had the impression there was some coolness there. I get on well with the Crandene set-up, so I didn't want to get drawn in if I didn't have to.'

'Suppose I said that that time might have come, but that I'm forced to be cagey too.'

Joan considered this. 'We can try and see how far we get. I'll tell you as much as I feel I can.'

'Done.'

'I was fond of Alice, very fond in fact, and we were close particularly in her last years, when I acted virtually as her carer. That's why I love this cottage. Alice left it to Henry since she had precious little else to leave and he had a family, but it was always understood between her, your grandfather and myself that if he sold I should have first refusal. It's worked out well.'

'You said you got on well with Crandene . . .' Rachel began hesitantly.

'And you think that prejudiced me against Aunt Alice? One doesn't rule out the other. The world is not black and white, as Alice herself discovered.'

'How?'

'She told me a few years before she died that she had viewed the world in black and white for many years, but suddenly she had discovered it was full of colour if one chose to look. The colour in her life had been given to it by Robert and Crandene.'

'I don't believe you,' Rachel said flatly. How could she? This would go against everything she'd discovered from the script.

'That is what she told me.'

'But she hated Robert Beavers.' She was on the point of spilling out the whole story, but held back.

'I wasn't privy to all her past secrets, but she certainly didn't hate Robert by the time I knew her. Of course, I was a teenager when I first met them both and by the time I came back to work for her in 1970 he was dead, and she was living here. She spoke of him very lovingly.'

'He was dead by then. It was hindsight, through rosy spectacles,' Rachel guessed. 'I've got evidence of how much she hated him when he was alive.'

256

'Now you have contradictions, Rachel. Alice is a calm logical person who can't find colour in life, but suddenly she wears rose-tinted specs. Are you referring to the recipe script by any chance?'

So Joan knew of it. Of course she would if she had indeed been as close to Alice as she claimed.

'Did you see the script?'

'I did.'

'Did Alice tell you what it contained other than recipes?'

Joan looked at her steadily. 'No. Other than that it represented the past for her, not the present. She didn't want to talk further, and I didn't press her. Your mother took it with the rest of the family papers. She asked me if I wanted it, and I said no. I didn't tell Margaret anything about the script. Let it die with Alice, was my view. It still is.'

If only it were that simple for her too, Rachel wished. Joan could choose to stand aside, but she herself was in too deeply to do that.

'Did Alice mention anything – letters and so on – that went with the script?'

'Yes.' Joan's face softened. 'She asked me to destroy it all, and I did.'

It had gone, everything she needed to cement the case against Robert Beavers, to bring Alice Carter's story to life, to convince John Foster that in Robert Beavers' case For Valour did not apply – and to leave herself and Adam in limbo. 'Can you tell me what there was?' She was aware that tears were running down her face.

'Alice gathered it up and gave it to me to burn. I did so without looking at it, all but one piece, which fell out. It was a page torn out from the Bible – the Book of Samuel, I believe, and a circle round one verse. At the top was a scribble which read, "Alice, he's done for me. Remember our windy hill, my lovely, darling Alice." I didn't want to destroy it, so I kept it till she died, just in case she mentioned it, but she never did.'

'And then?'

'I burned it. I do have one possession of Alice's though. Not what you're after, but you might like it. It's a book of poems by Rupert Brooke.'

257

Rachel took it from her, handling it carefully. It had been precious to Alice, and it would be to her too. It fell open at an early poem: 'Breathless we flung us on the windy hill . . .' So that's where it had come from. All the questions were answered now, save one. She came straight out with it.

'Joan, can you tell me what happened to Alice's child?'

'What child?' Joan looked puzzled.

'She was dismissed from Crandene for immorality.'

'And you assumed she was pregnant?' Joan looked amused. 'She used to laugh about that. She told me Robert was in love with her even then, and when he found her in the chef's arms one day, he sacked her. He wouldn't believe she was only comforting him because of the recent death of his son – and then she compounded her sin by going to live with him and his wife.'

'And that's all?' Rachel asked, reluctant to let go of yet another of her theories. The real Alice, it seemed, was determined not to be captured. She would remain enigmatic to the end.

1984

Alice tried hard to think straight about her life – and about the future. She was old now, and Henry had gone to live in France. She was glad she had taken him to the war cemetery so that he could see Harry's grave. All so long ago, so many twists of fate. He would know nothing, it was better that way. She should destroy the carbon script as she had all the evidence that went with it. She no longer had the strength to do so, however, either emotionally or physically, or even to ask Joan to do so. Henry had said he did not want it, but she would leave it here anyway so that either he or Margaret would take it, or even darling Joan. She had already told Henry and Joan it wasn't to be published, and Henry would tell Margaret. It hardly mattered. The evidence had been burned, and what use was the script without that? It could do no harm at all. No one would bother to go deeply into it, without knowing there was anything to find. Once, the script meant the world to her, now it meant nothing.

258

She had done all she could for Harry and for Robert. Crandene remained as her memorial to Robert, but what did Harry have? For him too she had left her legacy.

~

'It's all been thrashed out.' Adam threw himself down into an armchair. 'It was quite a do.' He had just driven back to Kent from Crandene after the Big Meeting and Rachel awaited him not in his home, but hers – her 'new' cottage, into which she'd moved back yesterday. So much had happened in the ten days since she had met Cousin Joan Parsons, discussions with Adam, meetings with John Foster, and finally organizing the move back into her cottage yesterday. She had longed to be present at the meeting between Lord Beavers, his solicitor, John Foster and his solicitor, and Adam, but Adam had cheerfully told her her presence would be a red rag to the bull. She had been hopping up and down waiting for his arrival, cooking a dinner she hoped was worthy of the occasion, and calming down Marjorie over the phone to assure her firstly that she hadn't abandoned her for ever and secondly that their Crandene contract was under discussion and she'd be ringing her as soon as she knew the position.

Which was now!

'How did he take it?' she burst out.

'He kept his cool. After all, no evidence.'

'So how *did* your uncle get convinced action was necessary? When we left him he was still thinking it over.' His summons to Adam for today's meeting came out of the blue.

'Your chum Julia. She talked in ciphers of her own, about balance of probabilities and what not, and advocated her compromise solution. So we went storming in there today and reached it.'

'What was it?' She had been kept in the dark about this, to her fury.

'Patience. It seems that the Beavers family had been told the script was destroyed, Robert Beavers had confessed to his son George about it, but had said there was no danger anymore. George had duly passed it on to *his* son.'

'Robert admitted not deserving the VC to his own son?' Rachel asked incredulously. 'That deserves the award in itself.'

'Yes, George took that view too, apparently. He didn't know all the ins and outs of the affair, however, so Alice Beavers became Public Enemy No. 2 if not No. 1 for him, whatever his father's view, even though the marriage appears to have been a happy one in later years. When Lord Beavers learned from you that another script was around he must have freaked out. All his worst suspicions confirmed. That script had to go.'

'Hence my burned house,' she said ruefully.

'Again no proof. You can't convict on the shape of a man's face and your neighbour's ID wouldn't be sufficient. Anyway a compromise has been worked out. The For Valour exhibition will be mounted, and Robert's VC duly recorded. Other men were saved by Robert, even if Rolfe wasn't. It is not our place to judge.'

'Whose is it then?' It still seemed unfair to her that Beavers' reputation should remain unblemished. 'History's?'

'I don't see how history can judge any better than us without evidence.' Adam hesitated. 'Would you go along with its being the man himself, Robert Beavers? He had to live with the knowledge of what he'd done.'

Rachel thought this over. There were surely flaws in this argument, but perhaps it was the conclusion Alice herself had come to.

'Yes,' she answered at last. 'I can.'

'What my uncle has insisted on is that the men's role gets to be seen as well as the officers. So Harry Rolfe and Peasbody come back into the picture, and the Tommies as well as the officers. Also you'll be pleased to know John insisted on there being photos of Alice herself in her restaurant and her recipes being displayed and cooked, with photographs of some of the pages. They'd mean nothing in themselves. Beavers went puce when he found out the script hadn't been burned, and it's now agreed that it won't be published. He wants a written undertaking from you.'

'I suppose that's reasonable enough. He doesn't know I can't publish it anyway.'

'You bet it is. He wanted the copyright made over to him first. John's solicitor told him to stuff it.'

'And he did?'

'He stuffed it. He also wants an undertaking from you that you won't publish the story of Harry Rolfe and Robert Beavers.'

'That's harder, Adam. It's the truth. I couldn't do that.'

'*Would* you publish it?'

Rachel hesitated. 'No.'

'Why not?'

'Don't laugh. I don't think Alice would want me to. She came to love Robert, according to Cousin Joan, which means she'd made her peace with the past. It's not my place to say she was wrong.'

He hugged her, then she felt his lips on hers. 'O wise young judge,' he murmured.

'Two wise young judges,' she pointed out. 'We've both gone for compromise. And so's poor old Lord Beavers. He must be spitting at the idea of glorifying Alice's role at Crandene.'

'He nobly said it would add some love interest linked with Harry Rolfe's name. Talking of love interest, John seems very taken with Julia.'

'You're joking. Does he knows she bites?'

'Uncle John is pretty good at biting back, for all his mild appearance. They'll make a splendid couple.'

'I take it the cooking contract for Marjorie is still in place?' She didn't want to think about 'couples' at the moment.

'It is. And you're still part of it. His Beavership doesn't seem to have anything personal against you incidentally. Maybe the unicorn's influence helped. Your chum Michael is hard at work on producing new copy for the exhibition, to cover the new angles, and a booklet to go with it on the story of the men. He's very keen on Harry Rolfe and Peasbody. You can help him out with our research into your family.'

'*He* is?' She was unreasonably annoyed that this was being taken out of her hands.

'Oh come, surely you don't mind. He said he'd be in touch.'

'The ways of fate are very strange,' she said crossly.

'You might get a small mention in the acknowledgements.'

'And what if he publishes the true story of Robert's VC while he's writing about Harry? I gave him a lot of stick about the historian's role.'

'No evidence again. Draw the line under it, Rachel. You've won recognition for your aunt and for her Harry. Isn't that enough?'

'I suppose so.' It was, but it left open another question. 'But is it enough for us, Adam?'

He didn't pretend not to understand. They were alike after all, they thought alike. Two of a kind. Was that good?

'Do you love this cottage, Rachel?'

'Yes. It's part of my past and I've come to value that.'

'You're leaving Alice behind. Can you leave this too?'

'Have you left Annie behind?'

'Yes. In a funny way, Alice did that for me. She took the risk of loving again, so are you going to live with me and be my love? You said you didn't do partners.'

François jeered in the background, as Rachel laughed at his memory, threw up her hands and surrendered.

'Do you know, I think I am. I could always keep this cottage and rent it . . .'

'No, you couldn't. I'm selling mine.'

This startled her. 'Then where—'

'You haven't heard the full story of the meeting yet.' And he told her.

'He's *resigning*?' she yelped. 'How on earth did John manage that?'

'Quite simple really. He told Lord Beavers that he wasn't going to give his money to a chief executive officer of a charity who knew he was fundraising on such shifting sand. He could take his choice. Either he could remain as CEO at Crandene and do without his money, or he could resign, become chairman of the board of trustees – and Crandene would find a new CEO. He chose the latter. Even after he knew who it would be.'

'Who?'

'Me.'

The day was fine, as they walked hand in hand along the village street of Aumale. It was a fine spring day and the breeze stirred

262

fields that could hardly have changed since 1916. Someone, Adam had remarked, had to tell Pops what had been going on. Surprised, she had instantly agreed – and then he had explained further just why this visit was necessary. He had used his absence from Rye to good purpose.

When she had telephoned to say they were coming, she had been told Pops wasn't so well. The lucid days were fewer now, and she was prepared for the change in him. She could see him sleeping in his chair by the window as they arrived, and he seemed even more fragile than when she was last here. Hearing them, he opened his eyes at the noise and smiled happily. 'Hello, Margaret. So you've come at last.'

'Rachel, Pops.'

'Oh yes. And you've brought that fellow with you again.'

'You'll have to get accustomed to me,' Adam said cheerfully. 'I'm a fixture.'

Pops heaved a sigh. 'What have you come for anyway, Rachel? Everything's left to you anyway. Take those china figures now if you like. Alice would have liked you to have them.'

'Would she, Pops?' she asked softly. 'I'm glad.'

'I was lucky to have Alice. And my parents too. Did I ever show you a picture of them? It's over there . . .' He waved vaguely towards his desk. 'Elsie her name was, and Edward was my father. Alice was so good to them, they said. Yes, we were a happy family, workhouse or not. Look after that picture, won't you? Wouldn't like anything to happen to that. One for the family album for your children. Got any yet?'

'We're working on it,' Adam replied gravely.

Rachel hesitated. Should she speak or not? Adam had left the decision to her. Pops closed his eyes. 'Do you know?' he said with some surprise, 'it's not been a bad old life.'

'We've been looking into Harry Rolfe's story, Pops. Do you remember that gravestone Alice took you to?'

'What about him?'

'Alice was in love with him.'

'Good for her. Killed at the Somme, I suppose. Never remember her mentioning him.'

263

'Yes, Pops. That's where he died.'

His eyes closed again. Rachel looked at Adam and shook her head slightly. How could they tell him that the reason he had possessed only the certified shortened form of his birth certificate was that Alice was not his sister, but his mother? That she, Rachel, had been right and Joan wrong? That Alice had been pregnant when she left Crandene, and that Henry had been named after his real father, Harry Rolfe? It would be too much, too late.

But it wasn't too late for her. She was Alice's great-granddaughter. In her, as well as Pops, Alice and Harry came together, and in her Alice's powers as a chef would carry on. She took Adam's hand and they stole quietly towards the door.

From behind them came Pops' voice. 'Funny thing,' he observed. 'I always had a notion that Harry must have been my father. Odd the ideas you get.'